THE TOMBS

CLIVE CUSSLER

AND THOMAS PERRY

G. P. PUTNAM'S SONS

NEW YORK

THE
TOMBS

G. P. PUTNAM'S SONS
Publishers Since 1838
Published by the Penguin Group
Penguin Group (USA) Inc., 375 Hudson Street, New York, New York 10014, USA • Penguin
Group (Canada), 90 Eglinton Avenue East, Suite 700, Toronto, Ontario M4P 2Y3, Canada
(a division of Pearson Penguin Canada Inc.) • Penguin Books Ltd, 80 Strand, London
WC2R 0RL, England • Penguin Ireland, 25 St Stephen's Green, Dublin 2, Ireland (a division
of Penguin Books Ltd) • Penguin Group (Australia), 250 Camberwell Road, Camberwell,
Victoria 3124, Australia (a division of Pearson Australia Group Pty Ltd) • Penguin Books
India Pvt Ltd, 11 Community Centre, Panchsheel Park, New Delhi–110 017, India •
Penguin Group (NZ), 67 Apollo Drive, Rosedale, North Shore 0632, New Zealand
(a division of Pearson New Zealand Ltd) • Penguin Books (South Africa) (Pty) Ltd,
24 Sturdee Avenue, Rosebank, Johannesburg 2196, South Africa

Penguin Books Ltd, Registered Offices: 80 Strand, London WC2R 0RL, England

ISBN 978-0-399-15926-8

Printed in the United States of America
1   3   5   7   9   10   8   6   4   2

Book design by Lovedog Studio

This is a work of fiction. Names, characters, places, and incidents either are the product of
the authors' imagination or are used fictitiously, and any resemblance to actual persons,
living or dead, businesses, companies, events, or locales is entirely coincidental.

THE TOMBS

1

PANNONIA, 453 C.E.

THE BARBARIAN ENCAMPMENT WAS ENORMOUS, A GREAT city that moved from place to place at the whim of its unquestioned ruler, the High King. But in the dim light of this predawn morning it was in chaos. Hundreds of thousands of warriors and their shrieking women and ungovernable offspring milled about. Hundreds of thousands of horses, cattle, sheep, and goats all bleated and neighed in the general alarm and made the dawn a cacophony of sounds. The stink of the livestock competed with the smoke of ten thousand fires being fanned to life at once.

Priscus's manservant had pulled him from his bed, certain that they were about to lose their lives in the sudden commotion in the barbarian horde. Priscus hurried along over the uneven soil, trying not to turn an ankle in a wagon rut or step in a hole. He followed Ellak, trying in vain to keep up with him in a pair of light sandals made for walking on the smooth pavements of Constantinople.

Ellak was a fighter, a man descended from famous warriors, who had lived to adulthood by the strength and speed of his limbs.

As Priscus caught sight of the huge animal-skin tent of the High King, its center pole as tall as a villa and its floor wide enough to hold hundreds, he could hear wailing and shouting and knew what must have happened in the night. He slowed enough to remain upright and maintain his Roman dignity. He was a diplomat, and, by default, the man who must write the history of this momentous day. Ellak, the High King's son, had come for him because Priscus was the most learned man for many leagues and might know of a way to save the High King's life. But the wailing might mean they were arriving too late.

Priscus hid his feeling of fear. The barbarians were in his way, running about, whipping one another into a fury. They could smell fear like dogs. They were trained and experienced killers from birth who had conquered their way from remotest Asia to Europe by sheer ferocity. When they'd heard shouting, they'd rushed outside, and would no more have come without their swords and daggers than without their hands and feet. Today, if any of them sensed fear in him—a foreigner—they would tear him apart without warning.

Ellak led him into the High King's vast tent. Priscus was nearly a head taller than most of the barbarians, who were from the distant east, short and broad, with wide shoulders and thick arms and legs, their faces like tanned leather. Priscus could see over the heads of some of the men who were blocking the inner chamber. That was where the King must be. The warriors standing nearest to the chamber were already pulling out their short daggers and cutting their cheekbones with deep slashes so the blood would run down in streaks like tears.

Priscus made his way by stepping sideways and slipping between the half-mad guards. Now he could see the High King's young bride, Ildico, crouching on the pile of rich carpets in the corner as far away from her husband as she could get. She was weeping, but nobody was comforting her. Priscus couldn't see anyone who even seemed to notice her.

As one of the guards turned to face his friends to let them watch as he mutilated his face with a short sword, Priscus slipped behind him into the chamber. He looked down at the body of the High King and could see why the young bride looked so shocked. The great barbarian, the *Flagellum Dei,* was sprawled on his back on the soft silk bed, his mouth open like a snoring drunk. Blood ran down from his nose and mouth into a wet pool at his head.

Priscus stepped to the corner and lifted the girl Ildico from where she cowered. He pushed aside the long blond hair from her ear and whispered, "It's all right. He's gone now, and there's nothing more you can do here. Come." It was all just soothing talk, just a human voice to comfort her without saying anything. Ildico was the High King's seventh wife, and in spite of her beauty she was barely more than a child, brought from her Germanic tribe to marry the conqueror. She understood Priscus's Latin as well as her own Gothic, but he wasn't sure which languages the guards spoke so said little. He helped her out into the light of the rising sun and the fresh air. She looked pale and weak like a ghost. He was hoping to get her away from the crowd before some warrior suspected the King's death was her fault. The ignorant were often suspicious, and even if a person died of a lightning strike, someone might have conjured it.

He spotted a few of her female retainers, the group of servants and kinswomen who had come with her for her wedding. They were standing a distance off, watching the proceedings anxiously. He turned her over to them and they hurried her away from the growing crowd.

Priscus was still looking in that direction to be sure she wasn't stopped when strong hands roughly gripped both his arms. He craned his neck to see his captors. He barely recognized either of them, although he'd seen them every time he'd come to meet with the High King. They both had fresh mourning cuts on their cheekbones, so blood covered the lower half of their faces. They had changed in demeanor since Priscus had sat with them last night, laughing and drinking to celebrate their lord's wedding. The two men dragged him into the King's tent, and the crowd of warriors parted to let them pass into the inner chamber.

Inside the chamber, the body had not been moved. Standing over it were Ardaric, King of the Gepids, and Onegesius, Attila's most trusted friend. Ardaric knelt and picked up the jug of wine that the High King had drunk before he'd died. He said, "This is the wine that Ildico poured him last night." Onegesius picked up the goblet lying beside the King.

Priscus said, "For weeks, he had a sickness that gave him nosebleeds. Maybe it got worse while he slept and he drowned in his own blood. That's what it looks like, doesn't it?"

Ardaric snorted in contempt. "Nobody dies of a nosebleed. He's been in battle all his life. He was wounded many times and never bled to death. It was poison."

"Do you think so?" asked Priscus, his eyes wide in shock.

"I do," said Ardaric. "And I've been thinking about you. Emperor Theodosius sent you to us four years ago with the ambassador Maximinus. Your interpreter, Vigilas, was caught in a plot to assassinate Attila. Instead of having all of you killed, Attila sent you back to your emperor in Constantinople. Maybe that was a mistake. And maybe Vigilas was not the only one who came to kill the King."

Onegesius poured wine into Attila's goblet, then held it out. "Prove you didn't poison him. Drink it."

Priscus said, "I don't know if it's poisoned or not. If the wine is poisoned, that won't prove I was the poisoner. I certainly wasn't in here with the High King and his bride on their wedding night. All my drinking it might do is kill me too."

"Your fear convicts you." Onegesius's free hand moved toward the hilt of his sword.

Priscus took the goblet. "If I die, remember I'm an innocent man." He lifted it to his lips and drained it.

The others waited and watched Priscus closely. Ellak stepped closer. "Well, Priscus?"

"I don't feel anything. It tastes like wine."

"Bitter? Sour?"

"Like all other wine—sweet like fruit, but with a few drops of vinegar."

Ardaric sniffed the goblet, took some of the wine on his finger, and put a drop on his tongue. He nodded to Onegesius, dropped the goblet on the carpet by the body of the High King, and walked out. He called out to the warriors, "There was no poison. He died of a sickness."

Priscus followed Ardaric out of the chamber and made his way through the milling crowd of warriors. With their anguished, blood-streaked faces, they made a frightening sight. These were men who had never done anything in their lives but kill. They fought, ate, sometimes even slept, on horseback. They had, in about three generations, conquered tribes from the grasslands beyond the Volga to

Gaul. This morning their greatest leader had been taken from them. Who could say what their grief and anger might make them do to a stranger from a foreign country?

Priscus walked briskly with his head down, not letting his eyes rest on any of the warriors streaming toward the High King's tent. He went to his own quarters and prepared an altar with a row of lighted candles for the purpose of praying for Attila's soul. After all, Attila had listened to Priscus and the other Romans when they talked of Christianity. And once he had met with Pope Leo at Mantua and made an agreement. Something might have planted a seed of faith in his mind. In any case, it was best to mourn him as visibly as possible. Priscus also vomited, and drank a great deal of water, and then vomited again, and found it settled his nerves.

Late in the day he left his own small tent and walked toward the center of the encampment. He saw that the High King's tent had been struck. Not far off, a large open space had been cleared. What had arisen on that spot was an immense white vision. He walked to it and touched it in wonder.

A vast tent made entirely of white silk had been erected. It moved and billowed in the breeze as he walked to the opening and looked inside. In the center was a bier that displayed the body of the High King, lying in state, in bright and costly clothes of purple and red befitting a warrior king, and with arms of the finest quality inlaid with gold and gems.

Around the bier rode the savage horsemen, the High King's best warriors, many of them kings of their own tribes and nations. They were riding around and around in a circle singing of his exploits and victories, their faces cut so the blood ran down their cheeks like tears. They sang that he was the greatest chieftain, a man who deserved not just the pale tears of women but the red tears of warriors. As they rode in their circle, Priscus could see that the blood soaked their beards and dripped from their chins onto their clothes and horses' manes.

Priscus knelt in the direction of the King and touched his forehead to the dirt so the warriors would see he was showing respect in his own way, then returned to his own shelter. He remained there for the next three days, writing about the life of Attila as High King and his death on his wedding night. Visitors came to Priscus and related the prodigious feats of mourning they had seen, and a few talked about the rivalry between Ellak, the oldest son, and Dengizich, the second oldest, and the resentment of Emakh, the third son, whom the two seemed not to take into account. Still others told him of Ardaric's disgust that the three sons couldn't remain united even until their father was buried.

Priscus went to the white tent the next day and found the High King being prepared for burial in the fiery light of a hundred flaming lamps. Attila's retainers placed him in a series of three coffins. The outer and largest one was made of iron. The coffin placed inside it was made of solid silver. The third was pure gold. The coffins were packed with the jeweled weapons of the many kings Attila had defeated. He had absorbed a hundred Asian tribes, beaten the Alans, Ostrogoths, Armenians, Burgundians, had savaged the Balkans, Thrace, Scythia, and Gaul. He had sacked Mantua, Milan, Verona, and taken most of northern Italy. He had defeated the legions of both the western and eastern capitals of Rome and Constantinople.

Also in the three coffins were breathtaking heaps of glittering gems and glowing gold, reflecting the flames of the lamps, and the coffins themselves were a great fortune. Priscus couldn't help thinking the inner one had probably been composed of the Eastern Roman Empire's annual tribute to Attila of two thousand one hundred pounds of gold. But he couldn't ignore the flashes of color inside—the cool green of emeralds, the blood-drop rubies, the deep blue sapphires. There were fiery garnets, indigo lapis, yellow amber, pea green jade, all competing for the eye's attention.

At nightfall a group of a thousand horsemen drawn from Attila's personal troop of bodyguards assembled. They placed the lids on the coffins, lifted them onto a huge eight-wheeled wagon that could carry the immense weight, and rode off, carrying no torches to light the way through the darkness.

Weeks later, Priscus was preparing a donkey train for the long trek back to report to the Emperor Marcian. It would take him a month to get from this savage country to the palaces of Constantinople, and by now he would have gladly crawled back on his hands and knees. Then in the afternoon another commotion swept through the camp, with people pointing fingers into the distance and yelling in their many tongues, so he went to investigate.

The elite horsemen of the burial detail were returning to the great encampment of the Huns. They came galloping, and the dust was visible across the plain for a long time before they appeared.

Ardaric, Onegesius, and the three sons of Attila—Ellak, Dengizich, and Emakh—and a great host of warriors, gathered at the edge of the encampment to greet them. When the thousand riders drew up, they dismounted and bowed to the assembled chiefs. In a singular honor, the chiefs bowed back. Ellak, the eldest heir of Attila, stepped up to the leader of the burial party, a man named Mozhu. He put his hand on Mozhu's shoulder and said, "Tell us."

Mozhu said, "We took the High King to a place in the bend of a river far away where travelers seldom pass. We built a crypt as deep as two men are tall, with a sloping entrance, and carried the coffins to the bottom. Then we covered the crypt and the sloping passage. We herded our thousand horses across the area many times until it was impossible to pick out the precise spot where the crypt was buried. Then we diverted the river so it will flow deep over the High King's tomb forever."

Ellak embraced Mozhu. Then he stood on an oxcart and made a speech to thank the thousand men who had stood with his father in battle and protected his body in death. Before he jumped down, he called out, "Kill them now."

The thousand men were engulfed by the great host of warriors around them. To Priscus, the thousand seemed to disappear like swimmers pulled under the water in a flood—a head here going down, a few heads there. They sank beneath the weight of the entire army. He saw none of the burial party resist or try to remount their horses to escape. He could not tell whether it was because their execution was a surprise or because they had certain foreknowledge that anyone who knew where Attila was buried must die.

Afterward, the burial party's bodies were covered with earth where they had fallen. Their leaders spoke of their loyalty, honor, and bravery. To Priscus it seemed the Huns considered the massacre simply a natural and inevitable part of the death of a great leader. It was all a single misfortune.

Priscus left the vast encampment at dawn the next morning with his train of a hundred fifty donkeys loaded with supplies and a few precious articles hidden among them—his written account of his mission to the barbarians, his personal books, a few souvenirs from barbarian friends. He also took with him the teenage bride-widow Ildico, whom he had promised to return to her parents in the Germanic territories when passage could be arranged.

When they were a day's journey from the barbarian encampment, he walked beside Ildico's donkey and talked with her. "See, child? I told you it was all perfectly safe. Once the barbarians were persuaded there was no poison, you and I could hardly be poisoners."

"I heard they made you drink the wine. Why are you alive?"

"The poison has to be given over time before it will cause bleeding and keep the blood from clotting. I've been giving it to Attila for weeks. Enough had to build up in his body so your final dose would make him bleed to death. But think more pleasant thoughts. You'll be very rich soon."

"Keep any gold that's coming to me," she said. "I did it for my people that he killed. Just get me home."

"The Emperor will want to send you home with a reward. What you and I did has probably saved the Empire from destruction."

"I don't care about the Empire."

He walked on ahead, thinking. He had done everything perfectly—gathered the sweet clover himself, patiently aged it to let it turn moldy, and then used it to make a poison that couldn't be detected and caused a death which looked like a disease. As he walked he composed parts of his account of his time with the Huns. He would describe it all—his mission four years ago with Maximinus, when the assassination plan was blamed on the interpreter Vigilas, the actions of the barbarians, the personality of their supreme leader.

He would, of course, leave out the particulars of the High King's death. Every trick not explained remains fresh for reuse. The Western Empire in Rome would be overwhelmed by its enemies before much longer. Its legions couldn't keep fighting off wave after wave of barbarians, each group more numerous and savage than the last. It was a simple game of numbers. The subtler methods of the Eastern Empire obliterated numbers—the Emperor had sent just one man to end the threat from the Huns, hadn't he? The Eastern Empire would live for another thousand years.

Ildico certainly was a beautiful young woman, he thought. The slim, graceful figure, the milky skin, and the golden hair were very appealing. In a way, having her for himself would make his quiet triumph over the great Attila complete. But no, he thought. That was exactly the sort of thing an emissary from Rome would do.

REMI FARGO HOVERED IN THE WARM WATER OF THE Gulf of Mexico, barely moving her fins as she worked. She finished filling her net bag with jagged pieces of a clay pot that had been nearly buried in the sand. She estimated that the original pot, as it had been over a thousand years ago, was about ten inches wide and four inches deep, and she thought she probably had gathered all of its fragments. She didn't want to risk scratching the smooth finish of the pot by putting anything else in the net bag. She looked up at the shape of the boat's hull, a dark phantom sitting sixty feet above her on the silvery underside of the water's surface. She exhaled, and the bubbles issued from her mouthpiece, then ascended, shiny globules shimmering up toward the light.

Remi caught her husband Sam's eye and pointed to the net bag, then gave him a thumbs-up. He held up what looked to her like a deer antler as though he were saluting her and nodded. Remi gave a couple of lazy kicks, and her slim, shapely body moved upward into a school of shiny bay anchovies that swirled around her like an ice storm. They left her, and she rose to the boat.

She broke the surface and instantly saw the other boat in the distance. She ducked under again, swam to the other side of the dive boat, and waited for Sam. She saw his bubbles coming up from beneath her, then his head and mask.

She took out her mouthpiece and breathed the air for a second. "They're here again."

Sam ducked under the surface and came up at the stern, keeping himself close to the outdrive so he remained part of the boat's silhouette. "It's them, all right—the same dive boat, a black hull and gray above." He looked again. "The same five—no, six people."

"It's the third day in a row," she said.

"They probably think we've found the city of Atlantis."

"You make a joke out of it, but it could be true. Not about Atlantis, but they don't know what we're doing here. It's the Louisiana coast. We could be diving on an old Spanish treasure ship that got blown here in a hurricane. Or a Civil War ship sunk in the blockade."

"Or a 2003 Chevrolet that somebody drove off a bridge upriver. We're in sixty feet of water. They were probably just out here drinking beer and rubbing suntan lotion on each other."

Remi drifted against Sam and held on to his shoulder so she could see the other boat. "Thank you for your lack of curiosity, Mr. Jokester. They're following us and watching what we do. Did you see that? A sun flash from a lens."

"Must be paparazzi taking my picture."

"Keep it up. But just remember, having strangers think we found something valuable could be just as dangerous as actually finding something valuable. Thieves attack you before they count your money."

"Okay," he said. "They've kept their distance for three days. If they come any closer, we'll have a talk with them. Meanwhile, we've got to get that sunken village mapped. The past few weeks have been interesting, but I don't feel like devoting the rest of my life to salvage archaeology."

Sam and Remi Fargo always claimed their reputation as treasure hunters had come from catching the attention of a few imaginative reporters on a slow news day. They shared a strong interest in history and the urge to go out and see it for themselves. This spring they had volunteered to do some diving for the state of Louisiana. An archaeologist named Ray Holbert had been on the shore, looking at the coast for damage from the oil leaks after an oil-drilling platform had burned, when he had found some potsherds washed up from the Gulf onto the beach. They were clearly of native origin and quite old. He had asked for a grant from the oil company to salvage what had seemed to be a sunken village. When Sam and Remi had heard about the project, they had offered to pay their own expenses and help.

Remi said, "Come down with me. I think I've found another hearth. Bring the camera."

Sam pulled himself up over the gunwale to reach the underwater camera, and they submerged again. Remi seemed to lose herself in the work. She led him to the stone hearth and let him examine it while she took the camera and photographed the site from every angle to record the positions of the potsherds around it. He watched the graceful movements of her body—in her wet suit looking a bit like her own shadow—and noticed a thin wisp of auburn hair had escaped from the hood of her suit at her forehead. He caught her bright green eyes looking at him through the glass of her mask, so he forced himself to relinquish the sight of her and look at the ring of charred stones she had uncovered beneath the sand. Then they filled their net bags carefully to bring more pottery up to be catalogued and mapped the site where they found them.

Suddenly Sam and Remi both heard the buzzing sound of a propeller. It grew louder, and as they looked up they saw the underside of a black hull speeding toward the anchored dive boat, throwing waves to each side. They could see the outdrive and propeller and the long spiral trail of churned bubbles behind it.

They watched the dive boat's hull rock and saw the anchor chain tighten to hold it, tugging against the anchor they'd sunk into the sand and then going slack when the other boat slowed down and idled within a yard of theirs. In a minute or two, the black hull sped up again and moved away at high speed, bouncing as it crested each wave.

Sam pointed upward, and the two floated to the surface. Remi climbed the ladder, and Sam followed. As they took off their gear, Remi said, "Well? That was a little closer, wasn't it? I'm glad we didn't surface just as they came roaring in."

She could see Sam's jaw was working. "I think they zoomed in to look at what we've been bringing up from the bottom."

"I hope they got a good look," she said. "I don't want to get chewed up by a propeller over a few potsherds and a middenful of thousand-year-old clamshells."

"Let's see who they are," he said. He started the engine and stepped to the bow. Remi took the wheel and inched them forward in the direction of the anchor so its two flukes would be pulled forward and freed from the sand. Sam pulled the anchor up and stowed it under the foredeck. Remi brought the boat around so Sam could scoop up the small ring buoy that held the diver-alert flag, red with a white diagonal stripe, and pull in its light anchor, then stow both in the stern.

She pushed the throttle forward and accelerated in the direction of the Grand Isle Harbor.

Sam moved forward to stand beside Remi and rest his elbows on the roof of the cabin while he held the binoculars and scanned the horizon. As they sped along the coast, Remi's long auburn hair whipped behind her in the wind. Sam said, "I don't see their boat. They must have put into the harbor. We may as well head in too."

Remi steered toward the harbor at top speed, but then, as they reached the harbor entrance, she slowed down rapidly. As they came around the breakwater, a Coast Guard boat moved across their bow at a distance.

"Good timing," Sam said. "You might have had to bat your eyelashes at him to get out of a speeding ticket."

"I don't get speeding tickets because I don't break the law," she said, and batted her eyelashes at him. "You can take the wheel."

She stepped aside and he took it, slowing down even more, to the speed of a walk. Remi bent over and ran her fingers through her long hair to straighten it, stood up and glanced at Sam. "You're still looking for them, aren't you?"

"I'm mostly just curious. I'm wondering how long we're going to have amateur treasure hounds, looters, and grave robbers following us everywhere."

"I guess you gave one too many interviews. It was probably the one with that TV girl from Boston with the long black hair." She smiled at him. "I could understand why you hung on her every word. She had such a cultured accent that the questions really sounded smart."

Sam returned Remi's smile but did not rise to the bait.

They both kept watching the slips they passed for the black-and-gray boat, but didn't spot it. When they reached the slip for the rented dive boat, they pulled in, tied up to the big cleats, and hung the bumpers over the side. While they were hosing off their wet suits and putting the tanks on the dock to be taken to Dave Carmody's dive shop to be refilled, they were still watching for the black-and-gray boat.

"Hey, Fargos!" Ray Holbert was waving as he walked out onto the dock, making it roll a little on its pontoons. He was tall and red-faced, and all his movements had a special vigor. His steps were long and his gestures were big.

"Hi, Ray," said Remi.

"Find anything?"

Sam lifted the cover on a cabinet near the stern to reveal several full net bags. "A few more potsherds we found near a stone hearth, some napped flint tools, a deer antler with some pieces chipped off, probably for projectile points. We've got the place nearly all mapped."

Remi handed up the camera. "It's all in here. You can download it to your computer and line it up on the chart from where the midden is."

"Great," said Ray. "We're catching up a little. I think we're going to get the three sunken villages along this part of the coast all identified, mapped, and given a once-over before the grant money runs out."

"We'll help out a bit when that happens," said Sam. "We can extend the work a bit."

"Let's wait and see," Ray said.

"Follow us to our cottage in your truck," said Remi. "We can hand over the latest finds. The charts and photographs are ready, the artifacts and bones are labeled and shown on the grid. I'd feel better if you have everything."

"Okay," said Holbert. "We're really learning a lot about these people. We knew just about nothing before. These villages were right above the beach. The carbon dates show that they must have been submerged by the rising sea level around the year 700. They all seem to be about the same size as yours—about five or six families in small dwellings with stone hearths. They used catches from the sea for food but also hunted deer inland. This first set of sites has been great."

"You're telling us it's time for the next set, aren't you?" said Remi.

"After tomorrow, I want to move everybody a few miles west. There's a couple dozen potential sites, and each dive team has just done one site. The day after tomorrow, I want every team to take an initial survey of a new spot along the coast off the Caminada Headland. That way, we'll get a better idea of what we've got to get done before we start to lose our summer volunteers. We'll probably eliminate most of the sites when we get a look underwater."

In ten minutes they were at the small cottage Sam and Remi had rented a block from the beach on the south side of Grand Isle. It was a one-story on stilts, with white-painted clapboard siding and a big front porch where they could sit at the end of the day and feel the breeze off the Gulf of Mexico. Sam and Remi liked to be anonymous when they traveled, and there was nothing about the cottage that would prompt anyone to think the couple renting it was a pair of multimillionaires. There was a low roof over the porch, a pair of big windows with an almost unobstructed view of the water, two bedrooms, and a small bathroom. They had converted one bedroom into a storage-and-work area for the objects they had brought up from the sunken Paleo-Indian village.

Ray Holbert entered with them, and Sam took him on a tour

of the artifacts while Remi took the first shower. Sam handed him the grid with the meticulously drawn objects found in various spots. There were also memory cards full of photographs that Remi had taken to ensure that there was a record of each object in relation to the others. The artifacts were stored in plastic boxes.

Holbert looked at the grid of the village and the artifacts. "With this number of deer antlers and bones, it looks as if the rising water changed the landscape a lot. There were probably forested ridges then. Now it's mostly bayous and sea-level flats."

"It's sort of a shame to move on," Remi said. She had showered and changed into Grand Isle evening attire—a pair of shorts and a loose short-sleeved polo shirt with a pair of flip-flops. "Although I won't miss our shadows."

"What do you mean?" asked Holbert.

"It's probably our own fault," said Sam. "There's another dive boat that's been following us. They watch where we go, then stare at us with binoculars. Today they came within a yard of our boat, as though they wanted to see what we had brought up."

"That's odd," said Holbert. "This is the first I've heard of them."

"Well, as I said, maybe it's just us. It's the price of having our names in the papers," Sam said. He looked at Remi. "Or maybe Remi's picture. Well, I'll help you load this stuff into your truck before I take my shower."

In twenty minutes Holbert's white pickup truck was loaded, and soon they were in the restaurant for a meal of shucked oysters, grilled shrimp with remoulade sauce, freshly caught red snapper, and a bottle of chilled Chardonnay from Kistler Vinyards in California. After they'd eaten, Sam said, "What do you think? Would you like to share another bottle of wine?"

"No, thanks," said Ray.

"None for me either," said Remi. "If we've just got one more day at this village, I'd like to get an early start. After tomorrow, we could spend the next few days swimming around, finding nothing."

"That's right, we could," said Sam. They said good night to Ray, walked home to their cottage, locked the door, and turned off the lights. They let the overhead fan turn lazily above their bed and went to sleep listening to the waves washing in along the beach.

Sam woke as the first ray of sun shone through the opening in the curtain, thinking he would tiptoe out of the bedroom to keep from waking Remi only to find her sitting on the front porch with a cup of coffee, dressed and waiting for him, looking out over the Gulf of Mexico.

Sam and Remi stopped at a coffee shop to buy croissants and coffee, then arrived at the marina, walked along the dock to the berth where they had tied their rented dive boat, and then stopped. "See that?" she whispered.

Sam nodded. He was already squinting, stepping silently out of his shoes and onto the foredeck of the boat. The cabin was closed, but the padlock's hasp had been knocked off with a heavy blow. He opened the sliding door and looked down into the cabin. "Our gear is all screwed up."

"Tampered with?"

"That doesn't quite cover it. *All screwed up* is the technical term." Sam took out his cell phone and punched in a number. "Hello, Dave? This is Sam Fargo. We seem to have a problem this morning. We're at the marina, and the dive boat we rented from you has been broken into. It looks like they broke our regulators, cut the rubber on the masks and fins. Can't tell what they did to the tanks, but I'd be really careful putting them under pressure. I haven't checked the engine yet or the gas tank. If you could get us resupplied right away, we could still go out. Meanwhile, I'll call the police."

Dave Carmody said, "Hold on, Sam. I'll be there in half an hour or so with everything you need. And better let me call the cops for you. Grand Isle is a small place, and they know me. They know they have to live with me another twenty years."

"Thanks, Dave. We'll be here." Sam put away his phone and went to sit on the foredeck. For some time he didn't move, just stared out at the open water.

Remi watched him closely. "Sam?"

"What?"

"Promise me you're not planning something out of proportion."

"Not out of proportion."

"Am I going to want to be carrying bail money?"

"Not necessarily," he said.

"Hmmm," she said as she studied him. She took out her phone and punched in another number. "Delia?" she said. "This is Remi Fargo. How are you? Well, that's just great. Is Henry in court or anything? Think I could talk to him? Wonderful. Thank you."

As she waited, Remi walked toward the stern of the boat. "Henry?" she said. "I just wanted to ask you a little favor." She turned her face away from Sam and lowered her voice while she said something Sam couldn't hear. She turned again and walked toward Sam. "Thanks, Henry. If you give him a little heads-up, I'd appreciate it. Bye."

"What Henry was that?" Sam asked.

"Henry Clay Barlow, our attorney."

"That Henry."

"He advised me we didn't need bail. Instead he's calling a friend of his in New Orleans, who will be prepared to come roaring down here in a helicopter with a suitcaseful of money and a writ of habeas corpus if we need him. Henry says he's slick as an eel."

"Henry would consider that high praise. What will that cost us?"

"Depends on what we do."

"Good point." Sam heard a sound and looked up the dock. "There's Dave from the dive shop."

Dave's truck stopped at the end of the dock. He came along the floating dock with a uniformed policeman beside him carrying a toolbox. The cop was big and blond, with broad shoulders and a potbelly, so the shirt of his uniform looked as though it might pop a button. "Hi, Sam," Dave said, then gave a slight bow: "Remi."

Sam got up. "That was quick, Dave."

"This is Sergeant Ron Le Favre. He figured he should look this over before we replace your gear." As soon as Dave's eyes passed across his boat he got distracted and pointed. "Look at that cabin door. That's imported hardwood, varnished so you could have shaved in it."

Sergeant Le Favre stepped onto the boat. "Pleased to meet you both." He took a camera out of his kit and began snapping photographs of the damage. As he did, he asked, "Mr. Fargo, what do you suppose is going on? Anything stolen?"

"Not that I can see. Just wrecked."

"Anybody around here mad at you?"

"Not that I know of. Everybody's been friendly until now."

"You have a theory?"

Sam shrugged. Remi glared at him, puzzled and frustrated.

"Okay. I'll write this up," said Sergeant Le Favre. "That way, Dave can submit it to his insurance company. First, I'll check around to see if anybody was sleeping on his boat last night. Maybe somebody saw something."

"Thanks very much, Sergeant," said Sam. He went to work help-ing Dave Carmody carry the damaged equipment to his truck and the new equipment to the boat. Next he started the engine, and he and Dave listened to it, opened the hatch, and looked at the belts and hoses. Before Dave left Sam said, "Dave, this is probably be-cause somebody got interested in what we were diving for. We've had some publicity lately, so this is probably the price. Just tote up the cost and put it on our bill. I don't want you putting this on your insurance and then having them jack up your rates."

Dave shook his hand. "Thanks, Sam. That's really thoughtful."

As soon as Sam and Remi were alone she said, "No theories, Sam? Really? How about the people in the black-and-gray boat who have been stalking us for days?"

"I didn't say no, I just shrugged."

"If something else happens, don't you want them on the ser-geant's record?"

"Well, if something happened to make those people upset, I'd find it inconvenient to have it in the police record that I suspected them of doing us harm."

"I see," she said. "This should be an interesting day."

Sam moved around the boat, taking an inventory of equipment, before casting off the lines. Remi started the engine and drove slowly out of the marina toward the Gulf. The world ahead was all deep blue sky and sea that met at the horizon and seemed to go on forever.

Sam stood beside her as she came around the breakwater and added speed. "I'm hoping to get this site finished today so that be-fore we move on to the next site we can feel we've got everything there is to find."

"Fine," she said. "That sounds like a peaceful ambition."

They moved westward along the flat green Louisiana coast toward the spot where they'd been diving. But as they came closer Remi said, "You might want to look ahead."

Sam looked over the cabin roof into the distance. He could see the black-and-gray boat anchored ahead. The red-and-white flag was up, and there were people in the water. "Interesting coincidence," he said. "Our diving gear gets sabotaged and now we find these people diving in our exact location." Sam took out the binoculars and stared in the direction of the black-and-gray boat for a few seconds. "They seem to be getting out of the water. Now they're pulling in their dive buoys and striking the flag."

"Well, of course," said Remi. "The famous treasure-hunting Fargos, it turns out, have been diving for broken pottery and deer antlers. Now these people have figured that out." She slowed the engine. "Let's let them get out of here. I'm not going down sixty feet and leaving them up here with our boat."

"Maybe that's not why they're leaving. If we can see them, they can see us. Let's try another approach. Keep an eye on them for a minute." He went into the cabin and returned with a chart. He held it up where Remi could see it. "Head along here toward Vermilion Lake. When we get there, I'd like you to take a winding course up into the bayou."

"That's a little vague."

"I don't want to stifle your creativity. Let's see if you can lose them."

Remi started to move forward, set herself on the proper compass course, and gradually pushed the throttle up, making the 427 Chevrolet engine roar. She shot past the black-and-gray boat at a distance, and kept going at the same speed. After a few minutes, Sam tapped her on the shoulder and she looked back. When she saw the black-and-gray boat coming after them at high speed, she threw her head back and laughed. "Not very subtle, are they? I guess it's a race." She pushed the throttle forward all the way, then tapped it with the heel of her hand to get the last bit of speed out of it. As she sped west along the Caminada Headland, she looked delighted.

Now and then the boat would reach a freak wave and leap over it. Remi would flex her knees to take the jump like a skier, cling to the steering wheel, and then duck to avoid the splash that the wind sent back at them. Sam stood close to her and said, "You can slow down a little bit now. If they lose sight of us this early, they might give up. We want them fully committed."

"Aye, aye," she said.

She drove on, keeping their pursuers barely in sight, until Sam said, "All right. Now go into Vermilion Lake."

She turned right, sped across the open water, and then headed for the bayous. As she shot into the first narrow, winding channel, she gradually pulled back the throttle. "Hey, make yourself useful," she said. "Get up to the bow and make sure I don't hit anything that's alive or puts holes in boats."

"Happy to," Sam said. He got up on the foredeck and pointed in the direction that was clearest. He studied the water for snags and shallow spots and kept her out of them. The water was dark and nearly opaque, the channel lined with reeds and trees hung with Spanish moss and vines. As they moved farther inland, the vegetation grew thicker, and the trees came together to form arches over the water. After a time, Sam called, "Idle the engine."

The engine went to neutral, and the boat coasted a few yards with a minimum of sound, then stopped and drifted into a shaded copse. Somewhere in the distance behind them they could hear the growl of the black-and-gray boat's engine. Sam and Remi exchanged a nod, and then Remi sped up again. They went on for another twenty minutes, and Sam waved at her again. She slowed down to a crawl while Sam came aft and looked at the chart.

"Get ready to anchor."

"Are you sure?"

"Something wrong with this spot?"

"It's a sweltering, mosquito-infested swamp where the alligators and the rare and celebrated American crocodiles can barely fight off the water moccasins. And I just saw an egret fall out of his tree from heat exhaustion."

"Perfect," Sam said. "Let's get our wet suits on. They'll protect us from the mosquitoes. Wear your booties, because we'll be walking. And we might as well bring flippers too, in case we need speed." Sam studied the chart, then put a big red X in a location about a half mile from their position.

"Isn't that a little heavy-handed?"

"They will have worked so hard to see it that they'll need to believe it."

When they were ready, Sam used the blunt end of the gaff to pole them to shore and used the hook end to hold the boat while they got out and took a few steps into the mud. Sam pushed the boat so it could drift out into the middle of the channel.

"Now what?" she asked.

"Now we go on a great big hike."

"Charming. Lead on." She walked along behind him through the reeds and muck.

Every so often Sam would turn back to check on her. She was stepping along at a steady pace, and her face was set in a quiet smile. After about twenty minutes of walking, Sam stopped. "You figured it out, didn't you?"

"Maybe."

"Why only 'maybe'?"

"Are you assuming they put a GPS tracker on our boat?"

He grinned. "I found it. I wondered why they didn't sabotage the engine, then realized it was so we wouldn't spend a lot of time looking around in the engine compartment."

"Then yes. I have figured it out. Let's finish the trek and see if they're out following our trail to the treasure."

He said, "Sometimes you amaze me."

"Really?" she asked. *"Still?"*

He led Remi deeper into the swamp and then along a wide right turn so they completed a vast circle. When they came back to their boat, she went a hundred yards up to the next bend and pointed. The black-and-gray boat was anchored up there to hide it from them.

Sam sat down on an old fallen tree trunk, put on his flippers, and pulled his mask down over his face.

Remi put her hand on his arm. "The alligators weren't just a figure of speech, you know."

"Don't tell them I'm here." He moved into the murky water and disappeared. He reappeared at the stern of the black-and-gray boat. He went to the bow, pulled up the anchor, and let the boat begin to drift downstream.

Remi moved quickly along the shallows to where they had left the dive boat, close to the shore among the dead trees. She used the gaff to push off, lifted the anchor, and looked up the watery channel at Sam, drifting slowly toward her in the black-and-gray boat. She could see he was working with a set of wires he had cut and stripped with his dive knife.

As Remi watched, Sam touched the two wires together, the engine started, and he began to steer the boat down the bayou toward her. She started the engine of their boat and moved along the bayou ahead of him at quarter speed, relying on her memory of where sunken logs and muddy bars had been. In a few minutes she was out into Mud Lake, then into Vermilion Lake, and then out into the Gulf. In a moment, Sam was coming up behind in the black-and-gray boat.

When they reached the open water far out from the Caminada Headland, they brought the two boats together and tied them. Remi climbed aboard the black-and-gray boat. "Sneakily done."

"Thank you," he said. They began to search the black-and-gray boat, concentrating on the cabin. In a few minutes, Remi held up a blue binder with a hundred pages in it. "They're a company. Have you ever heard of Consolidated Enterprises?"

"No," Sam said. "Pretty vague. It doesn't sound like anything specific."

"I guess they don't want to rule anything out," she said.

"At the moment, they're treasure hunters." He pointed to a marine metal detector on the deck, ready to be deployed.

"Why use that thing when you can just follow people who find treasures, wreck their equipment, and take over their spot?"

Sam looked around the cabin again. "There're six of them."

"Two women." She nodded and opened the binder again. "Here we go. They're a 'field team,' complete with pictures and names."

"Take it with you," said Sam.

"Isn't taking things crossing the line?"

"Isn't stranding six people in a swamp forty miles from home crossing the line?"

"I guess you're right." She closed the binder and went on deck. "What should we do with their boat?"

"Where's their home office?"

"New York."

"Then we'd better drive it back and dock it in the marina," Sam said. "It's probably rented from somebody who can't afford to lose it."

Remi swung her legs over the gunwale into their rented boat. Sam handed her his mask and flippers, then took off his wet suit and tossed it into the boat too. Remi cast off the line that connected the two boats. "I'll race you back to Grand Isle." She started the engine. "Winner gets the first shower."

Sam restarted the black-and-gray boat and got off to a fair start. Speeding up and heading for the marina at high speed, the bottoms of the boats rising to crest waves before smacking down into the troughs, they arrived almost an hour later nearly even. When Sam tied the black-and-gray boat to the dock, he climbed out wearing a purloined sweatshirt with the hood up over a baseball cap. He walked off the dock, then up the next one, where Remi was tying up their boat. She looked up. "You're looking smug in your stolen finery."

He shook his head. "I just smile a lot. It means I'm guileless and friendly."

She finished with the lines, then stepped to the cabin and tugged once on the new padlock. "Guileless? Being transparent isn't the same as being guileless. Take me to a long hot shower, a good restaurant, and then maybe we'll talk about the friendly part."

3

La Jolla, California

SELMA WONDRASH SAT AT HER DESK IN THE OFFICE ON
the first floor of the Fargo house on Goldfish Point in La Jolla.
It was still early evening in California, and she looked up from
the book she was reading to see the sun beginning to set over the
smooth expanse of the ocean. She loved the moment when the sun
seemed to sit on the horizon like the yolk of a fried egg. The long
Pacific swells came in below the house at the foot of the cliffs, and
she thought about how they came to her from across the world. She
seldom had time to read books for pure pleasure, but the Fargos
had been in Louisiana for nearly a month and what they were doing didn't require much research effort from her.

She ran her fingers through her close-cropped hair, closed her
eyes for a moment, and thought about the book she was reading—

The Greater Journey, David McCullough's book about nineteenth-century Americans who went to Paris. They were like her, people in love with knowledge. For them and her, to learn was to live.

She had, she thought, succeeded in finding the place for her.

As a child, Selma had sometimes imagined a painted portrait of herself, a mousy, uninteresting creature—*The Girl in the Front Row With Her Hand Up*. She had begun as a prodigy, a child who read at two, and kept reading, learning, studying, calculating, and here she was, a master researcher.

Catching sight of her reflection in the big shiny surface of the window overlooking the ocean, there she was, a small—perhaps compact—middle-aged—no fudging about that—woman, wearing a tie-dyed T-shirt and khaki pants. Well, these were Japanese gardening pants, and stylish.

She had been working for Sam and Remi Fargo for quite some time now. They had hired her right after they had sold their company but before they had built this house. Remi had said, "We need somebody to help us do research."

"On what?" asked Selma.

Remi answered, "On questions. On anything and everything. History, archaeology, languages, oceanography, meteorology, computer science, biology, medicine, physics, games. We want somebody who will hear a question and devise ways to answer it."

"I do that," she'd said. "I've studied many of those fields myself, and taught a few. When I worked as a reference librarian, I picked up some sources and know many experts on the others. I'll take the job."

Sam said, "You don't even know the salary yet."

"You don't either," she'd said. "I'll accept minimum wage for three probationary months and then you can name the figure. I assure you, it will be much higher than you know. You'll be much more appreciative then than you are now."

She had never been less than delighted that she'd chosen to work for the Fargos. It was as though she had never looked for a job but instead was to be paid for being a good Selma. She even helped Sam and Remi plan this house. She had researched architecture and architects, materials and sustainable design, and because she had already studied Sam and Remi she could remind them of things they liked and would need space to accommodate. She had also explained what was necessary for a first-rate research facility.

The telephone rang, and she considered letting Pete or Wendy, her junior researchers, pick it up. The idea lasted a half second before she became, as always, the victim of her own intense curiosity. "Hello. This is the Fargo residence. Selma Wondrash speaking."

"Selma!" came the voice. *"Meine Liebe, wo sind Ihr Chef und seine schöne Frau?"*

"Herr Doktor Fischer. *Sie sind tauchen im Golf von Mexiko."*

"Your German is better every day. I've made a fascinating discovery and I'd like to discuss it with Remi and Sam. Is there any way I can reach them right away?"

"Yes. If you'll give me a number where you can be reached, I'll ask them to call you as soon as I can get them above the surface."

"I'm in Berlin. The number here is . . ."

As Selma wrote down the number, she was already thinking she would put the McCullough book aside. Albrecht Fischer was a professor of classical archaeology at Heidelberg. It wouldn't hurt to spend some time this evening reviewing a few of his recent academic publications just to see what might be next. "Thank you, Albrecht. I'll get Sam and Remi's attention as soon as I can."

Late in the evening, after their romantic dinner of shrimp etouffee, softshell crab, and bread pudding at the Grand Jatte and a moonlit walk home along the Gulf, Sam and Remi had just gotten into bed when his cell phone rang.

As Sam dropped his feet to the floor to get his phone from the top of the dresser, Remi raised her head and leaned on her elbow. "Mine has an off switch."

"Sorry," he said. "I forgot it was on." He flipped his thumb across the screen. "Hello?"

"Sam?"

"Selma." He looked at Remi. She turned away and pulled the covers up to her chin.

"I hope I'm not calling too late."

"Of course not." He smiled at Remi. "What's up?"

"Albrecht Fisher called. He's made a discovery he wants to discuss with you and Remi."

"Is he at his university office in Heidelberg?"

"No, he's in Berlin. He gave me his number."

"Yes."

She read him the number, and he used the pen he'd left on the dresser to write it on a slip of paper in his wallet. "Thanks, Selma. How's everything at home?"

"Everything proceeds with the utmost serenity at the manor whether the lord and lady are in residence or not."

"You wouldn't call a man up in the middle of the night just to make fun of him."

"Never," said Selma. "Sleep tight." She hung up.

Sam went out to the kitchen and began to close the door, but Remi was already out of bed and put her hand on the door to keep it from closing. "I'm already awake. We may as well both be tired tomorrow."

"What time is it in Berlin?"

"Seven hours ahead of Louisiana."

"So it's eight a.m."

Sam tapped in the number and waited while the connection was established, then switched his phone to speaker. They listened to it ring.

"'Allo, Sam. *Wie geht es Ihnen?*"

"Fine, Albrecht. Selma said you had something to tell us, so we're both listening."

"I do," he said. "It's a find that I made only a week ago. I brought a few things here for testing and the results have come in."

"What is it?"

"My friends, I think I've found something incredible, and it has to be kept absolutely secret for now. It's so big, I can't excavate it alone. I can't even do a preliminary survey alone. Full summer will begin in a month, and again the need for secrecy in this situation doesn't even bear describing."

"We understand the secrecy, but can't you even tell us what it is?" asked Remi.

"I think . . . I believe that what I've found is an ancient battlefield. It seems to be intact, undisturbed."

Sam wrote on his slip of paper, "What do you think?" Remi took the pen and wrote: "Yes."

Sam said, "We'll come to you."

"Thank you, Sam. I'm in Berlin now, buying some things and borrowing others. Send me your flight information, and I'll meet you at the airport."

"Remi and I will be on a plane sometime in the morning, but the flight will probably add a whole day. See you soon." He hung up and looked at Remi.

"We should have asked what kind of battlefield," she said.

"All he said was ancient. So I guess we don't have to worry about unexploded ordnance."

"If it's in Europe, we may."

"He's in Berlin, but it sounded as though that was where he was doing tests, not where the site is."

"We'd better get packed."

In the morning, as they made the fifty-four-mile drive to New Orleans, Sam called Ray Holbert and said, "I'm sorry, but a friend called last night and needs some emergency help on a project, so we've got to go. I apologize for leaving in such a hurry."

Holbert said, "Don't think anything of it. You gave us a great month's work and we'll miss you. We don't have many volunteers who pay all their own expenses and plenty of ours too. But we'll keep in touch and let you know what else we discover."

"Thanks, Ray."

"Oh, and Sam? If someone were to go look for those people who rented that black-and-gray boat, where would you suggest they start?"

"I can't say for sure. Somewhere in the bayous inland from Lake Vermilion and Mud Lake, would be my best guess."

Selma had their itinerary waiting at the airport. Sam and Remi flew Royal Dutch Airlines from Louis Armstrong Airport in New Orleans to Atlanta and then on to Amsterdam. Sam and Remi slept on the transatlantic flight and then woke in time for arrival in Amsterdam. The final flight into Berlin was much shorter, and when they arrived at Tegel Airport in Berlin at 11:20 the next morning, there was Albrecht Fischer.

Fischer was tall and thin, with blond hair that was slowly lightening to white and once fair skin that had been tanned by the sun so many times that it had stayed that way, making his blue eyes stand out. He wore a gray sport coat that looked weather-beaten, with a dark blue silk scarf hanging loose from his neck. He shook Sam's hand and kissed Remi on both cheeks. It wasn't until they were walking toward the exit from the terminal that Albrecht Fischer spoke about his find.

"I'm sorry for telling you so little on the telephone. I think you'll understand when you see what I've brought to Germany."

"This isn't where it came from?" asked Remi.

"No," he said. "At the site, I sensed I was being watched. I needed to do lab work and examinations, but I didn't dare do them there. So I came back here. There are colleagues at Humboldt and at the Free University who have let me use their labs. I've been sleeping in the office of a colleague who is on leave and using the shower in his chemistry lab."

"Why not just go back to your own lab at Heidelberg?"

"A bit of a ruse to throw off anyone who might be interested in what I'm doing. I had some odd feelings while I was at work, and I've found that when you think you're being watched, you usually are."

Fischer took them outside the terminal, where he hailed a cab that took them to the Hotel Adlon Kempinski. While Sam checked them in, Remi took in the beauty of the hotel—the ornate carpets, fine furniture, vaulted ceiling—but she also noticed that Albrecht Fischer's eyes were moving constantly, scanning the steady stream of people coming and going through the lobby. He was agitated, impatient, and, at the same time, there was something else. He seemed to be afraid. Sam sent the bellman up to their room with the luggage, then rejoined Remi and Fischer. "Shall we go up?"

Remi shook her head. "I think we'd better go see what the good professor has been working on."

Albrecht brightened. "Yes, please do. I know you're probably tired from all the travel, but I've been keeping myself quiet about this until I'm half mad. And the lab isn't far."

Sam and Remi exchanged a glance, and Sam said, "Then of

course. Let's go." They stepped outside, and the doorman signaled a cab and opened the door for them. Albrecht waited until the door was closed to say, "Humboldt University, please." The cab let them off only a few blocks away at the statue of Frederick the Great in front of the main building of the university on Unter den Linden.

They walked quickly into a building that seemed to be all science laboratories—doors with smoked-glass windows with numbers on them. The ones that were open had young people inside, wearing lab coats and wandering among black boxes with screens, stands that held chemistry apparatus, and counters with centrifuges and spectrometers. As they passed, Sam kept looking into each lab. Remi took Sam's arm. "I know you're reliving the high points of your college years."

"What do you mean?" asked Albrecht. "I thought all American students did was drink beer and go to parties."

"Sam went to Caltech. They worked in labs, then drank beer and went to parties."

"I was just thinking about some of the people who went to this university. There was one student who was promising—a kid named Albert Einstein."

Remi said, "And before him, Hegel, Schopenhauer, the Brothers Grimm . . ."

"Today we're going to rely on Remi's specialties," said Albrecht. "A bit of history, a bit of physical anthropology."

He stopped at a dark laboratory, took out a key, and opened the door. They stepped in, and he turned on the fluorescent lights. "This is it." The room had black counters along the side walls, a whiteboard in front, and a half dozen large stainless steel tables. On one of them was a polished wooden coffin.

"Who died?" Remi asked.

"I call him Friedrich." He walked to the coffin. "Specifically, I've certified that he's my great-great-uncle Friedrich von Schlechter. When I found him, I didn't want to arouse curiosity, so I bought a coffin and hired an undertaker in the nearest city to put him in it, get the proper export papers, and ship him to Berlin for burial." He opened the lid. Inside was an age-browned skeleton with a few scraps of material that seemed to be rotted leather and a length of rusty metal like the blade of a sword.

Sam and Remi looked inside. Sam said, "He seems to have gotten his head disconnected during the trip."

Remi looked closer. "It didn't happen in transit. See the mark on the vertebra, right here?" She pointed at the back top surface of the last vertebra, where a deep chip was missing. "That's from an ax or a sword."

"Very good," said Fischer. "If you spend some time with him, you begin to learn more about who he is. Judging from the wear on the molars, and the good condition of the bones, I'd estimate he was at least thirty, but not yet forty. If you'll look at his left radius and ulna, you'll see some more marks. Those are clearly wounds that healed long before he died. The decapitation, of course, was his last injury. But these marks tell much more about him. He was a warrior. He was probably using some kind of two-handed weapon when an opponent swung a blade at his forearm. Or if he was using a shield, the blow got behind it. He lived and the wound healed."

"The swords and shields remind me," said Remi. "Have you run the carbon 14 yet?"

"Yes. We did one on a chip of his femur, one on a strip of leather that was with the body—a fragment of his shoe, a wrapping for a weapon perhaps. The reading was 82.813 percent of the carbon 14 remaining. I had also taken samples from another individual near him and tested them here. The result was the same, giving us a date of around 450 C.E."

"Four fifty," said Sam. "And where is the site?"

"It's a couple of miles to the east of Szeged, Hungary."

"Wow," said Remi. "And you think Friedrich here is just one of many?"

"Yes. How many, I don't know yet. A battlefield is essentially a very large mass grave. The place where the bodies come to rest is lower than the surrounding area, whether they're buried in the usual way or covered over time. I've detected remains as far apart as a hundred yards. Here. Look at this." Fischer went to another table and unrolled a large hand-drawn map with a grid on it. "This is the Tisza River, and here's the place where the Mureş joins it. This grid is where I found Friedrich, and this one, way over here, is where I found another individual at the same depth."

"Who could they be?"

"I'm tempted to assume they were Huns. The area of Szeged was the stronghold of the Huns at around that time. But when they fought a war, they would decamp as a group and go off to the enemy's country to fight. They fought the Ostrogoths, the Visigoths, Romans—both from Rome and from Constantinople—the Avars, Gauls, Alans, Scythians, Thracians, Armenians, and many smaller peoples whom they swallowed up in their conquests. They were also at some point allied with each of these groups against one or more of the others. Sorting out who was in this battle will take some time and examination."

"Of course," said Sam. "It's hard to say much about a battle after looking at two skeletons."

"Exactly," said Albrecht. "I'm eager to get back to begin an excavation. But there are problems."

"What sort of problems?" Remi asked.

"It's a big site—a large open field that at one time was a pasture, part of a collective farm under the Communist government, but has been lying fallow for more than ten years. It's out in the open near a road. Szeged is a thriving modern city, only a few miles away. If the word got out, there would be no way to stop people from coming out on their own and digging for souvenirs. And there have been enough stories of treasure being found in classical-era sites to attract thousands. In a day, everything could be lost."

"But, so far, everything is still secret," Sam said. "Right?"

"I'm just hoping that I'm imagining things. But I got the impression several times while I was exploring the district around Szeged that I was being spied on."

"There's a lot of that going around," said Remi.

"What do you mean?"

Sam said, "While we were in Louisiana, we were followed wherever we went to dive. It turned out to be an exploration team from a company called Consolidated Enterprises."

"That doesn't sound like archaeologists. It sounds like a business conglomerate."

"I'd say that's pretty accurate," said Sam. "Their business plan seems to be to wait for someone else to find a promising site and then push them off it and dive it themselves."

"Sam got them to follow us into a swamp on foot and then borrowed their boat."

Albrecht chuckled. "Well, you've become known for finding gold and jewels. I'm just a poor professor who studies people who lived a long time ago and whose idea of treasure was a good barley harvest. This battlefield is the most dramatic thing I've found. I'd been studying the contours of the land, looking for signs of a Roman settlement. At one point, the area was part of a Roman province.

The main reason I took interest in the field was that it wasn't covered with buildings."

"Do you have any idea who was spying on you in Szeged?" asked Sam.

"One day someone broke into my hotel room. I had my notes and my laptop computer with me. My luggage was searched, but nothing was taken. But on several days I saw a large black car with four big Eastern European men in dark suits. I would see them three or four times in a day watching me, and sometimes they would have binoculars or a camera."

"They sound like police," said Sam. "Maybe they suspected you were doing something illegal—like shipping Friedrich out of the country. If they knew you were an archaeologist, they'd want to know about any artifacts you'd found."

Albrecht looked at his feet. "I'm guilty of smuggling Friedrich out. But if I had stayed in Hungary to do the lab work, the word of my discovery would have been out in a day. Keeping a find secret is standard procedure. Everyone who has gone public prematurely has come back to a site that's been looted and trampled and all scientific and historical value destroyed. And this site is more vulnerable than most. The bodies I've found still had whatever weapons and armor they'd died with. There are textile fragments, bits of leather and fur. All that would be lost."

"Of course we'll respect your secrecy," Sam said. "And we're here to help you any way we can."

"We're good at secrets," Remi said. "But wouldn't it be a good idea to get Selma thinking about this? We may be able to use her help, and she has a way of anticipating what we might like to know."

"Do we have your permission?" asked Sam. "It would mean alerting the rest of our staff, but that's all."

"Of course," said Fischer. "The more good minds working on our side, the better. For now, I'm going to put Friedrich away."

"After we've had a chance to unpack and recover a bit, we hope you'll come to the hotel and have dinner with us," Remi said.

"Are you sure you wouldn't rather be alone?"

"We'd love to have a chance to talk some more tonight about your discovery," she said.

"I'd be delighted," Albrecht said. "What time?"

"Eight o'clock."

"Good. I'll just stay and lock up here, then get ready. I'll be there just before eight."

After they all shook hands, Sam and Remi walked out of the building, went past the huge statue of Frederick the Great on his horse, then turned right to walk onto Unter den Linden. At the distant west end they could see the Brandenburg Gate, and the Hotel Adlon Kempinski almost beside it. As they walked along the pedestrian mall under the linden trees away from the university, they passed famous streets one by one—Friedrichstrasse, Charlottenstrasse. They passed the Russian Embassy, and near their hotel was the Hungarian Embassy.

It was beautiful in the late afternoon, and Remi held her head high and looked at every sight.

"What are you thinking?" Sam asked.

"I was just wondering why we're being followed."

4

BERLIN

"WHERE ARE THEY?" ASKED SAM.

"Give yourself a few seconds," said Remi. "After that, take a look behind us at about the seven o'clock position. There's a young blond woman, and she's with a tall man with a shaved head."

Remi touched her shiny auburn hair as she walked. "A young blond woman in Berlin, eh? What could be more surprising than that?" Her body language said she hadn't been satisfied when she'd touched her hair. She took a small compact from her purse and appeared to look at herself, and brush a fine strand back into place with her hand. "It's one of the women from the team in Louisiana. And the man . . . Yep, him too. Their pictures were in that notebook we stole from their boat. How could they even get a flight to Berlin that quickly? We just got here a few hours ago and we knew where we were going."

Sam shrugged. "I guess they must have a corporate jet."

"Maybe we should get a job with Consolidated Enterprises. I wonder what other perks they get."

"Not the best time for them to show up."

"What do you think we should do?"

"I suppose we could ask a German lawyer if it's illegal to follow us around."

"Let's do that," Remi said. "Albrecht has gone to so much trouble to keep his discovery secret. I'd hate to have these idiots we brought with us claim jumping. Maybe we can get them deported."

"I'd rather have them in Germany than Hungary."

"Good point," Remi said. "We can talk to Albrecht at dinner."

"I'd like to do something before then."

"What?"

"I only see two. Let's split them up."

"After all the diving and flying, I could use an hour of pampering in the hotel salon."

Sam and Remi walked along the mall together. Then, when they reached the entrance to the Adlon Kempinski Hotel, Remi kissed Sam's cheek and went through the doors into the lobby. Sam walked alone for a few steps, then looked back to be sure the blond girl went in after her. He also saw the tall man with the shaved head stop suddenly and pretend to look back at someone in the other direction. Sam moved on.

He moved quickly past the Brandenburg Gate and entered the Tiergarten, the big urban park. He headed along the pathway under the trees toward the Hauptbahnhof, the big, shiny metallic building that was Europe's largest two-level railway station. He entered with the tall man with the shaved head still a distance behind, slipped into the crowd of travelers and commuters milling about, and bought a ticket for an S-Bahn train across the city. He hurried to the proper platform to arrive just as the doors opened up, stepped in, looked to see if his follower walked into another car, waited until the doors were about to close, and stepped off. He ran from the platform and disappeared down the escalator to the long-distance trains that ran east–west. He stood by the underside of the escalator for a few minutes, watching for the tall man with the shaved head.

When he was sure the man was not coming, Sam took the escalator up to the ground level, walked out of the Hauptbahnhof, found a comfortable bench in the shade, and watched the station exit.

It took twenty minutes before his tail emerged, looking glum. He'd stopped looking for Sam and kept his eyes on the ground a few feet ahead, his hands in the pockets of his thin raincoat. After he had a good head start, Sam stood and followed.

The man walked north onto Alt-Moabit, kept going until he reached the Tiergarten Hotel, and went inside. Sam slipped into a small bar across the street, sat at a table by the front window, and watched the hotel. It was a four-story building with no more than sixty rooms. A waitress came to the table, he smiled and pointed at the glass of beer the man at the next table had, so she brought him one.

He saw the young woman with the blond hair return to the hotel about ten minutes later. He kept watching. He saw the woman appear in a window on the fourth floor, open it, then draw the curtains. As he was finishing his beer, the front door of the hotel opened again, and, one at a time, the other four members of the Louisiana team emerged. There were three men and a woman with short dark hair. They paired themselves, two and two, and began to walk.

As Sam followed them through the Tiergarten, he decided they looked like a group of young accountants who had just come off work and were on their way to have a drink together. He was not surprised when he saw that they were heading toward the Adlon Hotel. After they arrived, two of the men split off and went into a nearby restaurant. The other two, now looking like a couple, walked into the lobby of the hotel.

Standing in the middle of the lobby, they looked a little uncertain. They stopped and turned, their eyes directed upward toward the curved ceiling with its crisscrossing of beams. Sam passed behind them and stepped into the elevator without looking back and took it to the floor above the Fargos' floor before walking back down the stairs to their room.

He knocked, and Remi opened the door, wearing an emerald green Donna Karan dress that he had admired when he'd seen it on a hanger. On Remi, it was hypnotic, making her skin glow and her eyes seem a brighter green than usual.

"Wow," he said. "I just had a dream that I was married to a woman who looked exactly like you. I hope I don't wake up."

"Flattery will get you everywhere. And you may recall I just spent two hours getting pampered. So what's the result of your sneaking around like a Cold War spy?"

"I completed the mission, but the news is not good," he said. "The whole bunch are here, all six. Two are watching the lobby now, and two are having dinner down the street. They're probably going to be the late shift. I don't think we'll see baldy and blondy again until morning."

"Okay," she said. "I'll take a turn worrying while you get showered and dressed. Your suit and white shirt are hanging over there in the closet. Albrecht will be here in a half hour."

"Right. While you're worrying, maybe you should call Henry again and see if he knows any great lawyers in Germany or Hungary."

"I already did and he doesn't. He's going to e-mail me a recommendation from a friend of his while we're at dinner. That reminds me. I'm starving, are you? I've been dreaming of smoked goose and champagne and marzipan cake since I heard someone talking about it in the salon."

"Don't. You're making me hungrier." Sam showered and dressed. Eight o'clock passed. When Albrecht was fifteen minutes late, Sam called his cell phone but it was turned off and the call went directly to voice mail. He called the front desk to ask whether their friend had come. Then he checked with the restaurant to find out whether Albrecht had been waiting for them there.

"Let's hope he got distracted with his friend Friedrich and forgot the time. If he's had colleagues here doing carbon dating, maybe he was getting other tests done and they distracted him," Sam said with concern.

"Let's try home." Remi took out her phone and dialed.

"Hi, Remi."

"Hi, Selma," she said. "We seem to have lost track of Albrecht."

"What do you mean 'lost track'?"

"He was supposed to meet us at the hotel a half hour ago, but he hasn't shown up, hasn't called, and isn't answering his cell. I thought he might have left a message with you, but I guess he didn't. Do we have any other numbers on file for him? He was staying at some professor's office at Humboldt University."

"Just his home and his office at Heidelberg."

"Probably that's a dead end."

"Anything else I can do?"

"Yes, actually. See what you can find out about a company called Consolidated Enterprises."

"Are they American?"

"I read something that said they were based in New York, but we just saw six of them here."

"I'll get on it."

"Thanks, Selma. They seem to be following us. And if they've already spotted Albrecht, we might have a problem. He's so paranoid, he may have decided to walk to France to throw them off."

"I'll let you know who and what they are."

"Good night, Selma." Remi put her phone back into her purse and turned to Sam. "Nothing. Any other ideas?"

"Well, you can either stay here keeping your beauty pristine or you can put on something practical and go with me to see if we can find him."

She shrugged. "I guess I've already shown myself to the only guy I was trying to impress. Take one last look before I put on a pair of jeans and sneakers."

"Sorry."

She kicked off her high heels and opened the small refrigerator, selected a chocolate bar, and took a bite. "Here. Have some dinner while I change." She gave him the bar, then turned around so he could unzip her dress.

A few minutes later Sam and Remi walked briskly back along Unter den Linden toward Humboldt University. The streets were full of people—locals and tourists—enjoying the beautiful walk beneath the double row of linden trees on an early-summer night. The fourth time Sam looked over his shoulder at the walkway behind them he said, "I don't see our stalkers."

Remi said, "They probably knew we had a dinner reservation at a Michelin-starred restaurant and figured we'd be accounted for over the next three hours."

"Are you getting worried?"

"More and more," she said. "Albrecht Fischer isn't an absentminded professor. He's used to running an academic department, teaching, writing, and putting together mental models of incredibly complex buildings with very little to go on. He doesn't ask friends to come halfway around the world and then forget they're here."

"Let's not assume anything," Sam said. "We're almost there."

They reached the laboratory building where Albrecht had taken them a few hours earlier. The outer door was still unlocked. They could see lights on in some of the labs on upper floors, but when they reached Albrecht's lab, it was dark.

Remi said, "Could we have passed him on the way?"

"Probably not. I was studying everybody I could see to spot watchers. But he might have gone somewhere to change for dinner, so we don't know which direction he'd be coming from."

Sam reached out tentatively to test the doorknob of Albrecht's lab and found that it turned. He opened the door, reached in, and turned on the lights. The coffin with Friedrich's remains was gone. The lab tables that had been lined up very precisely in two rows earlier were pushed aside at odd angles, and two had been knocked over. Two chairs looked as though they had been hurled across the room. As Remi and Sam moved farther into the room, they found several large splotches of blood in a trail leading toward the door. The scarf Albrecht had been wearing lay on the floor. Sam picked it up and put it in his coat pocket.

Remi took out her cell phone, dialed quickly, and clapped the phone to her ear.

"Police?" asked Sam.

"Uh-huh. In Germany they're 1-1-0." She heard something in German and said, "Hello. Can I speak to you in English? Good. I think a friend of ours has been kidnapped. Abducted. My husband and I were going to meet him at our hotel at eight o'clock. He didn't come, and so we're here at his laboratory at Humboldt University. There's blood on the floor, the furniture is knocked over, and things are missing." She listened. "My name is Remi Fargo. Thank you. We'll wait for them at the front door of this building."

Remi and Sam turned off the lights, left the laboratory, and walked down the hallway to the entrance. The on-off wail that European sirens make grew louder. When they opened the door, they saw the police car emerge from Friedrichstrasse and head toward them. The car stopped in front of the building, and two police officers got out.

Sam said, "Hello, Officers. Do you speak English?"

"I have a little English," said one of the policemen. "Are you Herr Fargo?"

"Yes. And this is my wife, Remi. Please come and see what we've found."

He and Remi led the two policemen into the laboratory and turned on the lights. As soon as they saw the condition of the room, the policemen looked more comfortable. They were on firm ground again: there had been a crime and so they were in charge. As they looked closely at the various physical signs of violence, the officers asked questions and took notes. "What is your friend's name? Is he a professor at Humboldt? If he's a professor at Heidelberg, why does he have a laboratory here? What is the nature of his work? Does he have a rival who would do something like this?"

Sam sighed. "Professor Fischer felt he had been watched while he was in Hungary. There were four men who followed him around in a car. He had no idea who they were."

"Anyone else?"

"We arrived today from an archaeological dive in the Gulf of Mexico off the state of Louisiana in the United States. There were six people there who work for a company called Consolidated Enterprises. They followed our boat to various dive sites and then sabotaged our equipment. As we were leaving here for our hotel this afternoon, we saw that two of the same people were in Berlin, following us."

"How would we find them?"

"They're staying at the Tiergarten Hotel," Sam said. "Fourth floor."

The two policemen conferred for a few seconds, and then the English speaker spoke into a hand radio briefly. Then he said, "We would like you to come with us."

"Where are we going?"

"The Tiergarten Hotel."

When they arrived at the Tiergarten Hotel, there were already six police cars parked in front and a high-ranking officer was waiting. The two policemen with Remi and Sam called him Hauptmann. He turned to them and said, "Mr. and Mrs. Fargo? I'm Captain Klein. I've got men upstairs speaking with these Americans who might have abducted your friend."

Sam said, "I'm a bit uncomfortable about the idea that these people could be the kidnappers. They're not ethical, but they don't seem to be violent."

Captain Klein shrugged. "You said they sabotaged diving equipment, perhaps endangering you. They've followed you from one continent to another. Sometimes criminals thrive because they don't seem to be the type. We'll know soon."

Klein's radio gave a blast of static. He said into it, *"Ja?"* There was a recitation by a male voice on the other end, and Klein replied briefly. He said to Sam and Remi, "Your friend is not in either of their rooms. We have some men searching other areas—the basement, storerooms, linen closets, offices, and so on."

"What about the specimens?" Remi asked. "There would be no legitimate reason for them to have any ancient artifacts or remains. They've been in Europe for only a few hours."

"Could you identify these objects if you saw them?"

"Some of them," she said. "Professor Fischer showed us the skeleton of an ancient warrior. There was a rusty partial sword or dagger, part of a leather wrapping or strap. And he had a map divided into a grid that showed the place where these had been found."

"Where did he find them?"

"Somewhere in Hungary," Sam said. "Captain, I would appreciate it if the description of the find and the location could be kept out of any public report. Professor Fischer has been keeping these things secret. If the word got out, the excavation of the site would be threatened. I personally assure you that the finds will all be reported to the government there and all permits obtained."

"Thank you both for your candor. I'll do my best to keep this information confidential." There was another blast of static, and he listened to his radio. *"Danke."* To Remi and Sam he said, "They're ready for us upstairs."

Sam, Remi, and Hauptmann Klein took the narrow elevator to the fourth floor and walked to an open doorway, where a police officer waited. He stepped aside, and they entered. The six Americans Sam and Remi had first seen in the boat off Louisiana were seated in the room, three on the couch and three at the small table by the window. Now that they were close and in a well-lighted room, Sam could see they showed red spots from mosquito bites, severe sunburns, and a number of scratches from struggling through thick foliage.

"Do you recognize these people?" asked Klein.

"I do," said Remi.

"So do I," Sam said.

"Yes," said Captain Klein. "As you predicted, they're carrying identification from Consolidated Enterprises in New York, and

I'm sorry to say all six are here. I had hoped one or two of them would be with your missing friend."

The young blond woman at the table stood up, angry. "What are these people doing here?"

"Mr. and Mrs. Fargo reported a professor missing. Do you know them?"

"Yes," she said. "They stole our boat and stranded us in a Louisiana swamp. We could easily have died out there."

"And now they've gotten you detained in a foreign country for a very serious crime. If I were you, I would stay far away from them."

"*Falsely* detained!" said the tall man with the shaved head. "I demand to have our lawyer present."

"Falsely or truly detained, still detained," said Klein. "We are simply attempting to eliminate one possible set of suspects. Trust me, if you are eliminated now, you will have good cause to thank us. Kidnapping a world-renowned German scholar is not something you want to be tried for in Berlin."

Klein stepped away from them and beckoned to the Fargos. They went out into the hallway and closed the door. He said, "My men thoroughly searched their rooms. They found no bones, no rusty objects, and no notes or maps."

Sam said, "I don't think these people abducted Albrecht Fischer. We saw two of them following us on Unter den Linden to our hotel. Then we saw the other four walk to our hotel and split up. They didn't seem to be moving against Albrecht, but they could have taken him soon after we left the laboratory."

"They could easily be a surveillance team for a much larger conspiracy," said Klein. "They've still offered no good explanation as to why they're following you and spying on you. They're clearly rivals looking for a discovery to steal, and Albrecht Fischer had a discovery. I'm going to take them to the station and spend some time finding out what they're up to."

"We certainly have no objection," said Remi.

"We'll also have officials watching the borders for the professor. If his kidnappers have had him for a couple of hours, though, he could be gone already." Klein looked at them shrewdly. "But you've figured that out. You're leaving Berlin too, aren't you?"

Sam said, "Someone kidnapped Albrecht Fischer and stole his notes, specimens, and photographs. I don't know if it was friends of these people or someone else entirely. But I do know where they're taking him."

"Then I wish you the best of luck. If it were my friend, that's where I would go. Good night."

5

Szeged, Hungary

SAM AND REMI CHECKED OUT OF THE ADLON KEMPINSKI Hotel late that night and took a cab to the Hauptbahnhof, where Sam had lost his follower that afternoon. They got on the south-bound Stadtbahn, but rode it only to Schönefeld Airport, where they caught a plane to Budapest. It was just an hour and a half to Ferihegy. They took a train from the airport to Nyugati Station in Budapest and then got on the next train that would take them the one hundred seventy kilometers to the city of Szeged near the southern border.

They walked out of the station in the morning to see lined-up cabs waiting for travelers. Sam left the suitcases with Remi and walked up the line saying to each driver, "Do you speak English?" When he saw a driver shake his head or look puzzled, he went to the next one. At the fourth cab, there was a dark, thin middle-aged man with sad-looking brown eyes and a mustache that looked like a brush. He was leaning against his cab, and there were three other drivers with him, listening to a story he was telling and laughing. When he heard Sam's question, he raised his hand. "Are you just curious or do you speak English?"

"I speak English," Sam said.

"Good. Then you can correct me if I make a mistake."

The man's English was perfect. His slight accent showed he had learned the language from a British teacher. "So far, you could correct me," Sam said.

"Where can I take you?"

"First, to our hotel. After that, we would like to take a look at the city."

"Good. City Hotel Szeged, then."

"How did you know?"

"It's a good, respectable hotel, and you look like smart people." He took their suitcases and put them in the trunk of his car, then drove. "You'll be glad you made time to see Szeged. It's the place where the best sausage and the best paprika come from."

"I like the architecture," said Remi. "The buildings have such interesting colors, mostly pastels, and baroque styles with all the intricate details that make them very distinctive."

"It's partly a good thing and partly bad," said the driver. "The bad part happened first. In March 1879, the river—the Tisza, over that way—flooded and destroyed the whole city. The good part is that afterward, the people thought hard about what they were building."

"It worked. For a city with a hundred seventy-five thousand people, it's gorgeous."

"You've been reading guidebooks."

She shrugged. "It's a way to pass the time on the train."

He stopped in front of the City Hotel, took the Fargos' two suitcases out of the trunk and set them in the doorway, and then handed Sam a card. "Here is my card. My name is Tibor Lazar. You can ask the people at the front desk about me and they'll say I'm honest and reliable. I know that because two of them are cousins."

"Thank you," said Remi. "Should we call when we're ready or will you wait for us?"

"I'll wait here."

A bellman was already carrying their suitcases to the front desk. They registered and went up to their room.

Sam sat on the bed and began to look at Google maps on his iPad. Remi whispered, "What are you looking for?"

"The field. We know that sooner or later, the kidnappers will take Albrecht to his find so he can show them where he's dug."

"Can you see where it is on the map?"

"I'm trying. It was on the east side of the Tisza River, north of the Mura River. I remember it in relation to the place where the two meet. He used that to orient his chart."

"I've got something you want," she said. "When we were in the lab and asked Albrecht if we could share the details with Selma, I took a picture of the chart with my phone so she'd know the spot we were referring to." She took out her phone and showed him the picture of the chart.

He kissed her cheek. "Perfect." He used his phone to call Selma and put her on speaker.

"Selma here. Fire away."

"Hi, Selma. Did you get the drawing of a site from Remi last night?"

"Yes. I assume that's the site Albrecht's been working on?"

"That's right," Sam said. "He said it would be fine to bring you in on this, so Remi sent it right away. The problem is that last night the reason Albrecht didn't come to dinner was that he was kidnapped from the lab in Berlin. The police have been watching plane and train stations, but I'm afraid these people got Albrecht out of Germany before we reported it."

"Was it those people from Consolidated Enterprises?"

"I'm not sure. I can't see that group of people doing something that would put them in a foreign prison for life. But the cops are detaining them for a while to be sure, which is fine with us."

"Are you in Szeged now?"

"We are."

"I used the computer to match the shape of the drawing to the shapes of the world's rivers to find out where Albrecht had been digging. I knew you'd be going to the find."

"Now we really have to," said Remi. "Nobody would grab Albrecht for ransom. He's not rich, just smart. They must want him to take them to his discovery and probably tell them all about it."

"What can I do to help?"

Sam said, "First, e-mail me a conventional road map with Albrecht's site marked on it."

"I'll have it for you in a minute."

"And abducting professors isn't something every criminal does. We need to know who is interested in the archaeology of this area, both legitimate and not."

"I'll see if Interpol will tell us who has been dealing in smuggled artifacts from Hungary, and the rest of Central Europe, lately. I'll also check with museum curators and antiquities dealers. If I got the date right, it was 450 C.E.?"

"That's right," Sam said. "And one more thing." He took out the card the cabdriver had given him. "I'd like you to check out a driver in Szeged named Tibor Lazar. He was waiting for a fare outside the train station when we arrived and he speaks English like the average Londoner. See if he's too good to be true."

"I'm on it. Another question for Interpol."

"Thanks," said Remi. "Meanwhile, we'll be here trying to draw attention to ourselves."

"Is that the best idea?"

"At the moment, it doesn't have much competition," Remi said. "If we do what Albrecht did, maybe we'll get a reaction from the same people who noticed him."

"Let's hope it's not the same reaction," said Selma. "I'll get this information to you as soon as I have it. The map is already on your iPad with the site marked. Good-bye."

Sam turned off his iPad. Remi said, "Ready to face the tour?"

"Eager."

They went outside to where Tibor was sitting in his cab. He got out and opened the back door. When they were in, he said, "You wanted to see the town?"

"Yes," said Sam. "Can we start at the river?"

"Of course," he said. "This is a good year for the Tisza. There are no floods, no droughts, no chemical spills upriver, no anything. Last year, we had everything."

Sam was watching his telephone, where Selma's map was on the screen. "It looks like a big river."

"It runs from north of Hungary, in the Ukraine, all the way down here, about a thousand kilometers, and empties into the Danube on the Serbian border. It's been important since ancient times. We don't get a lot of rainfall here on the southern part of the great plain. But the water comes south from the high country in the Ukraine, and the Mura River comes in from the east in Romania and brings the snowmelt and rain from the Transylvanian mountains."

Remi said, "I suppose the course of the river has changed since ancient times?"

"Many times. It was a slow, meandering river, with big loops going back and forth across the plain. But people never leave anything alone. In 1846, Count István Széchenyi started straightening it. He cut it down to about a thousand kilometers just by cutting across the loops. Now there are about six hundred kilometers of dead channels. They did more to improve it in the eighteen eighties, nineties, and the nineteen hundreds. Maybe there was some more that I'm not remembering or never heard about. But then in 1937 they realized that they'd better start fixing the parts that they'd ruined. Now the river is pretty straight, but it still floods—maybe worse than ever. The channels fill up with silt. But they'll keep fixing it as long as new politicians are born."

Sam said, "Up ahead, can you cross the bridge and show us the other side of the river?"

"Certainly," said Tibor. "We call that side Új-Szeged. It means 'New Szeged.' The old city was all on the west side."

"Is the east side really new?"

"It was always here, of course, but the city has grown mostly in the empty areas." He crossed the low, recently painted iron bridge, and they looked down on the river.

"Can you take us along this side a few miles?"

"Sure," said Tibor. "It's a beautiful, sunny day. We have the sunniest city in Hungary."

He drove them along until Sam could see they were near the spot that Albrecht had mapped. It was a large open field that was planted with alfalfa and left fallow.

"What is this land on the right?" asked Remi.

"This? Oh, it's just an old farm. It used to have cattle grazing on it. During the Communist times when I was a kid, it was part of a big farm collective. Since then, the government has been part of an effort by all the countries in the Danube basin to clean up the rivers. They haven't reopened the cattle farm. It's too dirty to be this close to the river."

"Can we stop and take a look?"

"Of course," Tibor said. He pulled over to the side of the road and parked. Sam and Remi walked a bit on the field by themselves.

"Well, we came," said Remi, "and I don't see anybody."

"No signs of recent digging either," Sam said. "Albrecht must have replaced the turf when he left and it hasn't been disturbed."

"Do you think Albrecht managed to persuade his kidnappers that his find was somewhere else?"

"I doubt it. All Selma needed was the outline of the river to find it, and Albrecht knew somebody had been watching him while he was here. I have a strong feeling they're keeping him somewhere close by. In order for him to be of use, they'd have to bring him here to tell them where to dig and what to look for or have him where they can bring the things they find to him."

"Maybe. But how do we find him?"

Sam looked past her. "I think the watchers have found us."

Remi turned her head to see a dark car that was stopped far up the straight two-lane road that ran along the river. A person with sharp eyes could detect that there were heads visible above the seats. She took out her phone and took a few pictures of the field, the river, and then up the road where the dark car stood.

Sam said, "Albrecht mentioned a big black car with four men in it. Do you think your phone will catch a license plate at that distance?"

"Maybe, but I have a feeling we'll get a closer look," said Remi.

They walked back toward the car, and Tibor said, "Do you know those men in the black car?"

"No," Sam said. "Do you?"

"I don't think so. I saw a reflection a minute ago. One of them seems to be watching us with binoculars. That's the right word, isn't it?" and he held both hands up to his eyes with the fingers circled.

"That's the word," said Remi. "They're probably just wondering what we're doing walking around an old cow pasture."

"All right," he said. He started the car and made a three-point turn and drove back to the bridge they had crossed, returning to the west side of the river. He kept looking in the mirror. "Are you sure you don't know them?"

"Positive," said Remi. "We've never been to Hungary before."

They drove to Arad Martyrs Square and saw the monument to the men killed in the 1848 revolt, the Musical Clock with sculpted figures from a medieval university, Klauzál Square, Schéchenyi Square, all in the city's center. The district was full of flowers and trees and pastel-colored baroque buildings that didn't look real.

As Tibor took them from place to place, Sam and Remi kept track of the black car. When they stopped abruptly near the center of the city, the car nearly caught up with them. Remi took another photograph through the rear window.

Tibor noticed. "Those men remind me of the way things were under the Communists. There were people who seemed to have no jobs except to follow people around and report them."

"I'd like to know who they're reporting us to," Remi said.

"I wonder if we can find out," said Sam. "Will the police tell us who owns a car if we have the license number?"

"I think they might."

Remi magnified the picture she had taken of the black car. She took a piece of paper from her purse and copied the license number on it, then handed it to Sam.

Sam said, "I'll double your fare if you'll find out. Here's the number." He handed the paper over the seat to Tibor.

He pulled the car into a parking space near the police station and disappeared inside.

Sam dialed the number at the Fargo house. "Hi, Selma," he said.

"Hi, Sam. I was just getting ready to call you with some of the information you asked for."

"Let's save most of it for later. I think we've reached the moment when we've got to know whether Tibor Lazar is a good guy or a bad guy."

"I have a tentative answer for you. He hasn't done anything to give him a criminal record or bring him to the attention of Interpol. He owns a small house and a small taxi company, and there are no suspicions that it's a front for anything. He has three cabs and owes money on all of them. He's too poor to be anything but honest."

"Perfect," said Sam. "Thanks, Selma."

After about twenty minutes, Tibor came out again. He got in the driver's seat and started the engine. As he backed out of the space and drove forward, he said, "Bako."

"Bako?"

"Arpad Bako."

"Do you know who he is?" asked Remi.

"I'll tell you all about my visit to the police while we're on the road." He moved down to the river and drove to the south. As he picked up speed, he looked in his rearview mirror as though he expected to be followed. "We must start with you. You are Samuel and Remi Fargo of La Jolla, California."

"We knew that," said Remi.

"Did you know that the local police knew that? They're operating on a directive from the national government. They have been asked to keep you under loose surveillance—when you leave your hotel, when you return, and so on. They believe you are here in search of ancient treasures. Is that right? Are you treasure hunters?"

Sam said, "We're amateurs who are interested in history. We have made some valuable archaeological finds, both under the sea and on land. But some of the most important were made of wood or bronze or steel and are treasures because they revealed things about the past. It's true that some of the artifacts we've found include gold or gems. But to dismiss us as treasure hunters is simplistic."

Remi said, "We never find a site and loot it, as treasure hunters would. We register it with the government of the country where we find it. We get permission from the authorities to dig and report what we find. In most places, the government owns whatever we find."

Tibor said, "They say you've become very rich. Is that a lie?"

Remi smiled. "Not a lie. A misunderstanding. Sam is an engineer. Some years ago, he invented a machine. It's an argon laser scanner that is used to identify mixed metals and alloys at a distance. We borrowed all the money the bank would lend us and started a company to build and sell the scanners. If we'd failed, we would've been in debt forever. But the company thrived. We're the only source for the scanners. Larger companies began to ask us if we would like to sell our company. When we got the right offer, we sold. All of that happened before we ever began to search for old secrets."

"So you're just very lucky," Tibor said.

"We have been so far," Sam said, nodding. "And I'd like it to continue. Maybe we should speak with the police if they're suspicious of us."

"It would be better if you didn't," Tibor said. "They're not interested in you yet, so let them stay uninterested."

"So were the four men who have been following us police officers?"

"No. They're creatures of Arpad Bako."

"Who is he?"

"Describing him taxes my poor ability in your language. I can say he's a greedy, evil man. But that's not enough. He's a thief. He's a pig, a dog, a rat, a snake, a cockroach!" Tibor shifted into Hungarian for another sentence or two, then subsided.

"He doesn't sound good," said Remi. "He's a zoo."

"I'm sorry," Tibor said. "I hate him. I've hated him since before I was born, and, since then, I've learned to hate him more."

Remi said, "Can you tell us anything about him that we'll understand? What does he do for a living?"

"He inherited the family businesses. The biggest one is a medicine factory. Pharmacology, you understand? They make pills and vaccines and things."

"We understand."

"It's a big company. There are people like me who think the way it got so big was selling drugs to people whose only sickness is their need for drugs."

Sam said, "You said you hated him before you were born. What did that mean?"

"His family and mine were on different sides for hundreds of years. His were against the revolt of 1848 and got members of my family arrested for treason. In World War Two, his family became Nazis just so they would be able to confiscate land and businesses.

They informed on my grandfather's brother to get him tortured and shot because he had a small farm the Bakos wanted. The next generation of Bakos were Communists to get privileges they then used to run the black market. When that government fell, they bribed people in power to let them take control of the medicine factory. Every time the world turns upside down, a Bako ends up on top and steps on other people's heads. Arpad is the worst of the worst. He was in the car when his driver hit my second son, going over a hundred kilometers an hour. Bako made up the story that my son was a pickpocket who had stolen something from a man and run into the street without looking. He got five of his creatures to swear to it."

Sam said, "Do you hate him enough to take a risk to deny him something he wants? Maybe to punish him?"

"I? Tibor? I would jump at the chance."

"A good friend of ours, a German archaeologist, was kidnapped yesterday in Berlin. He'd made a discovery near here and gone to Berlin to study what he'd found because he was afraid. He'd seen those four men in the black car following him."

"I understand," Tibor said. "Bako is one of those people who claim they're direct descendants of Attila the Hun. A few years ago, a bunch of them petitioned the government to have themselves declared an official minority group. It's just greed."

"Greed? I don't follow," said Remi.

"It's the tomb. He wants to find the tomb and claim it as his own."

"The tomb of Attila the Hun?" she said. "He won't have much luck. It's one of the great known tombs that have never been found. Does he claim to be a relative of Genghis Khan too?"

"Not yet."

She turned to Sam. "What do you think we should do?"

"What can anyone do?" Tibor said. "Bako doesn't just have money. He has his own little army of security people to guard him, his houses, his factories. There's no question he would kill to keep someone else from finding Attila's tomb or kidnap them if he thought they knew something he could use."

Sam said quietly, "We're not just going to stand by and do nothing."

"What will you do?"

"Find our friend and take him back," said Remi.

Tibor was silent for a moment. "Really?"

"Yes," said Sam. "He called us because he thought he might need help. He was right."

"Sam," Remi said. "Maybe you shouldn't—"

"No, I think Tibor's our guy, Remi. Tibor, I believe we can do this, but we need a man who's Hungarian, who's brave, and who hates Arpad Bako. We'll pay you well for your trouble and your time. If you're arrested, we'll get you the best lawyer. It won't be any extra trouble because he'll have to defend us too."

"Maybe I'd better show you who this man is before anybody does anything. I'm driving you to my garage to get a different car first."

"Wait," said Sam. "I'd like to get rid of those men who are following us. Let me drive. If I damage your car, I'll pay for the repairs and your loss of the use of it."

Tibor looked skeptical, but he pulled over and let Sam get behind the wheel. He sat in the passenger seat. Sam made a quick U-turn and then a left to pass behind the big black car. Tibor gripped the dashboard and stomped the nonexistent brake.

"You'll enjoy riding with Sam," said Remi. "He's barred from driving in four countries."

Sam accelerated up the road. When the black car followed and began to pull closer behind him, he let the left tires stray off the pavement onto the dusty shoulder and throw a big cloud of dust and bits of gravel into the air. The driver of the black car tried unsuccessfully to swerve to avoid it, almost lost control, and veered from side to side, overcompensating. Sam said, "He's not too good. Is there a place near here with very narrow streets?"

"There's a very old village about two miles ahead. It's too far from the river to have been destroyed by floods."

Sam accelerated more on the long, straight stretch across the plain, but roads like this were made for the big black car. It began to gain on Sam steadily. He delayed by weaving from side to side, then moving into the center of the road so they couldn't pull up beside him. When he saw the village coming up, he swerved to the left lane abruptly. The black car moved to the right, Sam stomped on his brake, and the black car shot past them.

Sam made a slow, safe turn onto the main street of the village, then went past a few stone buildings before he turned to the right into an alley so narrow that he could barely fit the taxi between the buildings. "Careful, careful," Tibor muttered. At the far end of the alley, Sam stopped.

Sam, Remi, and Tibor watched the back window and saw the black car, moving fast, flash past the opening of the alley. "Now we see if he's angry enough or we need to work on him some more," Sam said.

The black car made a tire-squealing stop, backed up rapidly into sight, turned, and sped into the alley after the taxi. Sam pulled forward out of the alley into a small open square. He got out. "Take the wheel," he said to Tibor. Then he stepped back to the open end of the alley. He picked up the handles of a wheelbarrow loaded with stones and prepared to push it into the opening.

Before he could, there was a bang, and then a loud scraping sound that rose to a screech, then stopped. Sam put down the wheelbarrow, ran to the taxi, and got into the rear seat with Remi. Tibor backed up to glance down the alley. He and the Fargos could see that the big black car had gotten wedged between the first pair of buildings. Its mirrors were gone, and it was jammed against the bricks on both sides. The engine roared, and there was a painful shriek of metal but little progress. Tibor pulled forward around the end of the row of buildings to the main street and drove back the way they had come.

They drove to a building that looked like a small warehouse. There were five men in overalls and work clothes. "Those two," he said, "the good-looking ones, are my brothers. The others are cousins."

Tibor got out and went to talk to a couple of them, then brought them back with him. A third man pulled a van out of the garage and left it running. Everyone smiled, shook hands, and pantomimed their delight to make one another's acquaintance. Tibor got into the van's driver's seat, and Sam and Remi got into the back. They were surprised to see that a man got in with them. He said, "I'm János. I'll be taking the pictures."

"Thank you," said Remi. She whispered to Sam, "What pictures?"

János snapped her picture. "You're welcome," he said.

Tibor drove them out to the east side of the city, then farther out onto the grassy plains. Five miles later they came to a large complex with five rows of white buildings. Most of them were long and low rectangles with no windows. János aimed his camera and began to shoot, clicking and winding automatically. He kept shooting as they drove along the tall chain-link fences with coiled razor wire along the top. They passed a guard gate that looked like the entrance to a military base, complete with armed guards in gray battle dress uniforms.

Remi said, "Why all the guards?"

"The reason they give is that they make and store narcotic drugs here, and they do research on new medicines, so competitors might steal their secrets. The real reason is so Bako can do as he likes and nobody asks questions."

All through the trip, Sam was silent. He looked closely at everything, but he said nothing.

When the van returned to the garage, Sam asked for a piece of paper and said to Tibor, "I'm going to make a list of things we'll need and give you money to buy them. If you can't get something, tell me and I'll have them flown here." He began to write as he spoke. "Four gray uniforms like the ones Bako's men wear. Four pistols with two spare magazines each in holsters on belts of black webbing. The ones they carry looked to me like Czech CZ-75s. If there's a Hungarian model that looks like that, it'll be fine. Black boots, four pairs, mid-calf height. We'll need to have the boots polished and the uniforms pressed. And remember, one set is for Remi, so get one size small. And get one short black leather dog leash and collar."

"Anything else?" said Tibor. "Anything to go with the collar?"

"A dog."

"A dog?"

"I'd like a German shepherd. If necessary, it can be a Rottweiler or Doberman. He needs to have a good nose and be well trained and obedient."

"There is a man in Szeged who trains dogs."

"And he's your cousin, right?" asked Sam.

"Not everybody is my cousin. This one is my wife's cousin. I'll see if he has a good dog right now."

"Can you take Remi to see his dogs and pick one out?"

"I could, but these are Hungarian dogs. Remi doesn't speak Hungarian."

Remi said, "I can learn as many words as a German shepherd."

"And all dogs speak to Remi," said Sam. He looked at Tibor. "Are you and János willing to do this? Have you made up your minds?"

"I'd rather go kidnap Bako and trade him for your friend. But, yes."

"If this doesn't work, we'll try that next."

6

Remi Fargo stood at the gate in the fence around the exercise yard, where there were several German shepherds. She said to Tibor's wife's cousin, "What's that one's name?"

"*Gyilkas,*" he said. "It means 'killer.'"

"And this one?"

"*Hasfel.* It's short for *hasfelmetszo.* It means 'ripper.'"

She went to the gate and reached for the latch. "Miss, you don't want to be in there."

"Of course I do. Why should they trust me if I don't trust them?" She stepped inside and closed the gate. She walked confidently up to each dog and let it sniff her hand, petted the thick fur at its neck, then moved on. She spotted the biggest dog in the compound, a tan male with a black head and tail. He had been sitting a distance away, watching. Now he approached her, and, as he did, the others all seemed to melt away.

"And who are you?" she asked the dog. He came up to her, looking directly into her eyes as he did. He sat in front of her, then licked her offered hand. She knelt and petted him, and he lay down so she could rub his belly.

The cousin said, "His name is Zoltán. It means 'Sultan.'"

"He's the big guy, eh?" she said. "The boss."

"Yes, miss. He doesn't usually do that with strangers." He corrected himself. "With anybody."

"He can read me. He knows I always fall for his type." She leaned down and spoke to the dog quietly. "What do you think, Mr. Zoltán? Do you want to do some work with me tonight?"

She seemed to get the answer she wanted. She stood, and the dog stood with her. He walked with her to the gate, and she brought him out with her. To Tibor's wife's cousin she said, "He's the one. Now, would you please teach me some proper commands in Hungarian so I don't embarrass him?"

THE BAKO Gyogyszereszeti Tersazag had ended its daylight shift hours before the new security van arrived at the front gate of the complex. It was dark, and the lights above the checkpoint were the brightest in sight. Two armed guards stepped to the van outside the tall fence. The young guard stood beside János, the driver, and looked past him into the van, and the other, the senior man, stood on the passenger side where Tibor sat. Sam had decided that Tibor should wear the high rank so he could be the spokesman. Tibor had gold hash marks on his right sleeve and a gold star on his baseball cap while the others had no insignia of rank.

When the guard asked a question, Tibor appeared to say what had been arranged earlier, that they had brought a search dog because one of the labs had reported an intruder. When the man asked him a second question, Tibor seemed to find the high-ranking officer that lived in the back of his brain. He turned a disdainful look on the man and answered wearily. The man began to say something else, but Tibor interrupted him, coldly furious. He gestured at the gate and shouted something in Hungarian that could only be, "Open up! You're wasting time!"

The other guard on János's side had been looking in the back of the van, smiling at Remi. Tibor's shout startled him, and then he heard a low growl, and saw the big shepherd start to bare his teeth, leaning toward the open window. The man jerked back, stepped to his post, and activated a circuit to make the gate swing inward.

János drove through the gate and kept going up the asphalt road, then made a turn beyond the first row of buildings so the van was out of sight of the two guards. He stopped and everyone got out. Remi and the big dog went first, János and Sam came next, while Tibor stood a little apart like a drill sergeant next to his marching platoon. As a group, they looked very formidable and professional. Sam's care in being sure all wore pressed uniforms, identical side-arms, boots, utility belts, and caps was paying off. Remi also had a matching black shoulder bag. She gave Zoltán a biscuit, patted him hard, murmured a few words to him in Hungarian, then reached into her leather bag. She pulled out the scarf that Albrecht had lost in his lab and let the dog sniff it. Then she said, *"Vadászat!"* Hunt!

Zoltán began to sniff, moving back and forth across the paved area between the rows of buildings. He seemed to be at a loss at first, but then he moved on ahead, pulling Remi with him. She spoke to the dog in English as they went, her voice barely above a whisper. "Come on, you big boy. You're going to use that big beautiful nose to find Albrecht."

The rest of the group followed at a distance of just a couple yards, giving Remi and the dog space to move or double back, but

Zoltán walked along at a slow, comfortable pace, holding his head up and turning from one side to the other, no more interested in one spot than another. Sam said, "Has he lost him?"

Remi said, "He's got the scent in mind and now he's hunting. We just have to let him search for another whiff of it."

"Look up there," said János. There was a low rectangular building at the edge of the compound farthest from the road. It had its own high chain-link fence around it with coiled razor wire on top. Inside that fence was a second one that had four strands of thinner, tightly strung wire.

Sam said, "It's an electrified fence." He pointed to a sign in Hungarian. "What does that say?"

"Danger. Contagious Disease Research Laboratory. No Unauthorized Personnel. Protective Suits Required at All Times. Gate Sets Off Alarm."

"Do you think it's real?" asked János. "If I kidnapped someone, I'd put him in a place like that."

"Bring Zoltán," Sam said. Remi brought the big dog close to the gate. He sniffed around dutifully and then moved on.

They kept going and then turned a corner, and, as they did, they came face-to-face with a pair of security guards dressed exactly as they were. The two men had AK-47 assault rifles slung over their shoulders. The one nearest to Sam lifted a flashlight to shine on their faces.

Sam's judo training made him move quickly. His arm shot out like a striking snake to snatch the flashlight out of the man's hand as he stepped into the man's body and put him on the ground, then shone the light in the other man's face.

Tibor was as shocked as the two sentries, but he recovered more quickly. He spoke loudly and harshly in Hungarian, and what he said was not a compliment. Sam and Remi could guess that it involved the guards' dress and deportment. Tibor took the flashlight and shone it on them as he found fault with their shaves, then tapped one man's shirt because its buttons did not line up with his belt. He didn't like their shoeshines either. Finally he waved them past with a final threatening growl.

Sam said, "Very well done."

"Thank you. But have you noticed we've been here only ten minutes and we've been stopped twice by men with automatic weapons?"

"It's an encouraging sign," said Sam. "This place is too well guarded to be an honest drug company. Let's hope one of the things they're hiding is Albrecht Fischer."

Suddenly the big dog surged ahead. His leash tightened and jerked Remi's arm, then pulled her relentlessly forward. "We've got a scent," she said. Zoltán tugged Remi along the roadway between the windowless buildings, and the others followed closely. Sam and János spread out on both sides of her and watched for obstacles ahead and either way, with their hands resting on their pistols.

They reached a building near the farthest corner of the complex, some kind of utility or storage building. There was one door made of steel, and around it was a steel cage with its own door and an electronic card reader on the latch. Zoltán went to the cage, nosed around it, trying to find a way in, getting more and more excited, sniffing under the grating and then jumping up to put his forepaws on it.

"*Ül*, Zoltán," Remi said. "*Jo fiu.*" She patted Zoltán as he sat. To the others she said, "This is it."

Sam said, "We can knock or we can wait for somebody with a card key."

"I'll knock," said Remi. "Take Zoltán out of sight with you."

The three men and the dog stepped to either side into the shadows while Remi went up to the cage and pressed a button next to the card reader. A loud buzzer went off inside.

A small window in the steel door slid open at eye level, then closed. The door opened. A man in the usual gray uniform appeared and asked her a question in Hungarian. She laughed as though he'd said something charming. He was clearly intrigued by the sudden arrival of an attractive woman. She smiled brightly at him and he pressed a button on the inner wall of the building that buzzed and unlocked the cage door.

As Remi stepped inside, the man saw Zoltán materialize out of the darkness beside her. He began reflexively to shut the steel door, but Zoltán was much faster and pushed in ahead of Remi.

There was a low growl as the dog's jaws closed on the man's forearm, and the man let out an involuntary yelp. As the door was swinging shut, Sam hit it with his shoulder, and he, Tibor, and János were inside, guns drawn. János shut the door.

"*Ül!*" Remi said to the dog: "Sit!"

The man in Zoltán's grip sat. When he did, Zoltán released him and sat too. "*Jo fiu,*" Remi said. "Good boy." The man remained seated on the concrete floor while János relieved him of his gun and kept it pointed in his general direction.

"Sam!"

They all spun and saw, across the empty floor of the building, an enclosure that looked like a tool cage, with a steel grating that went from the floor to the ceiling and a padlocked door. Behind it stood Albrecht Fischer.

"Albrecht!" called Sam. "Is he the only guard?"

"There are two others on duty now. They both have rifles. They left a few minutes ago to bring back some coffee."

As they hurried to the cage, Sam said to Tibor, "They're probably your friends with the flashlight and the badly shined shoes."

In the enclosure, Albrecht had a bed with a steel frame and a thin mattress over wire mesh like a military bunk and he had a portable toilet. He was wearing the same clothes he'd worn in Berlin, which looked worse for wear and had dried bloodstains on the front of the shirt.

Sam called, "Bring the guard over."

János spoke to the man and the man got up to walk over to the cage. Zoltán followed at the guard's heels, occasionally issuing a low growl.

Sam said, "Get the key."

Tibor gave the man the order in Hungarian, but the man shrugged and said something. János patted him down. "He doesn't have it." He ran to the desk near the door and rifled the drawers. He found a second padlock with a key in it, ran back with it, and Sam tried the key in the first padlock. It didn't fit.

Sam said, "Tell him to take his uniform and boots off." He added, "You strip down too, Albrecht."

The two men obeyed, and Sam said, "Albrecht, step back and get behind something solid. Everybody else, do the same. When I shoot the padlock, the clock starts running. We have to move quickly. We dress Albrecht like us and lock this guy up in his place. Then we move fast to the van and get out of here. If anybody we meet aims a weapon, shoot first."

The others got behind some wooden crates. Remi took the dog with her and covered his ears with her hands.

There was a loud bang as Sam shot the lock off the cage. Everyone began to move quickly. János pushed the guard into the cage and sat him on the bed. Albrecht came out and put on the uniform. As Albrecht was tying his shoes, Tibor put the guard's gun belt around him and clicked the buckle. Sam used the second lock to secure the cage.

Everyone trotted to the door. As Remi was about to open it, the buzzer sounded loudly and made her jump. Zoltán began to growl, but she whispered to him and he went quiet.

"Our two friends must be back," said Sam. "We've got to let them in."

Tibor stepped to the side of the door where the guard had pressed a button to open the cage before. He read the label, then nodded. The others all moved to the sides, backs to the wall, with guns drawn. Tibor pressed the button to buzz the guards in while Remi swung the door open.

The two men stepped inside, each carrying two paper cups of coffee, their rifles slung across their backs. As soon as they were in, Sam and János were beside them, holding pistols to their heads.

Tibor snapped some orders, and the men set down their coffee cups, set their rifles on the floor, stepped away, and lay down on their stomachs. János removed the handcuffs from the leather cases on their belts and handcuffed them to two steel girders that served to support the roof.

Remi and the dog went out, with Sam right behind. Albrecht followed, and then Tibor and János, carrying the two AK-47 rifles. When Sam looked at them questioningly, Tibor whispered, "Would you rather we had them or they did?"

They moved quickly, in loose formation, along the drive between the rows of buildings toward the spot where they had left their van.

There was the sound of a truck moving along the roadway on the far side of the buildings to their left and then a second truck coming along the paved surface outside the tall chain-link fence. They stopped in front of a building for a moment, using its bulk to hide from the truck moving along the fence. Sam and Remi moved to the corner of the building to see that it passed. The vehicle was a stake truck with about fifteen men inside, on two benches along either side, all in gray guard uniforms and holding AK-47 rifles, muzzle upward, between their knees.

When the truck had moved away along the outer perimeter, Sam moved close to the others. "So much for going over the fence."

Suddenly there was the sound of running feet somewhere to their left beyond the next row of buildings. Sam, Remi, and Zoltán began to run ahead toward the gate, and the others moved up with them. "We've got to keep from being boxed in," Sam said. "Stay ahead of them."

The group ran harder until they reached the double-fenced building with the warnings about Contagious Disease Research. Sam said to Tibor, "Go over one row and see if you can keep those guys from flanking us. I'll give them something else to think about."

He waited until the others were around the next row of buildings and out of sight. Then he ran up to the Contagious Disease building and threw his body against the gate in the fence. There was a loud ringing alarm and a louder electronic siren. The red lights above the gate flashed, and a set of floodlights came on, illuminating the outside of the building. Sam ran along the drive on their original route.

Ahead of him, a group of six security men from the next buildings ran into the long drive. One of them raised a rifle to his shoulder, and Sam sidestepped behind the corner of the closest building and pulled out his pistol. He reached around the corner, exposing just his gun arm and one eye, and fired five shots into the group, saw two men go down, then three others begin to drag them to safety. The last man laid down covering fire with the AK-47, spraying the area where Sam had been with bullets. Sam was already running around the building to the next paved drive.

Squads of men were moving along the buildings to get to the Contagious Disease building. The stake truck that had brought the guards waited fifty yards ahead of Sam. He ran up behind it, dashed along the left side, and flung open the door, pointing his pistol in the driver's face. He dragged the man out and pulled his sidearm from its holster. He knocked him to the ground, used the handcuffs on his belt to subdue him, then took his place behind the wheel.

Sam shifted the truck into first gear, turned left, then right, and saw Zoltán and Remi, János, Tibor, and Albrecht sprinting along the pavement. He shifted into second, gained a little speed, and then saw Tibor become aware of him. Tibor turned to face the truck and began to swing his rifle around. Sam switched his lights on and off, slowed, and waved his left arm wildly out the window. "It's me!" he yelled. "Get in!"

Remi was at Tibor's side in a second and Tibor lowered the rifle. The four ran hard to get to the truck as Sam drove to meet them. He stopped, and they clambered up onto the flatbed. He drove ahead.

Zoltán ran back and forth behind the truck, whimpering for Remi. The truck was too high for him to jump up. There was the sound of Remi pounding on the cab roof. "Stop, Sam!"

He stopped. Remi jumped down, ran around the truck, opened the passenger door, and stood on the step. She called, "Up, Zoltán!" The big dog ran and jumped up onto the truck seat, Remi spun herself around and sat, then slammed the door shut. "Hit it!" she said. She took out her pistol and rolled down her window as the truck gained speed.

Sam drove along the paved road between the buildings. They were now moving up the center of the complex, with rows on each side. A platoon of men ran out into the road ahead of them, knelt, and prepared to fire, but Sam switched on the headlights, and Tibor and János, standing up in the flatbed behind the cab, opened fire. They hit one of the men, and the others ran for cover.

Sam said, "We've got to crash the gate. Tell them to get ready."

Remi got up on the seat, hung her torso out the window, and shouted to them: "We've got to crash the gate!"

Tibor and János stood, leaning forward on the cab, replaced the magazines on their rifles, and looked ahead. Remi held her pistol in both hands, also watching ahead.

Sam lifted his pistol from his belt with his left hand. "I'm going to go through as fast as I can. It would be best if we could make the guards keep their heads down until we're out of their effective range."

"Good plan . . . as plans go," she said.

"I know you're the only pistol champion we have, but I'd rather they not see enough of you to hit. You're also the only wife I have . . ."

"You're so sweet."

". . . at the moment."

Zoltán looked at each of them in turn, not sure what to think.

Sam reached the last corner, slowed to make the turn, and drove past the van they had brought there. As they passed, two men hiding in the back of the van flung the rear door open. Sam, Remi, and the others were too far away to hit before the men jumped to the ground, pulled out pistols, and fired wildly in their direction.

"If one of us had opened that door, we'd be dead," said Remi.

Sam shifted from third to fourth as he drove for the gate. The two men on duty had closed the chain-link barrier, and now there were five or six others standing in front to guard the exit. To Sam it looked as though they were overconfident, assuming that nobody would actually try to crash the gate, so they were not really ready. Their rifles were slung across their backs, and they had done nothing to reinforce the barrier, even though they had another stake truck parked beside the gate.

"Slight change of plan," said Sam. He switched on the high-beam headlights. "Tell the guys to get down."

"Get down!" she shouted.

The three men lay flat on the truck bed, the brothers facing the sides with their rifles ready, Albrecht, in the middle, facing backward.

Sam kept adding speed as he approached. When he and Remi were twenty-five yards out, Remi held her right elbow with her left hand and fired, dropping the man in the guard kiosk, then fired several rounds at the riflemen, who were unslinging their firearms. Sam fired eight shots into their midst, but he was not the shot with a pistol that Remi was and all he was sure he accomplished was to increase the men's impulse to dive for cover.

Sam adjusted his course slightly, held the steering wheel steady, and passed just three feet to the right of the parked truck, missed the gate, and plowed into the chain-link fence. The fence was so high that as the cab ran straight into the mesh, it passed under the crossbar where the razor wire was coiled. The truck pushed a forty-foot section of the mesh ahead of it until the bottom links caught on the ground, the mesh was pulled flat, and the truck drove over it.

The guards fired their weapons on full auto but just managed to spray the kiosk, the parked stake truck as Sam passed behind it, and most of the nearby buildings. As soon as Sam's truck was outside the fence and gaining distance, he steered it over the bumpy ground onto the road again. Albrecht and the Lazar brothers opened fire at the guards at the gate, pouring such a steady stream of bullets in their direction that not one of them dared to lift his head above whatever cover he was hiding behind.

Sam drove hard out the driveway. He slowed only enough to make the turn to the road, then sped up again. After a few minutes, Tibor rapped on the cab roof and leaned close to yell to Sam, "Let me drive now! We can't take this truck into the city. I know where to go."

Sam stopped the truck, climbed up onto the truck bed, and let Tibor take his place. He drove no slower than Sam had, but before they reached the outskirts of Szeged he went down a narrow back road, took several turns that Sam couldn't even see, and arrived at the big garage where he had taken them earlier.

He pulled the truck into the garage, and the others all climbed down. Zoltán jumped from the cab to the ground and then sat calmly.

Albrecht said, "I thank you all sincerely. If you hadn't risked your lives, I would have lost mine. I'm sure of it. I owe my life to you."

"We had better do what we can to keep from being caught," Remi said. "I must have seen five men hit tonight. Some of them could be dead."

Sam said, "What about the van? Can they trace it?"

"It was borrowed."

"From who?"

"From a parking lot," Tibor said.

Sam called out, "Everyone change back into normal clothes in the shop."

They took turns washing powder residue and dust from face, hands, and arms, and came out in street clothes and shoes. Albrecht put on clothes that Tibor lent him. Sam said, "Can we dump the truck in the river? I know it's bad for the fish, but it could wash off any fingerprints."

Tibor said, "János can drive it. We'll pick him up and drop you three at your hotel."

Remi, Sam, and Albrecht sat in the backseat of Tibor's cab, and

Zoltán lay across their laps. They followed the stolen truck until János turned off the road to a wooded hillside above the river. He set the truck in gear, let out the clutch, jumped out, and watched the truck's momentum carry it forward a couple of yards, then over the crest of the hill. It picked up speed, went off an escarpment, and knifed into the river. It rolled onto its side, then took on water through the cab windows and disappeared.

János ran to the cab, opened the passenger door, and sat beside his brother. The cab moved off. The next stop was at the dog-trainer cousin's house. Remi got out with Zoltán and opened the gate so they could go into the enclosure. There were a few tentative barks as dogs awoke to the unfamiliar sights and smells of new people, then recognized Zoltán and quieted down. Remi knelt, held the big dog's face to hers, and whispered something.

When she came back to the car, Sam asked, "What did you say?"

"I told him I would probably never see him again, but that I would always remember what a good brave dog he is and that I love him."

"What did he say?"

"'Do you want me to bite that silly man before you go?' He loves me too."

Sam said, "I guess he and I are both jealous."

The cab pulled away, and Tibor drove them to the City Center Hotel. As they got out, Sam said, "Here, Tibor. I wrote this before we left." Sam handed him a check. "Take it to the Credit Suisse bank in the next day or two. They'll call our banker in the United States to verify it, but it will be in your account right away."

"Are you leaving Hungary?"

"Not yet. But I thought that if something happens to us, it will be better if you have this now."

Tibor shrugged. "Thanks." He put it in his coat without looking at it. "One more thing. Complain about your hotel room. Make them move you to a different one."

"I was just about to do that," said Sam. "I'll call you in a day or two." He watched the cab pull away.

While Tibor drove away from the hotel, he pulled out Sam's check and handed it to János. "I can't read it and drive too. What does it say?"

"Pay to the order of Tibor Lazar one hundred thousand dollars. It sounds like a lot of forints."

"It is," Tibor said, his eyes wide.

Sam, Remi, and Albrecht Fischer stepped to the front door of the hotel, but Albrecht stopped Sam from opening the door so no one would overhear. "The man who kidnapped me, that madman Arpad Bako. He thinks that what we're after is the tomb of Attila the Hun."

"It figures, I suppose. It's one of the great treasures that has never turned up," said Remi.

"And probably never will," said Albrecht.

Sam shrugged. "At least we're not getting kidnapped and shot at for pocket change." He pulled the door open and ushered the others inside. But he turned and took one last look at the street outside, paying special attention to the dark and secret places where a man could hide.

7

SZEGED, HUNGARY

SAM, REMI, AND ALBRECHT SAT IN THE LIVING ROOM OF their new suite on the top floor of the hotel, all showered, wearing clean clothes and finishing their room service meal of fresh bread, soft körözött cheese, and kolbász sausages. They had a bottle of Balaton Barrique 1991 Hungarian merlot.

"I lied, of course," said Albrecht. "I wasn't going to tell some glorified gangster about one of the most important discoveries in decades." He shook his head. "To be honest, I haven't figured out what it is I've found. I had no time to do much analysis or consult with colleagues before Bako's thugs kidnapped me."

"What did you tell him?"

"That I had been looking for signs of the Roman occupation force in this district. I carried conviction because, wherever I go in Europe, I'm alert to signs of Roman garrisons. Wherever they camped, they always dug in, and the structure of the place is virtually the same from England to Syria. This was Pannonia, a Roman possession until the Huns arrived."

"And that satisfied him?" Remi asked.

"He's a madman and nothing satisfies madness. He wants Attila the Hun's burial goods. The man thinks he's an heir of Attila the Hun. If he's not a literal descendant, he's certainly a spiritual one, and what he's searching for is a big thing here. In Hungary, people still name boys Attila. And here we are on the southern plain, where Attila made his stronghold."

Remi said, "I may not be remembering clearly, but isn't the treasure supposed to be the coffins themselves?"

"Yes, that's part of it," said Albrecht. "Supposedly there's an iron casket, and inside it a silver one, and inside it one made of solid gold. But they were supposed to be filled with the jeweled crowns and weapons and ornaments that belonged to all the kings and nobles and bishops that Attila defeated. That would make quite a pile."

"The story sounds like quite a pile," said Sam. "A pile of—"

"Sam!" said Remi.

"Sam's probably right," said Albrecht. "The only contemporary account we have of Attila's death is from Priscus, the Eastern Roman Empire's ambassador to the Huns. He describes the mourning and funeral, but mentions no treasure. The treasure is first described by Jordanes eighty years later. He was from one of the barbarian groups, possibly the Ostrogoths. People have searched for the treasure for fifteen hundred years and found nothing."

Albrecht sat in silence for a moment. "But Arpad Bako is not going to be put off or discouraged by odds or reason. He's convinced he's destined to find Attila's tomb. And he's obsessed with stopping anyone else from finding it."

"Let's step back and look at this from his perspective," said

Remi. "Is there any chance at all that what you found might relate to the tomb in some way?"

"I've just begun, but I doubt it," said Albrecht. "It's true that the carbon date of the remains is around 450 C.E. and Attila died in 453. And a battle here at the center of the Huns' territory may well have had to do with his death. What happened after the death of Attila was chaos. His three sons all had their own factions, and Attila's generals had their own kingdoms and armies. There could have been unrecorded battles among any of them." He shrugged. "All I can say for sure so far is that these casualties were not Romans. They didn't have the Romans' superb armor, nor did they carry the *gladius*, the short, wide-bladed stabbing sword, or the *scuta*, the big shield that Roman soldiers put together to form a wall against an enemy charge."

"So the bodies at the site could be Huns and the fighting could have been related to the tomb."

"It's too early to rule out very much, even that. And if anyone ever finds the tomb, this is probably the way it will happen—someone looking for something else will stumble on it."

Sam said, "Let's deal with the discovery you already have. We need to give you a chance to complete your excavation safely."

"I don't see how we can do that now. Some of Bako's men were shot."

Sam smiled. "Would that have bothered Attila?"

"Probably not."

"Then it won't bother Bako. He may even try to keep the incident quiet. He can't tell the police somebody stole his kidnap victim. And for the moment, your excavation is his best chance of learning anything new. He'll want you to get to work."

"He's too dangerous. We can't start excavating as long as he's here."

"Maybe you can. Do you know any important Hungarian ar-chaeologists?"

"A few of them. Dr. Enikö Harsányi is a professor right here at Szeged University. So is Dr. Imre Polgár. I had planned to consult them before I was abducted. They know this area's history better than I do."

"Then call them in now. What we need is not to hide this excava-tion. We need to make it as public as possible. We need to get lots of people involved, to be there on the site, and to help with the project. Three foreigners digging in a remote area are in danger. Fifty or a hundred local scholars digging are an expedition."

"Students and graduate students," said Albrecht. "Of course." He looked at the telephone. "I'll call them right— I forgot. I don't have my address book with their numbers. They can also help to guard the site."

Remi said, "Call Selma and tell her what you need." She yawned, looking at her watch. "It's still daytime there, and she'll be up. I'm going to pick this bedroom over here for Sam and me and go break it in. You can have the other one, Albrecht. Good luck with the calls."

The next afternoon, Albrecht, Sam, Remi, Professor Enikö Harsányi, and Professor Imre Polgár were standing beside a tour bus with Tibor Lazar. They were watching a cadre of six graduate students, each supervising ten volunteer undergraduates, laying out the field in a grid with stakes connected by lengths of twine. A little farther along, three more professors from the Institute of Archae-ology of the Hungarian Academy of Science were examining soil samples.

"In European spodosol, the base rate of soil addition is fifty-three years for an inch," said one. "We should expect about thirty inches of soil added here. But it's flat land, and we have a river nearby that overflows its banks."

Another said, "That would add alluvium to the thirty inches."

"How often has the Tisza flooded this high since 450?"

"I'd say every hundred to a hundred fifty years. Say ten times. And the most recent floods seem to have been worse than early ones. The one that destroyed the city of Szeged in 1879 was undoubtedly the worst. To be safe, we should expect remains to appear as deep as six feet or as shallow as thirty inches."

Sam saw Tibor get on the bus, so he left the others and followed him inside. As Tibor sat down in one of the front seats and picked up a newspaper, Sam said, "Good morning, Tibor. How are we doing?"

"I have two cousins on the road at that end and two down the road at the other end. They're all heavily armed and have telephones to warn us. I have a van with six men a mile off who can come up behind either group—my wife's brothers."

"That's great," Sam said. "We have to keep the diggers safe. Thank you."

"Thank *you*."

"For what?"

"For letting me help take something from Bako for once. And because your check wasn't a fake."

"Your help wasn't fake. You saved Albrecht's life."

"You saved Albrecht. I just said, 'Do as I say or this crazy man will kill you.'"

"You must have said it right."

Tibor studied him. "You're planning something else. What is it?"

Sam smiled. "They don't need me to dig up this field. But I think

I can do something that will fool Bako and keep his men busy so these people can do their work."

"Arpad Bako is a very big man. You saw just one of his businesses. He has money and power, and he has rich, powerful friends here and elsewhere. You have to be careful."

"He's after the tomb of Attila the Hun, just as you thought."

Tibor laughed. "Not the Fountain of Youth? Not the Ladder to Heaven?"

"I'm sure you know the stories. Attila was supposed to have been buried in secret with his treasure and then the Tisza River diverted to cover the grave."

"Ah, of course. We're all told that as little children," said Tibor. "Arpad Bako must be the only child who ever believed it. Besides, the Tisza is a thousand kilometers long, and it used to be even longer. Lots of it has been diverted, some parts cut off and left dry. All the swampy parts were drained."

"That's the beauty of it, Tibor. Remi and I are not going to find the tomb. We're just going to make Bako watch us look for it."

"I want to join you."

"Welcome aboard. Speaking of boats, do you have any relatives with boats?"

"Not a relative, a friend. He would rent it for, say . . . nothing."

"Are you sure you want to do this?"

"Well, you just risked your life to rescue a friend from a compound full of armed men and paid me a fortune for spending a day and a night helping you. It's good business to be your friend."

The next morning, a thirty-foot fishing boat, *Margit*, puttered up the Tisza River at five to ten knots. Sometimes it would idle, barely holding against the lazy current of the river, and then begin to make diagonal crossings. The *Margit* was towing something, but it was impossible to tell from the shore what it was because it never rose above the surface.

A sharp-eyed observer might have seen that there were five people aboard—a helmsman, two men who stood watch, a man who operated whatever was being towed, and a slender auburn-haired woman who watched the screen of a laptop computer on a shelf that was mounted just inside the cabin.

After less than an hour of this, a truck with an enclosed cargo space moved slowly along the road above the river.

In the cargo space were four men, sitting on a bench along one side. They used a camera with a telephoto lens, two marksman's spotting scopes, and a video camera with a powerful zoom lens, all mounted through holes in the side of the truck. The leader of the group was a man named Gábor Székely. He was in the first position behind the driver so he could direct the actions of any of the others.

His cell phone buzzed and he lifted it and said in Hungarian, "Yes?" He listened for a time and then said, "Thank you." He put the phone away and announced to the others, "The man in the stern with the cable in his hands is Samuel Fargo. He had some equipment flown in overnight: a metal detector, some pairs of night vision goggles, and a Geometrics G-882 marine magnetometer, which detects small deviations in the earth's magnetic field, especially those caused by pieces of iron."

"The iron coffin," said the man beside him.

Gábor didn't see fit to acknowledge that. "The woman must be his wife, Remi Fargo. They have been staying at the City Center Hotel."

The third man said, "We've got rifles here with scopes. We could easily kill anyone on deck from this truck."

"We don't want to do that just yet," said Gábor Székely. "The Fargos are experienced treasure hunters. They've found important treasures in Asia and the Swiss Alps and elsewhere. They have the boat and the equipment for the search."

"We're going to wait until after they find it?"

"Yes. That's what we're going to do. When they find the outer casket of iron, we'll move in before they can raise it to the surface. They'll have a terrible accident and we'll find the tomb. Mr. Bako will be a hero for finding a national treasure."

In the boat on the river, Remi Fargo studied the display from the magnetometer on her laptop computer screen. "This is insane."

Sam said, "What's wrong? Not getting anything?"

"The opposite. I'm getting everything. The riverbed is full of metal. I've got images that look like sunken boats, anchor chains, cannons, ballast, junk, bundles of rebar encased in cement. I think I've picked up a couple of bicycles, an anchor, and what looks like an old stove in the past five minutes."

Sam laughed. "I guess there's enough to keep it interesting. If you spot anything that's buried ten feet down and looks like an iron coffin, it might be worth a closer look."

"I assume we're going to dive the river no matter what we see."

"The more we do what Bako and his people think is getting us closer to the underwater tomb, the more they'll ignore Albrecht and the others."

Tibor said, "We may have Bako all confused and frustrated now, but don't let it make you too comfortable. He has enough men to do many bad things at once."

They spent several days on their magnetometer survey of the lower river. Each evening, they went to see Albrecht and his team at the building in the city center that they had rented as a lab.

"It's definitely a battlefield," said Albrecht.

"How could it be anything else?" said Enikö Harsányi. "So far, we've found six hundred fifty-six adult male bodies, all armed, and all apparently killed together and then buried where they fell."

Imre Polgár said, "Many of them—perhaps a majority—show signs of having serious wounds that had healed. We found impact fractures, stab and slash wounds that hit bone. These were career fighters. The term should probably be *warriors* rather than *soldiers*."

"And who are they?" asked Remi.

"They're Huns," said Albrecht.

"Definitely Huns," Enikö Harsányi agreed. "All of them so far."

"How can you tell?" Sam asked. "DNA?"

Albrecht took them to a long row of steel tables, where skeletons lay in a double row. "There isn't a DNA profile of a Hun. The core group in the first and second centuries were from Central Asia. As they came west, they made alliances with or fought, defeated, and absorbed each tribe or kingdom they met. So by the time they were here on the plains of Hungary, they still had many individuals with genes in common with Mongolians, but others who appeared to be Scythian, Thracian, or Germanic. What they shared wasn't common ethnicity but common purpose. It's like asking for the DNA profile of a seventeenth-century pirate."

"So how do you identify them?"

"They were horsemen. They traveled, fought, ate, and sometimes slept on horseback. We can tell by certain skeletal changes that all of these men spent their lives on horses. But there's much more conclusive evidence."

"What's that?" Sam asked.

"The Huns weren't regular cavalry, they were mounted archers. In Asia they developed this tactic with the help of an advance in the bow and arrow."

He very carefully picked up a blackened piece of wood with irregular curves. "Here it is. It's a compound bow, and the style is distinctive. See the ends where you nock the string? They're called *siyahs*. They're stiff, not flexible. The wood isn't just a piece of wood. It's layers of laths glued together. There are always seven *siyahs*, made of horn, and the grip is bone. It made for a very short bow that they could use on horseback and it gave much greater velocity to the arrow. This is probably as good a specimen of a Hun bow as exists today. So far, we've found over four hundred of them."

"Huns against who?" asked Sam.

"That, I'm afraid, is a more difficult question. The victims were all over the field together. They were laid out with no separation for affiliation, simply covered with earth where they fell. They all had the sort of armament that a Hun would use, primarily the compound bow. They also carried a long, straight, double-edged sword in a scabbard that hung from the belt, and a short sword, or dagger, stuck horizontally in the belt. They wore goatskin trousers and a fabric or fur tunic. Some had leather vests."

"There are still puzzles and mysteries," said Dr. Polgár.

"I can see some right here," Remi said. "Nobody looted the battlefield."

"That's one," said Dr. Harsányi. "A well-made sword was a prized possession. A compound bow made of wood, bone, and horn took a very skilled craftsman much preparation, a week of labor, and months of drying and curing. It's not the sort of thing one leaves on the field."

Remi pointed at the nearest skeleton. "And the wounds are peculiar, aren't they? They're not random the way they usually are in a blade fight."

"No," said Albrecht. "The Huns were archers, and yet we haven't found any arrow wounds—no arrowheads that stuck in a bone or pierced a skull. And we haven't seen the sorts of injuries usual to the battles of the period. No arms lopped off, no leg wounds that must have bled out. Every wound is a big, fatal trauma—there are nearly four hundred beheadings and a very large number of what I believe to be throats so deeply cut that the blade hit the anterior side of the vertebrae."

Sam said, "What it looks like to me is a mass execution. We don't see a second faction because the killers buried the victims and walked away."

"It does look that way," said Remi. "But if these men died so heavily armed, why would they let themselves be killed?"

"We don't know," said Albrecht. "We've just begun our work, but we're asking ourselves these questions as we recover the rest of the remains."

The next day, Sam and Remi arrived in the morning at the dock where the *Margit* was waiting to tow the magnetometer. Tibor sat, eagerly reading a newspaper. When he saw them, he said, "Sam. Remi. You have to see this article."

"What is it?" asked Remi.

Tibor spread the paper out on the dock so they could all look at it at once. On the front page were pictures of six people. The photographs looked like mug shots, with the subjects staring straight into the camera. Remi knelt on the dock. "Sam! It's them, the people from Consolidated Enterprises." She turned to Tibor. "What does it say?"

"Six people, all carrying American passports, have been arrested by Szeged police on suspicion of having committed an armed raid on the Bako pharmaceutical factory a week ago. In the raid, eight security personnel from the Bako company were killed."

"Eight?" said János. "It must be all of the five we hit and the three we tied up in that building. Bako must have had those men killed himself."

"It sounds that way," Sam said. "I was sure most of the five were just wounded and we didn't harm the other three at all."

"What can we do?" Remi asked. "We can't let these idiots take the blame for murder."

Sam took out his phone and dialed the house in La Jolla. The phone rang once.

"Hi, Sam. What's up?"

"Hi, Selma. The six people from Consolidated Enterprises seem to have been sent to Szeged to keep spying on us. They've been arrested for the raid on Bako's factory. But I think that at the time when that happened, they were still in the custody of Captain Klein in Berlin."

"You want me to straighten this out for them?"

"Let's put it this way. If they were to remain in jail for, say, thirty days, I would not be unhappy. If they were to be convicted of eight murders, I'd feel awful, and Remi would make sure I felt worse."

"You bet I would," she said.

"Hear that?" he said.

"I did," said Selma. "From what I've learned about Consolidated, they're awful people, but they don't deserve capital punishment just yet. I'll call Captain Klein in Berlin and get what I need to spring them, but I won't pass it on to Consolidated's New York office unless things get really ugly. How does that sound?"

"Great. Thanks, Selma." He hung up and looked at Remi. "I hope we haven't just made ourselves the only suspects."

"Us? I don't think we've got much to worry about," Remi said. "Remember? There was an order for the local police to keep us under surveillance. If they arrested us, they'd have lots of explaining to do."

"She's right," said Tibor.

"Get used to that," said Sam.

The excavation of the field grew much larger as the students and their professors worked. It was the next week that the lawyers arrived. Tibor's guards saw them first and called Tibor on the boat.

There were a half dozen of them in two big black cars. They pulled up along the road next to the excavation and got out. They all wore immaculate white shirts, dark suits, and striped neckties. When they walked, they were careful to step just on the pavement so no dust would dull the shine of their Italian shoes.

One of them, a shorter, thicker, older man than the others, came forward. He approached a blond female student who was running dirt through a screen with a wooden frame to find small objects. He said, "Go get your bosses."

"The professors?"

"Are they professors?" he said. "Then tell them class is in session and don't be late."

The student ran off along one of the narrow paths that had been left among the grids and stopped at a spot where Albrecht Fischer, Enikö Harsányi, and Imre Polgár were conferring with some other colleagues in khaki clothes. The girl delivered her message, and they all came back up the path.

Enikö Harsányi arrived first. "Hello," she said. "I'm Dr. Harsányi. Can I help you?"

The older man in the suit said, "My name is Donat Toth and I'm an attorney. I have an injunction here to make you stop digging on this land." He held out the paper.

A second woman stepped from the group and took the paper.

She glanced at it and said, "I'm Dr. Monika Voss. I'm the regional director of the National Office of Cultural Heritage. My office has granted this group a permit to carry out this excavation."

Albrecht Fischer held out an official-looking document. Donat Toth took it, glanced at it, and handed it to one of the other suits, who examined it and passed it on. When it came back, he said, "This is out of date. My client now owns the land and will be taking possession today."

"This is the property of the city of Szeged," said Dr. Voss.

"My client, Mr. Arpad Bako, has submitted a very high offer to the city of Szeged, which has been accepted." He held out some more papers.

Dr. Voss looked at the papers, then took out a pen and wrote something on one of them. She said, "The National Office of Cultural Heritage hereby voids this sale."

"You can't do that."

"I just did."

"No, you can't! We put cash money into this!"

"Get it back. Any land containing cultural treasures is under control of the Office of Cultural Heritage. Act number 64 on the protection of cultural heritage says so."

"Who says that what's on this land is cultural treasures?"

"The definition of a cultural treasure is in the law too—all goods of more than fifty years of age, including archaeological findings from excavation. I've identified some here, and no local government officials can overrule my determination."

"I'll go to court."

"Others have. They lost and so will you."

Two of the younger lawyers moved in close to Donat Toth and whispered to him with great concern. He waved them away. "What's to stop me from tearing up this permit?"

One of his legal advisers said apologetically, "Three years in prison, sir."

Toth threw the permit in the general direction of the professors, but it simply floated peacefully to the ground. One of the students picked it up, blew the dust off it, and handed it to Albrecht Fischer. The men in dark suits returned to their cars, turned around, and drove off. Just as they did, Sam, Remi, Tibor, and János arrived in Tibor's taxi.

When the boat crew had heard the story, Tibor said to Sam and Remi, "Defeating Arpad Bako's lawyers isn't the same as defeating Bako."

Sam said, "We need to buy the archaeologists more time."

"How much more?"

"Albrecht thinks they can finish here in another week," said Remi. "They've got the locations of the bodies mapped and most of them photographed and removed. In one more week, he thinks they'll have everything removed from the site."

Sam stared out at the excavation site for a moment and then said, "Here's what we do. Tomorrow we'll pick a spot. We'll stop going up and down the river, anchor, and then start diving. The next day, we'll go to the same place. We'll let them see us going down with markers."

"Then what?" asked Remi.

"Then we double down. We do everything we would do if we were bringing up something big and valuable. We want to rent a dredger mounted on a barge. We'll bring in bulldozers and dump trucks to build our own road to the riverbank right where we're diving."

Tibor said, "Are you sure you want Bako to think you've found the treasure?"

"I want him to think we know where it is, but that there's a lot of heavy work to do to recover it."

"All right," said Tibor. "I'll start with my uncle Géza. He has a construction company, and there are always equipment operators who need work."

The next day, Sam and Remi were out on the deck of the *Margit* in their wet suits, with compressed-air tanks and other gear in a rack near the stern. They set out buoys and flew a red flag with a white stripe to let passing boats know that there were divers in the water and then submerged.

They explored the bottom of the river together, finding an array of metal objects. There were broken pipes, anchor chains, a few hundred-gallon barrels that had held some liquid that had long ago leaked out through rusted holes. Interspersed with the familiar were the unidentifiable: heavily rusted ferrous objects that could only be described as round or long and thin or hollow. Their names and whatever they had been used for were long lost, but these objects were of greatest interest to Sam and Remi. Anything that looked very old and mysterious was a find. They gathered a pile of these objects under the silhouette of Tibor's boat and then surfaced.

Across the river, inside the cargo bay of the parked truck that shadowed them each day, the five men had been joined by Arpad Bako. The five all stood very straight, and all of them remained silent, while Bako looked through a spotting scope at the divers. Bako was a tall, muscular man who wore his curly hair long, so it draped across his forehead and hung over the back of the collar of his white shirt. His suit was a fine garment from a personal tailor he had flown in from Italy. His dark eyes were sharp and alert.

Gábor Székely, the squad leader, said, "You see, Mr. Bako? The whole operation is different now. We're wondering if all that digging being done up the river might just be a diversion from the real operation here."

"It told them the tomb was near, I think," said Bako. "Attila was buried near the Tisza and then the river was diverted to cover the grave. You know that."

"Anytime you give us the word, we can shoot them. With four rifles, we could get all of them in a couple of seconds and be on our way."

"Don't be stupid," Bako said. "The casket could be under twenty feet of sediment by now. The outer one is made of iron and the inner ones from heavier metals. That's why they're making these elaborate preparations—to dig down, attach cables and chains to it, and lift it to the barge. Then they'll move it from the barge to a flatbed truck on that road over there. That moment is weeks away and will cost them millions of dollars to reach. Let them do the work."

While Bako and Székely watched, the people on the boat swung the arm of an electric winch out over the water and lowered the cable. There were a series of sharp tugs on the cable, and then the winch began to pull something up from the bottom. Soon a large nylon net emerged, dripping and draining water. In the net were rusted objects, all of them unidentifiable.

Arpad Bako began to shift his weight, first to one foot, then the other, back and forth, in his excitement. "Look!" he cried. "Look! They're bringing something up!"

"It looks like a bunch of rusty junk."

"It's fifteen hundred years underwater!" he yelled and punched Székely's arm hard. "Anything from the Huns is what we've waited for. Those fools are doing our work for us." His hands kept clenching into fists. "Watch them! Don't let anything go unnoticed." He turned to the man with the camera. "Get clear shots of everything they bring up. Until they move the barge with the crane in over the tomb, they're working for us. When that happens, you can end their employment."

8

"WE'RE DONE," ALBRECHT SAID. "WE'VE EXCAVATED THE entire grid. The artifacts and remains have all been removed from the site, and most are properly packaged and catalogued. In a few days we'll move them to a temporary facility in Budapest for safekeeping while the museum there prepares space for them."

"That's a huge accomplishment in a few weeks," said Remi.

"We knew we didn't have years to do it, and thanks to my Hungarian colleagues and their students we were able to bring in at least fifty trained assistants every day, and as many as a hundred some days."

"That's probably what did the most to keep you safe," said Sam. "It's hard to commit a crime in front of that many people."

"How many warriors did you find in all?" asked Remi.

"A thousand." Albrecht turned away and took a step or two, suddenly interested in looking closely at the skeleton on the table beside them.

"You mean you just have a rough number?" she said. "You haven't done a final count yet?"

"Exactly one thousand."

Sam and Remi looked at each other. "That can't be meaningless," said Sam.

"No," Albrecht said almost under his breath, still staring at the skeleton. He looked up reluctantly. "In fact, before we were willing to accept that number, Imre and Enikö and I counted them again together. Our current theory is that these men were a unit of some kind. The Huns aren't known to have divided themselves into units of a hundred and a thousand, the way the Romans did. But there's no reason to think they never formed temporary units for particular tasks. A commander might have said, 'I need a thousand men for this scouting party and another thousand men to carry out a raid.'"

Remi said, "I hope I'm not being presumptuous, but Sam and I have been doing a lot of reading about the Huns since you called us in. I can't help wondering if you and the others aren't ignoring a possible explanation just because it's too good to hope for."

Albrecht sighed. "We don't want to jump at the idea you're alluding to because of its implications. Not only would it provide encouragement for Arpad Bako, but it could set off a gold rush among the public. Think of the implications."

"Think of the evidence," she said. "Here are a thousand men exactly, all of them Huns who were all killed apparently on the same day, around the year 450, but not in a battle. They're at the center of Hun power, where there were hundreds of thousands of allies but no enemies. They were killed without a fight."

Sam said, "And they were buried with their belongings, including their weapons. They weren't dishonored or mutilated after death. I think Remi has to be right. They were Attila's personal bodyguards. They were sent off to bury him and his treasures in a secret place and then divert the river over the tomb so it wouldn't be found. When they came home, they were killed to prevent them from revealing the location of the burial."

Remi said, "They'd need at least a thousand men to divert a river. They'd have had to dig across one of the loops to make a shortcut channel."

Sam said, "They were all heavily armed, all seasoned warriors with healed wounds. Why would they let themselves be killed without even drawing a sword unless—"

"Unless they were fanatically loyal to Attila, like personal bodyguards," said Remi. "They would feel they were dying with their leader as they had always expected to."

"Yes, it makes sense. Yes, it fits," said Albrecht. "But to accept that story would be a terrible mistake. The tomb of Attila would be worth billions. The Huns were like a giant broom sweeping across Asia and Europe, from beyond the Volga to the Seine, taking everything of value with them. If we announce we've found the men who buried Attila, this whole region will be dug up in a year. Other artifacts of incalculable value will be destroyed, and nobody will be any closer to finding the tomb than they are now. If you accept the old stories, the job of the guards was to take the body and the treasure far from here."

"You're scholars," Sam said. "I know you can't falsify your description of the find when you publish it. And as soon as it's published, others will immediately see what Remi and I see."

Albrecht looked down at the floor and shook his head. "Arpad

Bako thought I might be on the edge of confirming the myth of Attila's treasure. Should I make him into a genius?"

"But it's never been about treasure for you," said Remi. "It's about uncovering the past. As you already said, this doesn't bring anybody closer to the treasure. It just confirms one part of the story—that the guards were killed."

"I know," Albrecht said. "I just don't want to help the criminal who kidnapped me to end up with one of the greatest treasures in antiquity."

"All right," said Sam. "Now that your find has been secured, Remi and I will begin to pack up to go home. You and the others can release just the information you want to, on your own timetable. But I feel I should remind you that big secrets have a habit of finding their own way out. You and the other archaeologists aren't the only ones who saw this. So did hundreds of students. Most of them haven't gone far enough in their studies to interpret what they've seen. But in a couple of years, many of them will get curious and start doing research."

Albrecht threw his hands up in despair. "What would you have me do?"

"What scientists and scholars always do, in the end," said Remi. "Keep looking, and thinking, with an open mind, and reporting your best interpretation of what you see."

"You're right," said Albrecht. "I know it, and I feel ashamed for being so hesitant. Please don't leave us yet. If you could keep Bako and his men occupied for a few more days, we could get the finds to the National Archives."

The next morning, the work at the river continued. Sam and Remi dove in the murky water while Tibor's friends and relatives continued to level and grade a straight roadbed from the road to the river. All that day Remi and Sam scoured the riverbed for rusted objects of various sizes and shapes, lifting them onto the boat. At the end of the day, as usual, they unloaded the boat and trucked the objects to a storage building at the University of Szeged, always covered with tarps so Arpad Bako's watchers would be curious without being able to satisfy that curiosity.

In the evening, Sam and Remi joined Albrecht and his colleagues in studying the objects found in the excavation at the field. The remains of warriors that had already been given preliminary examinations, photographed with their possessions, and catalogued were being placed in wooden boxes, to be archived at the Aquineum Museum, part of the Budapest History Museum, which was housed in the huge Károlyi Palace.

Sam and Remi wandered among the skeletons that had been laid out on tables and tarps to be studied and photographed but which had not been professionally examined since they'd been exhumed. At one point, Sam stopped for a moment. He knelt by a skeleton, craning his neck to see the face from another angle.

"What's wrong?" said Remi.

"Have you ever tried to get people to keep a secret?"

"Sure," she said. "That's pretty much how girls spend sixth grade."

"Ever succeed?"

"No. Once you tell someone that what you're saying is a secret, that makes it valuable, a commodity to be traded. Once someone says he has a secret, it means he wants to tell. It's an invitation to nag him until he gives it up."

"Here are a thousand people who had a secret. Not one of them told?"

"Got to hand it to the Huns," she said. "They knew it's hard to talk when you're headless. We didn't have that option in sixth grade."

"Of course. But even if these men all knew they were going to be killed, they still had relatives they would want to help. I can believe they were all fanatically loyal to Attila, but by then he was dead. Without Attila, the Huns were a loose federation. Didn't even one of these guys hedge his bets?"

"Apparently not or we would have a history course about some other guy who came onto the scene with a boatload of treasure."

"I suppose you're right," Sam said. They walked along the rows of skeletons, passing dozens, then more dozens, a hundred.

"Wait," said Remi. "Take a look at this one."

Sam joined her beside the skeleton. The skeleton had a gold ring around his neck like a Celtic torque. Beside him was a sword with a scabbard with silver mountings. He was wearing a vest that had been made of sheepskin. There were but a few wisps of the shaggy wool left on the outside, and the whole inner leather surface had turned a deep brown.

Through the rib cage and past the backbone, they could see something that looked like rows of designs and, below it, a large and elaborate shape. Remi said, "Doesn't that look like print? And surely that's a picture of something."

"Kind of odd," said Sam. "While he was wearing the vest, you wouldn't be able to see the designs."

"Priscus wrote that they wore their leather clothes until they fell off them. The only time you'd see this is after he was a skeleton."

Sam raised his hand in the air. "Albrecht!" he called. "Can you spare a minute?"

Albrecht came from across the big room and joined them. He looked down. Then he knelt beside the skeleton, moving his head to see the vest through the ribs. Very faintly he breathed, "Oh, no."

Remi said, "Doesn't it look like writing?"

"It *is* writing," said Albrecht. "We've got to get the vest off him so we can see all of it." They carefully lifted the upper part of the skeleton, leaving the severed head on the tarp. While Sam held the torso, Remi and Albrecht slipped the vest down off the shoulders and then the arms. They laid it out on the tarp. Albrecht looked at the shapes closely.

"It's Gothic. It's an early eastern Germanic language, probably what half of Attila's troops spoke."

"Can you read any of it?"

"Quite a lot of it, actually," he said. "There was a nobleman named Ulfilas who commissioned a translation of the Bible just about when Attila died, so we know a lot of the vocabulary and structure. And it has a lot of similarities to other Germanic languages. In English you say *have*. In German it's *haben*. In Gothic it's *haban*. Generally, Gothic retains a *z* that German lost. Things like that."

He read. "'Two days and a half north, one half day west. He's where the fourth-night moon is widest.' Fourth-night moon. I have no idea what that means."

Sam said, "I do. The moon is on a twenty-eight-day cycle. If you start a cycle with the new moon or the full moon, the fourth night is always a crescent."

"Look at the picture," said Albrecht.

"That's the waxing crescent," Sam said. "The left edge is lit up."

"Do you think it's a calendar?" Albrecht said.

"No," said Remi. "This guy was the cheater. He didn't get to talk, but he made a map. The crescent is the shape of the bend in the river that they cut off when they diverted it. He's telling us where Attila is buried."

9

Szeged, Hungary

SAM AND REMI WERE IN THEIR HOTEL SUITE, AND SELMA Wondrash was on Remi's computer screen. "Wendy and Pete and I have done the comparisons and angle measurements and calculations many times and we're sure that we've found the spot that was indicated on the vest. The Roman soldiers of that era could cover twenty-five miles in a day on foot. The Huns were horsemen. When they wanted to, they could probably do twice that distance. But this time they had to transport a heavy load, so we've brought the estimate back to about twenty-five. That means we have a distance north along the river of sixty miles and a distance west of twelve miles. Using aerial photography and satellite images, we do find a dry channel with a crescent-shaped accumulation of alluvium on its west, or outer, side. And the later shortening and straightening of the Tisza left the spot not only dry but nowhere near the modern course of the river."

"You're using the same reasoning we are," said Sam. "The cargo must have weighed several tons, so it was loaded on a huge wagon, probably drawn by a herd of oxen. They would have gone across the plains east of the river, where they didn't need a road, and probably stayed out of sight of the river until the end. In fact, they probably had groups of outriders on all sides to be sure nobody came close."

"Agreed," said Selma. "So when we compare the map on the vest with the aerial photographs, we get a spot at 46° 25' 55" north and 19° 29' 19" east. That's about a hundred thirty miles south of Budapest."

"What's there?"

"Well, it could be worse," she said. "It's not a cathedral or a nuclear power plant. It's the Grape Research Institute, in Kiskunhalas. The *halas* part means 'fish.' In medieval times the town was surrounded by lakes, presumably fed by the river. They're long gone, but the memory lingers on, as does the sandy soil, which is terrific for growing wine grapes."

"How does a modern person get there?"

"From Szeged, you take Route 55 until you reach Route 53, then switch."

"We'll let you know when we've figured out how to do this," Sam said. "We've got a whole lot of activity going on at the Tisza River to make Bako's men think we've already found the tomb underwater."

"If I were you, I'd keep that up," she said. "Arpad Bako has been investigated for three murders besides Tibor Lazar's son. And I wish you good hunting. If anything comes to mind that I can do, give me a call."

"We will."

The next morning, Sam and Remi went down to the Tisza River

as usual and spent most of the day diving to keep up the pretense that they'd found something. It wasn't until after dark that Sam, Remi, and Albrecht saw Tibor arrive in an eight-year-old Mercedes sedan. "Is this your car?" Sam asked.

"My personal car?" said Tibor. "No. I own it, but we use it as a cab. We have a number of regular customers who don't want a taxi with a sign on it. We take them to restaurants and parties. In Hungary, the legal amount of alcohol you can drink and drive is zero, so they need to be driven. Me, I walk. I don't need a car."

Sam loaded the metal detector, three short-handled spades, and night vision goggles into the trunk and climbed into the sedan with the others. Tibor drove them north along the river, staring intently into the rearview mirror at times.

"Are we being followed?" asked Remi.

"I don't think so," Tibor said. "It's hard to tell on these country roads, though. If somebody is behind you when you leave one town, he'll stay behind you all the way to the next town. And it's dark, so all you can see is his headlights."

"But you don't think anyone is following us?"

"No. The one who's been behind us all this time drives like my grandmother. Anybody we have to worry about would be bold and crazy."

Sam and Remi caught each other looking out the back window and smiled. Sam said, "At the next town, let's double back and see if he does too."

"Good idea," said Tibor. He pulled up next to a restaurant at the next town, then drove around it along a narrow and winding road that would accommodate just one car at a time, emerging again near the restaurant. Then he pulled back onto the highway. They didn't see a car ahead of them, but they could no longer see the car behind them either, so they felt reassured.

Sam used the GPS on his phone and directed Tibor the rest of the way. When he saw they were nearing the edge of a huge vineyard outside the city of Kiskunhalas, he said, "Turn your headlights off." The road ahead went dark, and the car rolled to a stop. In the moonlight it was possible to see, on their left, a low hillside gently curving upward like an amphitheater. There were long rows of vines on weathered stakes connected by strands of wire for support. Sam, Albrecht, and Remi got out of the car, took the metal detector, the night vision goggles, and the short-handled, sharp-bladed spades for digging in the sandy soil out of the trunk and closed it quietly. Sam bent close to Tibor's window and said, "Wait for us somewhere out of sight, and keep your phone on. If you see someone coming, or the sun is about to rise, call."

"There are woods up ahead. I'll be waiting there." Tibor drove slowly off, turned, and disappeared into the night.

The three climbed a low rail fence and walked to what they judged to be midway along the crescent-shaped accumulation of soil. Then Sam turned on the metal detector and began to search. He bent over, to present a low profile, and walked up and down the rows of vines, stopping at the end of each row and then moving to the next.

Albrecht and Remi knelt at either end of the rows, watching through their night vision goggles for any sign of people coming. Occasionally they would switch to the infrared setting to see if they could pick up heat from a human being in any direction, then switch back to normal night vision. None of the three shone any light, and there was no sound except for the steady, faint summer breeze through the grapevine leaves and the slough of Sam's shoes on the soft ground between the staked vines.

Sam moved methodically from the upper end of the crescent down toward the flat land. The crescent framed a loop made in the river where the channel curved and the water slowed. The alluvial soil had been deposited there before the river was diverted—highest at the midpoint of the curve and tapering on both ends.

Suddenly all of the metal detector's readings changed. Sam saw the needle bury itself at the upper end. He moved a few steps and the needle dropped again. He came at it from the side and got a similar reading. He stood up straight and waved to the others, then knelt down. Remi and Albrecht came from their stations and knelt beside him.

"Is this it?" whispered Albrecht.

"It could be a lot of things," Sam said. "All I know is that it's metal and that it's big."

Remi rose and went to the end of the row, then came back with the spades. They began to dig, each moving apart from the others and digging quickly in the sandy soil. The work went steadily, and soon they were down about five feet, lifting each shovelful up above their shoulders to throw aside. Sam's shovel rang out as it hit metal. A second later, Remi's scraped a smooth, hard surface.

They set aside their spades and used their hands to clear the dirt off a metal plate. It was a flat rectangle, perhaps six feet long and three feet wide. Albrecht whispered, "There's rust. The material is an impure form of iron. This could be the lid of the sarcophagus."

"Let's clear around it to get a better look," Remi said.

Sam and Remi moved to the ends and began digging around the outside, so Albrecht began on the long side. They dug in silence, the suspense goading them to work harder and faster. But as they dug, each of them hit a second surface, just below the iron slab, that seemed to be stone.

Sam said, "Let's see if we can budge it."

All three stood at one side of the iron slab and used their spades to try to make it move. They strained, tried inserting the tips of their spades under the edge and pushing. The slab budged a fraction of an inch. "It moves. Let's dig a space beside it and push the lid in it."

They increased the size of the hole by three feet so that there was an empty space for the lid. They pushed again but made little progress. "Let's try something else," Sam said.

He climbed out and went to the nearest row of grapevines, where there were wooden stakes with sixpenny nails driven partway in to hold the wires for the vines. He began to pull the nails out. Sam looked closely at each one, twirled it in his fingers. He put some in his pocket and rejected some, pushing them back into the holes in the stakes.

"How many do you want?" asked Remi.

"Thirty or forty. Don't take any that are bent."

Albrecht and Remi collected nails until Sam said, "That's enough to test the theory." They all got back in the hole.

"Now we use our spades to try to pry up one end. A quarter inch will do."

They pried an end up, and Sam held his spade down with one hand and bent to insert a nail sideways between the iron sheet and its stone base. Once one was in, he could insert twenty others without much strain. They repeated the process on the other end of the slab. Albrecht said, "Your theory is sound. Let's hope your rollers are big enough."

Sam knelt at one side of the slab of iron and moved it easily aside, rolling on the sixpenny nails. The three looked down through the opening with their night vision goggles. Albrecht said, "This isn't what I expected. It looks like a stone room."

"Let's hope it's not an air-raid shelter," said Remi. "Or a septic tank."

Sam said, "I can see part of the floor." He took off his belt and slipped it over the handle of his spade and through the buckle.

"Each of you hold one end of the spade and I'll lower myself down a bit and jump."

Remi put her hand on his shoulder. "Sam, I weigh eighty pounds less than you do." She took the end of the belt and sat at the edge of the opening. She pushed off, rappelling down a few feet, then extended her arms and hung from the belt. Then she dropped into the darkness.

They heard the soft thud of her feet hitting the stone floor. There was silence as she walked into the part of the stone room where they couldn't see her.

"Remi, talk," Sam said. "Just so I know it wasn't full of carbon monoxide, or fifty-year-old nerve gas."

"It's full of . . . nothing."

"You mean grave robbers have been here?"

"I don't think so," she said. "Grave robbers are messy. Wait. There's another big piece of iron. This one's only tarnished, not much rust. It's got something carved in it. Looks like Latin."

"The Romans are my regular specialty," said Albrecht. "I've got to see it."

"Here. Hold on," said Sam. "Exactly the way Remi did it."

Albrecht held the belt and eased himself over the edge, then held on and rappelled a few steps, hung, then dropped the last couple feet.

Sam put the three spades together like spoons, slipped his belt around them and through the buckle, and propped them across a corner of the opening. He then lowered himself down.

The room was made of big river sandstone, worked roughly into rectangular blocks. They had been put together with mortar, so the room was waterproof.

Sam found Albrecht engrossed, standing beside Remi with his night vision goggles on and staring at the big piece of iron that had been burnished and then had Roman letters carved deeply into it. "Can you translate for us?" asked Sam.

"'You have found my secret but have not begun to learn it. Know that treasures are buried in sadness, never in joy. I did not bury treasure once. I buried treasure five times. To find the last, you must reach the first. The fifth is the place where the world was lost.'"

Sam said, "Remi, your phone has a flash. You'd better get a shot of this."

"But somebody could see it."

"Unless you want to carry that chunk of iron to Szeged, we've got to chance it."

She took off her night vision goggles, raised her cell phone, and took the picture. Then she said, "I'll send this to Selma as soon as we're aboveground and can send a signal."

They all heard a sound like footsteps coming from above and froze in place, barely breathing. There was a voice, male, speaking quietly as he walked. Then someone laughed once, like a cough.

Sam jumped up, caught the end of the belt, and pulled it overhand. The spades came with it and dropped into his arms. They made a slight metallic noise, but he hoped it hadn't been loud enough to reach the people above. He, Albrecht, and Remi crouched in the far end of the room, away from the entrance, waiting for the intruders to pass by the hole they had dug or come closer to examine it.

As the three watched, the steel slab was pushed across the opening, narrowing the faint rectangle of moonlight until it became a slit and then disappeared.

10

KISKUNHALAS, HUNGARY

THERE WAS THE SOUND OF DIRT BEING SHOVELED ONTO the iron slab that sealed the stone crypt. The shoveling continued. The first few loads of dirt were louder, and the ones after that quieter, but it was clear the dirt they had removed to dig down to the crypt was all being returned to the hole to cover it.

Sam whispered, "Stay still, and don't use more oxygen than we have to."

The three sat on the floor of the crypt, leaning against the stone walls, waiting. A half hour passed, then an hour.

"Do you hear anything?" whispered Remi.

"No," Sam said. "I think they've gone." Sam stood and moved to the space just below the slab of iron. "I think we can get out."

"How?" asked Albrecht.

"We dug down about eight feet. The hole was eight feet wide and ten feet long—six hundred forty cubic feet. This room is ten feet wide, ten feet long, and ten feet deep. That's a thousand cubic feet. We can let the dirt fall in here. We'll spread it on the stone floor as it comes in and it will raise us as it does."

"So simple," said Albrecht. "You think like a Roman."

"I just hope they haven't left guards on the surface to watch the site," Remi said softly.

Albrecht said, "I say we take the chance. We breathe about sixteen times a minute and consume about twenty-four liters of air. We'd better get started."

"Right," said Remi. "Let's lift Sam up to reach the slab."

"No," said Sam. "It would take both of you to lift me, but I can lift you both. If I brace myself against the wall, you can each step up on one of my knees, then to my shoulder. Push your shovel blade between the wall and the iron slab and pry it open an inch or two. That should be enough."

"He's right," said Albrecht. "The two of us can exert more force than Sam can alone."

Sam selected a spot, braced his back against the wall, and bent his knees. Albrecht and Remi took off their boots. Albrecht took a shovel, then stepped from Sam's knee to his shoulder. Remi stepped on the other knee and shoulder. They worked the blades of their shovels into the crack between the iron slab and the stone entrance. They moved both hands down to their shovel handles for maximum leverage. Remi said, "On three . . . one . . . two . . . three."

Sam didn't have to wait to find out if his plan had worked. The fine, sandy soil that had made this such a perfect place for viniculture immediately began to trickle from the narrow opening that they had made. It soon fell in an unbroken curtain, coming down steadily, in front of his eyes.

Remi came down from his shoulder and helped Albrecht step down. Sam raised himself up and sidestepped past the falling dirt.

Whenever the soil under the opening got to be a foot deep, the three would shovel it into the empty end of the stone chamber in front of Attila's message. As the minutes passed, the level rose steadily, and they stepped up on it repeatedly, rising higher and closer to the ceiling each time.

Filling the stone chamber with dirt left less and less space for air. When the floor level had risen about four feet, Sam lifted his shovel and worked it up into the narrow space between the stone and the iron slab, increasing the opening, and then scraped along the wall's edge, bringing more dirt into the crypt.

Remi said, "What are you doing?"

"Trying to speed up the process before the air in here gets too scarce. I've cleared a few inches of space so we can slide the slab into it and make a bigger opening on the other side."

The three stood about a foot apart and pushed the slab the other way with their shovels. The slab moved on its rollers, first closing the narrow opening they'd made, then going another few inches. A much wider opening appeared on the other side of the slab, and the dirt sifted in much faster than before.

"Let's rest for a while," Sam said. The others sat down while Sam spread the dirt around. The rate was much faster now, and when they were within four or five feet of the ceiling, the flow stopped. Sam pushed his shovel up into the opening and it broke through the last of the dirt above it. A shaft of sunlight shone through, illuminating particles of dust floating in the chamber.

They all took off their infrared goggles, blinking in the light. They listened but heard no sound of men above them. There were random chirps of birds, flitting from one row of grapevines to the next. Fresh air flooded in.

They gathered beneath the opening and worked to clear more room above that side so they could push the slab into the newly cleared space. When they rolled the slab back, there was enough of an opening to allow Remi to slip out. She climbed up, then called down, "It's still early morning. I don't see anyone. Pass me a shovel."

Sam pushed the shovel up through the opening and she worked for a few minutes. "Okay, push the slab another few inches."

Sam and Albrecht moved the slab again, and now there was enough room for them to slip through too.

"I can hardly believe this," Albrecht said. "We're out."

They used the shovels to cover the iron slab, but they didn't have enough dirt left aboveground to level it with the surrounding land. Sam looked around. "Hear that?"

"A car," said Remi. They all ducked low in the depression. Remi raised her head and peered out. "Wait. It's Tibor's car."

The car sped up and stopped and then Tibor got out. "Why didn't you call?" he asked. "Didn't you find it?"

"We'll explain later. Just get us out of here," said Sam. "And not toward Szeged."

They all climbed in and Tibor drove off. "I'll go the other way, toward Budapest."

"Perfect," said Sam. "We need to figure out what that message meant. We've got a head start. When those men dig their way into the chamber, they'll be expecting to find a tomb, just as we did."

"It wasn't a tomb?" Tibor said.

"It's more than that," Albrecht said. "Much, much more. How far is it to Budapest?"

"About fifty miles. Maybe an hour, if I push it."

"Then push it," Sam said. "We'll try to fill you in on the way."

11

TIBOR DROVE FAR ABOVE THE SPEED LIMIT, BUT IT WAS
early in the morning and they saw few other cars. Albrecht sat in
the passenger seat beside him and the Fargos were in the back.

Sam said, "Remi and I plan to go after the five treasures. How do
you feel about joining us?"

"This is my life's work," Albrecht said. "Of course I'm in."

"Five?" said Tibor. "*Five* treasures? I'm in five times."

"But how do we want to proceed?" asked Albrecht.

Sam said, "I've given it a little thought. First, we need to deci-
pher the message that Attila left us and be sure we understand it."

"Fortunately, it's only Latin." Albrecht took the newspaper Tibor
had left on the seat, then used his pen to write out his translation.
"'You have found my secret but have not begun to learn it. Know
that treasures are buried in sadness, never in joy. I did not bury
treasure once. I buried it five times. To find the last, you must reach

the first. The fifth is the place where the world was lost.' In this section he tells us where the most recent treasure is."

"Where can that be?" asked Remi. "When was the world lost?"

"There are a couple of good candidates for that description," Albrecht said. "Remember that, to Attila, the world meant the land between the Ural Mountains and the Atlantic."

"Let's call Selma," Remi said. "Maybe she and Pete and Wendy can help us sort this out." She pressed a key on her cell phone. There was a ringing sound and then Selma's voice on the speaker.

"Hi, Remi."

"Hi, Selma. You're being included in a very important discussion. Did you get the Latin inscription I e-mailed you?"

"Yes," said Selma. "It was like a puzzle—or maybe just the beginning of one. Are you going after it?"

"Yes," said Sam. "First, we need to know where 'the world was lost.' Albrecht was just saying there are a couple of candidates. Go on, Albrecht."

"Well, certainly if Albrecht—"

Albrecht interrupted. "We called because we want you to verify the facts, and, in the end, we'll want your opinion too. Our command of history and its principles will give us an advantage. But Mr. Bako has done a decades-long obsessive study of Attila's life. He's probably got an incredible command of the details. Buffs and fanatics can be powerful opponents in a contest of trivia."

"You said you saw two possible meanings for when the world was lost," Remi said. "What are they?"

"One would be the battle Attila fought at Châlons-en-Champagne, France, in the year 451. The Huns had advanced to the west through Germany and most of France, pillaging and destroying cities. The Romans, under Flavius Aëtius, along with a larger contingent of allies, raced to cut off the Huns' advance. They met on the plain at Châlons. Both sides lost many men, but there was no conclusive winner. This was the farthest west that Attila ever got. If he had won a clear victory, he would have gone on and taken Paris, and then possibly the rest of France. He would have ruled most of the area from the Urals to the ocean."

"What's the other candidate?" asked Selma.

"It's a bit more complicated story," Albrecht said. "It began a year earlier, in 450. Honoria, the sister of the Roman Emperor Valentinian III, was in exile, living in Constantinople, the eastern Roman capital, because at the age of sixteen she was pregnant by a servant. Now she was about to be married off to a Roman Senator she didn't like. Her solution was to write a letter to Attila the Hun, asking him to rescue her. Attila definitely interpreted the letter as a marriage proposal. He believed she would bring him a dowry consisting of half the Roman Empire."

"Was that really what she had in mind?" Remi asked.

"It hardly mattered, because her brother Valentinian wasn't going to let it happen. He hustled Honoria back to the Western Empire, to Ravenna, Italy, where he had his court."

"Attila wouldn't have put up with that," said Tibor.

"He didn't," Albrecht said. "In 452, after his disappointment in France, Attila and his men went south and east into northern Italy. They took Padua, Milan, and many other cities. Attila, at the head of his huge army, moved south toward Ravenna, forcing Valentinian and his court to flee back to Rome."

"And Attila followed?"

"Yes. Until a delegation met him south of Lake Garda, near Mantua. The delegation included noble Romans, led by Pope Leo I. They begged for mercy, asking him to spare Rome. History says he turned around and left for Hungary."

"That's all?"

"I said it was complicated. He had taken northern Italy almost unopposed. He wasn't a Christian and wouldn't have been interested in the Pope's request. Italy was at his feet. They had no army comparable to his. I think that his great army made the conquest of Rome impossible. The country was in the middle of a terrible famine. There was also an epidemic. The descriptions indicate it was probably malaria. If Attila pushed on for Rome, there would be no food to feed his huge army, and many would die from illness. So he left, planning to return another day."

"Is that what you think is the meaning of 'where the world was lost'?"

"Yes," said Albrecht. "He was already receiving annual tribute from the Eastern Roman Empire. He controlled most of Europe, from the Urals to central France. If he'd been given the Western Roman Empire, legitimized by the hand of the Emperor's sister, that was pretty much what he would have considered the world."

"Albrecht is the expert, but if my opinion makes a difference, I heartily agree," said Selma.

"It's a year later than the battle in France," said Sam. "At the end of his life, I think he wouldn't say the battle was the most recent loss, and ignore losing Rome when he had it in his hands."

"Exactly," said Albrecht. "Fighting to a standstill in France was important. But having Rome was having the world."

"Attila says he buried a treasure. So it's off to Italy."

"The place where the world was lost was where he stopped his army and went home," Albrecht said. "We'll research it carefully, but it would be south of Lake Garda near Mantua."

"All right," said Sam. "Beginning now, we're in a race. Arpad Bako will dig up the crypt, expecting to find us in there dead. He'll find the message, get it translated, and head where we're headed."

"If that's his interpretation of the message," said Remi.

"Right. What's the plan?" asked Tibor.

Sam said, "I think that Bako has more reason than ever to want to snatch Albrecht. Interpreting these ancient messages is going to be crucial. So we fly Albrecht to California on the next flight so he can work with Selma in the research center at home in La Jolla. It's also extremely important that we know what Arpad Bako and his men are doing and where they are from hour to hour. The only one who can hope to accomplish that is Tibor, so he returns to Szeged and recruits people he can trust to help him. Remi and I will catch the next plane from Budapest to the area south of Lake Garda and get started on the search. Other suggestions?"

"No," said Albrecht. "Perfectly right."

"I'll be honored to work with you, Albrecht," said Selma. "All right, everyone. Your plane tickets will be waiting at Ferihegy Airport at Budapest. Except you, Tibor. Might I be so presumptuous as to suggest that you take a different route home?"

"Thank you, Selma. I will."

"And Selma?"

"Yes, Sam?"

"See if you can get a scrambled satellite phone to Tibor, programmed with our numbers and yours."

"Right away." They could hear her computer keys clicking at a furious rate. "And while I'm at it, I'll get new ones for you too."

"Good idea," said Sam.

"And nobody forget," Remi said. "A few hours ago, Bako's men tried to bury us alive. Don't anybody ever stop looking over your shoulder."

12

SZEGED, HUNGARY

ARPAD BAKO SAT IN HIS OFFICE OVERLOOKING THE TISZA River and the bridge. On the other side of the river he could see the lights of Új-Szeged. It seemed to him that the lights brightened and extended farther every time he looked. He was in such high spirits that he began to feel a creeping sadness. He should have prepared some kind of celebration. A moment like this should not have been wasted. Gábor Székely and two of his men had reported good news from a vineyard on Route 53 at Kiskunhalas.

Somehow the two Americans and Albrecht Fischer had sorted out the twists and turns of the Tisza that had disappeared since Attila's time and found it. They had found the tomb. Székely had received the report from his surveillance team at three a.m. but had the consideration to wait at Bako's house until he had awakened at seven.

The surveillance team had followed Tibor Lazar's sedan all the way to the experimental vineyard, using a transponder they had attached to it. When they caught up, they found Fischer and the Fargos actually inside Attila's tomb. The two surveillance men had read the situation and made a quick decision not to try to drag them out. They had simply moved the heavy iron seal back over the opening, replaced the dirt, and driven away to wait for them to suffocate.

Bako could hardly believe his luck. He had the tomb of Attila, containing one of the great treasures of ancient history. And he had trapped inside it the only people capable of preventing him from retrieving it. Last night, Arpad Bako had won the prize of his life. But now it was night again. Why was Székely taking so long?

His telephone rang. It seemed terribly loud in the dark and solitude of his office. He reached into his suit pocket for it. "Yes?"

"This is Gábor Székely, sir."

"Good. I've been waiting."

"The news is . . . unexpected," Székely said. "We've dug down to the tomb, but it had been filled with dirt. We dug down into it carefully, brought in more men, and emptied it. There was no treasure, no body of Attila, and there never had been. Attila's men had simply buried an iron sheet with Latin writing on it. We've photographed it, and I just sent it to you as an attachment to an e-mail."

Bako whirled his chair around to face his desk and turned on his computer. "What about the Fargos and Professor Fischer?"

"They aren't here, sir. They must have escaped, which would explain why the underground chamber is filled with dirt. As the chamber filled up, they—"

"If you're sure you've found everything, close that chamber and bury it again so no outsider will be able to find it. I don't want some third party joining the hunt for the tomb."

"Yes, sir."

"And then come back here to my office. I'll have orders ready for you."

"Yes, sir."

Bako saw the e-mail, headed "no subject," from Székely. He opened it, downloaded the attachment, and saw the picture. He enlarged it so it filled the two-foot screen on his desk. The rough, tarnished surface was gouged deeply, and he could make out the letters easily. He had gone to the best school. While his Latin wasn't good enough to do justice to Livy or Suetonius anymore, this was the crude and simple Latin of soldiers. He translated it as he read.

"'You have found my secret but have not begun to learn it . . . The fifth is the place where the world was lost.'"

Bako laughed aloud and punched the air above his desk. "Five treasures!" He would be one of the richest men in Europe. His mind raced. Of course he knew the place where the world was lost. Anyone would know that. It was the site of Attila's defeat, the battlefield where Aëtius and the Visigoths joined forces to stop his advance on Paris!

Then he remembered something unpleasant. His enemies had been trapped in that stone chamber with the message scraped into the iron sheet. They had gotten out alive. They would be rushing to Châlons right now. There was no time to waste.

Bako snatched up his phone and dialed 33, the code for France, and then a private number. It was the cell phone of Étienne Le Clerc.

"'Allo?"

"Étienne!"

"Hello, Arpad," he said wearily. "You have caught me at dinner. Is there trouble?"

"There is only opportunity. I've discovered the location of one of Attila's hidden treasures. It's in a place where you can easily help me get it. But there are other people rushing to get there before I do."

"So you're planning to win the race by substituting a person who was born at the finish line? How much do I get?"

"You will have a third of this treasure, but I must see all of it—everything that is found—before we split it."

Bako could almost hear Étienne Le Clerc's shoulders shrugging. "*Oui, bien sûr.* But I'll need specific information on where it is. I'm not going to dig up half of France searching for it. Who, and how many, are the competition?"

"There are an American couple named Sam and Remi Fargo. They're amateur treasure hunters. They've joined with a German archaeology professor named Albrecht Fischer. I'll send you their pictures by e-mail. And there's a Hungarian taxi driver named Tibor Lazar. I don't think they'll bring anyone else. They'll want to slip into France, find the treasure, and get out."

"And where is the treasure to be found?"

"Before I tell you, are you sure you're willing and able to do this and to stick to my terms?"

"We must both look at everything and then each take half."

"I said one-third!"

"You said 'split.' To me, that means 'split down the middle.' I'm taking all of the risk and doing all of the work. And I'm doing it in my own backyard."

"Oh, all right. We don't have time to argue, and there will be more wealth than we can spend in our two lifetimes. Take half. But no matter what you learn during all this, it remains a secret."

"*Oui.*"

"The treasure must be buried on the field of the Battle of the Catalaunian Plains, at Châlons-en-Champagne. Look for a buried chamber on the east side of the high stone outcropping in the center of the field near the Marne River. It should show up with metal detectors."

"Will do, my friend. When we've dug up the treasure, I'll call you."

"Good," said Arpad. "And when the Fargos and their party arrive, please do what you can to solve that problem too."

"If they were to have a fatal accident, it would be a pity, but these things do happen sometimes. If it does, I'll expect additional monetary consideration. Men who can and will do this sort of thing don't come cheap."

"I'll be waiting. Thank you, Étienne."

Bako clicked his cell phone to end the call and put it in his inner coat pocket. He was feeling like a great general who had just committed a corps of foreign troops to the distant wing of his battle, neatly outmaneuvering his opponents and trapping them. He had acted decisively, even ruthlessly, a little like Attila.

He thought about Étienne Le Clerc. He was an unapologetic gangster, not a legitimate businessman who cut a few corners. He lived very well by a combination of several schemes that Bako knew about—money laundering, melting stolen jewelry into bars and selling the loose gems, counterfeiting several currencies and trading them outside their home markets for euros, smuggling Bako's prescription drugs into France—and probably other schemes Bako didn't know about. Le Clerc had dozens of operatives, dealers, smugglers, and enforcers in his organization and they were already in France, not far from the place where the world was lost.

Great conquests weren't made by battle alone but just as often by shrewd alliances. Attila would have understood that and recognized him as a kindred spirit worthy of being his heir.

13

VERONA-BRESCIA, ITALY

SAM AND REMI FLEW TO ROME AND FROM THERE TO VE-
rona. They picked up the rental car that Selma Wondrash had reserved for them and drove westward out of the city around thirty
kilometers to the resort city of Peschiera del Garda on the south
shore of Lake Garda. When they arrived, Remi put down the guidebook she had been reading and said, "Let's get out near the marina
and walk."

Rolling hills surrounded the southern end of the lake. The marina was large, with graceful sailboats rocking gently so that their
masts moved like metronomes. Sam and Remi could hear the soft
sound of rings and pulleys swinging against the aluminum masts in
the light summer breeze. The little town on the big lake indeed had
a vacation feel to it. From here, it seemed to be all boats and hotels.

"What did you learn in the guidebooks?" Sam asked.

"The lake is the biggest in Italy, thirty-four miles long. The upper end is surrounded by mountains, but down here there are lots of beaches. The water enters in the north and flows out in the Mincio River here in Peschiera del Garda, and a bit farther on it flows into the Po River."

"So we're getting close," said Sam. "The account Albrecht e-mailed us says Pope Leo I went with his delegation to meet Attila south of Lake Garda where the Mincio River meets the Po."

They walked along the pebble beach past several docks and a café. The buildings they could see were mostly two to four stories high, and old. They were painted white, pink, and yellow. There was a sixteenth-century brick wall around the old boundaries of the city, with walkways on top. They found a parking lot outside the walls that had a garden with *Peschiera del Garda* spelled out in flowers at the main gate and then a pedestrian mall where there were cafés and shops.

"How are we going to find the spot?" Remi asked.

"The usual ways, I guess. We start with the things that were already here in 452."

"The town was founded in the first century, so it was already three hundred years old when Attila arrived."

"It was just a little village along the shore. Without much warning, out of the north comes Attila the Hun, of all people, at the head of a huge army of horsemen. He had just devastated much of northern Italy on his way here."

"The people were probably too busy running to look at him closely," said Remi. "I know I would have been."

"Me too. That's how Venice was founded. People running from Attila as he came down from the north hid on the islands. When he left, they didn't."

"Okay, smart guy," she said. "The towns around here have

changed. But the place where the river leaves the lake must be the same."

"That's logical."

Remi said, "So Attila and about fifty or a hundred thousand warriors and their horses and wagons came this far south, loaded with the plunder of northern Italy. They camped south of here where the Mincio ran into the Po. Then the Roman delegation, consisting of Pope Leo, the Consul Avienus, and the Prefect Trigetius, arrived. What the two sides said to each other was never revealed. All the accounts are guesswork. What we know is that because Italy was in the middle of a famine, there was not much food for the Huns to steal. There was also an epidemic, and many of the Huns already had fallen sick. Marcian, the new emperor of the Eastern Roman Empire, was encroaching on the Danube, which would threaten the Hun strongholds. For whatever combination of reasons, Attila and his men packed up and returned north, giving up his chance to rescue Honoria from her brother and gain control of the Roman Empire."

"Let's think a minute," said Sam. "He's heading home. But he hopes to come back in a year or two and conquer Rome. He's loaded down with loot from northern Italy. So he leaves a treasure to resupply his troops on his next attempt. Where would he leave it?"

"At the place where he stopped to camp," Remi said. "It's as far south as he got. That's the place where he could safely and secretly bury whatever he wanted to. And if he was going to use it to resupply his army, the road to Rome is the place to do it."

"Right."

"So we agree. It's where the Mincio meets the Po?"

"I think so. The place where he turned back has got to be where the world was lost."

"Let's start with the west side of the Mincio. If you're coming down Lake Garda, that's the less mountainous side, so it's the most sensible way to travel."

"All right," said Sam. "Let's go check into our hotel. On the way, we can tell Selma to track down the equipment we'll need."

As they walked toward their car, Remi called Selma in California and put her on speaker.

"Hi, Remi."

"Hi, Selma. We're here in Peschiera del Garda and we think we know where to search. But we'll need a handheld magnetometer and a good metal detector."

"They're waiting in your hotel. I ordered two of each."

"Why, thank you, Selma," said Remi.

"Once I saw the pictures of the big iron slabs, I knew you'd be needing detectors. Anything else you want, just let me know."

"You got it," said Remi. "Has Albrecht arrived yet?"

"Not yet. His plane arrives in about two hours. Pete and Wendy are going to pick him up. We've got his room ready and plenty of space and computer equipment set up."

"Thanks, Selma," said Sam. "We'll start work this afternoon."

Remi added, "We'll call and let you know if anything turns up. Has Bako moved yet?"

"You're safe for the moment. Tibor says that Bako and his men are still in Szeged. If they understood the message, they're in no hurry to get to Italy."

"That's the best news of the day," said Remi.

"Glad to oblige. I'll talk to you if anything changes," Selma said and then hung up.

Remi put the phone away and they drove to their hotel, a white building on the beach with a cordon of bright red beach umbrellas that made it look as though it belonged a few miles to the east on the Adriatic. After checking into the hotel and examining their equipment, Remi and Sam went to see the concierge, a fifty-year-old woman wearing a tailored gray suit with the hotel's logo on the left lapel. "May I help you?" she said, her lightly tinted glasses glinting.

"I understand that this area is full of bicycle paths," said Sam. "Is there one that runs the length of the Mincio River?"

"Oh, yes," said the concierge. "It begins where the river flows out of the harbor and runs all the way through Mantua and beyond. I've done the ride myself many times. It's about twenty-five miles."

"When you say 'and beyond,' what do you mean? How far beyond?"

"There's a natural stopping point at Mantua where the river becomes three lakes. But you could continue eight miles to the place where the Mincio continues to the Po." She reached into the top drawer of her desk and handed Sam a map. "The bicycle route is marked and shows you just where to go."

"Thank you," said Sam. He gave a little bow. "*Mille grazie.*"

The concierge laughed. "You make a good Italian. Once you get to know this place, you might not want to go home."

"I'll try to be a good guest," he said. To Remi he said, "Let's get some bicycles."

They walked along an old canal, following the map, to a bicycle shop. At first, everything in the shop seemed to be the sort of gear used by professional racers. But when the proprietor saw Remi walk past a three-thousand-euro bike and ask for something a bit more comfortable for touring, he showed them some sturdy, practical mountain bikes with thick, knobby tires and well-padded seats. They picked out a pair, with his advice, bought backpacks, and threw in some visors to keep the sun out of their eyes. Sam also bought a variety of accessories—lights, reflectors, and other items that attached to bicycles, and a portable set of bicycle tools.

They rode their new bicycles back to their hotel, then walked them into the elevator and took them to their floor. When they had the bicycles in their room, he attached the magnetometers in such a way that no one looking at the bicycles would know that there was anything unusual about them. The telescoped magnetometer poles looked like reinforced bicycle crossbars, and the sensors extended just a few inches in front of the handlebars.

He removed the two metal detectors from their boxes but kept them stored unassembled in the two backpacks.

As they were preparing, Sam's cell phone buzzed. He switched on the speaker. "Yes?"

"Sam? It's me, Albrecht."

"Are you in California yet?"

"Yes. I'm in your house, with Selma. Since I left you, I've spent some time studying the available satellite photography and aerial mapping of the spot where you're looking, and I've rechecked some of the written sources."

"What can you tell us?"

"There are several versions of the story but a few things we know for certain. One is that Attila left a trail of destruction in the northern part of Italy and came down the west side. There were no roads on the east side until the 1930s, which is an indication of what the landscape is like."

"Remi figured that out," said Sam. "And since the Huns didn't leave a written history, we're guessing the best sources are the people who kept track of Pope Leo I. They list the cities Attila sacked and destroyed. Mantua is the last one."

"Leo met him on the Mincio where it empties into the Po. The

Pope had come from the southeast, and since he was the suppli-
cant, he went to Attila's camp."

"How will we know where the camp was?"

"Your coordinates are 45° 4' 17.91" north, 10° 58' .01" east. Attila had between fifty and a hundred thousand fighters. That means
at least a hundred thousand horses and innumerable cattle, sheep,
and goats. They would be lined up along the river, drinking and
grazing. The encampment would be on a fairly flat piece of ground,
but elevated to keep from flooding."

Selma said, "We put the camp's tents about two hundred yards
from the confluence, stretching west along the north side of the Po."

Remi said, "Why the north side?"

"Attila had just come down from the north, and they knew that
no force was left behind them. The only possible threat would have
been a Roman army somewhere to the south, so they would have
kept the river to the south of them as a barrier."

"Okay," said Remi. "North side of the Po, west side of the Mincio. Flattish ground, look for the highest spot on it."

"That's right," said Albrecht. "We're still trying to decide how
Attila's men could have buried the treasure secretly."

"We have a couple of ideas," Sam said. "We'll let you know if
we're right. What's the latest on Arpad Bako?"

"Still no movement. Tibor positively identified Bako going into
his office as usual this morning and coming back from lunch in the
afternoon. He had four of his security men with him."

"Great. Please let us know if anything changes. By now, Bako
should have read the inscription in the false tomb and he ought to
be moving."

"Maybe he's not as good at this as we are," Selma said.

"I'm just hoping he's not better."

"We'd better get going," said Remi.

"I heard that," said Selma. "We'll be waiting for news."

Early the next morning, Sam and Remi dressed in tourist clothes: shorts, T-shirts, and athletic shoes, with their sun visors and sunglasses. In another five minutes they were out on the road, heading for the Mincio River.

An old, level towpath bordered the river and made it a favorite ride for bicyclists. Sam and Remi pedaled along the paved path with dozens of others, admiring the beauty of the city and the equally beautiful Lombardy landscape, the flat fields nearby and low rolling hills in the middle distance, with a row of trees growing along each bank of the river. There were houses that must have dated from the Middle Ages and old vineyards with vines strung on poles and overhead wires. They stopped at a pleasant spot beneath the trees along the river and ate their picnic lunch.

They reached Lago Superiore, the first of the lakes, at one-thirty p.m. and rode along its southern shore into the center of Mantua. They found a sidewalk café where they could rest and have espressos and pastries in view of the second lake, Lago di Mezzo, then rode over the Via Lagnasco bridge to SS 482, the Via Ostiglia.

"Eight more miles," said Remi. "This is glorious. I don't feel tired at all."

"It occurred to me that we've been following the river downstream," said Sam. "Does that suggest anything to you?"

"Yes. That we'll be pedaling uphill all the way back to Peschiera del Garda," Remi said. "Or we'll have to find another way."

After an hour of easy pedaling, they could see the destination. The Po ran west to east and was wider than the Mincio. On both sides of the Mincio were cultivated vegetable and grain fields as far as they could see, except for the field at its confluence, which had been plowed but not yet planted. The trees were all along the riverbeds.

Sam and Remi dismounted from their bicycles and studied the landscape. "This is a good place not to be noticed," said Remi. "I can't even see a building on this side. Albrecht said to stay on the west side of the Mincio, north of the Po. All we need to find now is a fifteen-hundred-year-old campsite."

"Give me a minute to check the GPS." After a minute, Sam said, "We're on it. They would have watered their horses along the river-bed. And if I were a nomadic horseman, I would be sure to take really good care of my horses." He turned away from the river to face the field. "Fifty to a hundred thousand Hun warriors means something near two hundred thousand horses. It's hard to imagine what that must have looked like. The line of horses must have stretched along both rivers for a couple of miles."

Remi wheeled her bike to a nearby tree, leaned the bike against the trunk, stepped on the bike's lower bar, then the seat, and pulled herself up to the tree's first large branch. She reached up to the second branch for a handhold and then stood.

"What do you see?" asked Sam.

"From up here, it looks as though the highest part of the field is right over there." She pointed a hundred yards inland to a section of the field that was slightly elevated.

Sam stepped close and helped her down, then extended the magnetometers' poles so the sensors extended about three feet in front of the bicycles' handlebars and the boxes holding the gauges were between the handlebars and easy to read. They walked their bicycles, side by side, into the field and up the slight incline.

It was late afternoon, the sun's rays falling at a low angle on the field. As they walked they read the magnetometers, watching for disturbances in the magnetic field. There was little fluctuation in the readings until they crossed the highest point in the field, which was almost a dome. Then the needles jumped.

"Did you get that?" Remi asked.

"Got it," Sam said.

They both stopped. Sam said, "Let's see how big it is."

Remi laid her bike down to mark the place where the disturbance began and walked with Sam as he wheeled his bike a few yards. "There," he said and laid his bike down. They paced the distance together, then replaced the bikes with their sun visors. They rolled the bikes along a perpendicular path. "It's ten paces by fifteen," Remi said.

"That's what I get," Sam said. "About twenty by thirty feet. Let's try one of the metal detectors." Sam assembled the one from Remi's backpack and began to pass it back and forth over the area they had marked off. It gave off an electronic tone, then a squeal—a loud and unchanging shriek—as he walked the width of the spot.

Remi said, "It's huge—much bigger than the first chamber. Plan A or Plan B?"

"We'll have to mark it so we can find it again quickly, then ride back to Peschiera del Garda and get ready to excavate tomorrow night after dark."

"Where will we find a way to hold a hoard of gold twenty by thirty paces across?"

"We've got a navigable river right over there."

"Aha, Plan A," she said. "A big boat."

Sam marked the spot by taking the sensor off his magnetometer and laying the long aluminum pole flat on the ground. Then they rode their bicycles back along the towpath to Peschiera del Garda under the waning sun and then into the darkness.

As soon as they were in their hotel room and had a bath, they called Tibor's secure cell phone. "Tibor?"

"Yes, Sam."

"We need the three men we used as crewmen on the boat in the Tisza. They need to be at our hotel in Mantua by tomorrow evening at sundown."

"You have a boat?" asked Tibor.

"No, but by tomorrow night I will."

"They'll be there."

"Thanks, Tibor."

"I have to get off now, so I can talk to them. Good-bye, Sam."

Sam and Remi called the concierge again, and while she got them a reservation for a fine restaurant in Mantua, they drove the twenty-five miles to the city to shop in the best stores and find clothes suitable for an evening out. They began with a gray Armani summer suit for Sam, and, at Folli Follie, Remi bought a simple but striking Fendi jacquard sleeveless dress with a gold accent on the belt. They wore the clothes they had bought, left the clothes they'd worn in the trunk of the car they'd parked at the city walls, and made the ten-minute walk to Ochina Bianca, a restaurant just north of the city's center.

They ordered risotto alla milanese, redolent with saffron, as their pasta course, osso buco as their entrée, and their wine selection was Felsina Fontalloro 2004 from Tuscany. Remi said, "This is all so wonderful. Let's flip a coin to see which one of us goes to culinary school so we can have this at home."

"The cooking part is not my specialty," he said. "Think of me as your nutritionist and trainer. I'm just helping you build up your strength for tomorrow when the work starts again. In fact, I'm already thinking you might need some dessert. There's a local delicacy called sabbiosa, which is a plum cake soaked in Guinness. How can that be bad?"

"I have no idea," said Remi. "Maybe it can't."

"In fact, I'll even have some with you to be sure it's up to your standards."

"I'm sure you will."

After their dinner in Mantua, they walked to the city walls, got into their car, and drove along the country road toward Lake Garda. "I'm glad we did this," Remi said.

"Are you?"

"Yes. Tomorrow night at this time, if we're digging a deep hole with shovels, I can remind myself that while the world sometimes brings you dirt and hard labor it also brings perfect risotto."

"And a perfect date to share it with."

"You're getting awfully good at that," Remi said. "I'm going to have to keep a close eye on you to be sure you're not practicing compliments on other women."

"Feel free," said Sam. "I relish close attention."

"I know you do," she said, and leaned close to kiss his cheek as they drove in the starlight back to their hotel in Peschiera del Garda.

14

CONFLUENCE OF THE PO AND MINCIO RIVERS, ITALY

IT WAS TEN THE FOLLOWING NIGHT BEFORE SAM AND Remi walked into the field again. This time they arrived by car. Sam drove it off the road under the row of trees and bushes and covered it with a tarp to hide its shape. He and Remi wore dark clothes and carried shovels and crowbars, flashlights, climbing ropes, and infrared night goggles in their backpacks.

They quickly found the pole they had left behind and began to dig. The work went more easily than Sam had anticipated because the ground had been plowed recently, so it was loose for the first foot or more. Beneath it was rich black dirt from thousands of years of overflows from the two rivers, land cultivated by the Etruscans and then the Romans, then the Lombards and modern Italians.

It took them two hours to reach a rough stone surface. They dug away some of the dirt on top, moving only enough to make a path to the opening on top. This time, there was not an iron slab but a barrier of three big stones laid close together over the opening and mortared in place.

Remi looked closely at it and said, "This doesn't look like something we can move by ourselves."

"It isn't," Sam said. "I'll be right back."

"What are you doing?"

"Getting the car," he said over his shoulder. A few minutes later the car they had rented was bouncing along the plowed rows of the field with its lights off. Sam backed up to the edge of the hole he and Remi had dug. He got out, attached the climbing ropes to the tow ring under the car, and looped them over the first of the stone slabs. He took a hammer from the trunk and a crowbar to use as a chisel to chip away most of the mortar. When he was ready, he said, "You drive. I'll give the stone a little help from back here."

Remi got into the driver's seat and opened the window so she could hear Sam.

Sam went to the first of the stones, slid the bent end of the crowbar under its edge, then walked a few yards over to the long aluminum pole from the magnetometer that he had dismantled the day before and came back with it. He slipped it over the long part of the crowbar. The pole was about seven feet long, and he grasped it near the end. "Okay, Remi," he said. "Slowly."

She gave the car gas gradually, pulling against the weight with the doubled ropes, while Sam pried the stone upward, helping to free it from the mortar. There was a pop and then a scrape as the car pulled the stone free. The space that had been uncovered was roughly two feet wide and four feet long.

Sam set aside his elongated crowbar and knelt above the opening as Remi returned to kneel beside him. Sam went to his belly and shone his flashlight into the hole. There was a deep, burnished glow about six feet down, the soft shine of untarnished gold. "Eureka! We did it."

Remi kissed his cheek. "Fargos one, Bako zip."

Sam took out his telephone. He pressed a programmed number, then heard the slightly accented "Yes?"

"We've found it, Tibor. Bring the boat to the mouth of the Mincio, where it meets the Po. Go a few yards up the Mincio and then pull into the western shore. I'll be there to meet you. Don't show any lights."

"We'll be there in five minutes."

"Thanks." Sam ended the call.

"Well?" said Remi. "While you're playing Treasure Island with the boys, what do you want me to do?"

"Call Selma and Albrecht and let them know. Tell Albrecht to get in touch with his Italian colleagues so we'll have a safe place to store the treasure."

"Want me to move the car?"

"Not yet. I'll be back."

Sam walked to the river and waited on the high bank until he saw the big shadowy shape of the boat appear in the moonlight on the Po River. In a moment, he could hear the steady throbbing of the engine running at low speed. As the boat came abreast of his position he called out, "Beach it and throw me a line."

The boat glided into the sand and stopped. A silhouette appeared on the deck at the bow, threw a rope to Sam, and then watched him tie it to a tree. One by one, the four men jumped down to the sand and climbed up the bank. The last was Tibor. He patted Sam's back. "It's good to see you again. Is it real this time?"

"I'll show you." He set off into the field and the others walked with him.

Tibor said, "You remember my cousin Albert and my cousin Caspar from the Tisza diving boat."

"Of course." Sam shook hands with them. "Thank you for coming."

"And this is my cousin Paul. He speaks Italian."

"Pleased to meet you," Sam said. To Tibor he said, "If I had a family like yours, I could take over the world."

"In our part of the world we've had too many people try to do that already. The Lazars stay home, eat, drink, and make love. That's why there are so many of us."

They reached the spot where Remi waited, and Tibor repeated the introductions. The men all bowed to her in turn. Tibor said, "I reminded them she was a beautiful woman ahead of time so they wouldn't act like hermits who never saw a girl before."

"Thank you, Tibor," she said. "Let's get to work."

Sam, Tibor, and Paul used the climbing rope to let themselves down into the chamber. It was larger than the one in Hungary, and, as they stepped down, Sam could see that this was an even bigger treasure than he had expected. Most of the plunder that was taken from northern Italy in 452 must be here.

There were thousands of gold and silver coins, gold chains and armlets, gold chalices and crosses, the plunder of a hundred churches and monasteries. There were swords and daggers with hilts studded with rubies, sapphire rings, necklaces and torques in great profusion. There was finely wrought armor and chain mail, detailed carved cameos, ornaments of every kind, oil lamps and sconces, mirrors of polished silver with gold fittings. The sheer number and variety of objects was intimidating. Gold brooches, bracelets, buckles and studs, and a great number of objects Sam hadn't time to examine and identify, were strewn about randomly.

They used wooden crates to hold the treasure that Tibor brought from the boat. They filled the car's trunk, then the backseat and the passenger seat and the floor. Then Remi drove the car to the river with Caspar and Albert and they unloaded it onto the boat.

When Remi drove the car back to the treasure chamber, she had eight wooden boxes with rope handles. They usually were used for bringing fish to home port, so they had a slight fragrance, but with them the loading went quickly. Sam, Tibor, and Paul could fill the car, and while Remi drove to the riverside to load the boat, they were busy filling the boxes for her next trip.

It took three hours to empty the chamber and load the boat. When the treasure had been completely removed, Sam said to Tibor, "Take the boat up the Mincio and anchor it on Lake Garda. It's twenty-five miles, so we'll probably be there in time to see you arrive."

"All right," said Tibor. "But what happens if the police stop us and the boat is inspected?"

"Then tell Paul to forget he speaks Italian and call me."

With Attila's plunder aboard, the boat was heavier and lower in the water. It took Sam, Tibor, and the three cousins to push the bow off the sandy beach into the calm water of the Mincio. Tibor said, "I hope every ounce of gold is a tear for Arpad Bako."

"That reminds me," said Sam. "Who's watching him while you're here?"

"My brother is in charge. He has eyes on Bako and his five closest men day and night."

"Better than I could have wished," Sam said. "Have a pleasant voyage."

The engine started, and the boat turned slightly so Tibor could climb aboard. It straightened and began to chug up the quiet river toward the lake.

Sam and Remi drove to the open chamber one last time. They

used the climbing rope to lower themselves into the dark stone room, and then Sam turned on his flashlight and shone it on each of the plain stone walls. This time, there was no engraved iron plate. But on the floor, visible only now that the treasure had been removed, was a stone block with engraved letters. They stood over it, and Remi took several photographs with her cell phone, then reviewed them to be sure the letters were clear. Sam was busily copying the message on a piece of paper. When he saw Remi looking at him, he shrugged. "If we lose the phone, I'm not coming back to read this. Are you?"

"I wasn't thinking about that," she said.

"What were you thinking?"

"That this isn't like the huge iron slab we found in Hungary. I'll bet that, using the car, we could lift this thing out."

Sam knelt and tried to jiggle it but couldn't. Then he used his pocketknife to scrape at the mortar a bit. "I'll be right back," he said and climbed up the rope and out. He returned a few minutes later with the other rope, both crowbars, and the hammer. They went to work on the mortar, and in a short time they had freed the stone. They pried it up, and Sam tied the rope around it, first the short side, then the long side. He climbed up, and Remi heard him start the car. The stone was thinner and slightly smaller than the blocklike stones that made up the bulk of the room. It rose easily and then stopped. Remi climbed up the rope and joined Sam at the surface and then went to the car and used it to pull while Sam used the crowbar to help it over the edge and to the ground. The two of them used their crowbars to lift the stone up so they could slide it onto the backseat floor.

"You were right," he said. "This time we don't have to leave the message for Bako to see."

They used the car to drag the larger stone back over the opening to seal the chamber. Then they shoveled and pushed the mound of dirt over it. Once the ground was even, the chamber entrance was four feet under.

Remi turned and looked back at the plowed field. "Wow. Look."

It was just beginning to get light, so they could see their deep tire tracks running from the chamber to the riverbank and back. "I wish we could get rid of those tracks."

"We don't have a way," Sam said. "All we can do is try to make the damage look like a drunken joyride." They got into the car, and Sam picked up the empty wine bottle from their picnic lunch, wiped off the fingerprints, and tossed it on the ground. Then he drove up and down the field, turning and looping, backing up, making a random set of shapes that were not concentrated in one part of the field. Then he bumped up onto the highway that ran parallel to the river.

As dawn approached, Remi sent the photos to Selma and Albrecht. It began to rain. "I'm glad we didn't have to contend with that," she said. The rain grew slowly to a steady, strong downpour, and Sam drove them through every puddle, washing the mud and dirt from the rental car. When they reached a spot where they could park unseen close to the Mincio, they stopped and dumped the inscribed tablet into the river. "I'm going to take a picture of the spot," said Remi. "Once it isn't a threat to our lives, we'll come back one day for the tablet and donate it to a museum." When she had her pictures, they drove on.

They arrived in Peschiera del Garda before six a.m. and waited in the parking lot near the marina to see the big boat go under the last bridge into the lake. While they waited, Remi called the house in California and Selma answered.

"Hi, Remi," she said. "We got your pictures. Is the treasure as big as it looks?"

"Bigger. Have you and Albrecht read the message?"

"Albrecht has translated it, but he's been studying the situation." Selma paused. "He should be the one to tell you." After a bit of rustling, Remi heard Albrecht say, "Hello."

"Hi, Albrecht," said Remi. "Could you read the stone?"

"Yes. It's still just Latin. Here's what it says."

" 'You have my fifth treasure. The fourth is in the place where friends rushed to become enemies. While I buried treasure for the future, King Thorismund buried funeral goods for King Theodoric.' "

"What do you make of that?" asked Sam.

"It's a reference to the other possibility I referred to for the fifth treasure, the Battle of the Catalaunian Plains in 451," Albrecht said. "The friends were Flavius Aëtius, the Roman general, and Theodoric, the King of the Visigoths. Both had been friends of Attila but hated each other. When Attila invaded and looted much of France, they joined forces at Châlons-en-Champagne and became his enemies."

"What's that about funeral goods?"

"Theodoric was killed in the battle, but, as sometimes happens in big battles, the principal leaders lost touch with one another and Theodoric's body wasn't found until the next day. His son, Thorismund, buried Theodoric, presumably with his armor, weapons, and personal belongings, and the crown passed to him."

Remi said, "And this was your second choice for 'where the world was lost.' "

"That's right," Albrecht said. "This was the farthest west Attila got—roughly to the city of Troyes, France. The men who formed an alliance to stop him had once been friends of Attila's. The battle was huge and violent, but it ended in a draw. When it was too dark to fight, Attila withdrew to his camp. Flavius Aëtius didn't pursue the Huns when they left. Some historians believe he was afraid to destroy them because it would have left the Visigoths unopposed. I suspect the truth was that the Huns were still strong as ever and he didn't want to push his luck. This was the last major battle that the Romans could be said to have won and that was only because Aëtius was still on the field when the other armies departed. Theodoric was dead, and his son Thorismund set off for home as fast as he could to secure his place as the new king of the Visigoths."

"Good enough," said Remi. "So we know roughly where we go next. But we're still in Italy. Have you gotten in touch with the Italian authorities?"

"Yes. They understand the need for secrecy and the need for speed. They'll be in touch with you in a few hours to take possession of the artifacts and move them to Rome."

"Good," said Sam. "I'll be glad when they're somebody else's responsibility."

Selma said, "When you've finished with the Italian authorities, go to the airport in Verona. Your tickets to France will be waiting. Just insert a credit card in the machine for identification and it will print your boarding passes. While you're in the air, we'll be preparing more information for you."

"Thanks, Selma."

An hour later, they saw the boat pass under the last bridge and move out into the lake outside the marina. They called Tibor and told him the plan and then went to their hotel.

They had barely showered and eaten a room service breakfast before there was a knock on the door. Standing in the hall were five men in dark suits. "Mr. and Mrs. Fargo," said the leader. He held up a badge and identification card. "I am Sergio Boiardi. We're assigned to the Tutela Patrimonio Culturale of the Carabinieri in Naples. I understand you have requested our help."

"Come in, please," said Sam. When they were inside and the door was closed, Sam said, "We have made a major discovery, a treasure hoard from the year 452."

"We were told you want us to take custody and register it."

"Yes," said Sam.

"You are aware that the bilateral agreement between the U.S. and Italy covers the ninth century B.C. to the fourth century A.D.?"

"Yes. Technically, a fifth-century find is probably exempt from registration, but we're voluntarily asking for a license to transport the artifacts after they've been catalogued and photographed by the Italian authorities. To be open with you, there are other parties who have been actively trying to prevent us from making any discoveries and they're violent. Part of our intention is to ensure that they don't attempt to steal the find from us."

Boiardi nodded. "And where are the artifacts now?"

"On a boat we rented. It's anchored outside the marina in the lake," Sam said. "Our idea was to rent a trailer, load the boat onto it, and tow it to a secure spot where we could unload the artifacts into boxes and put them on your truck."

Boiardi said, "It's a good plan. We can borrow a barn in the countryside that will hold a truck and a boat on a trailer for a few hours, then all of us can be on our way without attracting unnecessary attention."

"Let's do it," said Sam.

They drove down to the marina in an unmarked white truck the Carabinieri had brought with them, then went to a nearby boatyard and rented a large trailer and a hitch for it. After they had backed the trailer down the boat launch and into the lake, Tibor's cousins piloted the boat onto the trailer, and the truck pulled it up into the parking lot. Within a few minutes, the boat was secured, the men were all in the truck, and one of Boiardi's men drove them to a large barn on a farm on the west side of Lago del Garda. The driver pulled the truck and trailer inside, jumped down to close the doors, and then everyone went to work.

Boiardi supervised his men as they placed the boxes of precious coins, ornaments, and gems from the boat into identical cardboard boxes that looked as though they came from a moving van. As the objects came to light and were put on the floor for repacking, both Remi and the Carabinieri took photographs. The rows of boxes grew higher in the back of the truck.

"It's astounding," said Boiardi. "Every object is an archaeological marvel, a bit of Attila's plunder. But plenty of the objects are much, much older than Attila. What he was taking were often masterworks, the museum pieces of their time, some of them from the beginning of the Roman era, some Greek, some from early Christian churches. We're all very fortunate that the diggers—the grave robbers who are always scouring Italy for antiquities—didn't find this before you did."

"We never expected it to be as good as this," Remi said. "But I guess we should have. The Huns had moved south through Italy, stopping at each city to plunder its wealth. We think he left so much here because this treasure was going to fund his next attempt to invade Rome."

Sam, Remi, and Tibor and his three cousins helped the Carabinieri repack and load the precious objects. The work went efficiently. When they were finished, Boiardi said, "We'll tow the boat back to the marina and then we'll be on our way. We're driving to Rome so the treasure can be stored in the safety of the Capitoline Museum."

Everyone climbed into the truck again and the Carabinieri driver started the engine. Two Carabinieri walked ahead of the truck and pushed open the large sliding barn doors. As soon as they did, they found themselves with guns held to their heads.

Sam, Remi, and Boiardi felt the truck stop abruptly. Boiardi opened the back door and they jumped out to see six men rush into the barn. They wore ordinary street clothes—sport coats or windbreakers, jeans or khaki pants—but they were carrying SC70/90 assault weapons, short-barreled submachine guns with folding stocks.

Boiardi stepped in front of Sam and whispered, "Take my gun."

Sam reached for the small clip-on belt holster at Boiardi's back and took the Beretta pistol and holster and pocketed them. As soon as Boiardi felt his gun slip away, he shouted in Italian—Sam couldn't understand all the words but he got the gist—"What are you doing here? We are national police on a mission. Put those guns down instantly."

The response from one of the men at the door was to fire a short burst from his weapon into the roof. When the two Carabinieri who'd had guns to their heads involuntarily jumped at the sudden noise, the interlopers laughed. They roughly pushed the two men back into the barn and then spread farther apart so that each of them had a better angle of fire at either the group of Carabinieri and Remi or at Sam, Boiardi, Tibor, and his cousins.

The man who had fired into the roof was a big, barrel-chested middle-aged man with a thick black beard. He charged forward, flung open the door of the truck's cargo bay, climbed in, and tore open a couple of boxes. He dragged one to the back of the truck and tilted it so the others could see the contents. He called out, "*È d'oro. È tutto oro antico!*"

Sam had no trouble understanding those words. The others exchanged quick glances and seemed to catch the man's joy like a virus. The leader jumped from the truck and stepped close to Boiardi, who said something quick and angry to him.

The man grinned. *"Ci avete seguito."* He moved off toward the place where the two Carabinieri stood and, while his friends aimed their weapons at the police officers, he patted them down. He found one officer had an extra pistol, took it, and brought his rifle across the man's face.

"Sorry," Sam said. "Remi and I must have been too visible."

"No, I'm sorry," Boiardi whispered back. "He says they didn't follow you. They followed us. They knew that the only cases our office handles involve finds of antiquities, so they waited until we left Naples and followed us."

The robbers were busy using the policemen's handcuffs on them and tying them to the vertical beams of the barn. Then two of them and their leader approached Boiardi and the leader frisked him.

The leader took his eyes off Sam while he was searching Boiardi and Sam noticed. He drove his left fist into the leader's face like a piston as his right drew Boiardi's weapon. He grasped the leader's coat and jerked him upward to act as a shield and held the pistol to his head. Boiardi snatched away the leader's SC70/90 automatic rifle and held it on the two men who had come over with the leader.

The two men set their rifles on the floor, stepped back, and raised their hands in the air. The two Carabinieri who had not been hand-cuffed yet knelt to pick up their own sidearms from the barn floor and then picked up the two automatic weapons.

One of the armed thieves saw the meaning of what was hap-pening and decided to stop it. He yelled, "No!" and opened fire. His rifle spat bullets, and his leader collapsed to the floor in front of Sam.

Sacrificing his leader served its purpose. The other thieves, see-ing their leader dead, no longer had a reason to give up. They turned and tried to take cover, carrying their weapons. Boiardi's two police officers fired on them, and one was hit in the leg and sprawled on the floor. No others offered resistance.

The man who had shot the leader was not about to capitulate. He fired a burst in the general direction of Sam and Boiardi, who had taken cover behind the boat trailer. Sam climbed over the railing into the boat and crawled to the bow.

As the man was stalking along the wall looking for an advantage, Sam swung his arm over the gunwale and fired. His bullet hit the man's upper torso at the collarbone. The man spun around to return fire, but his right arm went limp and he dropped his rifle. Two Carabinieri were on him, handcuffing him and forcing him to sit at the side of the barn with his wounded colleague and the man he had shot. The others quickly lost their weapons and joined him.

Boiardi telephoned the local police to obtain help, an ambulance and police cars to transport the prisoners. While they waited, he asked the prisoners questions. The answers were defiant and resentful. He was about to give up when Remi said, "Can you find out if they were sent by a man named Bako?"

He did, then translated. "Who is Bacco? Is he from Sicily? There are lots of Sicilians in the archaeology business lately."

"I guess that means no," Remi said. "Gold just attracts its own trouble."

In a few minutes they heard sirens, and the police cars began lining up in the barnyard. The ambulance arrived and the team of paramedics took the two wounded men, and a couple of police officers to guard them, and left. The three healthy thieves were transported. And finally a coroner's van came for the lifeless leader.

When they were back at the harbor and Boiardi was about to drive off to Rome, he stepped to Sam and Remi. "This is a disturbing development. The thieves have finally realized that the easiest way to find ancient treasures is to follow the national police officers who are supposed to verify and register the finds. We could be entering a period when no national antiquities officer will be safe. Anybody who doesn't retire is a fool."

"So you're retiring?" asked Remi.

"Me? No. Not right away. Not after your husband kept me alive. Maybe we'll talk about all this another day, but right now there's so much to do. *Arrivederci*, Fargos. Travel safe."

15

Selma Wondrash's voice came over the speaker on Remi's telephone. "The village of Châlons-en-Champagne has just two hundred twenty-seven people, and the spot Albrecht and I believe is the battlefield is five miles north near the hamlet of Cuperly on D994, La route de Reims."

"What are we looking for?" asked Sam.

Albrecht took over the phone. "Near the center of the battlefield was a rock shelf, a high outcropping, that rose from the ground at an angle. The Roman army, which also included the Visigoths, the Alans, and the Celts, rushed in, in a forced march, to control the high ground before the Huns arrived. When the Huns swept in on horseback from the east, they were greeted by arrows raining down on them from the rocks. The Huns made a tentative attempt to dislodge the defenders, then fell back to the east on lower, level ground.

They fortified their position by circling their wagons around the encampment."

"How far east from the shelf?" asked Remi.

"They would have retreated beyond arrow range," said Albrecht.

"How far was arrow range?"

"Well, I suppose you could stand on the top of the rocks and shoot an arrow off at a forty-five-degree angle and see."

"I just might do that."

"Or you could estimate. I'd say two hundred fifty yards would probably do it."

"We'll take the guess," Sam said. "Selma, could you send us another magnetometer and a metal detector at the hotel in France?"

"It's done. They should be there tonight. You're staying at L'Assiette Champenoise, an old estate with four acres of grounds and modern conveniences in the center of town."

"Thanks, Selma," said Remi. "If it's got a nice bathtub I'll be happy. And I think we could use some sleep. This has turned into a lot of night work."

"You're welcome. Pick up your car at Charles de Gaulle Terminal 1. Head east out of Paris on the N44 to Reims, about a hundred ninety kilometers. Then take D994, La route de Reims, to Cuperly."

"Got it," said Sam.

"Albrecht, what else can you tell us about the battle?" asked Remi.

"Well, after the initial skirmish, Attila could see he wasn't going to take the high ground on the rocky shelf. He fell back to await developments. In those days, that meant watching enemy troop movements and opening up a few birds to read their entrails. Attila let his enemies stew for most of the day. When the afternoon was nearly over, he attacked. The battle lasted until dark and left thousands dead on the field in about equal number for both sides. Attila's horsemen couldn't overcome the other side's advantage of holding the high ground. He fell back to his fortified camp. The Roman commander Aëtius got lost in the dark, separated from his Romans, and found shelter with some Visigoths, who had lost track of their own leader, Theodoric. His son Thorismund found his body the next day. Attila, apparently not knowing the poor shape his enemies were in, prepared to make a stand. He gathered a huge pile of the wooden frames of his men's saddles. If he were to die, he wanted his body thrown on them and burned. But then his men noticed that the Visigoths were leaving the field. They were going home so Thorismund could claim his father's throne. So Attila left, going east across the Rhine."

"Perfect," said Remi.

"Perfect?" said Albrecht.

"That's where the treasure will be."

"Why do you say that?"

"Sam and I have been thinking about this since we began. The treasures are always buried at some bad moment—a defeat, someone's death. How did they accomplish that? If we look at the accounts of Attila's death, there was a huge tent set up for Attila and his retainers, so big that you could ride horses in it."

"I don't think I see where you're going," said Selma.

"The saddle frames never got burned. They were a distraction, a show. Inside Attila's huge tent, where nobody could see, there were men digging another crypt, a treasure chamber like the two we've found. As soon as the hole was dug, the masons would disappear into the big tent to set the stones. Attila's trusted palace guards loaded the treasure into the chamber without leaving the tent. They sealed the chamber, covered it, and then struck the tent. Nobody had seen any hole or any digging. As they left, they probably herded their horses across the camp. Nobody but a trusted few knew where the treasure was or even that it existed."

"I think you've figured him out," said Albrecht. "From Châlons, he went to northern Italy and found new plunder on his way to invading Rome. He was probably already preparing to turn south into Italy the day of the battle. Rome was the biggest prize and probably always was his goal. Everyone knows Attila's enemies fought him to a standstill at Châlons. What they all forget is that he fought them to a standstill too."

Sam said, "The sources say Attila delayed his attack until it was nearly night. Maybe he was delaying until his chamber was dug and the stones brought from somewhere—probably the Marne River, which was right near the battlefield."

"I think you're right," said Albrecht. "If you can ascertain where Attila's tent was erected, you'll find the treasure chamber under it."

Their flight from Verona reached Paris in two hours and they picked up their rental car and drove out of the traffic and congestion of the city. Even with Sam's excessive speed, the one hundred ninety kilometers on the N44 took three hours.

Sam and Remi found their way to Châlons-en-Champagne, then the road to Cuperly, and drove the five additional miles to the tiny hamlet. Late in the afternoon they were among farmers' fields, various trapezoid shapes so closely interlaced that the land looked as though every inch belonged to someone and was under full cultivation.

"Let's keep searching from the road until we find the rocky outcropping or we run out of daylight," Sam said.

"Everything depends on finding that outcropping," Remi said. "There's no other feature mentioned in the old story we can use to orient ourselves."

They drove for miles on D994, La route de Reims, then went

north on D977, then north on D931, La voie de la Liberté. They were just northeast of the Marne when they saw the outcropping. From a flat field, it rose abruptly at a tilt, jutting higher as the eye moved from west to east. Sam pulled the car over to the side of the road and Remi took pictures with her cell phone and sent them to Selma.

"There," she said. "If this isn't it, then maybe Selma, Pete, and Wendy will be able to match the contours to some geographic source—satellite photos or something—and they'll be able to set us straight."

"I'm pretty sure this is it," said Sam. "If they could have done that, they would have. And we haven't seen a lot of candidates for the right spot before now."

Remi climbed up to stand on the seat of the convertible and then put one foot on the top of the door to raise herself a little more. "Uh-oh," she said.

"What is it?"

"I wish we had binoculars with us. I think somebody has been digging out there in the flat part of the field."

"Is it east of the outcropping?"

"Yes, and it seems about the right distance." She pointed at the spot. "Do you think that's beyond an arrow shot away from the rocks?"

"That would be my guess," he said. "If people were aiming at me, I'd certainly err on the long side." He stood on the seat beside her.

"See?" she said. "There and there. And over there."

There were small mounds of fresh dirt around holes in the vast green field. "That's just about what it would look like if Bako got here first. The small ones could be test holes, and that big one over there would be something they thought might be the chamber."

Remi hit a programmed number on her phone and put the call on speaker. "Tibor? This is Remi. I know you've been home only a few hours. But has anything changed with Arpad Bako?"

"No," said Tibor. "He and his security men are still here. It was the first thing I checked when I arrived. Why? Has something happened?"

"We're in France at the next site and it looks like someone has been digging."

"I don't like to hear that," Tibor said. "But we should have thought of another possibility."

"What?"

"Bako has been here in Hungary. But he has friends and business acquaintances in other places—customers and suppliers, both legitimate and criminal. Maybe he called one in France. I would be very careful if I were you."

"We will," she said. "Let us know if anything changes." She turned to Sam. "Well, you heard him."

"Tibor was right. We should have thought of this. If Bako has friends all over Europe, we've got a problem. While we're rushing to reach the next hiding place, his friends could already be on the scene digging."

"Now what?"

"Behave as though we can still win until somebody proves we didn't. Drive the rest of the way to Reims, check into our hotel, and spend the last of the afternoon preparing to come back here after dark."

AT HIS OFFICE in Szeged, Arpad Bako sat at the head of a long rosewood conference table, studying the executives ranged around it listening to a report by the director of foreign sales. He used such times, when they were paying attention to something else, to study them. They were smart men, all of them. Some were scientists— biologists, pharmacists, chemists—who worked to improve various medicines the company sold and discover new ones. Others had medical degrees and performed the drug testing and dealt with hospitals and universities. Still others were lawyers. Bako had gone to the university, but he was not their equal in education or intellect.

He was, however, a cunning man. It must be obvious to these men that the report they were listening to was impossible, a piece of fiction. The sales of narcotic painkillers and tranquilizers that had value in the underground economy of Europe were being over-reported. The numbers on the board showed they were being bought by legitimate foreign entities in far from proportionate numbers in every market. Even in countries that had famous hundred-year-old pharmaceutical companies like Switzerland and Germany, the doc-tors must all be prescribing Bako products. It was absurd. In a cou-ple of instances, the sales manager reported sales of Bako drugs in distant countries that must be larger than the number of prescrip-tions written for every other purpose during a year. Yet Bako's ex-ecutives listened to it without blinking. No numbers were kept secret from them. Everyone in the room had gotten rich by phan-tom sales, he knew, and they should be forced to hear the numbers. If they wisely chose not to compare the numbers with anything else they knew or to express doubts, then all must be well for the pres-ent. They were content with the status quo.

Bako's cell phone buzzed. A couple of the men jumped and then turned to look at the others with wry expressions, hoping some rival had been caught being rude and foolish in the meeting, but when they saw Bako taking his phone from his pocket they looked away. He read the number on the display and said, "Please excuse me, gentlemen. I need to take this call."

All of the dozen men stood up instantly, gathered items like laptops and tablets, pens and coffee cups, and filed out of the room. The last man out was the sales manager, who looked relieved. When the soundproof door was shut, Bako flipped his thumb to receive the call.

"Hello, Étienne," said Bako. "I've been wondering when you would call. Good news?"

Étienne Le Clerc chuckled. "It's such good news that you might think it's bad. We found the treasure chamber right where we expected it, in the middle of the old battlefield. It's big. Attila must have left Germany and France without two coins to rub together. You could have left me out of this, done it yourself, and made an extra hundred million euros."

"There's that much, eh? And you could be calling now to lie and tell me that there was no treasure—that someone beat us to it."

Le Clerc laughed. "I suppose this means we're both almost honest."

"Nearly so," said Bako. "Or maybe we choose our victims wisely. The treasure is wonderful news. Can you send me a photograph of the inscription?"

"Inscription?"

"The Latin message. Somewhere in each treasure chamber there is a message from Attila. Didn't you find it?"

"I suppose we must have taken it. I haven't seen it yet."

"It's hard to miss."

In Le Clerc's voice was a faint warning, just a small cloud forming on the horizon. He said, slowly and distinctly, "You haven't seen the contents of the chamber. It is literally tons of gold and silver, much of it ancient, even pre-Roman. If you want Latin writing, I've got plenty of that. There are whole books of it, with gold bindings studded with gemstones."

"I'm sorry, my friend," Bako said. "It must be different this time. The first one was deeply engraved into an iron slab the size of a door."

"We didn't find anything like that," said Le Clerc. "I'll look into it. Oh, and that reminds me. You said we should watch for the man and woman who would try to get there first. They were actually what prompted me to call. They're here. My men saw them drive up to the battlefield in a convertible and survey the field."

"Then things are better than I thought. If you can kill them, then we have all the time in the world to find that inscription."

"Don't worry," said Le Clerc. "I've still got men out at the site tonight removing the last bits before they cover everything up. We'll find the inscription. And, in the meantime, those people can be made to disappear."

AS SOON AS they were in the city, Sam inquired about renting a truck. He found an agency and rented one that had a bed eight feet wide and nearly twenty long, with a closed cargo bay. Remi took a photograph of a sign from a feed store and went to a printer to have it blown up and reproduced as magnetic signs and then stuck two to the truck's sides.

Sam and Remi went to their hotel, which was like a gated châtePau, and slept for a few hours before they woke to get ready. Sam assembled a metal detector and a magnetometer. They packed up their shovels and crowbars, night vision gear, and backpacks, and ate a dinner in the hotel consisting of duck l'orange with Rosé des

Riceys, a local wine that was reputed to be one of Louis XIV's favorites. They ended it with crêpes suzette.

At midnight they got into their rental truck. Sam drove and Remi sat beside him, trying to navigate. They drove along the curving rustic highway to the hamlet of Cuperly and then headed north. It was only a short time before they reached the field they had found in the late afternoon. Sam pulled the truck to the side of the road.

"Well, let's go see what they were digging out there," said Remi as she put on her backpack.

Sam replied, "Let's hope they just have big gophers in France."

They climbed a stone fence and walked into the field. Remi consulted the photos she'd taken that afternoon to guide them to the first hole they'd seen from the road. As they approached the hole, they put on their night vision goggles and knelt beside it. The sight was confusing, so they used their shovels to clear away some of the dirt.

"What is that?" Remi said. She reached down and touched it. "Steel. It looks like a cannon."

"You're right." Sam dug around it a bit with his hand, then stopped at the muzzle. "I think it's a French 75."

"That's a cocktail," she said. "Gin, champagne, lemon juice, and sugar, I think."

"Well, this is the cannon they named it after," he said. "Something about the hangover, I imagine. This is also why we have to be careful when we dig in France. The Marne is just to the south and east beyond that field. In the summer of 1918, General Ludendorff planned a big offensive to take the Champagne region. The allies got a copy of his plan, moved a lot of artillery around, and, an hour before the German attack, opened fire with over three thousand cannons. I'm guessing from the position and condition of this cannon that it probably got damaged in the return fire—or just got too hot."

"Whoever got here before us probably picked up a big spike on their magnetometer, dug down, and found it," said Remi.

"Let's go look at the next hole."

They moved toward the next one in the field, stopped, and looked in. At the bottom of the hole was what seemed to be the remains of a couple of wooden crates, both age-darkened and rotted-away. There was also the metal rim of a wagon wheel and the hub. Sam cautiously poked at the crates, which were as soft as wet cardboard. He saw the row of five cannon rounds, shaped like giant bullets, the brass casings green with patina from being buried for so long and the projectiles a uniform gray. "There's a find," he said. "Unexploded ordnance. It looks like a buried caisson. Let's move on."

"We should call somebody," Remi said.

"We will. There are so many bombs and mines and artillery shells from both world wars that France still keeps teams on the payroll to dispose of them when they turn up."

"This must have been quite a surprise to Bako's French friends when they dug their test holes," Remi said.

"Well, there's just one more hole dug in the field and it looks bigger than the first two," Sam said. "Whatever they found must be something that doesn't blow up." They walked toward the third hole.

They stepped up to the mound of earth that had been thrown aside in the digging.

"Look at the entrance," Remi said. "It's like the other—made of mortared stones."

"Let's see what's left in there," Sam said. Sam took a nylon climbing rope out of his backpack, tied a loop, put it over the shaft of his spade, then propped the spade in the corner of the hole's entrance to hold it. They adjusted their night vision goggles, and he lowered Remi into the chamber. After a few seconds, the rope went slack. There were a few seconds of silence.

"What do you see?"

"It's not empty, but I think it's been looted. There aren't any piles of gold down here. Come look."

Sam rappelled down the inner wall of the chamber. His feet touched a surface and he knelt. "It's cement," he said.

"The Romans had cement. Why not Attila?" Remi said.

"I know. If he wanted a mason, I'm sure he could have captured a thousand of them. It looks as though they made this chamber of timbers and then plastered the whole thing with cement, probably on both sides."

"Look," said Remi. She was standing a dozen feet away, beside a pile of metal that still had a dull gleam in the amplified green light of the night vision goggles.

Sam joined her. "I don't see any gold, but this is amazing— Roman shields, helmets and breastplates, swords, javelins. This must have been part of the spoils of the campaign."

"They're historically valuable," Remi said. "But still, it doesn't make me happy to know that Bako's French friends beat us here."

"Let's find the inscription, unless they took that too."

They searched the walls, looking for any faint scratches. Then, at the bottom of the pile of Roman equipment, they found a shield that was not like the four-foot-high rectangular Roman *scuta* that curves back at the sides. This was a round one with a steel boss at the center that stuck out like a spike. On the inner side, engraved around the rim, was an inscription in Latin.

Remi took a picture of it with her cell phone's camera, then had Sam hold the shield and took several pictures from different angles to bring out the carved letters in sharp relief. "There," she said.

"That should do it. Wait a second. It shouldn't be here. Bako's friends should know that this shield was important—maybe more important than anything else in the chamber. Why would they leave it?"

Sam shrugged. "They must have dropped in, seen lots of gold and silver and stones, taken them, and left. It's incredible luck for us."

"Let's get moving, then," Remi said. "You climb up and pull these things out with the rope and I'll tie the next load."

Sam ran the rope through the hand straps of the first two Roman *scuta*, then made a bundle of javelins and a bundle of Roman *gladius* swords, the standard-issue Roman short sword. He climbed to the surface, set the artifacts in piles, then threw the rope down to Remi.

After a couple of minutes, she called, "Haul away!"

When he pulled up the rope this time, there were five undeco-rated helmets belonging to common soldiers, two *scuta*, and four breastplates. He leaned down into the entrance, wearing a helmet as he stuck his head in the chamber. "Is that everything?"

"My heart goes pit-a-pat for a man in uniform," said Remi. "What was that?"

"What was what?"

"There was a light, like a beam, that went past in the air be-hind you."

He pulled back and looked across the field in each direction. "I don't see anything now. Probably just an airplane's landing lights as it came in toward Reims. It's not the year 451 anymore."

"Then you should update your wardrobe."

"Grab the rope and I'll pull you up."

16

WHEN THEY HAD REACHED THE SURFACE AND WERE IN the night air again, they sat on top of the chamber surrounded by the high pile of dirt from the excavation. Remi said, "We should probably take a couple rails off the fence and drive the truck here to load up, as we did in Italy."

"Not a bad plan," said Sam. "I'm not eager to walk back and forth to get it all."

"I love it when you have the sense to agree with me," she said.

"Really? I'll try to remember that."

"As long as you're not trying to flatter and manipulate me into doing nice things for you at some later time," she added.

"Oh?" he said. "Would that be bad?"

"Sort of bad. Not *I'm furious at you* bad, but certainly not your best behavior."

"Certainly not," he said. "But my best behavior? That's a very high standard."

"Of course," she answered. "Shall we do this?"

"Okay," he said. "Since it was such a good idea."

"Thank you."

She picked up a bundle of javelins he had tied together, strapped a gladius in its sheath around his waist, and picked up the shield with the message on it. They both climbed out of the excavation. There was a loud snap as a bullet passed overhead and they jumped back into the hole. A second later, there was the sound of another shot.

Remi raised her head over the edge of the trench and put her night vision goggles on.

"Get down," said Sam.

"Did you hear the shot? He's about three hundred yards out. He couldn't even hit a big target like you."

"Not on his first shot, but I'll bet he's zeroed in now."

A third shot plowed into the pile of dirt behind them, and Remi ducked down. "Do you have any ideas?"

"He may be able to find the range quickly, but hitting a running figure is a bit harder."

"I didn't ask for random musings. I wanted a plan."

There were three more shots in rapid succession, one of them very high, one to the side, and one in the dirt behind them. Sam peered over the rim of the hole toward the distant rocks. "There's a car—looks like a Range Rover—up by the rock shelf. There are three or four of them with rifles, aiming at us."

Remi said, "Has it occurred to you that they're using the same strategy as the Romans and Visigoths: arriving first at the high ground and then holding us down with fire from a distance?"

"If only they were shooting arrows," said Sam. "Here. Take

this." He put another Roman helmet on her head, picked up a Roman *scuta*, rapped it with his knuckles, then set it aside and chose another. "This one's better. It's got a layer of metal on the outside." He picked up a third *scuta*.

"This won't stop a bullet," she said.

"No, but they'll make us harder to kill."

"If you say so."

"I do. Hold it over your back like this."

"You look like a turtle."

"Success. That's the idea. It's hard enough to hit someone who's running in the dark at this distance. If you have this between you and them, it will be hard for them to pick out what's you and what isn't. Now, let's go before it occurs to them that they can advance." He picked up his bundle of javelins, the round shield with the message, and the *scuta* he had selected.

Sam climbed out of the trench, ran away from the road as though he had a miraculous new plan, then made a quick jog to the side just as the shooters fired again. Remi saw he was drawing fire, climbed up and held her *scuta* behind her as she sprinted straight for the parked truck.

Sam reversed his direction and ran after her. Not noticing Remi at first, the snipers fired at him again.

Remi was still dashing for the truck, her body low and the four-foot *scuta* on her right shoulder to keep it toward the snipers. She ran past the nearest of the test holes, the one filled with artillery shells. As she had feared, the snipers fired round after round at the hole, trying to set off an explosion. But, as she had hoped, from where they were, they couldn't do anything but hit the dirt piled up around it. Even after she was past the danger zone, she could hear them wasting rounds on the explosives, thinking Sam's approach was a second chance to hit the old shells.

After that, each of the shooters seemed to share his shots evenly between Sam and Remi, which showed her that none of them had any training. The sniper's stock-in-trade was to select a target and ignore everything else in the world until that target was dead. The American sniper's standard, "One shot, one kill," was far out of reach of most other services, but all of them were much better than this.

As she dashed past the next test hole that had uncovered the French cannon, a rifle shot hit the right edge of her Roman shield. It punched the *scuta* hard to the side, and she felt splinters bouncing off her helmet, but she was able to hold on to it and keep running. The shield's curvature had served its purpose and diverted much of the force of the bullet. Running even harder, she made it to the shelter of the big truck. She crouched on the street side, away from the snipers, climbed into the passenger seat, slid to the driver's side, and started the engine. The shooters fired at the cab, blowing one of the side windows inward. They hit the cargo box, then the frame of the truck. Remi kept her body curled in a low-profile crouch.

Then, just as she was beginning to feel hope, one of the shooters managed to ricochet a round off something at the edge of the ammunition pit, and there was a loud, fiery explosion in the field. She looked, saw Sam dive to the ground with his *scuta* over his back. He scrambled forward as three more rounds went off, then a volley of six.

A moment later, Sam, still carrying the two shields and the bundle of javelins, appeared on the safe side of the truck. To her surprise, he climbed into the cargo bay, slammed the door shut, ran to the small window that separated the bay from the cab, and yelled, "Get us out of here."

Remi sat up, released the hand brake, depressed the clutch and shifted into first gear, then let the clutch out too tentatively, the truck making a jerky start. It didn't stall, so she poured on more gas until the transmission whined that it was time to shift again. She worked her way up to fourth gear and kept her foot on the gas. Urging the big truck up to fifty along the dark country road with no headlights on, she just aimed for the center of the pavement. She took off the ancient helmet, threw it on the seat, and moved her head to keep catching the reflection of the moonlight on the dark, smooth surface of the road.

As soon as she could look in her rearview mirror and not see the rocky outcropping, she switched on the headlights and went faster. She kept adjusting in her lane to straighten the curves. She got up to sixty, then seventy, still climbing. She hoped there would be no cars coming from the other direction, but hoping seemed to make them appear. There was a glow in the sky above the hill ahead, and then a pair of headlights popped over the crest and came down toward her.

Remi moved as close to the right edge of the narrow road as she dared, trying not to lose any speed. The first car seemed to miss her left headlight by two inches. As its headlights went past and became a pair of red taillights fading into the distance, the driver leaned on his horn, a blare of protest into the night. The next three cars shot by in silence, maybe taking advantage of a slightly wider stretch of road or maybe just speechless with shock over her reckless driving.

She kept glancing in the rearview mirror, hoping the shooters hadn't decided to pursue her. Again, her hopes seemed to conjure what she most feared. On the road behind her, a pair of headlights appeared, accelerating toward her rapidly. When she went around a curve, she looked in the side mirror to get a clearer view of her pursuer. The vehicle was bigger than most, and higher—the Range

Rover they had seen parked partway up the rocky shelf on the battlefield. There was a larger vehicle behind it, a truck much like the
one she was driving. Of course there would be a truck, she thought.
The treasure chamber had been as big as the cargo bay of a truck.
When these men had taken out the gold and silver, it must have
been too much weight for the SUV to carry.

The Range Rover quickly moved up behind her, and soon the
truck was close. She knew the next move would be to come up
beside her so somebody could aim a rifle out the window and
shoot her.

The car came closer and closer, and she realized that the driver
was trying to hold his headlights to illuminate her tires so rifle
shots would bring her to a halt. She heard Sam fiddling with the
rear doors of the cargo bay. She steadied the truck and watched
the side-view mirror. The Range Rover was about as close as it
could be when the doors of the truck swung open.

An ancient javelin came flying out of the dark cargo bay. It had a
small, narrow, sharp tip at the end of a steel shaft that extended
nearly half its length, then about three feet of fragile old wood.
Flexible, it seemed to slither in the air, spiraling as it flew.

In Remi's rearview mirror, she saw the driver's eyes go wide and
mouth gape open as the metal shaft hurtled toward him. The tip
struck the windshield with an audible bang, and she saw the white
impact mark appear in front of the driver, the tip of the javelin
stuck in the safety glass. The wind made the shaft move back and
forth wildly, swinging the sharp tip around in front of the faces of
the driver and his companion.

The Range Rover weaved crazily for a moment, as the driver
fought for control, and then spun sideways. The truck had been
following the Rover too closely to avoid it and plowed into the

driver's side near the left front wheel and spun the car around before both vehicles stopped.

Remi kept driving. The truck crossed into Reims about ten minutes later, and she parked it at the rental agency. She and Sam put their Roman weapons and armor into the rental car they had left at the agency and drove to their hotel.

Dressed in black clothes covered with dirt from the field, they carried their heavy armloads of ancient war gear into the lobby. They both had dirt smeared on their faces and hands. When Sam stopped at the front desk, the clerk looked at the ancient helmet and seemed uneasy. "Sir?" he said.

"I'm Samuel Fargo from Room 27."

"Yes, sir. Is everything satisfactory?" He eyed the javelins and the shields.

"Oh, this? We were just at a costume party that got out of hand."

"Yes, sir. We've found that any party with a Roman theme seems to be trouble."

"I guess we should have asked before we went. Right now, I'd like to rent a second room. I'd like one on a different floor, different hallway. Is that possible?"

"That we can do." He looked at a computer screen, produced the papers for Sam's signature, and then the room key. "Room 315, sir."

Sam and Remi took the Roman arms to the new room and leaned the shields and javelins against the wall.

Remi shook her head. "Too easy to find. It's precious."

Sam picked up the engraved shield again, opened the window, and climbed out of the gable onto the steep roof. He walked to the nearest chimney and stuck the shield between it and the slate shingles at the peak. Climbing back inside, he locked the window.

Sam said, "We'll have to go out and look around. I think we should find the men who are trying to kill us."

Remi said, "I'd like you to repeat that to yourself and see if it sounds like a good idea."

"Not the men, exactly," he said. "What I'd like to find is where they're hiding the treasure."

"And how do you want to do that?" she said.

"Well, let's think about who they must be. They appear to be a group that isn't usually involved in stealing ancient artifacts. They didn't notice the shield with the inscription and they left extremely valuable Roman artifacts in the chamber just because they weren't made of gold."

"You're right," said Remi. "So who are they?"

"Friends and allies of Arpad Bako—almost certainly business connections. So what business is Bako in?"

"According to Tibor, the main one seems to be diverting prescription drugs he manufactures to illegal channels."

"I'm guessing these men are local drug dealers."

"Seems reasonable."

"So let's call Tibor." He took out his cell phone and hit Tibor's preprogrammed number.

"Yes?" a groggy voice answered.

"Tibor, it's Sam."

"I was asleep. What time is it? Where are you?"

"We're still in France. Bako seems to have called in some French crooks to do the searching, just as we feared, and they've beaten us to the treasure, but we found the inscription still in the chamber."

"Some bad, some good. Is there any way to get the treasure before they move it?"

"We managed to lose the French shooters who came after us. We think they're related somehow to Bako's illegal activities, so they're probably in the drug trade. I'm wondering if we can find the addresses in France where Bako ships his legal pharmaceuticals."

"I've been working on this since we suspected someone else was in France. I called a cousin who works for the shipping company Bako uses. I haven't found a place in France where he ships medicine. We think any legitimate sales are shipped into France by a Belgian company. But he has a supplier for chemicals called Compagnie Le Clerc. They send him chemical compounds in special containers and when he's unloaded them he ships them back. There are people who believe that when he ships the containers to France, they're not empty."

"Do you have the address of Compagnie Le Clerc?"

"Yes."

Sam took out a pen and a five-euro bill and wrote down the address. "6107 Voie de la liberté, Troyes."

They returned to the rental agency, parked the car, and took their truck again. "I was hoping I'd seen the last of this thing," Remi said. "How much do we owe them for the bullet holes?"

"They're still adding it up."

"And don't forget the broken window."

"I'll drive," Sam said. They drove out of town, and Remi used the map on her cell phone to find the route and distance. The two cities were just about seventy-nine miles apart, so the drive took them a bit over an hour and a half on the E17.

When they found the address in Troyes, their mood began to brighten. There was a small blacktop parking lot, a truck garage, and a medium-sized warehouse. As they approached, Remi said, "Slow down so I can look in the parking lot."

In the lot, close to the warehouse, were the Range Rover with its broken windshield and, beside it, the truck that had run into it. The truck was missing its front bumper, and the left front wheel of the SUV was out of alignment. Sam pulled over on the highway so they could study the complex carefully. There were no windows in either the warehouse or the garage, but each had skylights on its roof. There were no lights turned on and no men walking around on the grounds.

Sam drove onto the blacktop. They sat there for a few minutes with the motor running, but nobody opened a door or came out to see who they were. "Can they have all gone home?" asked Remi. Sam looked at the side of the warehouse, studied the slope of the roof, then backed in the truck so the cargo box fit neatly under the eaves.

He and Remi got out and exchanged a look. It took no words for them to execute the plan. Remi reached into the truck behind the seat, opened the toolbox, and found a tire iron and a rope. They stepped onto the front bumper, onto the hood, up to the cab's roof, then to the top of the cargo box, and finally onto the roof of the warehouse. They knelt by the closest skylight and stared down into the building.

There were white plastic containers the size of ten-gallon paint cans stacked nearly up to the skylight. On either side were open aisles on a concrete floor. There were two forklifts, and there was an office.

Sam said, "Look away," swung the tire iron to break the skylight, then reached in and cleared away all the broken glass stuck to the frame. Then he tied the rope securely around the steel strut in the middle.

"Here goes," Remi whispered and lowered herself on the rope to the top of a row of plastic containers. She tested them. "They're full of something," she said. "Pretty stable."

Sam followed her down. They made their way to lower and lower stacks of containers until they reached the last stack, which was only three high, and they got to the floor. They split up and began to search the warehouse. They kept at it until they'd checked every bit of open space and the office that occupied the end of the building.

Sam stepped close to Remi. "It was a promising idea, but promising ideas don't always pan out. I thought they'd hide the treasure where they store their drugs."

Remi shrugged. "We haven't found those yet either. These all seem to be chemicals." She was staring at a stack of plastic containers. She stepped to the nearest container and read the label, then tipped the container an inch, moved to another row and lifted another container, then another row and container.

Sam did the same. They all seemed identical, around forty pounds each. Sam and Remi moved from row to row, sampling the containers randomly within each row. Finally, just as Remi set one back down, she saw Sam using his pocketknife to unscrew the band around the top of another. Remi came close as he lifted the lid and they saw the familiar gleam of gold.

The two went to work, quickly lifting each container and setting aside the ones that weren't filled with an identical quantity of chemical. Some were heavier, some lighter, and many made noises if they were shaken. Sam pushed a wooden pallet close to the row and started putting the containers of artifacts on it. After about twenty minutes, the pallet was loaded, and he brought another. They were expert at spotting the off-weight containers now, and the pallets were loaded more quickly. When they had found every one they could, and all they checked were full of chemicals, Sam said, "Find the switch that opens the doors."

While Sam brought a forklift to lift a pallet loaded with containers of antiquities, Remi found the right button. As he approached the door, it rose and he drove out, and Remi ran to bring the truck to the front. Using the pallets and forklift, he and she loaded the rental truck within a few minutes. The load consisted of three pallets, each one four containers high and four wide. When they were done, Sam drove the forklift back inside and then returned. They closed the warehouse door, buttoned up their truck, and drove off.

They arrived at their hotel in Reims at four a.m. Sam said, "I'll get the weapons and things out of the new room and you get our belongings we left in the old. Then we'll head for Paris."

They hurried inside. When Sam reached the door of the second room, he could tell something was wrong. There was a light glowing under the door. It was about three minutes later when Remi arrived, pulling the one suitcase they shared. Sam was climbing in through the room's window. The armor and arms they'd left all seemed still to be there, but the expression on Sam's face told her all was not well.

"Oh, no," she said. "Did they get it?"

Sam held up his empty hands and closed the window. "While we were in Troyes robbing them, they were in Reims robbing us. They've got the shield with Attila's inscription."

17

"THE SADDEST TREASURE OF ALL IS THE THIRD. IT LIES in the grave of my brother Bleda, who was the one chosen to die on the River Mureş at Apulum."

"I have no idea where that is," Remi said to Albrecht and Selma.

"No, but I have no doubt that Bako will know as soon as he reads the shield," Albrecht said. "Apulum is the Roman name of the city that the Romans made the capital of Dacia, which was a province of the Empire from the time of Hadrian until around 271 C.E. Dacia was the first Roman province to be abandoned in the contraction of the Empire. It would have been a familiar place to the people of Central Europe during Attila's time, so it would be familiar to anyone obsessed with Attila. And, of course, the Mureş River is the same one that runs into the Tisza River in Bako's hometown of Szeged. Apulum is now called Alba Iulia and it's in Transylvania, a part of Romania."

"We'll have to try to beat him to it anyway," said Sam. "We've got a few more minutes before we board our plane for Bucharest. Now is the time to tell us anything you can about Bleda's grave."

"Attila calls it a sad story, and it is," he said. "In 434, Attila and his older brother Bleda became co-kings of the Huns when the last king, their uncle Ruga, died. Shared monarchies are fairly rare in history, and this one probably reflects the fact that the younger brother, Attila, was also a phenomenon that's rare in any population—a great fighter, great leader, and charismatic personality. The two brothers ruled for about a decade with immense success. They operated in complete agreement, as though they were a single mind with two pairs of eyes and the ability to be two places at once. Under their rule the Huns grew stronger and more numerous through conquest, richer and more feared by enemies. Then, during the years 444 and 445, there was a period of peace. Attila and Bleda, like other kings between wars, occupied themselves with hunting. In 445 Bleda and Attila rode eastward into the Transylvanian forests, apparently to hunt boar and deer. What happened out in the forest is still the subject of speculation. Some say Attila used this opportunity to set up a hunting accident that killed his older brother so he could be sole king. I've always preferred the other version, and the inscription engraved in the shield seems to indicate I'm right."

"What's the other version?"

"That the hunting trip was an attempt by the elder Bleda to get Attila out in the wilderness, where only their close henchmen were around, and kill him. The attempt was botched, Attila fought back and killed Bleda."

"Why that version?"

"A little something about sibling psychology. The older sibling—particularly a male heir—is a little king from birth, doted on by everyone in his world. When a younger male sibling comes along, the firstborn is supplanted at the mother's breast and feels threatened in every way. It is the older sibling who bears the resentments, who feels wronged and robbed by his own brother, by his family and society. So he's more likely to be the aggressor. The younger brother is usually the unsuspecting offender who's easily taken by surprise. What's different here is that Attila was not unsuspecting or easily defeated. It doesn't fit anything we know about him. He was a born fighter. He had lived at the Emperor's court in Rome as a hostage when he was a teenager and could probably smell a conspiracy from a hundred miles off."

"What evidence is in the inscription?" Remi asked.

"He said Bleda 'was chosen' to die. He didn't just die. Fate or the Creator chose one of the two brothers over the other. That implies that both were at risk, as in a fight. This is also the saddest of all the deaths of Attila's life up to that time. He had already lost his mother, father, uncle, and two wives that we know of. One thing that would make Bleda's death worse was if he forced Attila to kill him."

"It's horrible," said Remi, "but the more I think about it, the more likely it seems."

There was a call for passengers to board the flight to Bucharest. "Thanks, Albrecht. We'll talk to you when we're on the ground again." She quickly dialed Tibor's number.

"Yes?"

"It's Remi and Sam," she said. "The address you gave us in France was correct. It worked out. We've turned the treasure over to French authorities for safekeeping. The next spot is in Transylvania, on the Mureş River near Alba Iulia, and we're on the way. But Bako got the inscription too. Could you please—"

"We'll watch them every minute," said Tibor. "We'll know exactly where they go."

"Thanks, Tibor. They're already calling our flight. We'll call you from Bucharest." She turned off the phone, and they got up to join the line of people entering the collapsible boarding tunnel to their airplane.

The plane rumbled down the runway and rose into the air. When it leveled, Remi lifted the armrest between her and Sam, leaned her head on his shoulder, and promptly fell asleep. The uninterrupted race from one country to the next, the heavy physical labor at night and searching in the daylight, had finally exhausted her. After a short time, Sam slept too.

They awoke when the pilot announced the approach to Bucharest Airport. After clearing Romanian customs, they picked up their rental car. As they drove toward Alba Iulia, Remi read a history about Attila and his brother Bleda that she had downloaded to her phone at the airport in Paris.

"It says here that Bleda had a famous Moorish dwarf named Zerco in his retinue. Bleda was so fond of him that he had a special miniature suit of armor made so he could go on campaigns with him."

"If I were Zerco, I think I would have passed up the honor," Sam said. "It must have been like getting into a fight where everyone else is twelve feet tall and weighs a thousand pounds."

"I suppose having a king's favor and protection must have seemed worth the risk."

Sam was silent for a moment. "Is there any mention of what Zerco did after Bleda was killed?"

"No," she said. "But that doesn't mean much. This is a travel guide, not a serious history."

They drove directly to Alba Iulia without stopping until they reached their hotel. After checking in, Sam called Tibor on his cell phone.

"Yes?"

"We're in Alba Iulia," said Sam. "Any news?"

"Yes, but it's all bad," Tibor said. "Bako is still at home. He's working in his office at the factory right this minute. But his favorite five security men have all packed up and driven eastward into Romania. I have my brother and two cousins following them and, so far, they're heading straight for you."

"Thanks for the heads-up," Sam said.

"They're traveling in two vehicles, both American-made SUVs, both new, both black with tinted windows. They've been on the road since early this morning, so they might already be there. If you see them, don't let them see you."

"Thank you, Tibor. We'll look carefully before we do anything."

"Good luck." Tibor signed off.

Remi said, "We could find some central place in town and watch for them."

"Not this time. They know we had a chance to see the inscription on the shield before they did and they're rushing here. They must have gotten a call from the people at Compagnie Le Clerc and left within an hour or so. If Bako isn't with them, they won't be coming into the center of town for good hotels and restaurants. I think they'll be out searching until they find the grave even if it means sleeping on the ground in the woods."

They went back to their car, drove to the Mureş River, and followed the road that ran parallel to it, searching for any landmark that might signal an undisturbed piece of ancient masonry. They kept going for a couple of hours, then turned around and started to drive in the other direction. As they did, Sam's cell phone rang.

"Hello?"

"Sam, this is Tibor again. Bako just went home and came out with two of his men. They were dressed in gear like they were going on a safari. Then a third man pulled up in a truck. I think it means that Bako got a call saying that his men have found the burial chamber. I'm in a car following them at a distance, and I've got another car to switch places with me now to keep them from spotting me."

"This is the second chamber they've beaten us to," said Sam.

"You ended up with both treasures so far, and maybe we'll end up with this one," Tibor said. "It can still be sent to a museum and not melted down into bars in Bako's bank."

"We'll try to accomplish that much, at least."

"I'm calling my brother next to see what Bako's men have found."

"I'll be waiting for word," Sam said. He ended the call and said to Remi, "We might as well have lunch while we're waiting." He drove into Alba Iulia and stopped at a café, where they could see the twelfth-century cathedral and two of the seven gates in the city walls. The oldest city architecture had a hint of Roman influence to it, with rounded arches and square, multilayered towers. Sam set his cell phone on the table.

They had rosól, a stewed-duck-and-vegetable dish, and Băbească Neagră red wine, and had just begun their dessert of baklava, when Sam's phone rang. He and Remi looked at each other, then looked at the phone. Sam picked it up. "Hello, Tibor."

"They're in the forest on the east side of the town and it looks like they've dug a hole. They've stopped. Apparently they're waiting for Bako to arrive before they enter the chamber. I guess he wants to be the first."

"Where's Bako now?"

"He's still about thirty miles away, and we're driving along the Mureş. My brother and cousins are watching the crew at the chamber, but there's not much they can do. It's too late to keep Bako from getting there first."

Sam thought for a moment. "All right, then. Let's move our strength away from the treasure."

"*Away* from it?"

"Yes. Give me the location and then get everyone back to Hungary. Remi and I will see what we can do on our own."

"What are you going to do?"

"If it's too late to keep Bako from finding the treasure, we'll try to keep him from taking it home."

"How?"

"I'll think about it on the way."

"I have confidence in you. I have many friends, but not one of them has a mind like you—a machine for grinding out crazy ideas."

"He's got your number," Remi said.

"Thank you, Tibor. Please get your brother and cousins back to Szeged. And all of you, take a different, less direct route home."

"I'll call you with the exact location."

"Thanks." Sam looked at Remi.

"We both meant good crazy." She kissed his cheek.

The phone rang again, so soon it surprised them both. Sam picked it up and Tibor's voice said, "I'm close now and I can see where Bako has pulled over. It's five kilometers from the east city walls of Alba Iulia. It's a heavily forested area just past the beginning of a hiking trail. There's a parking lot and a picnic area. The two black SUVs and the truck are all parked there."

"Good," said Sam. "We're on our way."

"Are you sure you don't want me to stay?"

"Positive. Have you sent your brother and cousins home?"

"Yes."

"Excellent. Now head for the border a different way."

"I'm going now."

"Good luck."

"I give it back. You're the ones who will need it."

Sam and Remi drove past the place that Tibor had described and kept going. They found a second parking lot and a marked trail that might have been the other end of the first trail. They turned around and drove back past the parked vehicles toward the Hungarian border.

They drove past Alba Iulia, and then, a few miles on, they reached an area that was more mountainous. As they drove, the highway became a narrow road, with winding pavement and nearly vertical canyon walls that were a tangle of rocks, trees, brush, and vines. Sam kept driving, scanning the land for the perfect spot.

At last, he was sure he had found it. There was a quarter-mile ribbon of road that wound to the left and right, then rose and disappeared over a crest. The mountains of Transylvania held the largest remaining area of the virgin forest that had once covered most of Europe, so the vegetation was thick and wild. Sam stopped the car, then backed up at a high speed until he reached a turnout to allow cars to pass, killed the engine, and popped the trunk.

Remi got out too and retrieved the two shovels, climbing rope, and a crowbar. As she reached for the night vision goggles, Sam said, "We can leave the goggles."

"Good. That means we'll be done by dark."

"Come to think of it, we'd better take them." He took a shovel, the crowbar, and the rope and began to climb up the wall at the side of the road to the rocky slope above. Remi took the second shovel and began to climb beside him.

"While we're climbing," she said, "you can help me find a title for my memoir. Do you like *Remi: An American Woman in a Transylvanian Prison*? Or does that give away too much? Maybe just *Remi: Girl Behind Bars*."

"How about *One Lucky Girl: My Life With Sam Fargo*?"

She laughed, then climbed harder to get ahead of him. As they climbed higher and higher, she realized that the bulges in the rocky wall and the curve of the road made it impossible to see their car below them. On second thought, it also meant that while they were up here they were not visible from the road. Anyone on the road looking up would see only the rocks.

After more climbing, Sam walked along near the crest for a few hundred feet. Then he took his shovel and began to dig.

"I hope what I'm doing is undermining this boulder. If it rolls straight down the hillside, as round heavy things tend to do, then we'll have a fairly impressive landslide, block Bako's road to Hungary, and be on our merry way."

"Merry? Are you sure?"

"If it works, we will be merry. It just will take an enormous amount of work done in a hurry and a massive helping of luck." He turned his attention to shoveling away the dirt and small stones that seemed to be holding the four-foot boulder in place a hundred fifty feet above the road. Remi stood on the other side of the boulder and shoveled too.

They reached a moment when the boulder seemed to have emerged from the dirt of the hillside. They had freed more than half of its bulk, and its bottom was undermined. Sam walked a few yards to a sapling, selected a dead limb about ten feet long and two and a half inches thick. He then rolled a nearby rock in front of the boulder to use as a fulcrum.

"Okay, Remi. Go along the ridge until you can see what's coming from a distance. When it's safe to drop the hill on the road, give me a wave."

"I'm off." She trotted along the ridge, sometimes stopping to jump a gap in the rocks or avoid obstacles. Finally she stood far above the road a distance from Sam, raised her arm, and waved.

Sam set his lever horizontally against the fulcrum and pushed. He was ten feet to the side of the rock so he could use his entire lever. He pushed again and there was something behind the rock that began to groan as the boulder moved.

The first try failed to dislodge the boulder, so Sam set his limb again against the rock. He looked up and saw Remi waving her arms frantically. He waited.

Down below, he saw a bus laboring up the road, the driver making a groaning downshift as it struggled toward the crest. After a minute, Remi waved her arm once more. Sam moved his fulcrum closer to the boulder, set his shoulder against the lever, and pushed with both legs. The boulder rocked forward, rocked back, and then rolled out of the bowl where it had sat. At first, it turned painfully slow, rolling once and then merely sliding, the topsoil too loose to allow it to turn. The boulder scoured the ground and vegetation. It reached a vertical drop of about six feet. When it hit the next group of rocks, it seemed to shatter the shelf where they sat, propelling them forward and downward. The boulder outran the ground debris, but it had dislodged much of the hillside, so at first there was a slide of rocks and gravel, and then a layer of soil with mature trees growing in it started down the hill. The trees remained upright until the rocks and soil caught them by the roots and they plunged. The slide was all very noisy—tons of moving rock and dirt and cracking wood—and then near silence.

Sam looked down. His landside had covered the road from rock wall to rock wall. There were about ten more seconds of small, round dislodged stones bouncing down the last few yards onto the pile and then the silence was total.

Sam grabbed the shovel, rope, and crowbar and trotted along the ridge until he reached Remi. Without speaking, they used their spades to keep from falling and setting off a second landslide. When they made their way down, they ran along the road to their car, threw their tools in the trunk, turned around, and drove off toward Alba Iulia. It seemed to Remi that they were now seeing many more cars and trucks heading along the road than they'd seen at first. All the traffic was heading toward them now. It was after about fifteen minutes that Sam's driving brought them close to other cars going the same way.

"I hope the cousins all made it out before we wrecked the road," said Remi.

"I'm sure they did," said Sam. "We gave Tibor plenty of time. What we need now is a name and phone number of whatever group in Romania controls the smuggling of antiquities."

"I'll call Selma," Remi said.

"Hi, Remi," said Selma. "Tibor tells me you've decided to go it alone again."

"The other team beat us to Bleda's burial place. Sam pointed out to me—possibly because of our experience in France—that finding the treasure and bringing it home are two very different things. We are now broadening our game to include being tattletales. Who can we call in Romania to report Bako smuggling antiquities to Hungary?"

"We'd better have Albrecht do that through an intermediary," said Selma. "The federal police in Romania are run out of a place called the General Inspectorate in Bucharest. We'll call and say we've got a case for Interpol and they'll send the border police. I can use a computer for the call and run the signal through a couple of forwarding services to keep us out of it."

"Thanks, Selma."

"You're welcome. Bako'll get in trouble if they catch him. Romania's Law No. 182 of 2000 says everything found must be registered and given a classification certificate by the government. They consider any antique part of the 'movable cultural heritage.'"

"We'll call you as soon as we tie up some loose ends."

"It's not over?"

"I'm afraid not. We still have to see the chamber."

"Be safe."

They drove through Alba Iulia again, past the wooded area where they had found Bako's vehicles. They parked at the next parking lot and walked back through the forest. As they came close, they heard a voice shouting in Hungarian what seemed to be instructions. They crept closer, staying low behind bushes, until they could see Bako sitting on the edge of the chamber with his feet dangling in the dark void below. Four men held a rope that was tied around him under his armpits. A fifth man ran up and handed him a flashlight.

Bako pushed off and slid into the chamber. Sam and Remi could see from the twisting of the rope that he was moving around, trying to shine his flashlight into the chamber in every direction at once. A couple of times his men, exhausted from digging and moving stones, seemed likely to lose their grip on the rope and drop him.

At last he was in the chamber. The men relaxed and rubbed sore muscles while the rope went slack. There was a shout from the chamber. The men pulled up the empty harness, and one of the security men put it on and was lowered inside. The rope went slack again, and the men knelt by the entrance to hear the conversation of their superiors. They looked at one another in consternation.

Remi whispered, "Something's wrong."

There was another yell from the echoing chamber, and the men exerted themselves to pull their colleague up quickly. He spoke to the others and then they lowered a camera into the chamber. Several times light flashed from the dark entrance up into the surrounding trees. When they pulled up Bako, he stomped around, looking angry, muttering to himself. Suddenly he shouted orders at his men.

The security men worked at loading their equipment into the truck, but they didn't seem to be bringing many artifacts up from the chamber. There were a few weapons, some textiles, some pottery. There was much conversation in Hungarian, and Bako, his head security man, and two others got into one of the two SUVs.

Remi whispered, "They're not taking any of the artifacts in Bako's car."

Then one of the other security men came and opened the hatch at the back of Bako's SUV and lifted the rug and a panel to reveal the spare tire and jack. He slipped a sword in a sheath, a belt with a dagger, and a bullet-shaped steel helmet inside. He closed things up and shut the hatch.

"Thank goodness," she whispered. "At least now he's guilty of something."

The SUV backed up, then turned and drove off along the Mureş River toward the blocked road.

Two men had been left behind to clean up and then drive the other SUV and the truck back to Hungary. Remi and Sam crawled back through the brush and then walked the rest of the way to their car. They drove back to the last parking lot, playing the car radio so loudly that the men couldn't help but hear. They slammed the doors and began to walk up the path, making all the noise they could.

By the time they reached the chamber, the two men had gone. They had hastily covered the entrance with brush. As Sam and Remi approached, they heard the two vehicles start and drive off. Sam took the rope he had brought and quickly lowered Remi into the chamber.

Her feet had barely touched when she said, "I can see what's wrong. Come down quickly."

Sam joined her and they explored the space together. The skeleton of Bleda lay on a slightly raised bier, like a low bed. In a corner was the three-foot skeleton of Zerco, the dwarf. They both lay in the postures of the buried and both had broken skulls. They had obviously been hit with a heavy weapon. The only treasures in the tomb were much-decayed clothing, leather horse harnesses, and saddles.

"Albrecht was right," Remi said. "Bleda tried to get rid of Attila and lost."

"That's the way it looks," Sam said. "There's no treasure. It's just Bleda's own stuff. And his friend Zerco. If Bleda had died in an accident, Attila wouldn't have executed Zerco."

"We'd better find the inscription," said Remi. She looked at each of the walls, and Sam scuffled his feet around to see if he could uncover anything on the floor. He saw nothing.

From time to time, Sam checked to detect whether he could hear noises outside. As he did, he instinctively looked up and there saw the inscription. The words were engraved in the stone ceiling above their heads. He touched Remi's arm and pointed upward. "It's as though he wanted Bleda to see it."

Remi took three photographs with her cell phone, and Sam realized why they had seen the flashes when Bako had taken his photographs. He had been aiming upward.

They climbed back up their rope and quickly made their way back to the rental car. As they drove, they passed the SUV and the truck making their way back toward the still-open chamber. They were going to see if it was safe to finish their work.

As Sam drove, Remi sent her photographs to Albrecht and Selma in La Jolla. They continued toward Bucharest for a half hour before Remi's phone rang.

"Hello?"

"Remi, it's Albrecht."

"Did you get our pictures?"

"We did."

"You saw the way Bleda was buried?"

"Yes."

"I'd say your theory just got a boost. It was no accident. There was no reason to kill Zerco if Bleda died in an accident."

"True. But it doesn't prove which brother was the aggressor."

"Any news of Bako?" asked Sam.

"Some hopeful signs. Tibor just called and said that two of Bako's lawyers got on a plane for Bucharest. It could mean he was arrested. But they won't hold him for long on a charge like removing artifacts."

"And the inscription we sent?"

"That's why I called, actually. It says, 'The death of my dear brother was the saddest day of my life. Before this, the worst was when together we gathered our ancestors' bones.'"

"We've got to get back to Hungary fast," said Remi. "Bako saw the inscription and tried to leave in that direction. I think we should do the same. If we don't, Bako might beat us to another one."

18

"If we get there in time, maybe we can outsmart him," said Sam. "Bako should still be in Romania dealing with the charge for removing artifacts."

"But he's seen the inscription, so he could easily call in his security people to start digging," said Remi.

"Try to reach Tibor and ask him to watch for any unusual activity among Bako's men.

"And ask him to find us a helicopter."

"He's going to love this," she said as she autodialed the phone. "Hello, Tibor?"

"Hello, Remi. Am I going to be sorry I answered this call?"

"Probably, but for a short time only. All we need for the moment is for you to have Bako's men watched—all of them, not just the worst five. And we need a helicopter."

"A helicopter?"

"Yes. Please tell me you have a cousin."

"I have a friend. Where do you want him to pick you up?"

"Can he fly in Romania?"

"Yes."

"Then he can pick us up at Timişoara Airport. It's the closest airport. And ask him to bring a pair of binoculars."

"I'll call him now."

"Thanks, Tibor." She ended the call, then saw something on her phone. "Selma sent us an e-mail."

"Read it to me so I can keep driving."

"Okay. Here it is. 'The next treasure was buried in 441 on the north shore of the Danube River. That was the border between the land controlled by the Eastern Roman Empire and the land of the Huns. The Huns had been gone from the region for a couple of years, 438 through 440. The Romans—or the optimistic Romans, anyway—figured they were gone for good.'"

"That has to be one of the worst assumptions ever."

"About as bad as they could make." Remi continued: "'The Huns had gone east to join the Armenians in their war against the Sassanid Persians. When they came back to their strongholds north of the Danube in 440, they found that while they were gone the Bishop of Marga had crossed the Danube to loot some of the royal graves of the Huns.'"

"A Bishop did that?"

"The church must have had personnel problems. Anyway, 'The Huns came back and weren't very happy. Attila and Bleda demanded that the Eastern Roman Emperor in Constantinople hand the Bishop over to them. The Bishop was a pretty slippery character. He immediately realized that the Emperor would order that he be given to the Huns. So he secretly went to the Huns himself and betrayed the city to them. The Huns destroyed the city. Then they went on to take all of the Illyrian cities along the Danube, and Belgrade and Sofia.'"

"I can't blame them for being angry, but what about the Bishop?"

"I have no idea. Maybe they agreed to keep him alive or killed him, or both," she said. "'They reburied the remains of their people. The conjecture is that for funeral goods they used the artifacts stolen by the Bishop, as well as some of the wealth they picked up in sacking all of the other cities.'

"It doesn't say who was in the royal graves," said Remi. "But in the tomb message, Attila called them ancestors."

"So what happened after the reburial?"

"The Huns don't seem to have been in a better mood. In 443, they looted Plovdiv and Sofia again and then kept going. They made it all the way to Constantinople, where the Emperor Theodosius had to pay them nineteen hundred sixty-three kilograms of gold to leave and had to raise the annual tribute he paid to twenty-one hundred pounds of gold."

"I hope Bako is waiting to get out of jail and can't do anything."

Sam and Remi reached Timişoara and found it beautiful. The Habsburg-era architecture reminded them of Vienna. Airport signs directed them to Traian Vuia International Airport, where they were able to return their rental car to the Bucharest-based agency. They found their way to the heliport.

The helicopter was already on the pad, and a middle-aged man with a sand-colored mustache and sand-colored hair and wearing a sand-colored leather jacket met them at the gate. "Mr. and Mrs. Fargo?"

"Yes," said Sam. In spite of the man's smile, Sam was not ignoring the possibility that he had been sent by Arpad Bako. Bako was probably sending men out in every direction looking for them by now. But he couldn't have known they wanted to rent a helicopter. He waited for the man to say something convincing.

"Tibor said you were in a hurry, so I came right away. I'm Emil."

"You speak such perfect English," said Remi.

"English is the universal language of fliers," said Emil. "If a pilot is Swedish and the air controller in Bhutan is from the same Swedish village, they speak English on the radio. Tibor and I both studied English to qualify for pilot training."

"Tibor is a pilot?" Remi said.

"Much better than I am. He was an airline pilot. He retired only a couple of years ago and started his taxi business."

"I wonder why he never told us."

Emil chuckled. "Tibor is one of those people who wants to know about you but thinks it's a waste of time to tell you all about himself." He opened the door on the side of his helicopter. "You sit in those two seats," he said, pointing out two sets of earphones. "You can listen but don't talk until I tell you. All right?"

"Right," said Sam. He and Remi climbed into their seats, belted themselves in, and put on their earphones.

Emil radioed the control tower, told them his course, and immediately started the rotors moving. As the engine whipped the rotors around faster, the noise grew, and then they rose into the air, tipped and leaned forward slightly, and headed up, out, and away from the airport and its pattern of runways. Emil headed southwest, climbing gradually as he went. After a while, he reached a ceiling, flew low and steady, but when he was a couple miles from the airport he climbed again. "Now we're away from the flight paths. You can talk now."

"Can you head for the north side of the river, along the bank?" asked Remi.

"We're looking for a place where somebody is digging."

"Digging?"

"Yes," Sam said. "It'll probably be a group of five or six men digging holes with shovels. If we get there early enough, we may find them still searching the ground with electronic equipment. We'd like to get a good look at them but not give them the impression we're interested in them."

"Ah, that reminds me," said Emil. "Tibor said you wanted binoculars." He opened a compartment and lifted the straps of two pair and handed them back to the Fargos.

"Thank you, Emil," said Remi. "We're very glad you were available."

"So am I," he said. "I don't usually get to do anything this interesting. Most of the time, I take tourists up to look at the same sights they saw from the ground the day before. Now and then there will be a businessman who needs a quick ride to Budapest or somewhere."

"Let's hope this doesn't get too interesting."

After a short time, Emil said, "We're just about at the Hungarian border," pointing to the river. "Now we'll swing down along the Danube."

The Danube was wide and curved, regularly moving around high points in the land. There was plenty of boat traffic, and the river ran through heavily populated areas, with tall buildings almost up to the water's edge. "The river is an international border, but we'll be over Hungary on the north side."

"Stay over land if you can," said Sam. "We're looking for ancient graves. We think they'll be on higher ground and back a bit from the river so they wouldn't get washed out by floods."

"I understand," Emil said. They flew along the Danube from

east to west. Where there was an area that looked as though it had been disturbed by digging or had an assortment of trucks and equipment, Sam and Remi would ask Emil to hover so they could take a better look.

They passed near an area that looked peculiar and hovered. About a hundred yards north of the river was an old-fashioned building, painted a buttery yellow, with high roofs and an extensive network of paths leading through formal gardens. There were at least a dozen men with shovels digging holes in the grass, in the middle of flower beds, in the paths. There were another dozen men walking the site with metal detectors and a couple of men pushing magnetometers mounted on wheels along like lawn mowers.

Emil took a second pass above the estate, and what Sam and Remi saw was shocking. Bako's men had already found several graves and opened them. There were big stones lining open-topped pits and beside them human skeletons thrown aside and piles of metal being loaded into crates. Sam got on his telephone.

"Hello?"

"Albrecht," said Sam. "We've got bad news. I don't know how Bako did it this time, but my delaying tactics didn't work. He's got twenty or thirty men at an estate on the north shore of the Danube. They're digging up graves and looting them. So far, they've got four or five open."

"We've got to move fast," said Albrecht. "I'll call our friends at Szeged University and have the authorities move in and put a stop to it. Can you give me an exact location?"

"Our friend Emil probably can."

"Tell them it's Count Vrathy's estate on the south end of Szeged. It's a museum now. It's probably closed at this time of day and they must have overpowered the watchman."

Albrecht said, "I've got it. Thank you," and hung up.

Sam got on his phone again. "Tibor, we're with Emil in the helicopter."

"I'd have to be deaf not to hear the rotors."

"Bako's men have found the Hun royal graves above the north bank of the Danube at the Vrathy estate. What can you tell me about Bako and the group he took to Romania?"

"They haven't returned from Transylvania yet."

"He seems to be substituting quality for quantity, using twenty or thirty men from his businesses to do the digging. We need to prevent them from hiding the treasure."

"Sam!" said Remi.

"Hold on, Tibor." He turned to Remi. "What's wrong?"

"They've moved a big boat up to the shore."

"Tibor? They're going to load the treasure into a boat. From up here, it looks like a fifty-foot yacht. They're still digging, so this will take a while. But we need to know where that yacht is from now on."

"I'll send men to the river above and below the Vrathy estate to watch where it goes."

"Good. Thank you. And Remi and I are going to need the equipment we left with the boat on the Tisza. We'll need our scuba gear, the tool kit, and a covered truck."

"I'll call my cousin."

"And ask him to be sure the air tanks are full."

"I'll call when we're ready."

Sam, Remi, and Emil kept returning to the airspace above the estate and then flying off into the distance as though they were transporting something on a route that passed over the estate. After about an hour and a half, the boat was loaded and the men with shovels and other equipment had begun getting into trucks to drive away.

Sam leaned forward to talk to Emil. "Emil, you've done a wonderful job. We may call on you again. Is there a place where you can set us down within a couple of miles of here without being seen?"

"Yes," he said. "There's a landing space near the university. I can put you down there."

He took them a short distance over the city and set the helicopter down on a large X at the end of a parking lot. "This is it," he said.

Sam said, "What do we owe you?"

"Nothing. Tibor already paid me for the day."

Sam handed him five hundred dollars. "Then please accept a small gift with our thanks."

Emil handed Sam his business card. "I know you can't read Hungarian, but you can read the phone number. Call it anytime of the day or night. If I can't help you, I'll find someone who can." They shook hands, Sam and Remi got out and the helicopter rose and flew away.

Remi said, "You know, I can't stop wondering what finally happened to the Bishop who robbed those graves the first time."

"I think his reputation for shrewdness may have been exaggerated."

"You think Attila and Bleda killed him?"

"To his people, he was a traitor. To the Huns, he was a grave robber. I'd be surprised if he died in bed."

"Let's see if doing the same brings bad fortune for Bako."

Sam's phone buzzed. "Hello?"

"It's me, Tibor. Where are you?"

"At the helipad by Szeged University."

"Stay there."

Five minutes later, a white-colored truck with a covered cargo bay appeared at the far entrance to the lot and drove straight across all the lanes to them. When it stopped, Sam and Remi climbed into the cab to join Tibor.

He said, "My cousins tell me the yacht is anchored offshore. Bako's men loaded fifteen wooden boxes onto the lifeboat and then they took them to the yacht and loaded them onto the deck. So we think they're getting ready to take the artifacts somewhere by water. The Danube runs through Germany, Austria, Hungary, and Romania to the Black Sea. Many rivers feed it. They could go anywhere without setting foot on land."

"Have the police arrived?"

"Nobody has seen them yet."

"All right," said Sam. "Let's go see if we can make Bako unhappy."

Tibor clapped his hand on Sam's shoulder. "I'm glad I lived to meet you two. Nobody has made me laugh so much since I was a kid."

Sam rubbed his shoulder. "Okay. Let's get the truck to a place where we can see the yacht."

Tibor drove them down to the road that ran along the Danube and turned east. After a few minutes, the road swung inland a bit to avoid a row of old estates along the river. When it swung back to the river, Tibor pointed. "There. See it?"

"The one with the high bridge?"

"That's the one." It was sixty-five feet long, with an aluminum lifeboat hanging from davits in the stern.

"All right," Sam said. "Remi and I need to put on our scuba gear."

"I have nephews in the back of the truck. I'll get them out and let you get changed." He stopped the truck by the side of the road and opened the back, summoned the two young men out, and let Sam and Remi in to put on their wet suits and organize their gear.

Sam tested the underwater light and examined the tools that he'd requested. He put them in a net bag and attached it to his belt. "We'll drift with the river's current. When we get there you'll have to hold the light so I can see what I'm working on. I'll try to work quickly."

Remi looked at him suspiciously. "You're not saying what you're working on?"

"I know how much you like surprises. But don't surface no matter what. Stay as deep as you can."

Tibor's nephews helped Sam and Remi go down a path to the water on the far side of the truck, where they couldn't easily be seen from the yacht. They put on their flippers and stepped backward into the dark water of the Danube. As soon as there was enough water to cover them, they submerged.

The big white yacht was at least a hundred yards from shore, anchored just at the edge of the channel where much larger boats and small freighters traveled. Sam and Remi headed for the yacht, staying deep in the murky water and checking their progress occasionally by shining the light on the riverbed below them and ahead of them.

Finally Remi's light found the anchor chain approximately where they had expected it, a straight diagonal line from the upstream end leading up to the dark shape above them on the silvery surface.

Sam gestured to Remi and slowly rose, coming up under the hull, but not touching it. He swam along the keel to the stern and looked up at the propeller protruding on its shaft from the lower part of the stern.

Remi clutched his arm and in the light she held he saw her shake her head. He could see the anxiety in her eyes through her mask.

He put his hand on her shoulder, patted it gently, took her hand, and aimed her light at the propeller. They both knew that if the men in the boat started the engine, Sam could be chopped to pieces in seconds.

Sam proceeded methodically. First, he found the cotter pin and removed it from the nut with a pair of needle-nose pliers. He used the pliers to lift the tabs that held the locking ring, returned the pliers to his net bag, and wedged a wrench between a propeller blade and the stern to keep the propeller from turning while he used an adjustable wrench to remove the nut. He placed his feet against the stern and pulled the bronze propeller off its shaft, then carried it a distance into the deeper channel before he dropped it.

He returned to the stern of the yacht and surfaced cautiously. He took off his flippers, his tanks, and his mask and hung them on the bare propeller shaft and climbed the stern ladder to get aboard.

Just as he reached the rear deck, his eye caught a sudden movement to his left. He spun and saw a man by his left shoulder swing what looked like a pipe. He ducked into the man's torso so the pipe went over him, gave the man a quick jujitsu punch to the jaw, and held him in a choke hold until he was unconscious. He found a length of rope on a cleat, used it to hog-tie him, and then tore the man's shirt to make a gag.

Sam saw the wooden crates on the rear deck covered with a tarp. He pulled back the tarp and quietly lowered ten of them into the lifeboat at the stern. They were heavy, and it took nearly an hour of backbreaking work. Then Sam draped the bow rope in the water and freed two pins on the davits to lower the boat to the river. The lifeboat made an unexpectedly loud ratchet sound as it hit the water with a splash. Behind Sam there came a sound of running feet and a call: "Stashu?"

Sam jumped from the stern, grabbed his tanks, mask, and flippers from the propeller shaft and put them on and cleared his mask as he sank deeper.

Remi had seen the loose bow rope and now she held it out and they both grasped it and pulled. She and Sam swam, diving deeper and pulling the boat along the surface above them. As they went, Sam kept looking behind them and around the yacht to be sure none of the crew were jumping into the water after them.

First came the muffled sounds of shots from the yacht above the surface, but with each shot they heard a *chuff* sound as a bullet plowed under, leaving a line of churned water and bubbles behind it. Each one pierced straight into the water until it exhausted its momentum at about four feet, then simply sank into the dark water below them.

Next Sam and Remi heard the engine start and knew the propeller shaft was spinning freely. Without the propeller, the engine was just noise. The helmsman didn't seem to understand at first because he just gunned the engine harder and louder while the crew at the bow used a power capstan to weigh anchor.

As soon as the anchor was off the bottom, the yacht began to drift downstream, powerless to fight the current or to steer. The anchor kept rising nonetheless, and the boat drifted farther and farther from Sam, Remi, and the lifeboat. At some point the engine stopped, but by then its noise was so far away that Sam and Remi had lost it among the many passing engines above them on the Danube. Sam guessed that they would drop anchor again, but the yacht was too far away to pick out in the murky water.

Sam and Remi arrived at the shore and hauled the lifeboat up onto the mud. Almost instantly the two brawny nephews were beside them, taking the heavy crates out and loading them into the back of the truck. Sam and Tibor joined them. The crates were heavy with precious metal, but ten crates took no more than a few minutes to load. Sam and Remi got in the back, the boys got into the cab with Tibor, and the truck rumbled off into the big, busy city.

As Remi took off the wet suit and set her gear aside to put on street clothes, she said, "We're not done yet, you know. We've still got to find the message from Attila. It will be in one of the graves."

"Let's hope the ones waiting for us there are Albrecht's professor friends and not Arpad Bako."

19

AS THE POLICE OFFICER HELPED REMI CLIMB UP OUT OF the open grave, she smiled and waved to Sam. She jogged across the damaged garden to Sam's side. "It was engraved on the wall. I'm sending the pictures to Selma and Albrecht."

"The bad part is that Bako's men probably read it hours ago."

"I know," she said.

Tibor said, "If he's got it, then it didn't make much of an impression or he didn't understand it. He's back in his office at the pill factory, looking innocent."

Sam said, "If he gets arrested, we won't be able to prove anything unless somebody else saw his men excavating here. And if he ends up in court, so will we. He could send his security men ahead to the next spot, wherever that is."

"I'd better go," said Tibor. "It's my turn to take charge of the surveillance crew. When they translate the message, let me know what it says." Tibor got into his car and drove up the gravel drive to the highway.

Sam and Remi walked back toward the open graves, looking at the careless devastation that Bako's men had left behind. They had apparently been ordered to find just the gold and simply thrown everything else aside. There were human bones and fifteen-hundred-year-old fabric, pots, implements, weapons strewn about the gardens and lawns of the estate.

Sam's telephone buzzed. "Hello?"

"Hi, Sam. It's Selma."

"What have you learned?"

"I'll put Albrecht on."

"Hello, Fargos," said Albrecht. "I'll read you the message from Attila: 'We buried our father Mundzuk along the river outside Talas. He faces west, the direction he was leading our army. His brother Ruga now leads in his stead.'"

"Where is Talas?" asked Sam.

"Talas was the oldest city in Kazakhstan. A Hun named Zhizhi Chanyu founded it, and it was the site of a battle in 36 B.C.E. It was an important stop on the Silk Road that ran through China, India, Persia, and Byzantium. It was destroyed in 1209, but it's now a modern city called Taraz. Its location is 42° 54' north, and 71° 22' east, just north of Kygyztan and east of Uzbekistan."

"It doesn't sound too hard to find," Remi said. "I assume we can fly there."

"As you can see, while we've been moving backward in Attila's life with each of the treasures he buried, we're also moving east. Kazakhstan is probably where the Huns became the nomadic horseback power they were. It also seems to be the place where they launched themselves toward the Roman world. The name Kazakh means 'free spirit,' meaning a nomad of the plains. The country is about one-third dry steppe, and the distances there are enormous. Kazakhstan contains more area than all of Western Europe. Selma will tell you about the travel arrangements."

"Hi, you two. I've made a reservation for you to fly from Budapest Airport to Moscow this evening. From there, you'll fly to the capital of Kazakhstan, Astana. You'll pick up your visas and letters of invitation there. From Astana, you'll fly to Almaty, the largest city, and on to Taraz."

"Sounds like a long trip," said Remi.

"It will take a while, but maybe after all the running around you two have done, it will give you a chance to rest up. At least sitting in an airplane will help you catch up on your sleep before you reach Taraz."

A FEW MILES AWAY, Arpad Bako sat in his office in a rage. He had just learned that the diligence and care he had expended and the risk he had faced to excavate the royal tombs of the Huns had been wasted. His weak and stupid security men had allowed two people, a husband and wife from America, to rob him of ten crates of gold and gems, much of it finely wrought ornaments, chalices, and crosses from the oldest churches in Europe. The rest were Roman-made ornaments from the garrisons along the Danube. This was the plunder the Huns had taken from the whole Balkan region. Some of it was from even farther away and longer ago, probably worn on the wrists, necks, and fingers of Central Asian warriors and their wives and buried with their descendants after reaching Hungary.

It had taken years of study and considerable luck to find this treasure, but he had done it. And now he had been robbed, as he had been in France. He couldn't even get the culprits arrested because he'd had no legal right to dig on the museum grounds. His foolish men had even fired at the Fargos and the stolen lifeboat, so they'd had to throw their guns in the river before being arrested.

The telephone gave an abbreviated ring on the other end, then some mysterious clicks and disconnection sounds, like doors opening and closing. Finally a female voice with a singer's lilt to it said in Hungarian, "The offices of the Poliakoff Company are closed for the day. If you would like to leave a message, wait for the tone." Bako knew that the machine was simply programmed to speak Hungarian to a Hungarian phone number.

He said, "This is Arpad Bako. Please call me back." He ended the call, then set the cell phone down on his large, highly polished rosewood desk and looked at it expectantly. The telephone rang almost immediately and he picked it up. "Hello, Sergei."

"I was surprised to hear your voice, Arpad. You're a fat, lazy plutocrat to call me at night."

"Ideas come to me like birds flying in my window. When I see a good one, I snatch it out of the air regardless of the hour."

"I like ideas. You can tell me yours. This is a scrambled line."

"All right," Bako said. "I have found a treasure hidden by Attila the Hun."

"A treasure," said Poliakoff. "Are we using metaphors now?"

"I say the word *treasure* the way Attila would have. A collection of coins and jewels, works of art, and ornaments made of gold and precious stones. They will be in a burial chamber."

"Attila's?"

"Attila's father's. You will get a third if you help me."

"A third of what?"

"A third of whatever we find," said Bako. "I can tell you we've found some of the treasures already. There was one in Italy. There was one in France with so much gold it took a truck to carry it out. There was a smaller one in the Transylvanian forest, and one on the north bank of the Danube that was ten shipping crates of gold and gems."

"You have all of this gold and jewelry? Send me pictures of yourself standing with it and send me a small sample in your next shipment of pain pills. A ring, a necklace, anything in your next shipment of pills. I'm expecting one by air tomorrow."

"I can send you a sample. Not much more. While my resources were devoted to searching in France, some competitors went and found the one in Italy. That treasure I never saw. I only read about it in the newspapers. The one in France was dug up by our friend Étienne Le Clerc. He took pictures, but those competitors stole it from his shipping warehouse. The one along the Danube, my men dug up today, and they took pictures. The actual treasure is now in the hands of the Hungarian government."

Poliakoff said, "So you know these treasures exist, but you don't have them. Who are these competitors who took these treasures from you?"

"It's an American couple named Samuel and Remi Fargo. They're rich treasure hunters, and they've found some magnificent riches in other parts of the world, but never anything like this. There can't be many treasures like these. Attila swept out of Asia across the Ural and the Volga all the way to France, robbing cities. And I found out where he hid most of those riches."

Poliakoff said, "This is just two people—and one of them a woman—robbing you and Le Clerc of a treasure worth millions and millions?"

"Billions. But it's not just two people. When Fargo needs men, he hires them. When he doesn't, they vanish like smoke. He also has the help of Albrecht Fischer, one of the world's leading scholars on the late Roman Empire. And when Fargo believes he's about to be outmaneuvered, he calls in the national police to take charge of the treasure."

Poliakoff said, "Arpad, you must never again tell this story to anyone. If any of the people we both deal with heard it, they'd think you were weak. They'd turn on you like wolves and eat you up."

"Are you interested in my offer or not?"

"Oh, I'll do it for you," said Poliakoff. "Where is your wonderful treasure now?"

"It's buried in a chamber in the city of Taraz in Kazakhstan. I'll send you a map."

"And where are the Fargos? Do they know where it is?"

"They were here in Szeged this afternoon, but they've had several hours to learn the next location and I'm sure they'll be leaving as soon as possible."

"Find out how they're planning to get to Kazakhstan from Hungary and let me know immediately. Do you have photographs of them?"

"I have men watching the airports and train stations and men watching the Fargos. I'm sending you the photos right now."

"Call me the minute you know their flight number and destination. Minutes and seconds will matter." He hung up.

FROM THE TOP TOWERS of Sergei Poliakoff's estate outside Nizhny Novgorod, he could see the Volga, and along its banks the lights of the city of more than a million people were like a galaxy of stars miles away. The city was huge and modern and had long been a center of aerospace research, but here in the calm and quiet of his estate it could easily have been the 1850s. When he sat in the gardens, he could listen to the winds and hear no interruption but for the calls of birds that had come to eat from his currant bushes.

Outside, an American-made Hummer with armored door panels waited with two of Poliakoff's bodyguards inside. Next came the family's big black Mercedes with tinted windows and then the follow-up, a white Cadillac Escalade. His wife, Irena, and the children went past the Mercedes and entered the Escalade. If any of Poliakoff's detractors were to attempt to cause trouble, they would attack the armored Hummer with its guards or the elegant Mercedes that looked as though it held the family. The men in the front seat of the Escalade would drive on through.

Sergei watched them leave, and then the front door closed with a resonant thud and the steel bolts snapped into place. Poliakoff was a good match for Irena. Her parents had been important intellectuals during the Communist era, and, unlike most of the others, they had never gone out of favor.

He picked up his cell phone and clicked his way through the pictures Bako had sent him of golden bangles and trinkets. Then he came to the pictures of the Fargos. The wife was not merely attractive, she was a genuine beauty, he thought. He knew, from his experience with Irena, that living with such a prize was a wonderful thing in daily life. In a fight, it wasn't such a good thing at all. It gave a man something precious, but also made him fragile and vulnerable, making him love his wife so much he didn't want to risk her in a fight.

Bako was essentially a merchant—greedy as a tick, but he didn't love a fight. He thought of enemies as competitors. And Le Clerc, at the bottom of his soul, was the same. Like Bako, he was capable of hiring a few ruthless men and keeping them around, but what he watched were the reports his accountants brought him. They were just dishonest business types, not tough men after real success. Poliakoff had lived in a harder world than the others. Only he seemed to see this situation clearly at a glance. The woman was the treasure.

20

FERIHEGY AIRPORT, BUDAPEST

SAM AND REMI WERE AT BUDAPEST AIRPORT, WALKING toward the boarding tunnel for their flight to Moscow.

"Astana is supposed to be all shiny and new," said Remi. "That should be interesting. The whole place was rebuilt in the past fifteen years."

"We'll probably have to spend some time in the capital seeing the people who have authority over antiquities," said Sam. "This time, I'd like to get them in on everything before we start digging."

"Do you think Bako will beat us there?"

"I can't predict," said Sam. "At times, he seems to begin ahead of us. He's already thinking about every site where Attila ever was and he picks the one he thinks fits. Other times, he seems to turn things over to people who don't know what they're doing."

"We're getting back in time to when Attila was young and to the part of Asia where the Huns came from."

"We'll see," he said.

The flight from Ferihegy to Sheremetyevo Airport took just an hour and forty-five minutes. From there, the fastest available flight from Moscow to Astana, the capital of Kazakhstan, would take eight hours and five minutes. As they taxied to the end of the runway, Remi gently put her hand on Sam's as she always did until the plane had taken off. When the plane leveled, she took her hand off his and began to read the book about Kazakhstan she had bought.

They sat together in near silence for the remainder of the short flight. Since they couldn't tell whether they were being watched by people Bako had placed on the plane, they communicated mostly by touch and whisper. When they got off the plane, they looked up at the electronic boards to find their flight to Astana.

They saw that their plane was expected to leave on time in three hours. They went to sit in a waiting area not far from their gate, and Sam took out his phone to look at a map of their route. After a few minutes of watching Sam, Remi said, "You seem a little jumpy. What's up?"

"Oh, I don't know." He watched a small group of men across the cavernous room, talking quietly among themselves. "I've noticed over the years that when you feel uneasy, there's often a good reason."

"That sounds a little too much like ESP," she said.

"You know, I'm not a believer in things that don't have causes. I just think that we're picking up tiny clues in large numbers all the time, and, once in a while, they add up to trouble that you haven't quite understood yet."

"I can believe that. But here we are in an airport designed and built by . . . let's say a very controlling government at the height of the Cold War. It's practically a machine for keeping an eye on people. You're probably just picking up on features of that design."

"Maybe," he said. "But please do me a favor and be just a little bit paranoid."

"If it helps, I've been observant," she said. "And I haven't seen any suspicious-looking men. I'm off to the ladies' room."

Remi walked across the open floor to the concourse and went toward the sign with the international symbol of the little cookie-cutter lady in a dress. As she walked, she heard the sound of high heels on the hard floor and noticed that a couple other women were converging on the restroom behind her. She glanced subtly to each side as she went, reassuring herself, just a couple young women with carry-on bags. She pushed on the door to enter and saw two large, middle-aged women in uniforms and aprons in front of her. One was at the row of sinks, handing out towels. The other, with a mop stuck in a bucket on wheels, was moving closer to the door. As Remi stepped in, the mop woman let the next couple of women in and then pushed a sign on a plastic cone in front of the door and turned a knob to lock it. She went to work, mopping the floor.

Remi went into an empty stall. When she came out, things seemed to happen all at once. As she opened the door, the two uniformed women stepped to her from both sides. The mop woman threw her arms around Remi and held her in a crushing embrace and the other one reached between two of her hand towels, pulled out a hypodermic needle, and injected Remi in the arm.

Remi drew in a shallow breath and prepared to scream, but the woman held a towel over her face. The sound began as a muffled yell but quickly died in a fight for breath. By then, Remi had begun to feel weak and helpless from the drug, and in a moment she lost consciousness.

Sam sat in his seat in the waiting area. He had been watching people go by for some time and now he picked up the book Remi had been reading about Kazakhstan, read a few pages but couldn't keep his mind on it. He went back to watching passersby. Moscow's airport was an open place, where any number of travelers from every continent were always visible. He picked up her book again, but after a time he realized he had been posing as a reader rather than reading. His book was merely a mute explanation of how he was passing his time and an assurance to others that he was harmless. Where was Remi? Too much time had passed. He pulled out his cell phone and called her, but her phone was turned off, probably since they'd boarded the plane in Budapest.

Sam knew that women's restrooms in public places often required waiting, but this felt wrong. Sam got up and, shouldering Remi's bag along with his, walked in the direction he'd seen her go. Down the concourse were restrooms. He walked directly there, but kept scanning the nearby shops and crowds for Remi.

He saw a large, heavy woman, dressed like a cleaning lady, come out of the restroom, pushing a wheeled cart with a couple of large barrels on it. She picked up the sign on the cone that had been blocking the door. Another woman in a janitorial dress came out and helped her push the cart. They went off down the concourse and turned into an alcove that, he supposed, led to some of the innumerable doorways where passengers couldn't go.

The fact that the cleaning ladies had closed the restroom for a few minutes reassured Sam, but not entirely. He stood across from the door and waited but kept looking up and down to see if Remi might have chosen another restroom and would be returning.

He had a memory of a restroom at O'Hare Airport in Chicago that had two sets of doors, one opening onto the concourse, where he'd entered, and the other, on the opposite wall, opening onto a different concourse. Could this ladies' room have two entrances? He saw a woman coming out, speaking on a cell phone. He said, "Excuse me."

She stopped walking, the phone still to her ear.

He said, "Does that restroom have two exits?"

The woman looked back at it and then at him, as though she were wondering what he could possibly mean.

He answered for her. "I guess not." He hurried on. He had wasted too much time. He called Remi's cell phone again, but it was still off. He listened to part of the message and hung up. He came to a gate where there were two women in airline uniforms, talking in Russian as they stood at a counter.

"Hello," he said. "Do you speak English?"

"Yes, sir," said one. "How can I help you?"

"My wife went to a restroom but didn't return. And it's not like her. She would call me on her cell phone if she went anywhere else. I've been calling her, but her phone is turned off. I'm very worried about her. She would never do this."

"Is she . . . perhaps ill?"

"She wasn't a while ago when we arrived from Budapest. Can you get in touch with airport police?"

The two women looked at each other uncomfortably. "Yes, I can," said one. "How long has she been gone?"

He glanced at his watch. "About a half hour. I know it doesn't sound long, but, I swear to you, she would never do this without telling me."

"It's a big airport. Could she be lost?"

"Anyone could get lost. But if she were, she would be even more likely to call me."

"Let me page her."

"Sure. But please call the police too."

The woman picked up a telephone, pressed a button, then held the receiver against her arm. "What's her name?"

"Remi Fargo."

"Would Mrs. Remi Fargo please pick up a white courtesy tele-phone or go to any Aeroflot desk. Mrs. Remi Fargo, please pick up a white courtesy telephone." She hung up the phone and smiled reassuringly. "She should be calling us in a moment."

"Please call the police."

"We should wait a few minutes to give her time to call."

"She's had plenty of time to use her own cell phone to call," Sam said, getting agitated. "Please call the police." He spotted two uni-formed police officers walking along the concourse. "Excuse me." He turned and ran after them.

As he came up on the two cops, he saw them look quickly over their shoulders at him, their bodies tensed for an attack. He smiled as well as he could. "Do you speak English?"

They looked confused, so he began to walk back toward the air-line desk, beckoning them to follow. When they arrived, he said to the airline woman, "Please, tell them my problem."

The woman spoke to them in rapid Russian, a quick exchange during which she gestured at Sam, at the telephone, and at the con-course and which included shrugs, head shaking, and apologies. Both cops spoke with the monotone formality of cops all over the world.

The woman said to Sam, "Do you have a picture of Mrs. Fargo?"

Sam brought one up on his cell phone and held it up for the oth-ers to study. The cop who did most of the talking used the radio on his belt, then put it back. Through the airline woman he said, "We'd like you to come with us. We'll try to help."

Sam thanked the women and hurried off with the police officers. They went into another of the nondescript, unmarked doors off the concourse. They took Sam into an office with several police of-ficers at desks and others watching television monitors. One of the cops, a young man with blond hair and a scholarly demeanor, said, "Sir? Please sit here and I'll take your report."

Sam was relieved to see a police officer who spoke English. "I'm not filing an insurance claim or something. My wife has disappeared and that means something has happened to her."

"We have to start with the report and then the help." The next ten minutes were taken up by Sam recounting what had happened, describing Remi and then showing the cop and others the picture on his phone.

"I took that picture only a few hours ago, before we got on the plane in Budapest."

The young man asked Sam to e-mail him the picture, then downloaded it. He explained what he was doing as he sent it to various police substations in the airport, then to the cell phones of patrolmen and plainclothes officers around it.

Sam felt his hopes rise. They knew what they were doing. They knew how to find someone. They had a good chance of spotting her. He felt a little foolish for feeling so pessimistic about them at first.

The cop asked more questions—about his flight to Moscow, what gate he and Remi had used to deplane, and when exactly she had gone off to the restroom. He was transmitting this information to someone. He seemed to read Sam's mind. "There are investigators looking at the surveillance tapes of those areas to pick out your wife and see where she went."

For the next half hour Sam sat in the office, waiting. The cops came in and out, answered phones, and conferred with one another. Nobody spoke to him, but he occasionally caught one of them looking at him surreptitiously. He was painfully, fearfully aware that in this kind of emergency, seconds counted. He didn't want conversation, he wanted them to find Remi, so he remained silent and watched. Then the half hour was an hour, then two hours. He called the house in La Jolla and left a message, explaining what was happening.

When two and a half hours had passed, several cops came in who had different uniforms—outdoor uniforms. The fabric, boots, belts, and hats were black. These men were also more heavily armed than the airport police.

When Sam had first come in, officers had smiled at him. "Don't worry. This is the most important Russian airport. It's like a bank vault. Nobody can steal a woman from here." Later on, another had said, "This place is more heavily guarded than anything in your country. Even if a woman were kidnapped, they'd never get her out of the building." Still later, it became, "They could never get her past the airport gates."

When it was time for the Fargos' plane for Kazakhstan to board, Sam and two of the new police officers went to the gate and scanned the waiting area, showed the airline personnel pictures of Remi but were greeted with head shaking and pursed lips. They stayed until the door to the jetway was locked, the jetway was retracted from the plane, and the plane was pushed out onto the tarmac.

Sam looked in every direction, hoping to see the slender, graceful form of a woman far off in the distance, running to catch the plane. He just saw thousands of busy, preoccupied passengers, trying to keep track of their belongings and their children, as they made their way toward other boarding gates.

21

NIZHNY NOVGOROD, RUSSIA

REMI FARGO WAS HALF AWARE, NOT AWAKE BUT STRUG-
gling toward consciousness, as a free diver struggles upward toward
the light, striving to burst through the surface to gasp that first
breath of air.

She was in a dark place that was so soft that she couldn't feel her
muscles push against anything solid, and she seemed to have sunk
into it. After a huge mental effort, she realized that she was inside
a big cardboard barrel, on top of some rags or cloths, and that
more had been dumped on top of her and then the barrel closed.
There must be airholes, she thought, but she saw none, and her
few minutes of effort made her lose consciousness again.

An unknowable number of hours passed before Remi approached
consciousness again. This time when she tried to open her eyes, they
opened. She now knew she was in the big barrel of hand towels the
woman had been handing out at the airport restroom. She righted

herself with gravity so she was kneeling on a layer of towels, pushed up with her hands, and felt the top of the barrel give a little, but it wouldn't budge at the rim. She ran her hands along the rim and pushed, but the top was tightly secured.

"Hello?" she called out.

There was no response.

"Hello? You out there. Open up." She thought about what had happened to her. She had been kidnapped from a ladies' room in the Moscow airport. The audacity of that was breathtaking, but her mind had no interest in the details. The two big women had drugged her and put her in this barrel, taken the barrel out of the airport, loaded it into what was likely a linen supply truck, and driven off with her.

She had probably been on the road before Sam had started wondering about her. Poor Sam. He must be absolutely insane with worry by now. She could picture him pacing in that waiting area, watching people boarding their plane for Kazakhstan, wondering what had happened to her. He would be driving the authorities mad by now too, and that was a good thing. He wouldn't let them forget about her—some unknown foreign woman who had gotten herself into trouble and had no powerful connections to make their lives really uncomfortable.

Remi considered calling out again but decided to wait. The time to yell would be when she heard people or felt them moving the barrel. There would be some chance of making an outsider hear her if they were in some kind of depot. An hour later, the truck turned off the smooth surface it had been on and bounced a little as it went over another surface, this one still smooth but feeling like something with a rougher texture, maybe gravel or dirt.

As she sat in the dark, she began to face the possibilities. Most likely, someone had seen her and Sam showing American passports and decided an American hostage was a good thing to have.

The truck stopped. She heard a set of double doors squeak open. Her mind took a second to follow several paths to their ends. She was much more athletic than they would suspect, and a highly ranked fencer and pistol shot. She might be able to pop out and—what?—get them to shoot her? She could pretend to be unconscious, listening to what they said in a language she didn't understand. She decided to be rational, open, and try to appear unafraid. Appearing unafraid might be difficult, but not beyond her acting ability.

She heard a clasp being undone and then an aluminum hoop being sprung open and lifted off the lip of her barrel. Hands popped the top off and then lifted the layer of loose towels on top of her. Remi stood up.

She recognized the two large women from the airport. They both wore coveralls now instead of the loose work dresses and their hair was pulled back and knotted. Behind them were two men. They might have been the ones driving the getaway truck and possibly helped lift the barrel on and off vehicles. But now one of them held a short, nasty-looking Stechkin APS machine pistol like those made for Spetsnaz units of the old Soviet army. She knew they were still used by police because they fired cheap, readily available ammunition and had low recoil. She could see these two were fitted with silencers. They hadn't been manufactured with tournament accuracy, but, at six hundred rounds a minute, they could certainly hit a girl in a cardboard barrel.

There were two other men in blue jeans and windbreakers. They both carried short-barreled Czech Škorpion machine pistols. A few feet beyond all of these men was another man, this one wearing a light gray tailored suit that fit him perfectly. He was clearly the man to watch. He nodded and smiled at the four people in coveralls, then said something in Russian to the whole group. They moved quickly, first to help Remi out of the barrel and off the truck, then to put a pair of plastic restraints around her wrists to bind her hands behind her.

The man in the suit maintained a cheerful smile through these proceedings and an easy manner that belied the military obedience and discipline of his underlings. He looked to Remi like a prerevolutionary aristocratic gentleman spending the summer on his country estate. He wore a crisp white shirt and a blue silk tie, and, while she watched, he lit a cigarette and turned his attention to her. "You looked like Botticelli's *Birth of Venus* being lifted out of your scallop shell, Mrs. Fargo."

He waited a moment, then said, "You're not speaking to me?"

"I don't want to prompt you to say anything that will make you think you have to kill me."

He nodded. "Very wise, in general. But kidnapping in Russia is about the same as it is in the United States—if I'm caught, I'm dead. I'll tell you what you need to know. You will be treated well and respectfully, but locked in your room. Every day someone will come, have you hold up that day's newspaper, and take your picture. We will be in touch with your husband. When he meets my demands, you will be freed."

"What are your demands?"

"Ah," he said. "So you are interested."

"Of course I am."

"I know about the search for Attila the Hun's five treasures. You and your husband found the one near Mantua, Italy. You stole the one at Châlons-en-Champagne, France. You got Arpad Bako arrested for finding Bleda's tomb goods. You stole the treasure buried along the Danube. You were on your way to find the final treasure when I stopped you." He watched her. "Aren't you going to deny any of this?"

"Would you believe me?"

"So you and your husband now have control of at least three very large hoards of ancient riches—ones from Italy, France, and Hungary. All came after prolonged campaigns of conquest and looting by the Huns. I've been told that each of them had to be moved by trucks." He was studying her reactions closely. "I believe your husband will trade those three treasures for you. It's a simple exchange."

"We don't have possession of any treasures now," she said. "We have made finds before. You can look them up. We always follow the international treaties and the national laws of the countries where we find things. Most of the time, the rules prohibit exporting any archaeological treasures from the country. In instances where the governments approve sale of any artifacts, we donate our percentages to our foundations. We don't keep any of it. The three finds that you mentioned have all been taken into custody by the Italian, French, and Hungarian governments. It could be years before we know what the disposition of the artifacts will be."

"Then your husband will have to enlist officials in those governments to help him, I suppose." He smiled. "This is an interesting chance for you both to see how much gratitude your generosity to governments over the years has bought you."

"What happens when my husband can't give you all those precious bits of those countries' histories? Are you going to kill me?"

"Am I? Of course not. I have people who do that kind of work for me. And I can tell you, I'm not a lunatic or a fool. If your husband delivers enough of these hoards so I know he's sincerely done his best, I'll release you."

Remi said, "You don't strike me as a man who cares about museum pieces. What about asking my husband for a simple ransom instead? He would certainly pay a million dollars for me." She saw his look of derision. "Say five million, then. And it would be so much less trouble and risk for you. He could transfer the money into your account electronically and you could transfer it instantly to another account in a country that won't allow it to be traced. No trucks, no border searches, no risk, no selling stolen antiquities for a hundredth of their value."

"Thank you, but I've heard enough," the man said. "My friends will show you to your quarters. Regardless of how things go, you and I probably won't see each other again. But I'll be hoping for your husband to come through for you." He turned and walked away. She could see he was heading toward a large garden a few hundred feet from a large mansion.

One of the men with the Škorpion machine pistols led the way. The two women guided Remi by the arms, and the other men walked a few paces behind, their Stechkin pistols ready. They took her through the opulent house, which looked as though it had been built between 1850 and 1870. There were old, dark paintings on the walls—some dramatic, stormy seascapes, some battles, and portraits of bearded men and bejeweled women.

The furniture was graceful and most certainly French, with silk upholstery and highly polished wood. They entered a large kitchen, then passed a butler's pantry. She assumed they were conducting her to a dungeon-like basement, but instead they led her, single file, up a set of narrow back stairs past several landings to the top, fourth floor. This was a route that had been designed and built for servants and led to a hallway of tiny rooms that had probably housed chambermaids and kitchen help.

They led her to a room halfway down the hall and to the right that had no windows, only a big, thick wooden door. In the room there was a single bed, a table and chair, a small dresser. There was a second door that led into a bathroom. From her experience of old houses, Remi suspected that the windowless bedroom had been for an upper-level servant and the bathroom had been the room of another servant. The remodeling had produced a comparatively comfortable cell with no means of entrance or exit, and no way to know if it was day or night.

The two women backed Remi up against a bare wall, lifted a Russian-language newspaper off the dresser and put it in her hands, and then one of the men took her picture. After they checked to be sure the picture was clear, they all left.

Remi listened as the door closed. It was solid, not hollow. She heard the key turning in the lock but no snap of a dead bolt. Good news.

Remi sat on the bed. She knew that the thing she was entitled to do now was to cry, but she refused. The right thing to do was to search the suite for any surveillance equipment—pinhole cameras, peepholes, any place where a camera might be hidden. There were none. Next she began her examination of the furnishings, especially the bed and the plumbing, for pieces of metal she might remove and use as tools.

These people had no idea, she thought. That man, that character out of the Romanov era, thought of her and Sam as victims, people he could simply rob or hold for ransom or kill as he wished. But since the Fargos' business had become successful over ten years ago, they had become potential kidnapping targets. They had known it was possible that at some point either one of them might be taken and had planned their response carefully, agreed on every move each of them would make as soon as they were separated. The prisoner would never stop learning about the place and the captors, always preparing to signal his or her location when the time came, and to facilitate a rescue. And the one outside—Sam this time—would simply never stop looking. If no break ever came their way, he would still be searching, a year from now or twenty years from now.

Sam would never give up, never let a lead go uninvestigated, never let a day pass without progress. She thought about Sam and tears welled up. Right about now he would be appearing to let the Moscow authorities handle the problem but would actually be quietly, relentlessly pressuring the U.S. authorities to help him.

22

MOSCOW

SAM SAT PATIENTLY IN THE U.S. CONSULATE'S WAITING room, not pacing or drumming his fingers or showing irritation. In the glaring evening sunlight, the room looked like a waiting room in a Midwestern doctor's office with leather easy chairs, a couch, and a lot of magazines on a table, even though the consulate on Bolshoy Deviatinsky Pereulok was an aggressively modern and efficient-looking eight-floor box.

He knew they were observing him, running a slapdash background check to see who he really was, and they needed time to accomplish it. Just as he was beginning to wonder whether the result had been negative, the door across from him opened. A man in a dark suit came in, his face set in a flexible expression that was not a smile, but was not unfriendly. "Hello, Mr. Fargo. I'm Carl Hagar, Diplomatic Security. Sorry to keep you waiting."

"Thank you for seeing me," said Sam.

"I've been briefed on what happened," Hagar said. "And I'm very sorry and very concerned. We haven't experienced this kind of thing in Moscow since the Cold War. The idea that an American citizen could be kidnapped from Sheremetyevo Airport is unprecedented. There have been terrorist attacks there, and times when people coming in at the airport have been arrested at customs, but never kidnappings."

"I don't think this was the Russian government. It's more likely to be some underworld group that's learned of our attempts to find a series of treasures from the fifth century."

"That's what we think too," said Hagar.

"You've been looking into my wife's disappearance already?"

"As soon as we heard about it. We always investigate the disappearance of any U.S. citizen from Moscow. But when we began asking questions about who you were, we ran across your years at the Defense Advanced Research Projects Agency. They make your story more credible and make you a potential military asset. Rube Hayward had flagged your record, asking to be notified if you got in trouble. I'm sure you can imagine what that means to us."

"I'm sure I can't," said Sam. "I've known Rube for twenty years, but, whatever he does, he doesn't talk about it with civilians."

"Let's just say you have friends in high places. We've been in touch with our contacts in Russian law enforcement, letting them know we're extremely interested and won't go away if they ignore this. I'm convinced they've given us what they know so far." He placed a file on the table, opened it, and pushed five photographs across to Sam.

Sam could see they were fuzzy black-and-white screen grabs from surveillance cameras mounted in the airport.

Hagar pointed at the first one. "Here is Mrs. Fargo entering the ladies' room at the airport. Next you see the two female janitors let two other women in after her, then put out a sign that says 'Closed for Cleaning' and lock the door. Here's what happens when the door opens." The photograph showed the cleaning women pushing out a flatbed wheeled cart with two big cardboard barrels on it.

"I saw those women," said Sam.

"What did you see?"

"They came out, pushed the cart around the first corner, and then went out through an unmarked doorway."

"The Russian police don't know who these two women are. They've blown up their pictures and they don't match the photo ID of anybody who works there. They've fast-forwarded their way through about eight hours of tape, and Mrs. Fargo never comes out that door. We think they had your wife in one of those barrels."

"This is awful," said Sam. "I wasn't really worried yet when I saw them. They didn't register as out of the ordinary because I didn't know what was or wasn't ordinary."

"Of course." He brought out another photograph. It showed the women outside the big terminal building, rolling one of the barrels onto a hydraulic lift at the back of a truck operated by a man in coveralls. There was Cyrillic script on the side.

"What does that say?"

"*Len Sluzhby*. Linen Services," he said. "They got into the truck, left the other barrel and the cart, and drove off. There really is a company with trucks like that and they do supply linens for the airport. The police say this truck isn't one of theirs."

Sam said, "I have a suggestion. I think the people who did this must have a connection with a man named Arpad Bako, the owner of a pharmaceutical business in Szeged, Hungary. He has been attempting to find the treasures before we can and he's shown he'll do anything to succeed. The people who did his searching and shot at us in France worked for a man named Le Clerc, who has been buying illegal prescription drugs from Bako. Somebody here must be importing Bako's drugs to Russia or supplying him with raw materials."

Hagar said, "I'll find out and get the results to you."

"Thank you."

"There's one more thing," said Hagar.

"The ransom," Sam said.

"Right. If they took Mrs. Fargo so they can exchange her for the artifacts you found in these hoards and tombs across Europe, they'll be getting in touch with you. They might already be watching you, so they'll be aware you went to the police at the airport and probably that you're here too. They'll threaten to kill her if you have anything more to do with us. You'll have to appear to go along with their demands."

"I've considered that."

Hagar reached into his pocket and then handed Sam a cell phone. "We're giving you a new phone. At some point they'll try to separate you from your cell, so, when they do, give them the old one. We'll use this cell's GPS to keep track of your location. We'll also try to watch you in other ways, so if you don't have a phone, we don't lose you."

"Okay," Sam said. He put the new cell phone in his pocket. "I should find a hotel and wait for them to call me. We weren't planning on stopping in Russia except to change planes."

"We'll put you up at the Hilton Moscow Leningradskaya Hotel. It's a building Stalin put up near the Kremlin in 1954 and it's big, with a lot of clear space around it. While you're going there to check in, we'll see who follows. That probably won't be what pays off, but something will."

"I'm sure it will," said Sam. He got up and shook Hagar's hand. "Thank you."

"There will be cabs outside. Take the first one that pulls up. I wish we could have met under happier circumstances. Rube Hayward was right. He said you'd be coolheaded and not afraid of anything."

"I appreciate Rube's compliment, but he's wrong," he said. "These people have found what I'm most afraid of on the first try."

Sam went out the front door of the consulate and saw a line of cabs. He stepped to the curb and the first one pulled up. Sam said, "Hilton Leningradskaya Hotel?"

The driver said, *"Da, da,"* and gestured for Sam to get inside. The driver seemed a bit impatient, as though he had other appointments to occupy him.

Sam got in and the man pulled out into traffic. Sam had to keep himself from looking behind him out the rear window to try to spot the tail the kidnappers would have on him and the American surveillance team trying to identify the tail. He had been awake all night and all of the following day. Now the exhaustion was beginning to slow his brain and made it hard for him to focus on the challenges he needed to see coming.

As he rode through the city streets, the evening sunshine seared his eyes and reminded him that Moscow was much farther north than the major cities of the United States and the sun would stay out longer. He might be able to use the time.

The driver pulled up in front of the tall-towered hotel. "Six hundred rubles." Sam knew that was about twenty dollars. He shuffled through the rubles he'd bought at the airport and handed him seven hundred as he took the carry-on luggage he and Remi had brought and got out. The cabdriver accepted his money and handed him a small wrapped package.

"What's this?"

"Take it," the driver said.

Sam accepted it, then turned to look behind them up the road. If any car was following, he couldn't spot it, and he knew that knowing wouldn't help anyway. He heard the cabdriver hit the accelerator and he turned again to get the license number. He stared at the rear plate, but it was caked with dirt. After a second, he realized the dirt was probably spray paint or a mixture of rubber cement and dust applied an hour ago.

He checked in at the hotel and went up to his room and sat on the bed. He set the package on the bed beside him and looked at it. He dialed his home number in La Jolla.

"Hello, Sam," said Selma. "Any word yet?"

"I think I'm about to get word. I'm going to leave this cell on while I open the package I just got. I'd appreciate it if you could listen to what happens, but don't speak until I tell you it's clear."

"All right."

Sam unwrapped the paper around the box, looking closely around the sides for anything that might be a wire attached to an initiator. As he raised the top, he scrutinized it from the side, but there wasn't anything that didn't belong. "It's a cardboard box, plain, like a candy box. There are no trip wires, no explosives. The cabdriver gave it to me a few minutes ago. There is a cell phone. There is also a picture of Remi holding a Russian newspaper. The numbers for the date indicate it's today. She's wearing the same clothes as last night and she seems unharmed. There's nothing else."

The cell phone in the box rang. Sam picked it up and said, "Hello."

"Hello, Mr. Fargo. Since you received this telephone, then you also must have the picture and know we have your wife. She's very beautiful, and seems to be very intelligent too. You must miss her terribly."

"What is it that *you* want terribly?"

"Right to the point. All right. You have recovered three hidden portions of the loot that Attila the Hun stole from European cities when he conquered them in the fifth century. You have one found in Italy near Mantua, one from Châlons-en-Champagne, France, and one from the shore of the Danube in Hungary."

"I don't—"

"Don't interrupt and don't argue. I know that you have taken them, and now you will give them to me. I want those finds."

"All three have been turned over to the national archives of those countries," Sam said. "There are treaties and laws that prevent people from—"

"I told you not to argue with me. Do I sound to you like someone who cares about treaties between foreign politicians? Getting the ransom is your problem. As soon as you have the three hoards in your possession, call me by pressing the programmed number on your new phone that says Remi."

"What happens if I can't get the three treasures?"

"Why make yourself afraid and unhappy? I hope I don't need to think of something terrible to do. I don't want to promise you some horrible last videotape of your wife if you fail. Succeed. I would rather have you confident and strong, thinking only about collecting my gold and delivering it."

"Even if I can do this, it will take some time."

"Time is not weighing on me. If you don't want her back for a week, take a week. A month? Take a month. Take six months."

"Where can I—" and Sam realized that he had prolonged the conversation as long as he cold. The kidnapper had hung up. He turned off the new cell phone, took it to the bathroom and wrapped it in a towel, closed the door, and went back to his own telephone. "Selma?"

"I'm here," she said. "I recorded that. But I didn't learn anything except that he's Russian, speaks English well, and isn't afraid."

Sam said, "How about you, Consulate? Do you have anything?"

The voice was calm, quiet, and American-accented—not Hagar, but someone who was a lot like him. "We have determined that a Russian trading partner of Arpad Bako is a man named Sergei Poliakoff. The Russian police are putting together a file for us."

"Where does he live?"

"Nizhny Novgorod. He has an import-export business, and an estate west of the city. The Russians haven't tipped us on what they know ahead of their report, but the officer who passed me the information implied that he's a pretty unsavory character. He has people in a lot of places, possibly even the U.S."

"Thanks. I'll have to get started on this right away. I'm going to leave both cell phones in my room. If you can, please get somebody to move the kidnapper's phone around a bit—drive it around, ship it to friends in Italy or France. He'll be tracking the GPS to find out where I am."

"But where will you be? You can't go off alone in this country. You don't even speak the language. You can't operate without the Russian police and that means dealing through us. I want you to promise me that you won't try to do anything like that." The man, whose name was Owens, stopped talking and listened. There was nobody on the line.

He switched to an internal line. "We're about to lose track of

Fargo. He's left the hotel. He'll probably turn up near Nizhny Novgorod in a week or two. He left our cell phone and the kidnapper's cell in his room. Send somebody to pick up both. Then send the kidnapper's phone on a vacation to Rome, Paris, and Budapest. It'll keep the poor guy's wife alive for a while."

23

SAM IS COMING. SAM WILL COME FOR ME NO MATTER what. He's coming for me already. He will have found something to trace.

Remi lay in bed even though she suspected it was late morning. She had read somewhere that experimenters living in caves without sunlight or clocks would gradually lengthen their sleep cycles to a twenty-six hour day. She heard the quiet knock of the girl who would be bringing her breakfast. She was sensitive to Remi's feelings. She knocked even though Remi was locked in and she had the key.

The girl's name was Sasha—a boy's name, usually, but maybe it was a nickname, or even a name that she'd assumed because she worked for a criminal and didn't want to be identified. She was about eighteen, slim and blond, with pale green eyes. She had come in about five times now. Each time she entered, Remi would make sure to talk to her.

Remi said, "Good morning, Sasha. What a nice breakfast you've brought me. Thank you very much."

Sasha put the food down on the small table and pulled out the chair for Remi as she always did. The girl never let on during the first few visits that she spoke English, but Remi had tested her. Remi had rattled on in English each visit as though the two were friends, and had planted ideas.

Once she had said she missed being outside and seeing the sun, and, most of all, she missed flowers like the ones that she had seen growing on the estate when she was brought here. The next visit Sasha put a bud vase on her tray with a small yellow rose in it. Remi had expressed great gratitude, and she repeated her thanks just as enthusiastically the next time a flower appeared. Remi liked the strong-brewed Russian tea Sasha brought in a glass with sugar in it. But the second time, she'd decided to sacrifice it. She had said, "It's too strong for me. Would you like it?" and with a reassuring expression gave the tea to Sasha. Remi said that what she liked best was coffee sweetened with a little honey. The next day, Sasha brought the strong tea as usual and kept it as her own, but she also brought coffee and honey. Sasha sat on the bed with her tea and stayed with Remi while she ate.

Each breakfast included coffee and tea, each lunch had a flower. When Remi talked, she would ask Sasha questions about the world outside. When there was a particularly beautiful purple-and-white tulip, Remi asked where it grew, and Sasha used cups, napkin, plates, and silverware to make a little map of the estate. As she placed the pieces she called them "house . . . garden . . . road . . . stables . . . pasture . . . garage" in English.

With every visit, Remi kept trying to solidify the friendship and learn whatever she could about the house, the grounds, and its occupants. Sasha didn't volunteer much information. Instead she listened to Remi, took a minute or two to ask herself whether the information could be dangerous, and then invariably devised some way to answer without saying anything that might get her in trouble.

Four days—twelve meals—passed this way. In the end, Remi knew—partly from observation the morning she'd arrived and partly from Sasha—the approximate layout of the house and grounds. She knew that there were twenty men on the estate who were not usually there and that they made Sasha's work much harder since they required much more cooking, cleaning, laundry, and dishwashing. And they were the sort of men who gave Sasha the creeps.

What Sasha didn't know was that Remi had slipped a fork up her sleeve the second day. Sasha would never have suspected that Remi had used a hole drilled in the steel bed frame to bend all the tines on the fork but one, that she had a husband who had taught her to pick a lock, and that she had broken one tine all the way off to use as a tension wrench.

During her sixth day of captivity, Remi unscrewed a small metal strut that strengthened the corner of the bathroom cabinet and tested its utility tapping on the pipes to make noise. That way, after using it, she could leave it where it belonged and never have it found if the room was searched.

She further endeared herself to Sasha by dividing her first dessert evenly and sharing it, all the while talking about what city they were near and which direction was Moscow in. When she was sure the house had gotten quiet for the night, she used her tine pick and tension wrench to line up the pins on the door lock's tumbler and open it. She practiced again and again until she could do it easily and quickly. It occurred to her while she did that Sam would be amazed at how good she was at picking locks now that it mattered.

She slipped out and spent about five minutes exploring the quiet, dark hallway to find the back stairwell she had climbed to get here, looked out two different windows at the large estate and the big black river beyond, and found the room at the top of the stairway where she could hear two guards snoring. Then she had the feeling that she had ventured as much as she dared and went back to her room, relocked the door by poking the pins out of line, and slept.

On the seventh day she practiced the Morse code that Sam had insisted she learn for this kind of occasion despite her protests that no military organizations still taught it. She abbreviated her message to "Remi 4th floor" and began to tap it on the pipe that fed her sink. The taps had to be soft and at a low volume and continued for long periods so the regular occupants of the house got used to them and didn't notice anymore. She and Sasha had a conversation in English about the mild, clear weather outside and the pretty view of the Volga from Sasha's room. When the house was dark again, Remi picked the lock of her room and went out again into the dark hallway.

Remi had a light and agile fencer's body, and her husband had taught her a few tricks about walking in a dark building. One was that boards tended to creak more near the center of a hall and that the way to walk silently was to move ahead a bit and then stop at the first creak and wait so that any listener would not associate it with the next creak that came, classifying the two as unrelated. Most noises made in this way would be thought of as having no human cause—just an old house standing up to a sudden wind or maybe a branch moving against the outer wall of the house.

Each day while Remi did her exercises to stay strong and limber, she reviewed all the tasks she had performed. She made certain that she had not neglected any of the preparations that Sam had made her practice in advance. During the long, happy times at the house on the Pacific at La Jolla, it had been hard to take all of the pieces of this drill seriously. Sam had kidded and cajoled her into learning the dull parts, but as she thought about them now, ticking them off in her mind, she realized that they had been helping her to stave off the terror that had been waiting to paralyze her. The drill had given her purpose and kept her occupied constructively from the very beginning of her captivity. Everything she did reminded her that she must not give up hope, but it also reminded her of Sam and made the tears threaten to come if she allowed them. *Sam is coming, getting closer. I've got to be ready.*

24

MOSCOW

MOVING THROUGH MOSCOW ALONE ON FOOT AT EIGHT
in the evening, Sam was unidentifiable, a shadow, indistinguishable
from the hundreds of thousands of Russians ending their work-
day and going home. Some were happy to go, and spoke to one
another and laughed boisterously. Maybe a few had spent some
time having a drink together. Others were just like Sam—tired,
solitary men, getting onto buses that headed out into the distant
suburbs where ordinary people lived. Sam waited until a line of
them had boarded the bus and he'd seen how much they paid, and
paid the same.

He had left the two cell phones in his hotel for the CIA, so he
hoped the kidnappers were following the progress of their cell into
and around Europe. Sam went east for as far as the bus went and
then followed a few of the passengers at a distance. They entered

high-rise apartment buildings collected together like the projects in big American cities.

The summer night was warm, so Sam managed to find a place to sleep outdoors at a construction site. A foundation had been dug, and there was a high pile of dirt with a tarp tied over it with several lines attached to grommets. Sam assumed that was to keep down the dust or prevent rain from turning the topsoil into a pyramid of mud. He climbed halfway up on the tarp so he wouldn't be seen from the street and lay down. He hadn't slept in two days and fell asleep immediately and woke only when the sun was high enough to shine on his face.

He got up and dusted himself off. As he was looking down at his clothes to be sure he had gotten them clean, he realized they were all wrong. He had bought them in Germany and Hungary and they didn't quite look like the ones the men had been wearing on the bus the night before.

Sam climbed down and walked east, staying with streets that looked as though they might be commercial zones. As he walked, the army of ordinary people heading to work appeared and he tried to stay among them. Late in the morning he found a block-long street market. There were numerous small shops with tables in front of them, extending out across the sidewalk. He bought a flat tweed cap with a short brim like the ones American workers wore during the Depression. He had seen just a few of these on the streets of Moscow, mainly on old men, but he needed a hat to make it harder for the people who were watching for him to see his face. He bought a wool-and-polyester sport jacket in a faux herringbone tweed, because he had seen many of these. The cut was too short and too wide for him, so it made him look broader in the shoulders and a bit more muscular. He bought a pair of pants to go with the coat that had a loose cut too. The pale blue shirt he bought was an exact match with some he'd seen on the bus. His last purchases were a pair of shoes with a wide box toe that were comfortable for walking and a bag with a shoulder strap like the ones European students use to carry books. He changed into his new clothes in a curtained dressing stall. And then, as he was walking past another shop, he saw a display of used books in a bin.

Sam leafed through the piles of books, pretending to be casually browsing but actually searching desperately for something in a language other than Russian. He picked up and even pretended to leaf through many that were set in Cyrillic before he finally saw something different, a tourist's guidebook in French. He immediately clutched it to his side and went to find the cashier.

After a few minutes of leafing through his French book, he found a map that seemed to show the area he was in. He walked away from the market, and kept walking, until he found a small urban park where he could sit on a bench and look at the maps of the Moscow area. After some study, he found that the various stations in the city had trains that went only to specific destinations. The one for Nizhny Novgorod was out of the Kursky Station, which was on the east side.

He folded down the corner of the page of his guidebook so he could easily find the map again, put the book in his shoulder bag with his extra clothes, and began to walk in the direction of the station. He walked steadily, stopping for food and drink at the sort of establishment where he could point at what he wanted and then hand someone a bill with a reasonable expectation of getting the right change.

It took him a whole day of walking to reach the right neighborhood and then he had to approach a family on the street, show them his French map, and say, *"Ou est la gare Kursky?"* He chose a family because it seemed safer for him than approaching either a woman, who might be afraid, or a man, who might be a cop. They pointed him in the right direction, with many friendly Russian words he couldn't understand.

Sam made it to the Kursky Station in the evening, but it was still quite full and busy. Trains were leaving regularly for distant cities. He found a schedule board and looked up at it for a long time. To his great relief, he saw that the words were written in the Latin alphabet as well as Cyrillic. He recognized most of the names—St. Petersburg, Odessa, Vladivostok—but he couldn't see anything that said Nizhny Novgorod. At first, he assumed that his exhaustion and his eagerness had combined to make him skip right over the name. He looked over and over, but still didn't see it. He walked along the line of counters and cages where station employees helped customers, studying their faces. Should he try one of the women because women are naturally softhearted or would they be ready to feel irritated by his approach? The pretty ones must get asked for dates and flirted with all the time, and who knows what the others would feel?

Then he heard words in English. There was a man behind a counter who wore a uniform reminiscent of a train conductor's. He was telling a couple who looked American that their fare was nine hundred rubles. Sam turned his head to be sure he wasn't cutting in line in front of someone and then stood in front of the man.

The man looked at him, expecting him to speak.

Sam said, "Sir, I can't seem to find Nizhny Novgorod on the schedule."

"Gorky," the man said. "The city used to be called Gorky and the railway never changed it. All Russians know that, so we don't have any trouble. Just people from other countries."

"Oh, thank you very much," said Sam. He was genuinely relieved. He had imagined another day walking to some other distant station.

"I'll help you. When would you like to go?"

"As soon as possible."

"Very good. There is a train at 2204. Would you like a ticket?"

"Yes, please."

"It will be nine hundred rubles. One hundred eleven U.S. dollars and fifty cents for a one-way second-class ticket or fifty-five dollars for a third-class ticket."

"And first-class?"

"I'm sorry, but those seats are all reserved already. It's four hundred sixty-seven miles and takes eight hours and ten minutes, so people reserve the best seats ahead of time."

"Second-class, then." He added, "Two tickets." *Never miss a chance to mislead,* he thought. *Couples are less suspicious than lone men.*

"Very good, sir."

Sam counted out two hundred forty dollars. "Thank you so much."

The man handed him his change in rubles. "And can I see your passports?"

Sam had his passport in his coat, but it occurred to him that he didn't want his name on the record, either for the Russian police, who would come and get him, or Poliakoff's men, who would kill him. He patted his pockets, a look of horror on his face. "Oh, no. My wife has our passports." He turned and craned his neck, searching for the imaginary woman. He also ascertained that the line behind him had grown to about fifteen people, many of whom were looking anxious.

"Never mind," the man said. "Here." He handed him two tickets. "If anyone asks on the train, just show him your passports then."

"Thank you again." Sam rushed off.

Sam had only twenty minutes to wait and so he went to the platforms and spotted a sign in Latin letters that spelled Gorky. He stood eagerly waiting for the chance to get on the train. He saw pairs of policemen walking up and down the platforms, occasionally stopping people to talk, sometimes even asking to see a ticket. Sam reminded himself that this was perfectly normal behavior. When he had ridden the subway in Los Angeles, there would often be pairs of sheriff's deputies, in their khaki pants and shirts, stopping people with the same half-friendly authority: "Didn't forget to get your ticket, did you?" The main thing was not to look furtive or frightened.

When the doors to the train opened, he held his ticket in his hand and stepped in. He walked from car to car until he found one that said "2me" which he hoped meant second class. He found a seat beside a window toward the back of the car. Almost immediately a man about his age sat next to him. There was alcohol on the man's breath, and he was broad and took up a bit more than his seat. Sam contemplated moving but was reluctant to draw attention to himself, and one by one the seats all filled up. Sam waited for a few minutes until the train doors closed and the people around him began to get settled. He leaned his head against the window for a time, looking out as the train moved slowly through the station, past the platforms, and then the open train yard, with its dozens of parallel tracks, under the evening sky. There was a disorienting feeling as a train clattered into the station on the track just to his left, giving him the unsettling impression that his train was suddenly traveling at high speed.

His train did gain speed from then on, heading out toward the farthest eastern reaches of the city. He hoped the man beside him was not going to try to chat the time away. If he did, Sam planned to smile stupidly, produce his American passport, and say he just spoke English. But there was no talk. The man folded his arms, leaned back in his seat, and fell asleep. After a few minutes, his deep breathing became a snore when he inhaled and a hiss when he exhaled. Sam stared out the window for an hour until the gray buildings floating by turned darker and were farther apart and then disappeared into the night.

Sam had walked most of the day, had many tense moments that he'd had to get through, and had finally gotten into a secure, comfortable place, a train that was taking him toward Remi. The repetitive sound of the wheels on the tracks, the gentle rocking of the car, even the soft sound of two women talking quietly, were reassuring. After a time, he succumbed to sleep.

He slept for seven hours and woke to a still-dark car full of sleeping people. He remembered seeing on the schedule that the train would arrive in Gorky at five forty-five. He checked his watch and saw that it was five. Somewhere far ahead of the train, the sky had become darker than night in preparation for the first light of dawn. He couldn't see the sun yet, just sense its energy. He had time to think about his next move. He realized he had been desperate and foolish to climb aboard a train that would take him unerringly to the train station in his enemy's hometown. How could Poliakoff not have photographs of Sam to hand out to whatever shadowy figures he could hire to watch for Sam and warn Poliakoff when Sam got off the train?

Sam was sitting passively, letting the train carry him straight into a place where his enemies were watching and waiting for him. From the moment he bought his ticket, he had been like a steer walking down one chute to the next on his way into the slaughterhouse.

Each turn he made closed off another alternate route and brought him closer to the end. He could see the open fields beside the train now and the telephone poles slipping past. The fields of alfalfa looked inviting, but he could tell the train was going too fast to permit him to jump. Maybe if there were a turn, or a hill, the train would slow down, but this area was as flat as the American Plains. There was no reason for a train to do anything but barrel into the bright morning. And then he felt the train slowing down.

He held his hand over his ticket inside his pocket and sat on the edge of his seat, looking out to see what was happening. People around him seemed to be waking up, poking or shaking one another, whispering. Then there was a definite slowing, and a recorded voice announcing a destination. People took that as a signal to stand and get their belongings off overhead racks or put on their jackets against the morning chill.

The train pulled into a station that was simply a pair of outdoor platforms, one on either side of the tracks, and a plain-looking brick building. He had no idea what the sign said. The train stopped, the doors opened, and people struggled with heavy luggage and children and their own stiff-leggedness from sitting eight hours. They got out the open door and started to walk.

Sam had instinctively tried to stick with crowds, but this wasn't a crowd. A trickle of people who didn't look much like him crossed a platform to a rural road that looked empty. He thought, *It's time. It has to be now.* He got up and stepped out the door with his schoolboy bag and his cap and began to walk. He heard the doors close behind him, then a muffled Russian announcement from inside the train, and the big diesel engine began to pull it away. He kept going. He looked at his watch. It was 5:08. If the train was on time, it was thirty-seven minutes from Nizhny Novgorod.

He knew he must be subjecting himself to a very long walk,

but he also knew that he had probably just saved his own life. He thought about his route. The train had gone pretty much due east for hours, and there was no reason to imagine it wasn't designed to go due east the rest of the way. He could see the sun rising at the eastern end of the road, so he headed toward it. He pushed his hat's brim down to protect his eyes and stared ten feet ahead at the ground alongside the road. He was going to get to Remi.

He knew he wasn't getting there quickly, but he decided it had to be that way. He didn't want to draw attention to himself, to be the one who was different. When he got there, he wanted to be like a drop of water in a rainstorm. He was just another Russian worker making his way.

25

IT WAS LATE THE FOLLOWING NIGHT WHEN SAM SAW THE big farm that a woman on the road had pointed out. There were large fields surrounded by fences, but there didn't seem to be anything growing except grass. He could see the big old manor house about half a mile back from the road and a number of white buildings beyond that he supposed must be barns and stables. There were no lights on that he could see. He could tell there was a stream that ran from somewhere in the back part of the farm down under the road and off in the direction of the Volga River. Most of the field was just short grassy vegetation that he couldn't identify in the night, but along the stream were tall reeds, and its course was marked by a long line of bushes and trees that grew there because of the abundant water.

He went down to the streambed and stepped along it toward the big mansion. He knew the vegetation would make his silhouette difficult to pick out, and the lower elevation of the stream would hide about half his body from the house. He also guessed that any guards stationed there would expect trouble to come from the road, not the little stream.

Sam walked patiently, listening and watching for trouble. Once, he froze, and felt his heart pounding, because he'd heard a noise up ahead, but then he realized it was just the sound of a bullfrog jumping off a rock into the water somewhere upstream. He listened to the night birds calling, trying to detect any note of alarm that men were approaching.

And then he reached a low arched wooden bridge that led from the fenced field to the lawn of the mansion. He climbed up the bank and sat beside the bridge to hide himself as he studied the building. There were four stories and a French mansard roof, but he still saw no sign of lights in the front. He searched for sentries. As he did, a pair of men appeared far to his right, walking toward the house from an area that looked to him like a formal flower garden. They passed the house, and he could see that both carried machine pistols on slings. They also carried small, powerful LED flashlights, and one of them took his out and ran its bright beam along the shrubs in front of the house as they walked. He shone the light up the side of the house to the second floor, and Sam noticed that there was a window open there at what must be the end of a corridor.

The two men turned the corner and walked on. Sam waited only a couple of seconds to be sure they were gone and then trotted up the lawn to the end of the mansion they had just passed. He tested the drainpipe running downward near the open window to see if its supports would hold a man's weight. Then he began to climb. He reached the second floor, put his hand on the window frame, and pulled himself in over the sill. He crouched near the window and listened. He didn't hear the sound of footsteps.

He thought he heard something else in the total silence, a faint tapping of metal on metal. Beside him was an open door. He moved toward it and saw it was a bedroom. He moved in farther to the next door, which was a bathroom. He could hear the tapping clearly now, and, after a moment, he knew exactly what it was.

Remi 4th floor.

.-. . --.. ....--.... ..-. .-.. --- --- .-.

Remi 4th floor.

.-. . --.. ....--.... ..-. .-.. --- --- .-.

She used the metal strut she had taken from the cabinet to rap on the pipe for what she imagined must be the thousandth time. Each night, when the house was silent and she was sure the others were asleep, she would begin signaling again. First, she would pick the lock on the bedroom door, leaving the separated fork tine in it so she could lock it by raking the pins aside on the tumbler and hiding the tine. She would open the door, listen carefully, and then make her way along the corridor to a window so she knew for sure it was night and all were asleep. Then she would go back and signal.

She always left the door closed but unlocked so she would be ready for Sam. It would be very difficult for him to find her, but she knew he would. He was a brilliant man, and he loved her as much as he loved breathing. He had once promised her that if they were ever separated this way, he would simply keep coming for her until he had her. Nothing would stop him while he was alive. She had no idea when he would arrive at this remote Russian manor house, but she knew he was on his way.

Most nights, she kept up the signaling on the pipes until she judged it must be around five a.m. and nearly light outside. Then she would look down the hall to confirm it was predawn, close and lock her door, and sleep. She had become nocturnal in the past week, sleeping during the long periods between meals except while she was exercising, bathing, or interrogating Sasha about the world outside.

And then he came. Remi was tapping on the pipe as usual when she became aware that something had changed. She had been in this small space so long that adding another human being changed everything—air, sounds, a new vibration on the floor as he walked in the door.

Remi sprang up instantly, hurried to Sam and threw her arms around him. She held him as tightly as she could for a full ten seconds, tears welling in her eyes. She recognized the familiar contour of his shoulders under the bulky jacket. Then she looked up at him and whispered, "What took you so long—enjoying being single?"

"No. You just forgot to tell me you were leaving."

"Oh. Sorry."

"Ready to get out of here?"

"Almost," she whispered. She sat on the bed and put on her shoes. "We've got to go that way and down the back stairs to the second floor, which will get us past the family's floor and the bodyguards. Then we use the main staircase to reach the first floor, so we miss the kitchen, where the night guards go for their breaks."

"You know that?"

"I made a friend—a girl who works in the kitchen. How did you get into the house?"

"I saw a second-floor window that had been left opened. It turned out to be a hallway. I heard your signal, and from there I went up the back stairs."

"Dumb luck. That was about the only way that was clear." She stood. "I'm ready." She opened the door and walked out, waited for Sam, and locked it behind them.

She led him down the spiraling stairs for two stories, then silently and carefully moved up the hallway to the broad main staircase. She stopped for a moment to listen for the two guards in their room snoring, then moved onto the stairs. The steps were carpeted, so their footsteps were muffled. They descended to the ground floor, where there was a large foyer with a marble floor with a round escutcheon mosaic at the center. As they stepped onto its surface, three men seemed to materialize from a shadowy doorway somewhere beside the stairs.

One man pulled back the charging lever on his Škorpion machine pistol, but the man beside him grasped his shoulder and said something in Russian that made him lower the weapon. Sam said to Remi, "They need us alive, to turn over the treasure."

"Do you promise?"

The three rushed toward Sam and Remi, who separated and dodged them. Sam faked to the side and redirected the first man's momentum into the staircase railing, then gave the second a glancing punch along the side of the head as he went by.

Remi backed up to the large fireplace that dominated the foyer. As the third man came toward her, she snatched up the poker. He took a tentative step toward her, but she didn't budge. "You just came after me because I'm the only girl."

He smiled.

"Bad choice." Remi performed a fencing thrust with the fireplace poker, which extended it at least a foot farther than the man had anticipated and poked him hard in the stomach. As he bent over to grasp his stomach, Remi swung the poker overhand and hit him on the head. He straightened and charged for her, knowing that in close quarters he could overpower her. She swung as she stepped to the side, bashed the back of his head as he went by, and put him out, unmoving, on the floor.

She saw the other two had recovered and were beginning to rush Sam and so she thrust the poker between the ankles of the nearest man. As he tripped, she withdrew the poker and brought it across his head as he fell. The third man, the one who had the Škorpion machine pistol on a sling, started to raise it toward her, and Sam delivered a kick to the side of his knee. The sudden pain brought the man down, and Sam was on him to wrest the gun away.

The gun went off, firing an unaimed burst into the floor, the far wall, and the staircase. Then it was empty, and Sam delivered a punch to the face that bounced the man's head off the floor. He took the gun and pulled the spare magazine out of the leather case attached to the sling, ejected the spent one and inserted the spare.

Remi was already halfway across the foyer to the dining room. They both could hear the thunderous sound of many booted feet coming down the stairs from the second and third floors.

Sam caught up with her, and they dashed through the huge formal dining room, with its thirty-foot table, and then ran into the kitchen. Sam whispered, "Do you know where we're going?"

"We need to get out, but we can't go outside yet or they'll get a clear shot at us."

"We'll have to try to make a splash from here." Sam bolted the door to the dining room, ran to the other side of the kitchen and bolted the door to the back stairway, then locked the door that led outside. They could hear running feet outside as men got into position.

Sam went to the big restaurant-sized gas stove and turned on the burners. There was no sound except the electric starters clicking repeatedly as they produced a spark. "They turned off the gas," he said. "Electricity's still on because they expect to catch us in the lights."

Sam flung open the pantry door, turned on the light, and looked inside. There was a barrel about five feet deep and three feet in diameter. He took off the top. "Flour," he said. He tilted it and rolled it to the middle of the floor.

"What are you doing?" asked Remi.

"I need two ounces of flour per cubic yard of air," he said. "Help me." He pushed over the flour barrel, lifted flour with both arms, and tossed it into the air. Remi did the same. He ran to the far side of the kitchen, where there was a big fan on a five-foot stand. He turned it on and aimed it at the big pile of spilled flour. In a couple of seconds, it was blowing it into the air, filling it with the fine white powder, turning the air in the kitchen into a cloud. "Get in the pantry," he said, then picked two pie pans off the counter, knelt on the floor, and tossed panfuls of flour into the air as fast as he could.

He looked around him, seemed to judge that things were going the way he wanted, and ran to the pantry to join Remi. He shut the door, flopped down beside her with the light still on, pushed some dish towels under the door, and put his arm over her. She said, "A flour bomb, Sam?"

"Almost anything explodes if you treat it right," he said. "Once there's enough flour in the air, the electric stove starters should ignite it. Close your eyes, cover your ears, and open your mouth. Do not raise your head."

They lay still. Then there was a terrible moment when the light in the pantry went dark. There was no longer a sound of fans or the clicking of the electric starters on the stove. "Well, that's that," he said.

"That's what?"

"They turned off the main circuit breaker. No igniter."

In a single avalanche of sound, the doors on both sides of the kitchen banged, assaulted by men using heavy objects as battering rams. They heard many footsteps outside, men dashing toward the back of the house. Sam used the charging lever to load the first round into the chamber of the Škorpion he had taken from the guard. He reached up to turn the knob of the pantry door and opened it a crack. The fans had stopped and the white flour was suspended in the perfectly still air, so thick it was difficult to see across the room, difficult to breathe. In an instant, Sam foresaw what was about to happen. He yanked the door shut, held Remi down and kept his body over hers. "Stay down."

A kitchen window shattered onto the floor, and a machine pistol began to spray bullets and sparks of burning powder into the room—*Bwaah!*—and those sparks were enough.

The flour suspended in the air exploded in a huge, fiery blast. It blew the kitchen doors outward, one into the dining room and the other into the back stairway, tearing the wood from its hinges and knocking the six or seven men senseless who had been trying to batter the doors in. The men at the rear of the kitchen fared worse because in the instant that the explosion blew the glass out of the windows, much of the wall blew out too, and was burning. The parts of the kitchen that still stood were burning too.

Sam pushed off the floor, lifting the pantry door off his back. Remi struggled to sit up. They were both white as ghosts, every inch of them covered with flour. He looked out at the damage. "Can you run?"

"Like a scared rabbit."

They dashed from the pantry, ran for the hole that had been the back wall, and then they were out into the night. The fire was already growing inside the mansion, and as they ran they could hear battery-operated smoke alarms going off all over it in a growing chorus. They sprinted across the garden behind it, running for the darkness.

Remi grabbed Sam's hand. "The stable is over there," she said as she veered toward a long, low building. Sam ran harder.

Behind them there were injured men being dragged out of the smoke-filled building into the air, many of them coughing and many battered and cut by flying doors and windows.

Remi and Sam slipped into the stable, where they could see a row of ten stalls with horses in them. The big noise had startled the animals, so they tossed their heads and looked at the two intruders with big rolling, frightened eyes. Far down the row, there was a horse kicking the gate of his stall, making a sound like gunshots.

Remi walked along the stalls, talking to the horses. "Hello, boy. What a big, smart boy you are. And handsome too." She reached up and patted each horse, murmuring sweet words to all of them. In a short time they seemed to be calmer, but outside the disturbing human noises continued—shouts, running feet, smoke alarms.

Sam held the Škorpion in his hand as he watched through the partially open door. "They're not turning on the power."

"Would you?"

"Probably not. The dark should help us get out the back of this building and into the fields."

"What would help more is if you'll saddle your own horse."

"Horse?"

"We can't outrun them, we don't have a car, and can't get to one without getting shot. A horse can run across country where there are no roads. Sasha says the railroad tracks are that way and they lead to a station." She swung an English saddle over the horse and cinched the strap. "Be good, big guy. Be calm."

"I'll do my best," said Sam.

"I wasn't talking to you, but be calm anyway."

Sam went to the wall of the stable where the tack hung, selected a saddle, blanket, bit, and bridle. He approached a horse and it reared and kicked the wall.

"Over here," Remi said. "I've got a good feeling about this one."

Sam went to the other stall and said, "All right, you big, beautiful monster. You and I are going to be best buddies." He saddled the horse and put on the bridle. "Now we're going to run away from about a thousand Russian guys before they kill your nice new friends."

Sam and Remi led the two horses to the far end of the stable, away from the house, the fire, and the commotion. Remi led her horse outside, mounted him, and waited. Sam, a far less experienced rider, hoisted himself up into the saddle, and his horse spun around. He needed to hold the reins with both hands to control the horse, so he tossed the gun aside. "Hold on, buddy. I'm your friend, remember?" The horse seemed to decide then he would be willing to go away from the house and set off at a canter.

They were in a large pasture where the horses no doubt were allowed to run during the day, so the horse's newfound calm was probably familiarity. Sam patted the horse and talked to him. In the next paddock, Sam could see barriers for steeplechase jumping and he felt a twinge of anticipation that things were not about to get better for him. Apparently these were jumping horses, and as a child Remi had been an avid rider. The only one in the paddock who had no idea what he was doing was Sam.

Sam again heard voices shouting, but this time it sounded as though they were near the riding area. Several times Sam heard the crack as a bullet passed nearby and then the rattle of machine-gun fire. He saw Remi's horse speed up, galloping toward the fence at the end of the field.

Remi's horse soared over the white rails. Sam spent a second noticing that the whiteness of the fence, reflecting some of the light
from the fire, made everything beyond it look black. He couldn't
make out Remi and her horse very well. Sam's horse followed with
him astride it, willing the horse to believe, against all reason, that
Sam was confident and experienced. To his amazement, the horse
ran up to the fence and leapt into the air. As Sam became airborne,
he heard Remi yell, "Lean forward!" so he did, and then the horse
landed, front hooves first and then the back, and Sam managed to
hold on.

The horses ran on, not as fast as they had at first but still about
as fast as Sam could tolerate. The field looked to him like an endless sea of blackness. The horses ran for two miles or so without
meeting an obstacle. In the distance, far to their right, Sam and
Remi could see lights on a roadway. It was hard to tell whether the
occasional headlights had anything to do with them, but the road
never got any closer and the lights never turned toward them or
stopped. Remi and Sam slowed down, and then they dismounted
and walked the horses in the darkness for a while to let them rest
and cool down. When Remi felt the horses were ready, she mounted
her horse and began to ride forward, slowly picking up speed again.
Sam mounted and followed.

S ERGEI P OLIAKOFF walked outside the burning manor house,
keeping a distance of thirty feet from the flames that were licking
up its sides and flickering along the peak of its roof. The back of
the house seemed to have been kicked outward by the explosion.
What there had been to explode, he had no idea. Since the fire had
begun, it had set off a couple of caches of ammunition, but they
had been quick, rapid-fire volleys, like strings of firecrackers, not

big explosions. Maybe the gas had not been turned off completely. He would probably never know.

The explosion was an outrage, an insult so egregious that he hadn't quite found a way to react to it. His handpicked, highly trained, well-paid squad of bodyguards and operators had failed utterly against one man on foreign soil, arriving on foot, to take back his wife.

The word *wife* set off a new set of concerns. His wife, Irena, and his children had been in Moscow, visiting her parents, and he felt relieved knowing that. But in a few days she would be coming home. And this—this ugly, horribly damaged building—was home.

His stupid men had formed into squads now and had begun fighting the fire with garden hoses. He watched them imitating well-trained troops, and felt affronted by their tardy and useless discipline and their lack of professionalism.

Next, faintly at first, and then louder and louder, he heard the wails of sirens. His men looked at one another, grinning at the realization that help was coming, and kept spraying water. Poliakoff ran across the yard and clutched the arm of Kotzov, the head of his bodyguards. "Hear those sirens?"

"Yes. They'll have these fires out in a few minutes."

"No, you donkey. Don't you remember what's stored in the basement? Get your men to stop spraying water. Get them to soak what's left of the ground floor with gasoline. Block the road from the highway to delay the fire trucks. We've got to give the house time to burn before the firemen and police get a look at those drugs."

Poliakoff stood in isolation as his men stopped fighting the fire and ran to siphon gasoline from the cars and trucks to add to it. This too was part of the outrage. These Fargo people had forced him to burn down his own house. What an indignity. He should have killed the wife as soon as he'd seen her.

* * *

MILES AWAY on the steppe, Sam and Remi saw train tracks across the road from them, the rails gleaming in the moonlight. "Sasha was right," Remi said. "Here are the tracks."

"Yes," said Sam. "But which way is the station?"

"Both ways, silly. That's how railways work."

"I meant the nearest station. But I guess it doesn't matter. Nizhny Novgorod is that way, so we've got to go the other way."

As they started to lead the horses across the road, they saw the first headlights they'd seen in hours. The car originally appeared far away and then came closer and closer. They could tell immediately it was like no car they'd ever seen. It had three headlights— the usual pair, and then another one right between the two on the nose of the car. As the car came around the bend and pulled to the side to pass, the center headlight moved, pointing in the direction it was going.

The car slowed and stopped in front of Sam and Remi. It was a dark bronze color, long and low, with a body that tapered and narrowed at the back, streamlined like a fantasy spaceship. It was brand-new-looking, but somehow the eye knew it was antique. It was a futuristic design from the past.

At the wheel of the car was a man who had white hair and a neatly trimmed white beard. He was wearing a colorful Hawaiian shirt that was illuminated by the light from the dashboard in the dark Russian night. He got out of the car and walked up to Sam and Remi. They could see he was very tall and straight. "Can we help you?" he asked quietly in Russian.

"We're Americans," Sam replied hesitantly in English.

"If you don't mind my saying so, you look as though you could use a hand," the driver answered in English. Sam and Remi were reminded that their clothes and faces were covered with flour and soot and dust, stuck to them with sweat.

The passenger door opened and a tall, beautiful woman with hair that was a platinum blond as light as her companion's hair stepped out of the car. "What gorgeous horses," she said. "Where did you get them?"

"We stole them," said Remi. "We're running away from a Russian gangster and his men. They kidnapped me."

"You poor things," she said. "We'll get you two out of here. But we'll need to do something about the horses first."

"Janet likes animals," the man explained. "That pasture over there is fenced, and I see water reflecting the moon. We could set them loose inside."

The man helped them remove the top two rails. They led their tired horses inside and put up the rails again. They removed the saddles and bridles, then left the gear on the fence. Sam and Remi gave the horses a pat and a hug, and then Remi whispered to them for a moment.

Sam and Remi came back to the road, and the man opened the door for them to get into the backseat. He got in front and drove off down the road.

Remi said, "What kind of car is this?"

"It's a Tucker," the man said happily.

The woman said, "He likes cars."

"Yes, I do," he said. "And we both like to travel. So when I learned this one was for sale, we decided to come pick it up ourselves. It'll make a nice addition to my collection."

"How did a 1948 Tucker get to the middle of Russia?" Sam asked.

"So, you know about them."

"I know they just had a year in production," said Sam. "I've never seen one before."

"Tucker made fifty-one of them. Up until now, there were only forty-four left. This is going to be the forty-fifth. An astuté Russian official in 1948 realized the Tucker was something special and had somebody buy one for him in the United States. I think he wanted to take it apart and copy it, but by the time the car got here he had gotten into trouble and was sent off to Siberia. The car has been in storage all these years."

"How are you getting it home?"

"By rail from here to Vladivostok, by ship to Los Angeles, and we'll drive from there," the man said. "You're welcome to ride along with us for as far as you'd like to go."

Remi said, "We'd be honored and delighted. We're headed for the eastern end of Kazakhstan."

"I know this is going to sound odd," said Sam, "but do we look familiar to you? I think we met you once before in Africa."

The man looked at them both in the rearview mirror. "Not that I recall. Lots of people think they remember me from someplace, but I think it's probably just my beard. Anybody can grow a beard."

"Just sit back and enjoy the ride," said the woman. "If you'd like a snack or something to drink, just speak up."

"Thank you very much, but I think I'll just try to doze off a little," said Remi. "Dawn is my bedtime."

As the sun came up, the 1948 Tucker drove on toward it, cruising smoothly, pushed along by its converted aircraft engine. Sam sat in the backseat, quietly marveling at the feeling of having Remi back again, leaning her head against his chest as she slept. Before too long, he would fall asleep too, but not yet. A moment like this was too good to cut short.

26

The Russian steppes

In the morning, they reached a small station east of the Volga, far enough from Nizhny Novgorod so that the stir the Tucker caused was not likely to reach the wrong ears. The tall man in the Hawaiian shirt opened the trunk in the front of the car and showed them two leather suitcases. "They won't let you get on a train like that. You'd better take some clothes to the restroom and get cleaned up and changed." He opened the suitcase monogrammed CC, and Sam chose some men's clothes. The one marked JC contained women's clothes for Remi. Mr. C. closed the suitcases and the trunk while Sam and Remi went into the station to change. The clothes were long on both of them, but they rolled the pant legs up a bit and came out looking nearly normal in time to see C.C. supervising the loading of his car.

The Tucker was loaded onto a special railroad car used for moving heavy equipment, chained down, and covered with a tarp to protect it from dust and rain, then locked inside and sealed.

The Fargos and the Cs, who had rescued them, waited a few hours in the terminal for a train called *Rossiya* No. 2, which was the Moscow-to-Vladivostok run. It would take seven days and cover 6,152 miles. Their new friends, the Cs, who seemed knowledgeable about every spot on earth but didn't mention when they'd traveled there, watched the special railway car added to the train and then helped Sam buy two berths on the first-class sleeper, called a Spliny Wagon, as far as the Russian city of Omsk.

As soon as they were on the train and moving steadily across the Russian steppes, Sam asked C.C. if he could borrow his cell phone. He went into his private sitting room, sat beside Remi, and turned on the speaker. He called the number that the man in the American consulate in Moscow had given him and said, "This is Sam Fargo."

"One moment, please."

The operator switched him immediately to another line.

"Hi, Sam. This is Hagar."

"Hello," said Sam. "Thanks for taking my call."

"Where are you?"

"I'm on the Trans-Siberian Railway with my wife, who is perfectly healthy and unharmed. I also thought you should know that the gentleman who was her host, Mr. Poliakoff, had some bad luck. There was a fire at his house, and some injured employees."

Hagar said, "I understand it burned to the ground and the police are investigating mysterious substances stored in his basement."

"Interesting. Well, thanks very much for helping me when I needed it."

"We would have liked to do more, but I guess Mr. P. wasn't as big and bad as he thought. Our mutual friend at Langley sends congratulations to you and his respects to Mrs. Fargo."

"Thanks." Sam ended the call, and then dialed the house in La Jolla.

"Sam! Is it you?"

"It is. And Remi's here with me, on a train."

"Thank God. Where are you going?"

"The next stop. Where we were headed when all this happened."

"Are you sure you want to—"

"We don't feel as though we ought to quit just because the other side got nasty. So we're still heading in the right direction. Our route may be just a bit less predictable."

"Can I send Pete and Wendy to help?"

"Just send some equipment, for the moment. Get us a hotel in Taraz, Kazakhstan, and send everything there. We'll need an industrial fiber-optic inspection borescope with rigid telescoping metal tubes. It will need a camera and a light, no more than six millimeters wide. We might need about five meters of extension. Also, a laptop and a magnetometer."

"Consider it done."

"And load onto the laptop anything you can find out about the city of Taraz or Attila's father or the archaeology of that part of the world. We're going to need a sharp learning curve if we hope to accomplish anything."

"We'll get back to work on it right away," Selma said. "When Remi disappeared, we set aside the treasure hunt."

"Thanks," said Remi. "Now I'm free, and we're both fine, so we can get back to what we were doing."

"Terrific," said Selma. "Let me give Albrecht and the others the good news, and we'll be in touch as soon as we can."

Sam returned the phone to C.C. Soon, Sam and Remi sat still, watching the steppes outside the window, the land near the train sliding past but the view in the distance unchanging. The plain was always in motion, the winds blowing across the acres of grass and rippling it like the waves of an ocean. The distances were enormous. Sam and Remi would fall asleep, and when they awoke there would be the same sights—the grassy flatlands, the sky, and what seemed to be an endless supply of rails and railroad ties making the wheels clatter beneath their car.

After a few hours, with no warning they could detect, the train would slow down and come to a small station. There would be local people on the platform, all of them gathered to sell local delicacies and staple food—fresh fruit, bread, hot tea, and various kinds of pastries.

The first time this happened, their new friends the Cs came to their sitting room. The woman said, "Let us pick some things for you. I promise you'll like all of them." The man whispered to Sam, "Stay here. Station yourself by a window and see if you recognize anybody you've seen before."

Through the curtained windows, Remi and Sam watched the transactions on the platform at the first stop. There were peasant families with their fresh-baked goods and fruit, and plenty of other dishes to choose from. The Fargos' new friends returned with a picnic for them. They did the same a few hours later at the second stop. Sam and Remi scrutinized the faces but spotted nobody who was familiar, and nobody who was making it his business to study the passengers.

After dinner, when they had spent nineteen hours on the train, C.C. came to their sitting room and held out his phone. "It's a woman named Selma." Remi took the call. "Hi, Selma," said Remi.

"Hi, Remi. Gather whatever belongings you have because you'll need to get off at Ekaterinburg."

"Any trouble?"

"No. A chance to leap ahead. Sam didn't say anything about your passport. Do you still have it?"

"Yes. He had my carry-on bag when I was grabbed. All I lost was my phone. Sam lost his too."

"They're easy to replace. I'll send each of you a new one at your next hotel. At Ekaterinburg, we have you on a plane to Astana. We want to get you there as quickly as possible."

"What's in Astana?"

"Your papers have been waiting for you there. We also want to get you out of Russia. It will be harder for Poliakoff to operate there, harder to find you, and harder for him to do anything to you if he does. He's as much an alien there as you are. Call when you're at Ekaterinburg Airport."

Sam and Remi had little to pack and they did as Selma asked. They went to the berth of their friends and told them they would be leaving at Ekaterinburg and thanked them for their help. Just before they pulled into the station, Sam said to the tall man with the white beard, "C.C., I think I should tell you that I don't believe that the next time I get in trouble a pair of good-hearted strangers will just happen to be passing by to pick me up in a rare antique car."

The man with the white beard looked at him sagely. "I think that's probably wise, given the odds."

"Are you CIA?"

The man shook his head. "I'm a man who was taking a car to Vladivostok when somebody I met at the American Embassy in Moscow called to say that two Americans might be coming along that route who could use some help."

"Just that?"

"Just that." He looked out the window. "You'd better get going.

People will be flooding the platform in a minute and you might want to slip out with them."

"We will," said Sam. "Thanks for the ride, Mr. C."

Remi popped up on tiptoe and gave the white-bearded man a kiss, and they slipped out onto the platform, moving quickly with the rest of the crowd. They found their way to a stand outside the terminal that had a sign with a picture of an airplane on it and boarded the bus that stopped there. Sam watched how much money the other people were paying the driver and did the same.

In a short time, they were at the airport. Without talking about it or making a plan, they had changed their way of traveling. They were much more watchful than they had ever been before. They went together to the counter, where they saw the names of destinations printed in both the Cyrillic and Latin alphabets, bought their tickets together, and then went toward the departure gates. If one of them went to a restroom, the other would wait just outside the door, noting each person who went in and listening for any sound of a scuffle.

Their plane for Astana, Kazakhstan left after five hours. They were both quietly but deeply relieved to get airborne toward Kazakhstan. It seemed to them to be a step away from the conspiracy of criminals who had been trying to harm them since they'd arrived in Berlin weeks before.

The city of Astana was all new and very busy. The airport had two terminals, international and domestic, so they went through the customs office, picked up their written invitation to enter the country and their visas, then made reservations on Air Astana for Almaty, the old capital in the southeast of the huge country.

When they told the airline's English-speaking representative what their ultimate destination was, they learned that getting to

Almaty was easy but that there was just one flight from there to Taraz a week. The Scat Air flight from Almaty to Zhambyl Airport in Taraz took only a couple of hours, but those hours were always five-fifty to seven-fifty p.m., on Thursday. They boarded their first flight for the six hundred five miles to Almaty and later checked into a hotel there to wait for Thursday to come.

They called Selma from the hotel to let her know where they were: the Worldhotel Saltanat Almaty.

"I'm sorry for the delay," she said. "But, so far, that's it. I'm working through a jet charter service to arrange an earlier flight, but I'm worried about attracting too much attention when you get to Taraz. Maybe we can get you in late at night."

Sam said, "We've just about decided to hire a car to drive us there. It's just another six hundred miles. That's two days."

"See who you can find," she said. "Just don't hire someone who will drive you into the wilderness and then cut your throats."

"We try not to," said Remi. "We check their knives for stains."

"We'll see what our hotel's concierge can do for us," Sam said. "If that doesn't work, Thursday always comes."

"Very stoic," said Selma. "Good luck. I'll be working on the plane. And I'll get new cell phones delivered to you at the hotel right away."

It took Sam and Remi an hour to work with the concierge at the Worldhotel Saltanat Almaty to find a driver. His name was Nurin Temirzhan, and the concierge said he was twenty-three years old and eager for the job of driving to Taraz. But like most Kazakhs, he spoke no English.

Sam said to the concierge, "Are you sure he understands what we want him to do?"

"Yes, sir. My English may not be perfect, but my Kazakh is impeccable. He will drive you to Taraz and wait for you to come back here for up to one week. If he waits longer, he will prorate your bill by one-seventh per day.",

"And the pay has been agreed to?"

"Yes, sir. Seven hundred, American, for the week." The concierge looked a little uneasy.

Sam smiled reassuringly and leaned closer to him. "Is there something that is still worrying you?" He paused. "If you will tell me, I won't blame you for it."

"Well, yes, sir. There have been several recent incidents in Taraz. Muslim fundamentalists have been shooting people, and one blew himself up. The American Peace Corps has left because of safety concerns."

"Thank you for your honesty and your help." Sam gave him a two-hundred-dollar tip and left his new cell number and Remi's in case people couldn't reach them directly for some reason.

Sam and Remi changed dollars for Kazakh tenge tenge at a bank, then went out in Almaty and shopped. An American dollar was one hundred forty-seven tenge. They found their way to Arbat Street, where the Centralniy Universalniy Magasin sold a wide range of merchandise. They bought clothes that would not strike Kazakhs as foreign or overly expensive. They took special care that Remi's were not formfitting or short-sleeved and that she had scarves to cover her hair, both to keep from offending Muslims and to disguise her if any of Poliakoff's people had come here to search for them.

They bought food in a modern supermarket in Almaty, concentrating on foods that their driver, Nurin, probably would eat too—fruits, nuts, bread, hard cheese, bottled water and tea—all things that wouldn't have to be refrigerated on a two-day trip.

The next morning, Nurin drove up to their hotel with a smile on his face and, with gestures and a constant monologue in Kazakh, got them into his car with their backpacks and their food. His car, a Toyota sedan of an odd gold color, was about ten years old. Sam listened to the engine for about ten seconds, then assured Remi that it had been maintained and would last a couple of days. While Nurin put the bags in the trunk, Sam popped the hood just in case, looked in, and reassured himself that the belts and hoses were all still all right.

Nurin drove out of the crowded city and headed west, and, to Sam and Remi's relief, he kept the car at a sensible but efficient speed, kept its wheels on the pavement and in its own lane. He paid attention to the traffic coming the other way into Almaty, which was still the largest and busiest city in the country despite the fact that it was no longer the capital.

Nurin stopped every three hours in small towns, bought gas when he could, and walked around the central market for a few minutes. He liked to keep the tank full, give his passengers a chance to use the public restrooms, and buy small dishes of food. He was black-haired and handsome, with the thin, strong body of a man who had done physical work, but his expression and manner were prematurely serious, like a man about twice his age.

When people saw Sam and Remi with Nurin, they would speak to them in Russian, but that was of no use. For the next two days Sam and Remi lived with whatever characterization Nurin might be giving them in the Kazakh language.

At one stop, Sam showed Nurin his international driver's license and his California license. Nurin was curious to look at them, but, no, he wanted to continue to do all the driving himself.

On the first night away from Almaty, Nurin stopped at a small Western-style inn, but he refused to go inside with Sam and Remi. Instead he slept in his car.

"Why do you suppose he wants to do that?" Remi asked.

"I think he's afraid somebody will steal his tires or something," Sam said.

They slept well in their room upstairs, and Nurin appeared rested and ready when they awoke the next morning and came outside. During the second day, Nurin took advantage of the flatness of the country to increase his speed. He drove hard until late afternoon, when the sun was low in the west and driving became difficult. And then they were passing larger rows of houses than they had in the little towns along the way, and soon there were streets with curbs and sidewalks. Finally there was a sign that said "Tapa3" and they knew they were in the city.

Nurin drove them up to the Zhambyl Hotel on Tole Bi Street. It was a four-story building that looked a bit like an American high school, but when they went inside they found it was very pretty and well decorated, with patterned marble floors and blue-and-gold Kazakh rugs. There was a clerk at the desk who spoke French and told them there was a pool, a restaurant, a bar, a beauty salon, and a laundry.

Sam rented a room for Nurin as well as one of their own. He asked the clerk to explain to Nurin, in Kazakh, that he was allowed to sign for his meals and any services he needed while the Fargos finished their business. He also asked if there was a secure parking place for Nurin's car.

The transaction made Nurin happy. He hugged Sam and bowed deeply to Remi, then went outside to drive his car around to the gated lot in back of the building. The clerk announced that Sam and Remi's equipment had arrived and was being moved to their room.

It was five, still early enough to be sure of three hours of light, so

Sam and Remi asked the clerk if he could direct them to the green market, or *kolkhoz*. The clerk marked it on a map of the city and the Fargos thanked him and set off on foot so they could get a glimpse of the place before darkness came. Sam wore a hat and sunglasses and Remi wore sunglasses and tied a scarf over her head. When they reached the market, they wandered among tables and bins of vegetables and fruits, baked goods and wine, pretending to evaluate the merchandise while all the time studying the people and the layout of the place.

Remi said, "Sam, do you believe this is the site of the old fort?"

"I doubt it. The ground is too low. If you build a fort, you want to use everything that gives you an advantage—altitude, steep approaches, water. I believe the archaeologists in the thirties found something here, but not a fort."

"That's what I think," Remi said. "We'd better call Albrecht and Selma."

They kept walking at the same pace, gradually making their way around the market to where they'd started. They kept scanning from behind their sunglasses, and then Remi said, "Bad news at two o'clock."

Sam looked in that direction and saw four men, wearing khaki pants, work shirts, boots, and baseball caps, sitting at an outdoor table, nursing tall drinks. They looked like oil riggers or heavy-equipment operators. "Who are they?"

"Some of Poliakoff's security guys. The short one with the blond hair is one of the four people who took me to Nizhny in a barrel. He and another man helped the two women. The really tall one I saw the night we escaped from the place."

"I suppose it was inevitable that they'd get here first," said Sam. "Did they see us?"

"I doubt it. They didn't show any sign, and none of them struck me as the type who would pretend not to see us. They'd be more likely to chase us."

They took a roundabout route to their hotel, stopping now and then to see if they were followed. When they reached their room, they opened the package with Remi's new cell phone, plugged it in to charge, waited, then called La Jolla.

A voice they hadn't been expecting said, "Hello?"

"Hi, Albrecht. It's us."

"Are you at your hotel in Taraz?"

"Yes. We hired a driver who got us here, but he speaks no English."

"What does he speak?"

"Kazakh, and a little Russian."

"Sounds adequate. Tell me what's happening."

"We just came from the green market that historians think is the site of ancient Taraz. We spotted four of Poliakoff's thugs at a café. We don't think they saw us. We also don't think the market looks right. It's too low to be a fort. It's also not on the river. Maybe there are springs or wells in town, but we haven't seen them."

They heard Albrecht typing on a computer keyboard. "Give me a moment to get a better perspective on this computer map. There. No, I think you're right. The old Chinese sources say that five hundred men worked two years to build the fort. They were in the middle of the Sino-Xiongnu War. Xiongnu was the Chinese name for the Huns. Zhizhi, leader of the Huns, was expecting a Han army of up to three hundred thousand men to arrive at some point, so the fort would have had to be strong. It would be built in the heights, and it would need a water supply. We know it was high-walled because when the Chinese did come, the only way they could storm it was by piling dirt up beside it until it was even with the wall. The fight was furious, and even Zhizhi's wives shot arrows from the battlements. The Chinese overwhelmed them and won. I don't think the fort was at the modern marketplace. The ruins under the market are more likely to be either a habitation or a cemetery."

"What will Mundzuk's grave consist of?" asked Remi. "What do we look for?"

"I'm sending you pictures of the known burials of the earliest Huns in Mongolia. They were buried under mounds. There's a burial chamber made of stone, and then over it are layers of stone, soil, and logs of Siberian larch."

"That's close to the sort of thing we found in France. It had been made of logs plastered with mortar."

"Look for any natural feature that could have been a mound. Most likely, it was leveled intentionally or by time, the wind, and the river. But Mundzuk would never have been in the fort, which was destroyed three hundred years earlier with Zhizhi's defeat. It was a ruin long before Mundzuk's time. Remember, we're looking for a king who died just during the migration to Europe. If the market is over a burial complex, Mundzuk's grave would be one of the last."

Remi said, "Is there any way to know how his father's death affected Attila?"

"We know quite a few facts," said Albrecht. "Mundzuk was buried in 418. Attila was born in 406, so he was twelve when his father died and his uncle Ruga became King. I've sometimes thought that even in that generation there might have been dual kings—that Mundzuk and Ruga might have shared the throne the way Bleda and Attila did later. At the time of Mundzuk's death, the Huns were making a big leap historically. The great migration, their conquest of much of Asia and Europe, was already well under way. We know that they were in contact with the Romans near the Danube around the year 370, so it's almost certain Mundzuk's body was brought back to the eastern homeland for burial only. Attila would have stayed for it and then returned west. In those days, young princes from all over the Roman Empire and beyond were kept in Rome for a few years at a time to encourage their families to keep their treaties with Rome, and Romans were sent as hostages to neighboring kingdoms. Once Attila's father was dead, Attila became a convenient choice as a hostage. He was sent to Rome."

"That must have been quite an experience for a twelve-year-old," Remi said.

"Yes, I'm sure it was. Either before or during the trip, he learned Latin, which the Huns and others considered a soldier's language, something likely to be useful to members of a ruling family. Later, Latin would help him communicate with allies and subjects from hundreds of tribes and with emissaries of the Empire. Attila met lots of aristocratic Romans, saw how the Romans governed, and certainly came away with lots of information about the Roman armies." Albrecht paused. "But I'm going on, aren't I? What we need to do is find the tomb of Mundzuk. Do you have any ideas yet on how you'll proceed?"

"Cautiously," said Sam. "We're in a town where we don't speak the language and just a few speak ours. We know there are anti-American groups operating here. We've just been to the supposed site, which is a central market in a big city, so there's barely space to stand on, let alone to perform an excavation. The problem is that by the time we get it done, the treasure will be gone, split among Poliakoff and his friends, and the gold melted down and converted to cash. This is like salvage archaeology. Either we do it now or we'll never get another chance. And this is the final treasure, the one Attila's message said we had to find to get to his tomb."

"I know," said Albrecht. "But treasure is never something worth getting killed for."

"Agreed," said Sam. "We've already pushed our luck to the limit. But we may have a way to push the limit."

27

THAT EVENING, SAM WENT TO NURIN'S ROOM AND INvited him to join him and Remi for dinner. He communicated this by a mixture of pantomime and gesture, finally walking to the elevator and beckoning Nurin to follow. When Sam had ushered him to the room, he and Remi presented him with a room service menu.

They asked him to use the telephone to order what each of them wanted for dinner. They had drawn pictures of farm animals and vegetables on a piece of paper. He got the idea, and performed the task. While they waited for their dinner, Remi picked up a magazine from the coffee table and showed him pictures of a fashionable Kazakh woman wearing flat shoes, a flowing dress, and a *hijab* that covered her hair. She pointed to what must be the address of a store in Taraz. She also showed him an ad for baby furnishings, clothing, and equipment and pointed to that address. Later in the evening, after they'd eaten, she took a notepad and showed him a set of pictures that Sam had drawn. Sam was an engineer, so the drawings were clear and neat, with numbers to show the dimensions.

Sam's first pictures were of a machinist with a tapping-and-threading machine taking a series of tubes and tapping and threading them on both ends so they could be screwed together. He took out the metal tubes and showed them to Nurin. Next there was a diagram of a large wooden box with dimensions written on it and a man painting it black. Nurin studied the pictures and diagram. Then Remi pointed to both and handed him several thousand tenge. Nurin, who was already eager to do something to stave off the boredom of sitting in a hotel for a week waiting to drive them back, accepted his assignment with pleasure. They could only hope Nurin would buy what they wanted and find a machinist to do the modifications.

Two days later, in the morning, a fashionable woman and her husband in a Kazakh-made business suit walked along the streets of the city pushing a large old-fashioned baby carriage. As it was a bright summer day, the carriage had a silk shawl draped over the carriage's awning and secured at the foot so the baby inside would be shaded and protected from the dust of the streets. The couple pushed the carriage through the green market, passing by every table or bin in a very systematic way. They went all the way to the end of one aisle, turned, and came back up the next, not skipping any part of the market.

The baby in the carriage was remarkably quiet. Just once, when the mother reached in under the silk shawl to adjust his blanket, did he cry. She reached in again and patted him, and after a minute or so he stopped crying and, a few fretful gurgles after that, went back to sleep.

The couple, when they spoke to each other, did so quietly in French or German. After they had explored the whole market, they moved on. They walked a few blocks surrounding the market and then walked back to the Zhambyl Hotel. A few minutes later, their driver, Nurin, came out to the enclosed lot, folded their carriage, and put it in the trunk of his car. At the same time, had anyone been interested, they could have seen the wife carrying a laptop computer and the husband a lesser-known piece of equipment called a magnetometer up to their room wrapped in the baby's blanket.

Once they were in their room, Sam and Remi used the laptop computer to convert all of the magnetometer data to a magnetic map of the central market of Taraz. They sent it to Selma and Albrecht at their house in La Jolla. Then they went down to the hotel restaurant for lunch.

The Kazakhstan diet was very dependent upon meat. Sam and Remi managed to avoid horse meat and horse sausage, sheep's brains, and *kuyrdak*, a dish made of the mixed innards of several animals. Instead they ordered kebabs, which had pieces of meat that they believed they recognized as fowl, and *tandyr nan*, a kind of bread, and they were very happy.

When they were back in their room, Remi's new phone buzzed. "Hello?" she said.

"Hi, Remi, it's Selma. Are you both there?"

"Hi, Selma. Yes. Sam's with me."

"I loved the baby crying. Where did you get that?"

"I found it on YouTube and recorded it on a disk. I just reached into the carriage and played it once and then turned it off."

"I've got Albrecht on now. He's getting impatient."

"Okay," said Remi. "Hi, Albrecht."

"Hello, Remi. Hello, Sam. You two have succeeded admirably. You've mapped the entire central market, or what's under it." He laughed. "I didn't tell you this before, but I was afraid Attila might have been referring to some burial ground outside the city. The early Huns in Asia used to pick a remote valley and bury people under mounds there. If that was the case, we might never find it. But, fortunately, this is different."

"Do you think the big rectangle near the center is the tomb?"

"I see several notable subterranian features—a long wall, which was at some point reduced to a line of rocks a man could have stepped over, a few outlines of early buildings, and a solid rectangular stone box. I compared its magnetic signature with the one on the Po River in Italy and the one we found in the vineyard at Kiskunhalas in Hungary. I also checked the dimensions of the tombs along the Danube and compared them. We don't have readings for the chamber in France or the one in Transylvania. But this one is the same shape and presents the same magnetic anomaly, the same disturbance to the earth's magnetic field, as the ones we have. Like the others, it's apparently a hollow room or it would have a much stronger signature."

"Did you happen to measure the exact spot?"

"We did. It's in the area that you surveyed. On your third pass, you went left to right. At four hundred seventeen meters on that aisle, you passed over the first wall of the crypt. It's around seven feet below the present surface. At four hundred twenty-two meters, you reached the end of the chamber."

Remi said, "Do you know if it was a buried chamber to begin with?"

"We can't know from this data. But it's below the features around it, as though it were already underground before they were built. And it's the only structure in the area that fits our experience of a Hun burial of the fifth century."

"Do you have any questions for us?" Remi asked.

"When you were walking the area, did you see any indication that the ground near this area had been disturbed? Any signs of digging?"

"We didn't see any," Sam said. "We don't even know if Poliakoff's men are here looking for Mundzuk's tomb or just hunting for us."

"Do you know what you're going to do yet?"

"We're working on it," Sam said. "We'll call you if we accomplish anything. Good night."

Sam and Remi went to Nurin's room and examined the large wooden box he had made. It was about five feet on a side and had a hinged lower section. It was held together with dowels fitted into holes and could be taken apart and moved.

Sam explained, with gestures and the clock, that he wanted Nurin to drive Sam and Remi to the market and help them set up the box for one-thirty a.m. He plugged in their electronic equipment to recharge and then they went to sleep.

They awoke at one, dressed, packed up their fully charged equipment—computer, battery-operated drill, steel drill bits, lights, fiber-optic unit and tubes—into their backpacks and went to Nurin's room. He was awake and ready, with the five-piece box already lying flat in the car trunk. He drove them to the green market and helped them carry the pieces to the deserted spot.

The awnings of the stalls were still up, but the tables and bins were now empty. Stores along the edges of the market were all locked up, with sliding gates across their fronts to prevent burglaries. There were lights on in some of the streets beyond the shops, but the contrast kept the marketplace in deeper darkness beneath its awnings and roofs.

Nurin helped Sam and Remi assemble the black box, and then

Sam patted Nurin's arm and pointed in the direction of his car and Nurin walked away.

As soon as Nurin was gone, Sam took the magnetometer out and Remi connected the laptop to it. They walked a few yards up the aisle and back to recheck the exact spot where the variance in the magnetic field began and ended. They repositioned their black box in a space directly above the anomaly. It looked exactly like one of the market's stalls. Then Sam lifted the hinged section of the box to let Remi crawl in while he packed the magnetometer into his pack and removed other equipment and then joined her inside the box.

The space was cramped, but he had designed the box to give himself just enough space for the moves he would need to make. He attached a drill bit with a four-foot shaft that had been designed for drilling through thick logs and beams. Then he positioned the bit in the ground and began to drill. The market was mostly fine, sandy dirt that had been packed down by the weight of many shoes. It took him little time to get down to a depth of four feet. When his drill was almost to the ground, he loosened the chocks to eject the shaft, then took the next shaft, which Nurin had paid a machinist to attach a screw to, and attached it to the first shaft. Then he attached this extended shaft to the drill and kept drilling. About six feet down, he reached a hard surface.

Sam pulled back on the drill and carefully removed the extension and the original bit. Sam inserted the rigid fiber-optic borehole viewer into the hole and extended it downward. The image of what the viewer was seeing was visible on Remi's laptop screen. The end of the viewer was a color video camera and a bright light, so the image was very clear and natural. After Remi had turned the viewer on and gotten the picture, she moved it up and down a little. "I think we're in luck," she said. "You're all the way to the top of the rectangle and either you cracked the upper stone surface with the drill or just pushed between two stones. The next layer looks like wood. It has a grainy texture."

She turned the screen toward him. He said, "It looks like wood to me too. There's no bark on it, so it may be thick planks instead of tree trunks."

"Then get back to work."

Sam reinserted the bit and attached its threaded extension and began to drill. The wood was hard and had a dense grain, but he definitely could tell he was drilling through wood and not stone. He was cautious because if he broke the drill, he didn't have another. At the end of about ten minutes, it abruptly sank a few inches. "We're through the wood," Sam said. "We're there."

He removed the drill and its extension and set them aside. He and Remi fed the fiber-optic rig down into the new shaft while Remi watched the image on the screen. When the tip light and camera reached the place where the drill had sunk suddenly, the space opened up and the computer image changed.

As they lowered and turned the rig, they could see the inside of the rectangular space clearly. "It's the tomb," said Remi. "I'm recording it." With difficulty, Sam turned his body in the narrow space of the box to join her in front of the computer screen. They could see a body, now a skeleton, lying on a mat at the rear of the tomb. He was dressed in a rich red costume, with a cape, a pair of high boots, and a piece of headgear unlike anything they'd ever seen. This hat, or helmet, was at least two feet in length, shaped like a narrow cone, with a complicated design of gold that protruded an inch or two from the front above the forehead. He wore a belt with a long straight sword in a scabbard and a dagger that was about half as long. His coat was held in place by gold buttons, and then more gold buttons studded his outfit. The chamber was well supplied with weapons, including a round shield with a silvery plated surface, bows, and quivers full of arrows. They could see jade and gold jewelry, carved ivory boxes, saddles and bridles decorated with more gold.

They manipulated the fiber optics, the size and brightness of the computer image, and searched for the most important part of the treasure, the message from Attila. After twenty minutes or so of recording every item in the tomb, Remi whispered, "I haven't seen anything that could be it, have you?"

"No. I'm going to try something else." Sam pulled the rigid rig up, then went to work on it. He removed the metal tubes that housed the cable and then he removed the extension. What he had left was a long, black, insulated optical fiber. On the far end was the rounded tip with the light and the tiny camera. Slowly, carefully, he inserted the flexible cable into the drill hole. Many times he had to pull it back an inch or two to straighten it or twist it to get around a snag. At last, after many minutes of feeding it in, it cleared the drill shaft, then curled a bit so they could see the sides of the stone chamber. "Wait. I see something."

"There," said Remi. "There it is."

She took the fiber-optic cable and twirled it with her fingers so she could aim it. The image was a set of deep scratches made with a knife on the wall. *Ego Attila filius Munzuci.* It went on, and Remi made sure to get every bit of it recorded, then sent it to Selma's computer, and then copied it on the disk, which she took out and put into the deep cargo pocket of Sam's pants. They began to dismantle their equipment and put it into their backpacks. As they began to open the hinged bottom of the box, Sam stopped.

"Wait," Sam whispered. "I hear something. Footsteps."

Remi closed the computer, turned off the fiber-optic light, and pulled it out of the hole. Sam put it into one of the backpacks, with the drill and bit, while Remi put the computer into the other backpack.

They listened. Remi lowered her head to the ground and squinted through the opening at the edge. "It's men. Five—no, six. They're coming this way, of all the million ways."

The footsteps grew louder and louder, as did the men's voices. There was laughter. They were loud and jovial. There was the clank of a bottle dropping into an empty steel drum used as a trash barrel. Sam and Remi remained motionless, barely breathing.

The footsteps passed by so close that Remi thought she could pick out each man from the others. There was one who seemed to have a stone in his shoe because his walk was *scrape-thump, scrape-thump*, trying to get it out from under his foot. He called out to his friends as they moved off.

Next there was a creaking sound. The man had sat on top of their box. He took off a shoe, and when he shook it to get the stone out, they could hear the squeak of the dowels in the holes. He put his shoe back on and tied it, and then they heard him trot off after his friends.

Remi exhaled and leaned on Sam. They sat still for a few minutes, and then she looked out again. "It's clear."

They opened the hinged section of the box, crawled out, put their backpacks on, then unhooked the box's sides and top and made it into a pile. Sam took a cap from the end of the fiber-optic machine, pushed it a couple of inches into the hole he had drilled, and then poured dirt over it and walked across it a couple of times.

They began to walk away from the spot toward the edge of the green market, carrying the pieces of their box. As they did, they heard the sound of a car starting. They stepped close to a wall in the shadows and waited until the car pulled up, its headlights off, and stopped. Nurin got out and opened the trunk. They put the collapsed box inside and then the backpacks. They got into the car and Nurin drove off toward the Zhambyl Hotel.

Sam took out his telephone and called Selma. "Sam?" she said.

"Yes," he said. "It's around five in the evening there, right?"

"That's right. And five a.m. there."

"Remi just sent you the video of the inside of the tomb, including the message."

"We've got it and it's unbelievable. Here's Albrecht."

"Sam. Does the other side know where the tomb is?"

"No. When we saw them, they seemed to be waiting for something, not searching with archaeological equipment. They were just sitting around a table at an outdoor café."

"Then I implore you, don't try to excavate. It's not essential that we be the ones to excavate Mundzuk's tomb and attempting to do so could easily get you both killed. As soon as we're there, I'll send a letter, with the magnetic map and the exact position marked, to Taraz State University and the national government in Astana. The country takes enormous pride in its heritage and they have more right to the burial you found than we do."

"As soon as you're where? Here?"

"Rome, Sam. Rome!"

"What?"

"That's right. You haven't read the message. It says, 'I am Attila, son of Mundzuk. My father is dead and so I am to be sent to the Romans to secure the peace, but one day I will conquer Rome. You find my father here, but I will be buried in Rome, guest of a daughter of the Flavian emperors.'"

"Does that suggest a location to you?"

"I know exactly where it is," said Albrecht. "I've been there."

Selma cut in. "Sam? I've already chartered your plane. It will be waiting for you at Taraz Airport at noon today. It's shockingly expensive, but it will take you to Rome, where we'll be waiting for you. We'll be staying at the Saint Regis Grand Hotel."

Remi said, "We'll try to manage it in our busy social schedule. Good-bye, Selma. See you there."

Nurin pulled up in front of the hotel and let them off and then drove on to the car lot behind the building. Sam and Remi went up to their room. They opened it and stood still in the doorway, looking in.

The room had been thoroughly searched. The mattress and springs were leaning against the wall, all of the drawers from the dressers were stacked in two neat piles, the chairs had been overturned so someone could look beneath them. The cushions were all unzipped. The towels that had been piled neatly in the linen cabinet were draped over the shower curtain. The Bokhara rug had been rolled up.

Remi said, "The expression *having your room tossed* doesn't really apply, does it? This is the neatest break-in we've ever had."

"They're pros. They were quiet so the hotel guests and employees wouldn't hear anything."

"What do we do about it?"

Sam said, "Nurin." He stepped back toward the door.

"Oh, no."

"Bring the laptop and leave everything else."

They closed the door and hurried down to Nurin's room. They knocked, but there was no response. They ran outside and around to the back of the building. There was Nurin, backed up against his car. Two of the men they had recognized from Poliakoff's estate were with him. One of them held a gun on him, while the other punched him. Nurin was bent over, unable to do anything but use his arms to try to protect his vital organs.

Sam and Remi came closer and closer, moving quietly and hoping the sound of Nurin's groans would cover their footsteps. At home, he and she had trained together for years and practiced for every unpleasant situation they could think of. They both knew that the only one to fear was the man with the gun and that both of them should attack him at once.

As soon as she was close enough, Remi took two running steps and leapt. She had the laptop computer raised above her head with both hands, tilting it so the thin edge would come down on the back of the gunman's head.

In the last half second, the man heard or felt the Fargos' presence. He half turned in time to have the computer hammered against his head right at the eyebrow. Remi's trajectory brought the computer downward from there to break his nose while its flat side obscured his vision for an instant.

As the man rocked backward, Sam's powerful punch to his midsection broke two ribs and bent him over. Sam grasped the man's gun hand and wrist, spun him and twisted his arm behind him, and ran him face-first into the car as he wrenched the gun out of his hand.

The man who had been punching Nurin raised his hands and stepped backward, but Nurin used his feet to push off from the car and drive his head into the man's solar plexus like a linebacker and run him into the side of the building. The man's injuries could not be determined, but he lay on the blacktop, clutching his thorax and shallowly gasping for air. Nurin's foot delivered a soccer kick to his face.

Sam quickly dodged in front of Nurin and pushed him away from the man, shaking his head. "No, Nurin. Please. We don't want to kill anybody." Sam's soothing tone restrained Nurin and seemed to bring him back to his usual calm. He nodded and leaned back against his car, touched his mouth, and looked at the blood on his hand.

Sam pointed at the two men, then held up his hands as though the wrists were tied. Nurin opened the trunk of his car and pulled out a length of nylon rope. Sam hog-tied the two men, then used a length of electrical tape from the trunk to secure some rags in their mouths for gags. Then he opened the driver's door and pushed Nurin toward it. "We've got to go now. Please, drive us." He pretended to be steering a car.

Nurin got in and started the car, then looked at them, half dazed from the beating and not sure he understood what Sam wanted. As he started out of the lot, Remi opened the laptop computer.

"Amazing how tough these things are," she muttered as she typed the word *airport* into the Internet browser search engine. There was a large color photograph of a major airport that looked like Heathrow, with a varied group of airplanes shouldered up to the terminal. She tapped Nurin on the shoulder and tilted it toward him.

After that, he drove with speed and confidence, heading toward Taraz Airport, beyond the southwest edge of the city. Nearly all of the traffic was heading in, bringing workers and merchants and country people into the busy city as the day began.

As Nurin drove, Remi typed some more. She brought up a map of southern Kazakhstan, then adjusted the screen so it showed the route from Taraz to Almaty. When Nurin reached the airport, she held it up so he could see it. She pointed at Nurin and then the map and said, "Go home to Almaty, Nurin." Then she pointed at herself and then Sam and then at the airline terminal, and said, "We're going away." She used her hand to imitate an airplane taking off.

Sam took out all of the tenge from his wallet and his pockets, and then almost all of his American cash, handed it to Nurin, and then patted his shoulder. "Thank you, Nurin. You're a brave man. Now go to Almaty before somebody finds the two Russians." He held the computer and ran his finger from Taraz to Almaty.

He and Remi got out of the car, waved to Nurin, and stepped into the terminal. Remi stopped when Sam went to the ticket counter and went back to look out the door. Nurin was pulling his car away from the terminal. As he reached the turn onto the highway, she saw him put on his sunglasses and turn to the east toward Almaty.

IN MIDAFTERNOON, Sergei Poliakoff got off his airplane at Taraz Airport. He hated leaving Nizhny Novgorod now that he was middle-aged and financially comfortable. He would not have minded going with Irena to Paris or Barcelona or Milan, but coming to this godforsaken place had taken him a whole day and night and, here he was, on a pile of sand and rock. All he had learned before he had left home was that Sam and Remi Fargo had been spotted in Taraz. He could hardly believe that they were simply continuing their hunt for the spoils of the Huns as though nothing serious had happened to them.

Poliakoff was aware that the Fargos often solicited help, or even backup, from various allies and authorities. But coming here was insane. Fargo had just finished rescuing his wife and forcing Poliakoff to burn his own house down. Had they never heard of revenge?

The police who had been digging around in the smoking ruin of Poliakoff's house had thought the chemical content of the ash and debris in the basement to be unique in their archive. They had no idea what it contained, and Poliakoff hoped that they had not enough patience to analyze it. He had been born a Russian and so he knew that an "unknown chemical substance" recorded on a police report could always one day be made to look like just about anything—even something worse than the truth. So he had not allowed the substance to remain mysterious. He had said in his deposition that the mess was the residue of various medicinal compounds because he had been working in a chemistry lab in his basement to concoct lifesaving drugs.

The two jumping horses belonging to his daughters had been found safe in a farmer's field seventeen miles from his house, so that part had worked out without trouble. But he hated that this couple, the cause of all his misery, seemed not to be afraid that they might fall into his hands a second time. They were wrong not to be afraid. He'd had four men here for days, watching for them. He also had a group of oil drillers from Atyrau searching for the tomb of Attila's father in the hills.

As he came into the baggage area, he saw two of his men waiting for him. One of them—the blond—had helped with the kidnapping of Remi Fargo, the last thing Poliakoff could recall that had been done right. As he approached, he said, "Tell me what's going on now."

"They were here," said the blond man.

"They 'were' here? Where are they now?"

"They took off about two hours ago."

"For where?"

"They filed a flight plan for Odessa."

"Odessa?" he said. "That's not their destination. That's a refueling stop." He reflexively looked up and away from them toward the terminal building. He would have to dream up some way of finding out the plan they would file in Odessa.

"There!" The blond man pointed. "Danil and Leo. They were at the hotel, searching the room. They must have found something."

Poliakoff saw the two men get out of a cab and begin to hurry toward him. He could see that one man's face was bruised and the other man could barely walk. He didn't need to speak with them and ask what had happened. He knew.

BEING AIRBORNE was a relief. Sam and Remi lay, with their seat backs tilted and their legs up, in big leather seats like overstuffed easy chairs. After the private plane landed in Odessa, Sam sat looking out the window as the ground crew chocked and grounded the plane and then hooked up hoses and began to refuel. He pressed the button for Tibor Lazar's number in Hungary. It rang once and there was Tibor's voice. "Sam?"

"Yes."

"How is the search going so far?"

"It's done. Let's leave it at that. Do you remember the morning when we were in your car on the way to Budapest and all agreed to be partners in this project?"

"Of course."

"Well, now is the moment for all of us to come together one more time. We've read the fifth message," said Sam. "We're going to find and open the tomb of Attila."

"Woohoo!" Tibor called out. It was a wordless shout, a celebration.

"Come to Rome," Sam said. "There will be a room for you in the Saint Regis Grand Hotel. You can bring János and anybody else you want. Just be sure Bako's men don't follow you and nobody knows your destination."

"I will bring János, but we'll need to leave the others here to warn us if Bako or his men move."

"All right. Come as soon as you can."

"We'll leave tonight. I wouldn't miss this if I had to walk to Rome."

Sam hung up. "Well, he seems enthusiastic."

"Without that enthusiasm, the rest of us would be dead—Albrecht, you, me."

"True," said Sam. He watched the two fuel men disconnect the hoses from the private jet. "It looks as though we're almost ready to head to our last stop."

"I am," she said. "I want a view of Rome, a nice hotel, a bath, and a dress that shows how little I've eaten since Moscow. And I want to sleep in a bed for at least one night instead of being out digging holes."

"That all sounds within our reach," Sam said. "Just one last dig and we're done."

28

ABOVE ROME

SAM AND REMI'S PLANE DID NOT COME IN TO LEONARDO da Vinci–Fiumicino Airport, the huge international hub with forty million visitors a year. Instead they flew into Ciampino Airport, fifteen kilometers southeast of Rome. They had no luggage except a laptop computer, so they passed through customs quickly.

It took much longer to get through the Roman traffic to reach the St. Regis Grand Hotel. The hotel was spare and elegant on the outside but luxurious inside, with ornate public spaces adorned with vases of flowers. At the desk was a message from Professor Albrecht Fischer, inviting them to his suite on the tenth floor. Remi said, "I'm going to buy myself some clothes, take a bath, and then I'll be ready to see people." She looked at Sam, who said nothing.

"And I'd better get you some clothes too," she said. "You look as though you've been digging for bones like a dog."

"A noble beast engaged in a noble profession, but I'd better go with you," said Sam.

They checked in, then asked the concierge to get them a driver to take them to the right stores for buying the best-quality ready-made clothes. They both bought new casual attire, and Sam bought a suit while Remi bought a cocktail dress, shoes, and purse. They took a cab to their hotel and retired to their suite for an hour before they came to Albrecht's room and knocked.

The door swung open, and it looked as though a party was in session. There was Albrecht, and Selma Wondrash was across the room carrying around a tray of hors d'oeuvres. Pete Jeffcoat and his girlfriend and coresearcher, Wendy Corden, were acting as bartenders. Tibor Lazar and his brother János sat on a couch. There was a large table set for dinner.

"Sam! Remi!" Albrecht called out as though announcing them. "Welcome to our humble abode." People stood up and surrounded them and then put wineglasses in their hands. Remi whispered in Sam's ear, "This is like a dream."

"It is," he said. They took seats at the big table. "Sorry we're late," he said. "We arrived wearing the clothes we wore in a fistfight."

"We've been eager to talk about the tomb," said Selma. "Albrecht wanted to wait for you."

Albrecht stood. "All right," said Sam. "Go ahead."

Albrecht said, "Well, what I believe we're going to find is the chamber containing Attila's remains. His message to us—to the people who found the five treasures, whoever they turned out to be—was very clear. He wanted to be buried as the guest of a daughter of the Flavian emperors."

"Which were the Flavian emperors?" asked Sam.

"Vespasian, Titus, and Domitian, a father and two sons, who ruled Rome from 69 to 96 C.E. They built the Colosseum. Vespasian was a general commanding the eastern forces who essentially took the throne by showing up in Rome at the head of his army. That made him a hard man to argue with. Titus and Domitian inherited."

"Why would Attila care about them?"

"I'm not sure. They were strong emperors who ruled near the height of Rome's power. They were the first emperors who tried to take over Dacia on the Danube as a colony, and that was near the Huns' territory, but it didn't happen until some time after the Flavians died."

"Then it doesn't seem like enough," said Remi.

"Connections are tricky. As everyone here knows, the Roman who fought Attila at Châlons, France, was named Flavius Aëtius. He was not an aristocrat from Rome but was born in what is now Bulgaria. He was sent as a young man to be a hostage of the Huns at the court of Attila's uncle Ruga. He and Attila were friends. The name may be part of the attraction. Maybe it symbolized the ruling class of Rome for Attila."

"And you said that Attila was a hostage too," said Remi.

"Yes. Attila was sent to Rome by his uncle, King Ruga, at the age of twelve in 418. He was there for at least two years, I believe. What he saw was extreme wealth, along with extreme corruption and murderous conspiracies. He saw that Rome was the ultimate prize for a conqueror. He also observed and studied the practices and strategies of the Roman army, the best in the world—its strengths, methods, and its weaknesses. Since he was from a warlike people, this was probably of most interest to him."

"And that made him want to be buried like a Roman?"

"It made him realize that Rome was the greatest empire of his era and that it was vulnerable to him. He wanted to conquer it. The burial would have been secondary, a sign he had won."

"And you said you knew exactly where he wanted to be buried in Rome."

"A crucial point is that none of the early Roman emperors were buried. The custom was to cremate them. If Attila wanted to be buried, as his father, uncle, brother, and other relatives were, as well as Huns as far back as we know about them, his choices were limited. For nearly all of Roman history, it was illegal to bury a body anywhere within the limits of the city."

"So what happened?" asked Tibor.

"What happened was, the catacombs. The early Christians believed in the resurrection of the body, so they wanted to be buried, just as the Huns did. They began to dig tunnels at the edge of the city and bury people there. The first were the Catacomb of Domitilla. She was a daughter of the Flavians, a niece of Vespasian, and first cousin of both Titus and Domitian. The land originally belonged to her. Like all of the forty other catacombs that came after it, this one was dug along one of the major roads."

"How long will it take us to find the Catacomb of Domitilla?" asked Tibor.

"Not long," said Albrecht. "The address is 282 Via delle Sette Chiese. It's just west of the Via Ardeatina and the Appian Way."

"You mean it's that simple? It's right there in the open?"

"Not exactly," said Albrecht. "With Attila, nothing ever seems to be simple. The Catacomb of Domitilla held one hundred fifty thousand burials. It's fifteen kilometers of underground passages on four levels. Each tunnel is about two meters wide and over two meters high, with shelves, or platform-shaped depressions, that hold the bodies of the dead. There are offshoots and rooms, each of which has more shelves dug into the rock. This kind of rock is called tufa, which is a soft volcanic stone that hardens after it's exposed to air. It's what is under all of Rome. If you wished to bury someone, you would find an unused spot or extend a tunnel to make one, then hollow out a shelf in the wall and put the deceased in it. Next, you would seal the space with a slab. Carved into the slab was the name of the deceased, his age, and the date of his death."

"But why did Attila choose a catacomb?" asked Remi. "And how would he even know about them?"

Albrecht said, "I'm sure that elucidating and explaining what Attila did will take up most of the rest of my career. Rome was the most famous place in the world. People talked about it. Attila was probably taught to admire the Flavians, two of whom are included in the group historians call the five good emperors. Many of the Flavian family were buried in the oldest parts of this catacomb. He also knew that the desecration and looting of monarchs' graves was a concern. We know he left instructions, going to great lengths, to hide his grave. We know Attila was very cunning. Because Rome was full of people from every country in the Empire, he probably knew it would be possible for a small burial party of Huns to look innocent long enough to enter a catacomb that was outside the city limits. To hide his grave among the graves of a hundred and fifty thousand, most of them Christians who owned little that could be left as burial goods, seems to be very much the sort of thing Attila might do. And of course we have his word that this is what he did."

"The word of a twelve-year-old?"

"One of the things we know is that people who underestimated this man usually died. And there is another reason to have faith in the young Attila."

"What's that?"

"That year, Attila was the one chosen as hostage, not his older brother Bleda or anyone else. This was Ruga's best chance to get a spy into the most important court on earth. It was also Rome's chance to form a relationship with the youth whom they believed would one day be leading the Huns. Both sides agreed on who that would be—the twelve-year-old Attila."

"All right," said Sam. "We know where the tomb is, and all the members of the partnership are here. Let's plan how we're going to accomplish this."

"I'd like to have all of us there for the finish," Remi said. "Even if we're fifteen hundred years late and the tomb has been looted, we all work to follow his instructions to the end."

"Remi is right to mention the possible end," said Albrecht. "Some of the catacombs were looted by Visigoths, Lombards, early medieval scavengers. It's possible we'll find nothing. But the Catacomb of Domitilla is the least compromised."

Sam said, "What are the legalities?"

Selma said, "We've done some looking into it. The people of Rome abandoned the Catacomb of Domitilla by the ninth century, then forgot it existed. In 1873 it was rediscovered. Because most of the catacomb was an early Christian cemetery, it was placed under the ownership of the Catholic Church. In 2007 the Pope appointed the Divine Word Missionaries, an organization of priests and monks, to act as administrator. At the moment, about sixteen hundred meters are open to the public, but they've been cooperative about projects to explore, map, and photograph the rest of the catacomb for historical purposes. It's by far the oldest and biggest, and the one that still contains the bones of its original dead. We've called Captain Boiardi of the Carabinieri Tutela Patrimonio Culturale. He has agreed not only to provide security but also to intercede for us with the Divine Word Missionaries. He's telling them about the way you called in the authorities after the Mantua excavation."

"Wonderful," said Remi. "He's somebody we want on our side."

"He called a while ago and asked for you and Sam. I told him I worked for you, so he said to tell you he would be here as soon as he could. He has the Ministry of Culture approving this as a joint project. Anything that's dated before the ninth century B.C. or after the fourth century A.D. will be granted a license for possible export to the U.S. Anything else will be negotiated case by case."

"Those are generous terms," said Sam.

"It will be good to have official backing," Albrecht said. "Going into a catacomb is like a cave expedition. The floor is hard, smoothly finished, and reasonably level and dry. But beyond the areas open to the public, it's not very different from the way it was in 300 C.E. There will be no electricity. None of the deceased will have been removed from their crypts and sepulchres. We'll use what we bring and, when we go, we'll leave nothing behind. This is a fifteen-kilometer archaeological site. We map and photograph, but, to the extent that we can avoid it, we touch nothing. We'll have to be very deliberate, attentive, and patient because the tomb will be hidden somehow. What we're after is one of the great treasures of the ancient world. Attila started thinking about this tomb when he was twelve and didn't stop until he died thirty-five years later. All we can assume is that finding it will not be easy."

Sam said, "I think we'd better all decide how we'd like to do this. I suggest that before we go down there, each of us think about our capabilities. If you don't think you're up to walking ten miles on a stone surface carrying a backpack, then you should remember that going there and back is twenty miles. If you have a hint of claustrophobia, it's better to realize it now. There's nobody in this room who hasn't earned the right to be down there. But we'll also need a team to remain on the surface to watch the vehicles, take charge of anything we bring up, deal with the authorities, and so on."

The group all looked at one another appraisingly, but at first none of them spoke. Finally Selma said, "I'll be worth more upstairs."

"I'll go down," said Tibor.

"So will I," said János.

"I think I need to be down also," said Albrecht. "I know what we're looking for."

"I'm going down," said Sam.

Remi said, "Me too."

Wendy said, "I'll stay with Selma."

"Thank you," said Selma. "I was beginning to wonder if I was going to be all alone."

"I'll stay up too," Pete said.

Sam said, "Unless I have Boiardi wrong, I think he'll supply a couple of Carabinieri to serve up on top too. If we find the treasure, the police will be the best ones to guard it. Next, let's plan the equipment we bring down there. There will probably be Tibor, János, Remi, Albrecht, and me. I figure Boiardi and two Carabinieri will make it eight. We should each have a wheeled pushcart. The wheels should be large and inflated, like the tires of a small bicycle. That way, nobody has to carry a seventy-pound pack, and, if we find the tomb, we can begin removing objects on the first trip to the surface."

"If carts like that aren't available, I'll have some fabricated," said Selma.

"When do you think we'll be ready?" asked Remi.

Selma said, "Today is Thursday. The catacomb is closed to visitors on Tuesdays. If we can complete the negotiations with the administrators by then, that would be the time to start."

There was a knock on the door and then several waiters with carts brought in their dinner. The whole group adjourned to the large table and continued their planning over a feast. Selma had ordered a wide variety of dishes and the wine to go with them. There were seafood dishes, others of carved beef, lamb, chicken. There were pasta dishes and several kinds of salads. The next knock came about ten minutes into the feast. Sam went to the door.

In the open doorway stood Captain Boiardi, dressed in a dark civilian suit instead of a black uniform. Sam said, "Captain. I'm glad you could come so soon."

"If you would save more policemen's lives, I'm sure you would always have excellent service." He embraced Sam heartily and slapped his back. "Good to see you, Sam." He took Remi's hand and kissed it. "Remi, it is a delight to see you again. You soothe my eyes after the long drive."

"Please come in and make yourself part of the party, Captain," she said. "Do you have any of your men with you? They're welcome to join us too."

"No," he said. "You remember the trouble we had last time because we were noticed leaving Napoli. This time we've split up and divided the stops we must make. I gave myself the most pleasant."

"Thank you," said Sam. "Let me get you something to eat and drink. If we don't yet have what you like, we can order anything. We're in a hotel, after all."

"I'll have a soft drink," he said. "Otherwise, water. I still have meetings this evening."

Sam gave him a glass of ginger ale, and they sat at the table. Boiardi said, "The Ministry of Culture has approved our proposal of a joint project in the catacomb. They have also granted a permit to excavate, secured the cooperation of the Divine Word Missionaries, and sent my squad to assist. When do we go in?"

"We'd like to start Tuesday, when the catacomb is closed to visitors."

"Perfect," said the captain. "We'd rather not waste men on crowd control."

"How did you get the Ministry to act so quickly?"

"You placed the first treasure—the one from Mantua—with the Ministry voluntarily and that showed you to be responsible and legitimate. You fought and saved Carabinieri from criminals, proving yourselves to be true friends of the nation, of historical study, and of me, Sergio Boiardi."

"I'm certainly glad we did," said Sam. "We plan to ask the Ministry to take physical custody of what we find this time too."

"Excellent," he said. "We'll be prepared to transport any finds to a space in Il Museo Archeologico Nazionale di Napoli right away."

"Will you be coming down in the catacomb with us?"

"Yes. I and two other men will join you. I will also have three men at the entrance with trucks, a radio link with the Rome police, and a first-aid station."

"Thank you," said Sam. "Can you be ready to go in on Tuesday?"

"We could go tomorrow."

"Tuesday will be fine," Sam said. "What time do you think we should start?"

"Four a.m. would be good. The traffic in Rome became impossible the day Caesar was assassinated," said Boiardi. "We're waiting for it to clear."

29

BENEATH ROME

AT FOUR A.M. TUESDAY, THE MEMBERS OF THE EXPEDI-
tion gathered inside the walls of the Catacomb of Domitilla at 282
Via delle Sette Chiese. It was not yet light out, but a representative
of the Divine Word Missionaries named Brother Paolo was there to
admit them. He wore the brown robe of a monk, but his bespecta-
cled face seemed more like that of a businessman than a monk, and
his socks and shoes were like those someone might wear going to
an office. The total effect was like a man caught in his bathrobe
before leaving for work.

They followed him down a set of narrow steps to the front doors
of a fourth-century church. Only the roof and a single row of windows were visible above ground level, and the interior of the church
seemed very old. It was bare, more a relic now than a place of
worship. The group brought their gear down into it, and Brother

Paolo showed them its three naves, then pointed out the doorway that led to the catacomb and sent them on their way.

It took the explorers about a half hour to get their carts down the first three sets of stone steps to the level where they were to begin their search and then to fill it with their equipment and supplies, which was in backpacks. In the days of preparation, the quantity of these items had been gradually pared down to the essentials—light, photographic gear, tools, water, and food. Now each of the explorers strapped a light to the forehead with an elastic strap.

As they made their way through the first tunnels, what they saw were empty shelves, a few small Roman frescoes plastered and painted over stone or brick, a few empty rooms built as crypts. There were shrines, chambers that were painted, but most of the burial places were unadorned, shiny tufa stone. As they went on, they saw more and more spaces that were still occupied. Now there were large stones to seal the tomb niches. Albrecht began to deliver lessons. "In this section we can relax a bit. The tombs are from the period around 550 to 600 C.E., long after Attila was buried. He can't be in a tunnel that hadn't been dug when he died. We want the sections with tombs that were dug before the year 453. You will notice that none of the seal stones gives the date as a number. During that era, the Romans used the Julian calendar, which began in 45 B.C.E. Years were not numbered. Instead they were given the names of the two consuls who took office on January first. The year Attila died, the consuls were Flavius Opilio and Johannes Vincomalus. Remember those names. Attila was still encamped at his stronghold by the Tisza River when he died, meaning it was too early in the year to go off to war. That means he probably died in *Januarius*, *Februarius*, or *Martius*."

Remi said, "Will it give his name?"

"Almost certainly not, unless it's disguised in some way. He was cunning, clever. He would not want a Roman to find his tomb. But I think he wanted it to be found some day."

"Certainly he gave us all the clues," said Remi.

"He made us work backward, from his most recent treasure to his very first. I believe he wanted a Hun to find the treasures and then use the wealth to do something in the world—but first to conquer it. Perhaps he wanted a descendant to find it. Apparently none of his three sons was up to the task of ruling the world and he undoubtedly knew it."

"Now that we're here, I feel as though I must have missed something along the way, some way of distinguishing his tombstone from the others," Remi said.

"Finding the tomb is part of his test too. We'll use what we've got—date and age—and see what else there is. The catacomb was used between the second and the seventh centuries. His will be somewhere in the earlier ones. And I'm guessing that there will be something that outsiders wouldn't recognize—maybe a linguistic signal, something that's not in Latin."

"I hope he didn't make it too hard for us non-Huns."

"I have faith that he didn't. Think about what you and Sam have just been through. He's been teaching you about himself. He's been forcing you to go and stand in each of the places where his life was changed. He's taken you from the final days, when he was at the height of his power, marrying the beautiful Gothic princess Ildico in his stronghold on the Hungarian Plain surrounded by his hundreds of thousands of fanatical followers, all the way back to the very first moment of his career. Now we know that the start wasn't a triumph. It was the moment when an orphaned twelve-year-old stood in his father's grave, about to be sent away as a hostage. And what he did was vow to conquer Rome and be buried here."

"But he didn't conquer Rome."

"He reached the point where it was in his power to do that but chose instead to preserve his overpowering army for another day."

"And he died before he could come back."

"True," said Albrecht. "His death was a complete surprise to everyone. During the long period while he was burying his hoards of pillaged treasure and leaving messages, I'm sure there was never a doubt in his mind that he would take Rome and declare himself emperor. When he turned back at the Po River in 452, he was aware that there was nobody left who could stop him. Flavius Aëtius, who had prevented him from extending his kingdom to the Atlantic coast, no longer had an army that could stand against him. It turned out that Aëtius's nominal victory at Châlons-en-Champagne was the last victory by any Western Roman army anywhere, and I believe Attila was astute enough to see it that way. I think that in 453, in late spring or early summer when campaigning season began, he would have gone back to attack Rome. Instead he died."

They walked along the dark catacomb, the lights from their foreheads the only illumination except when one of them shone a flashlight on an inscription or there was a flash when someone took a picture. From the rear of the group Sam called out, "Keep reading every seal stone you come to. Take pictures to help record our route."

They walked on, along gallery after gallery. At one point, Tibor and János turned to look at an offshoot of the corridor they were in, then scurried to rejoin the group as the light moved on ahead.

Sam stopped and whispered to them. "Did you hear something too?"

Tibor said, "It sounded like footsteps somewhere in the dark behind us. You heard it?"

Remi said, "You think that Attila's men came down here and took over an earlier burial?"

"Exactly," said Albrecht. "We think they found a tunnel, or even a district of the catacomb, that was old enough so nobody ever visited it anymore. Then they probably removed a sealing stone and whatever human remains were behind it. Next they did what some Roman families did—dug much deeper and wider into the stone to make a chamber. They would have made a very small, narrow opening so the tomb looked like the thousands around it. But if the treasure is anything like what we've read, the chamber would be much larger than any of the crypts we've seen so far."

"We've got to think more about recognizing it," said Remi. "Is there a family symbol, or a pun on Attila's name, or a nickname?"

"Even the name itself is a controversy," said Albrecht. "Some people think Attila is derived from Gothic and meant 'little father,' *atil* meaning 'father' and *la* being a diminutive. The idea is that the Huns were Asiatic and a bit smaller than the Gothic peoples of the future Germany. We also have Priscus's account, which says Attila was on the short side."

"Do you accept that?" asked Tibor.

"No. I think it contradicts much of what we know about him. He was a charismatic leader and an absolute ruler—a tyrant, if you will—and a ruthless warrior. At times he pursued strategies that would preserve his armies, but at other times, if it suited his purpose, he hurled his cavalry at fortified positions and accepted huge casualties as the price of victory. He wasn't the sort of person who is called 'little father,' and certainly not the sort who would use that name."

"So what is your favorite theory?"

"I think that the Hunnic language was closest to that of the Danube Bulgarians, a more recently extinct Turkic language. In Danube

Bulgarian, *attila* means, literally, 'great ocean' or 'universal ruler.' It fits the role of a king of the Huns, whose job was to bring victory, and therefore prosperity, to the people. It also has no hint of an origin in a distantly related language or a Western point of view."

The group walked to the first three galleries that were candidates for Attila's grave. They had all been dug and filled before the year 400. There were carved inscriptions, but none that contained all three necessary elements—the right names of consuls for the year 453, the age forty-seven, and a date of death during the first three or four months of the year.

Captain Boiardi asked, "Why do we assume Attila would tell the truth about anything? Why not put a fake name, year, and day?"

Albrecht said, "Because it doesn't fit with what we think his purpose was. We think he wanted the tomb to be possible for the right person to find—one with determination and cunning and persistence. We think he wanted the wealth he buried here and elsewhere to be used by a future leader of the Huns to rule the world."

They went to the fourth district on Albrecht and Selma's list, a place of intersecting galleries like the streets of an underground city. All turns were right angles at the ends of blocks. The explorers read inscriptions and took photographs, as they had for many hours, and then, without any audible surprise, came Remi's voice out of the near dark. "I think we've found him."

Albrecht stopped. "What?" He pivoted to face her.

Remi was standing beside a space where there were several openings covered with seal stones. She pointed at one and repeated, "I think this is Attila."

Albrecht moved closer to the big stone she was examining. His single headlight added to hers and lit it brighter. The others gathered around. Albrecht read aloud to them. "'*Fidelis Miles*,' meaning 'Loyal Warrior,'" he said. "'*Obit die annus Flavius Opilio et Io-*

hannes Vincomalus vicesimo quinto Ianuarii. XLVII.'" He laughed loudly and put his arm around Remi. "I think you're right. I think that behind this stone is the man we're searching for."

There was a general round of handshaking, backslapping, and hugging. Sam said, "Let's all stand back a little so the seal can be photographed. From this moment on, everything gets documented, measured, and photographed as it is before it gets touched. Albrecht will be in charge."

The next two hours were spent on documenting the seal stone and removing it successfully. In the carved shelf space was the skeleton of a Hun warrior of the fifth century, much like the ones Albrecht had found in the field in Szeged, Hungary, early in the summer. "Presumably this man is the loyal soldier." The man, who was now a skeleton, wore leather pants and a tunic. He also carried a dagger and a long, straight sword.

Sam and Albrecht placed a board under the skeleton and the textiles and weapons, then carefully slid it outward so it could be placed in a rigid airtight plastic container like a flat coffin that was held by Tibor and János. They moved it out of the way.

Now Albrecht and Sam began to examine the back wall of the man's narrow berth carved into the rock. Sam took out his pocketknife. "Can I test it?"

"By all means," Albrecht said. "I think it should be a false wall made of plaster."

Sam prodded and scraped at the wall for a few seconds and then brought out a chunk about an inch thick. "It's a layer of plaster that hides a second stone."

"Let's photograph it before we remove it." Sam and Albrecht stepped back while Remi photographed the plaster. Then they carefully removed pieces, examining them for paint or scratches.

Albrecht leaned into the opening and stared at the piece of tufa fitted into the back beyond the plaster. "It's a second seal stone. Oh, yes. This is it!" he said. "'*Sepulcrum Summi Regis.*' The Tomb of the High King. '*Magnus Oceanus.*' The Great Ocean. '*Rex Hunnorum.*' Ruler of the Huns."

The others applauded, probably the loudest sound heard in this spot in over a thousand years. As it died down and stopped, Sam leaned close to Captain Boiardi. "Was that an echo?"

Boiardi listened for a few seconds, then nodded. "Let's go see." He turned off his headlamp.

The two stepped away from the side of the tomb and went back the way they had come, their flashlights turned off. As they quietly walked back, from time to time one of them would stop and they would wait and listen for a few seconds, then continue. As they came to the second turning, there was a larger opening that had been dug for a family crypt. Sam and Boiardi made the turn, Boiardi flicking on his light to see where they were.

Caught in the light were four men who leapt out of the blind corner and grappled with them, trying to overpower them and bring them to the floor of the crypt. Sam, who had been training in judo for most of his life, put the first man down in his initial moment of surprise and delivered a debilitating punch to his chest. The second man had thrown himself on Sam's back and clung to it. Sam ran hard at the wall, pivoted and hurled himself into it. The man slumped down the wall to the floor.

Captain Boiardi was a police officer trained in hand-to-hand combat and a tall man who was stronger than either of his attackers. He put the first one down with combination punches to the jaw and belly, then put the second out with a choke hold.

As Sam squatted to pick up the flashlight Boiardi had dropped, he saw that two women were crouching in a shadowy corner of the crypt.

Boiardi shouted something in Italian and they looked frightened. Both held their hands up. "We don't understand you."

"Don't shoot just yet," said Sam. "I know who they are."

"Who?"

"They work for a company called Consolidated Enterprises, based in New York."

"How do you know them?" asked Boiardi.

"They seem to be following Remi and me around. They're supposed to be commercial treasure hunters, but I don't know if they are or not."

"Why would they assault a captain of the Carabinieri?"

"You'll have to ask them. They were following us when we were diving off Louisiana and then again in Berlin. They got arrested in Berlin and then Hungary. I don't know how those arrests were resolved, but we can call Captain Klein of the Berlin police."

"You framed us," said the young woman with the short blond hair who had followed Sam and Remi in Berlin. "Of course the charges were dropped."

The tall man with the shaved head said, "They held us for two weeks!"

One of the other men said, "Don't say anything else until we have a lawyer."

"What's wrong with you Americans?" Boiardi said. "Do you watch only American movies? The whole world doesn't require a Miranda warning. And if you want legal advice, I'll give you the best. Don't attack any police officers."

Sam nodded. "I've found that to be excellent advice. How did you people even get into the catacomb?"

The brown-haired woman said, "We followed you. We went into the church as soon as we were sure you'd be in the catacomb.

When that monk saw us, we said we were part of your group and we were late. He was really nice and showed us which way you'd gone."

"Very clever," said Boiardi. "Trespassing for the theft of national treasures, but still pretty good."

"What are you going to do?" asked the man with the shaved head.

Boiardi waved the six prisoners over and said, "Come this way if you like treasure. You'll get to see the biggest find of your life."

Sam and Boiardi walked behind the six American interlopers so they wouldn't try to run away, directing them to turn one way or another to get back to Attila's tomb.

When they made the final turn and reached the opening, János, Tibor, and the two policemen set the second stone a few feet from the opening.

Sam looked through the opening. Beyond was a much larger space, a whole room carved out of the tufa. The ceiling was about eight feet high and five feet wide. He could see that the left side of the room had been opened and then bricked up to close it off again. He could see it was Attila's burial chamber. There, in the middle of the room, surrounded by randomly strewn piles of gold coins that had once sat in baskets or leather sacks that had rotted away, as well as jeweled swords, belts, daggers, and ornaments, was a seven-by-four-foot iron casket.

The two Carabinieri guarded the prisoners while, one by one, Remi, Sam, Albrecht, and Boiardi all climbed in through the narrow passage and began to photograph and chart every inch of the tomb, making the original location of each item clear. After three hours, they began to remove the items around the coffin. They were boxed, listed, and loaded on the eight carts.

Boiardi stepped close to his prisoners, who were sitting on the floor of the tunnel, looking glum. "Well? What do you think of this?"

The blond girl shrugged. "I'm glad I got to see it."

Boiardi said, "So you have curiosity and an adventurous soul. So do I. How about the rest of you?"

The other five nodded and mumbled various forms of assent.

"Good," Boiardi said. "Because I'm going to give you a job. It'll give you a chance to begin working off your debt to the people of *Italia*. You can help us carry these priceless artifacts up to the surface."

"That can't be legal," said the man with the shaved head. "You can't make prisoners work unless they're convicted."

"Okay," Boiardi said. "This gentleman is excused from work. The prosecutor will be told he didn't want to make up for his crimes. He's not sorry yet. Sergeant Baldare, handcuff him. What would the rest of you like me to tell the prosecutor?"

The others all said, "I'll work," or, "Okay," or, "Tell him I helped." The man with the shaved head said, "Wait a minute. I'll help."

Boiardi nodded at Sergeant Baldare, who removed the handcuffs. "One warning, of course. My men are not fools. You will be thoroughly searched at the top and the contents of all the boxes will eventually be compared with the photographs we've taken. If anything has stuck to you or in you, there will be a very picturesque and ancient prison in your future. Understood?"

"Yes," said each of the six in turn.

An hour later, the first carts of gold, precious gems, and jewel-studded weapons that once belonged to conquered kings began to make their way on the long corridors and up the long stairways toward the upper world, where they had not been since the year 453.

It took five days of careful yet grueling labor to complete the exhumation of Attila's treasure. At the top, where Selma, Wendy, Pete, and three Carabinieri worked to verify and load the artifacts, things worked smoothly. The first truck left for the National Archaeological Museum at Naples at three a.m. on the first night, accompanied by two unmarked police cars, and a new truck was moved into its place.

The Divine Word Missionaries lived up to their name by issuing the true story only, that the Catacomb of Domitilla was the site of some archaeological investigation and would be closed to the pubic temporarily.

On the sixth day the team brought in four chain hoists and lifted the lid of the iron coffin. Inside was a coffin of pure silver surrounded by more of Attila's treasures. There were the crowns, scepters, daggers, and personal ornaments of a hundred kings, princes, chieftains, sultans, and khans. It took a whole day to empty and catalog the artifacts.

On the eighth day the team lifted the lid of the silver coffin. They found the old accounts were true. The last one was made of gold. It was surrounded by colored gem stones—emeralds, rubies, sapphires, garnets, jade, coral, lapis lazuli, jasper, opal, amber—stones from everywhere in the ancient world.

On the last day, they opened Attila's gold casket. Inside was the skeleton of a man about five feet four inches tall, wearing a red silk tunic and trousers, knee-length leather boots, and a fur cap. His bony hand held a compound bow made of horn, and he wore a sword and a dagger. On the inner side of the gold coffin's lid was an inscription.

"You have found the tomb of Attila, High King of the Huns. In order to stand before me you must be a brave and cunning warrior. My last treasure will make you a rich and strong king. Only time, failure, and sorrow can make you a wise one."

30

THE ST. REGIS GRAND HOTEL, ROME

"PLEASE, EVERYONE, MAKE THREE ROWS." THE PHOTOG-
rapher from the *New York Times* waved them into place. Seated
in the front row were Albrecht at the center, flanked by Selma and
Wendy. The second row was János, Tibor, and Pete. In the back
row were Sam and Remi Fargo, and Captain Boiardi of the Italian
Carabinieri Tutela Patrimonio Culturale.

Dozens of shutters clicked in a complicated volley, with flashes
that fluttered like strobe lights. The reporter from *Der Spiegel* was
delighted because he could take many close-ups of the famed
German historian and archaeologist Albrecht Fischer while he was
posed as leader. Reporters from the Italian papers *Giornale di Si-
cilia*, *Il Gazzettino* of Venice, *Il Mattino* of Naples, *Il Messaggero*
of Rome, *Il Resto del Carlino* from Bologna, and *La Nazione* all
jostled one another to get pictures of a sampling of the magnificent
treasure, which had been laid out on a white sheet on the carpet

and was being guarded by the tall, serious Italian Carabinieri in their dress uniforms. The Carabinieri just looked upward, immune to the allure of the glittering gems and crowns and swords on the sheet.

After the photographs, the interviews began. Sam and Remi moved off to the far end of the hotel meeting room, but reporters from *Le Figaro*, *Le Monde*, the *Daily Telegraph*, and *The Guardian* still found them.

The Guardian's reporter, a woman named Ann Dade-Stanton, cornered Sam. "Everyone I've talked to privately says you were the leader of this series of expeditions and that most of the time the only ones even present were Sam and Remi Fargo. Is this some kind of a dodge? A tax strategy or something?"

Sam said, "Everybody here traveled, took risks, and worked at some point in a deep hole. Some of us contributed by doing research, making arrangements for travel and equipment, and so on. Others spent more time on the scene. But I wasn't the leader."

Remi said, "The one Sam and I considered our leader and guide to the ancient world was our friend Professor Albrecht Fischer. He has spent his career studying Roman times. He telephoned us after he had made the initial discovery in a field in Hungary and asked us to come and help him. We did."

"But you're world-famous treasure hunters and adventurers. And I understand you paid all the expenses."

"We and Albrecht Fischer and Tibor Lazar were partners from the morning when we found the first stone chamber in Hungary. Albrecht had the most knowledge of history and the archaeology of the late Roman Empire. Tibor was born in the part of Hungary where Attila had his stronghold and could get people there to help us, including those with equipment and vehicles. Sam and I had some experience with historical research and donated some money. We all contributed what we had and we all brought in other people who could help."

"That's right," said Sam. "And along the way, the culture ministries of a number of countries helped us and provided physical protection and preservation of our finds where the world's scholars will be able to study them—particularly Hungary, Italy, and France. We also had help from the police forces of Berlin and Moscow."

"Sam?" Selma whispered. "The website."

"Oh, that's right," said Sam. "This is Selma Wondrash, our chief researcher." He nodded to her.

Selma said, "We will be putting up a website containing the complete catalog of all the artifacts in each of the treasure hoards and the tomb of Attila. It will include photographs of all of the items inside the treasure chambers in the positions where they were found, as well as close-up pictures made under museum conditions. From time to time, as scholarly articles about them are produced, the articles will be added to the site. We also expect to reproduce this information in a book, under the editorship of Professor Albrecht Fischer."

The reporters all dutifully wrote down what they were told and then joined in the celebration. The party went on late into the night. When Captain Boiardi and his men had packed the sample artifacts into their locked cases, they prepared to leave.

"Sam, Remi," he said. "The news will be in every major newspaper in the world tomorrow. Before the early-morning online editions come out, we've got to take the last of the treasure and transport it to the museum."

"Do you have to go so soon?" Remi asked.

"The longer we wait, the more dangerous it will be. Ancient

treasures capture people's imaginations, and not always in a good way. In the 1920s, Tut's tomb was a huge fad. And who was Tutankhamen? A rich teenager. This is *Attila*." The captain grinned, kissed Remi's hand and shook Sam's. "This has been a great pleasure, and the greatest accomplishment of my career."

"It has been for us too," Remi said. "I hope you didn't mean it when you said you were retiring."

"If you don't retire, I won't," he said. "I want to see what else you can find."

"We'll call you," said Sam.

The Carabinieri left the hotel, and then the reporters and photographers. Soon the only ones left in the banquet room were Albrecht, Sam and Remi, Tibor and János, Selma, Pete and Wendy. Sam picked up a spoon and tapped it against a champagne glass, making a musical tinkling. Everyone stopped talking and looked in his direction. "All right, everyone. We've had a great party. Now Remi and I are going off to get some sleep. Please meet us in the lobby downstairs at nine a.m. with your packed bags. We have drivers coming to take us to the airport. We're giving you a ride home."

As they walked lazily to their suite, Remi yawned. "You're flying everybody home on a rented jet?"

Sam shrugged. "Selma, Pete, and Wendy live at our house and we'd have to pay their airfare anyway. Tibor and János saved our lives at least twice each. And Albrecht invited us to be part of one of the great treasure hunts of all time. It's just two stops."

"I don't want to sound like an ingrate and a shallow woman, but it's been a long time since I've been alone with my husband when I didn't have a shovel in my hand and nobody was shooting at us."

Sam put his arm around her as they walked to the elevator. "Now, that's true. The first thing it does is make me glad that I married a beautiful woman who likes my company. The other thing is, it makes me glad that most criminals are such terrible marksmen."

She stood on her tiptoes to plant a kiss on his cheek. "I can't wait to get home."

"You'll get no backtalk out of me." He unlocked the suite door and they stepped inside.

The next morning, at nine, they met the others in the lobby, then got into their rented limousines for the fifteen-kilometer drive to Ciampino Airport. The jet Selma had ordered was waiting on the tarmac outside the small private terminal. The group waited until their luggage was loaded and then climbed the steps to board.

It was just five hundred ninety-six miles from Rome to Frankfurt, where Albrecht left them. "Well, you've given me something to think about," he said. "If I lived two lifetimes, I still wouldn't be able to complete my study of what we've found. I thank you one and all."

It was another six hundred ninety miles to Szeged. When they landed at the airport, Tibor and János Lazar stood up and Tibor said to Sam, "Are you coming?"

Sam took Remi by the hand and said, "Everybody, we'll be back in just a few minutes."

Remi looked at Sam with curiosity, then watched her step as they climbed down from the plane and caught up with the Lazar brothers.

Remi said, "Tibor, János, I hope we see you again soon. You're welcome to visit us in La Jolla, you have our phone numbers and e-mail addresses."

Tibor said, "We may, but not yet. We've decided to stay home for a while and rest. Now and then we'll get up to laugh at Arpad Bako. But only for that."

"I don't know how much your share of the treasures will be," said Sam. "A lot of it will never leave a museum. But you'll get millions of dollars from what's sold."

"See?" Tibor said. "I told you that it was a good idea to be your friend."

The four walked into the terminal and there, on the other side of the waiting area, was a man sitting beside a very large plastic carrier on a wheeled cart. Remi said, "Sam—?"

The man seemed to hear her voice and turned around in his seat to look at the newcomers from the plane. Remi's eyes widened and she ran toward him. She came around the large container, looked inside, and sank to her knees. She began to cry. *"Jo fiu,"* she said quietly. She popped up to her feet and threw her arms around Sam. "Oh, Sam. I don't believe this."

"I thought you deserved a present," he said. "But Zoltán deserved a present too and what he seemed to want was you."

Tibor, János, and Tibor's wife's cousin the dog trainer helped Sam push the cart to the plane. At the foot of the steps, Remi said, "We can't carry him up those steps in a box."

She knelt, opened the cagelike door, and out came Zoltán, first the big black snout and then the broad head and long-furred neck and then the muscular shoulders and body. She put her arms around the dog's neck and held him for a moment. *"Jo fiu,"* she whispered. "Good boy." She stood. *"Fel,"* she said. "Up." She began to climb the steps and Zoltán followed her up into the plane.

Tibor helped Sam carry the big travel carrier and set it down, then used its straps to secure it to an empty row of seats. Then he said to Sam and Remi, "We'll see each other before long," and went quickly down the steps and into the terminal.

As Remi and Zoltán walked back into the passenger area, Selma eyed the big dog. "Oh, good. He's finally bought you a pony."

Remi said, "Selma, this is Zoltán. Come here and let him sniff your hand. He won't hurt you."

Selma put out her hand for Zoltán and then patted his thick neck.

"—unless I tell him to."

Pete and Wendy laughed as Selma retreated. "He's just right," Pete said. "If you go to Alaska, he can pull the sled by himself."

"Okay," said Remi. "Now you two." Pete and Wendy approached Zoltán and patted him. He stood still and tolerated the attention.

Remi went to her seat beside Sam. To Zoltán she said, *"Ül."* The dog sat at her feet. She tickled him behind the ears.

The refueling and the preflight inspection were completed and the steward closed the cabin door. Sam got up, went to the carrier, and came back with a bag of dog treats.

"Good idea," Pete said. "Those will buy us time if he decides to eat us."

"Don't worry about him," said Sam. "He's better educated than we are. He's trained to recognize which people need eating and to protect the rest of us." Remi leaned down and hugged Zoltán again, then gave him a treat.

The pilot started the engines and the passengers fastened their seat belts. As the plane moved ahead, taxiing over the pavement, Zoltán looked watchful and ate his treat. The plane reached the end of the runway and turned into the wind. While the plane accelerated along the runway and then rose into the air, Remi kept her hand on Zoltán's shoulder to reassure him. "Don't worry, Zoltán. I'm here with you." Her safe, calm, musical voice seemed to relax him. As the rattles and vibrations ended and the plane lifted off the ground, Zoltán let his big head rest on the carpet and settled in for a long flight.

Remi leaned close to Sam and whispered, "I love him. And I love you. But this is so extravagant. A dog like him, with his training, costs as much as a Rolls-Royce."

"A Rolls-Royce is a great machine. But it won't trade its life for yours."

Sam tilted back his seat and so did Remi. She rested her head on his chest. Zoltán looked up at them once, then surveyed the cabin and laid his head down again and closed his eyes.

31

GOLDFISH POINT, LA JOLLA
THE FIRST FLOOR

IT WAS SUNSET WHEN REMI AND ZOLTÁN WENT OUT FOR
their evening run along the beach. In the weeks since the Fargos had
returned from Europe, Remi had devoted a great deal of time to
working with Zoltán. She had wanted him to get used to the part
of the world that would be his home.

So far, Zoltán seemed to like La Jolla. He was utterly calm and
peaceful. When she walked, he walked. When she ran, he ran.
Today she had run to the little protected beach at the south end of
La Jolla that was called the Children's Pool. Lying on every inch of
the beach and the concrete breakwater were about a hundred seals
and sea lions. She knew there was no way Zoltán could have seen
seals or sea lions in Hungary, but he seemed no more inclined to
bother the resting sea mammals than he had been to bother a tree
or a park bench.

They turned back and ran along the concrete path toward Gold-fish Point, then up onto the green lawn and past the palm trees of the park to the Valencia Hotel. As she looked out beyond the park's vast lawn to the ocean, she thought about what an incredible place this was. La Jolla meant "the Jewel," and it was the right name. She and Sam had chosen to build their house up above Goldfish Point, at the north end of the little district. The point was the entrance to the surf-splashed caves along the rocky part of the coast and was named for the bright orange Garibaldi that swam in La Jolla Cove.

When Remi and Sam had designed their house, they had just spent six years devoting all their time to building and running their company, which produced and sold the argon laser scanner that he had invented. They had been offered an astonishing sum for the company and its patents and had made the sale. For the first time not only could they afford to build a large and expensive house, they had the time and energy to devote to it.

When it was finished, the house was twelve thousand square feet on four floors planted above Goldfish Point. The top floor held Sam and Remi's master suite, two bathrooms, two walk-in closets, a small kitchen, and a sitting room with a wall of windows that looked out on the ocean. The third floor held four guest suites, the main living room, the main kitchen, and the dining room. They had decided to use the second floor for a gym, an endless lap pool, a climbing wall, and a thousand-square-foot strip for Remi's fenc-ing and Sam's judo.

The only place for an office was the ground floor. It had open work spaces for Sam, Remi, Selma, and up to four researchers. There were more guest bedrooms, a lab, and a fourteen-foot-long saltwater aquarium with plants and animals from the California coast.

As Remi and Zoltán took their evening jog home, she looked out beyond the cove and saw two yachts she had not noticed there earlier. They sat offshore about a half mile and, from her perspective on the path above the beach, they looked as though they were almost touching. They were both big, fast cruisers in the 130-foot class, a kind of yacht that she had seen European celebrities charter in the western Mediterranean. They were commonly capable of about sixty knots, and a few were faster. She'd seen a few like them in the San Diego Harbor in the past couple years, but they were extremely expensive and better suited for speeding people between the Greek islands or along the French Riviera than plying the Pacific.

She and Zoltán were past the hotel now and beginning to make their way up to the street that led to the higher wooded plateau where their house stood. She could see it from where they were, perched up on the hillside, its walls of windows facing the ocean on three sides. The lights in the house were warm and welcoming to her. Sam had designed and installed a system of individual sensors that automatically turned on a few lights on each floor at dusk. Because there were few interior walls, that gave most of the house a golden glow.

Remi kept trotting up the hill, which was the hardest part of her daily run, when she noticed that, all at once, Zoltán became oddly agitated. He leapt forward and then stopped abruptly at her feet and stared ahead with his amber-and-black German shepherd eyes. Remi stopped and stood beside him, trying to determine what he was staring at. Something ahead on the winding street was worrying him.

Remi was concerned and now even more impatient to get home. She knew enough about Zoltán's sense of smell, his training, and his predator's ability to detect the presence of living things hidden from human view to know he was evaluating something he considered unusual and important. She considered putting his leash on. Maybe she had discovered a situation where he was unreliable. She'd heard stories of shepherds going after postal workers because of the smell of dry-cleaning fluid on their uniforms. It could be something like that. Actually, no, it couldn't. He was exquisitely trained, and using the leash would have seemed to her to show a lack of faith in him.

While she was waiting for him, Zoltán began to move forward again. He didn't trot, as he had before. His head was low, his nose sniffing the air and his eyes fixed on something Remi couldn't see. His shoulders flexed as he began to stalk. His whole body went lower now, compact like a compressed spring.

Remi didn't talk to calm Zoltán or rein him in. He wasn't investigating now. He was sure there was a threat. She walked along behind him, marveling at his single-minded concentration. He stopped again, and then she heard the sound. She felt it in her body, the nerves in her hands, because she had heard the same sound so many times when she pushed a loaded magazine up between the grips and into the receiver and it clicks into place. She heard the slide being pulled back to allow a round to pop up into the chamber.

Zoltán took four steps at a dead run and leapt into the foliage ahead. He came down halfway into a privet hedge, gripping a man's arm in his teeth. He shook it until the man lost his grip and the gun clattered on the pavement. Zoltán charged forward, pushing the man backward so he couldn't retrieve his weapon.

Remi ran forward, kicked the gun off the road into the darkness, and kept going. Now Zoltán was ahead of her again, running toward the house. He didn't wait for the driveway but instead took the shortcut through the pine woods, and she followed him. He tore ahead of her in the darkness, running silently on the thick layer of needles. Twice as she ran, she saw him veer off, heard him tear into something with a growl, and then heard the scream of a human voice join his snarl. She sprinted to catch up and then she saw a silhouette. It was the shape of a man making a quick dash across the path. Zoltán collided with him, not changing his pace and throwing his big body against the man, shunting him aside onto the ground.

Then Remi and Zoltán were through the woods and running across the lawn, then up the concrete walkway, then up the steps. She heard the men running after her, and they were fast, only a couple of steps behind her now. Zoltán turned, growling, and charged. She heard the sounds of the fighting as she flung the door open and Zoltán ran inside with her. She slammed the door and as she slipped the bolt she let out a scream: "Sam!" There was a thud against the door as someone tried to shoulder it open.

Zoltán barked, and Remi screamed again as she ran deeper into the house. "Sam!"

On the ocean end of the first floor, where the open office space was, Selma called out, "Remi! What's wrong?"

"Men are here! They chased me and tried to ambush me on the path in the woods."

Selma ran to Remi, then stopped and stared at Zoltán in horror. Remi looked too and saw that his muzzle was dripping blood. He turned to stare at the door and crouched, his teeth bared.

As they looked, the whole house went black. There was the sound of men running up the steps and then a loud boom as they swung something that sounded like a battering ram against the steel door. The impact set off the battery-operated alarm system, so there was a loud, pulsing tone that kept on as the ram hit again with another boom.

The house's emergency generator was running now, and a few low-watt lights came on, so they could see. *Boom!* There was a whining sound as the vibration from the battering ram turned on the motor that lowered the steel shutters on the first floor. Now the whole floor was lit only by those few bulbs, deprived of the moonlight and the glow from the rest of La Jolla's electric lights.

Then Sam was in the room with them. He went to the metal control box built into the wall, opened it, turned on the monitor for the cameras over the door, and looked for just a second. "Selma, call the police."

He used the intercom to speak to the men outside. "You, on the porch. Get the battering ram out of here or you'll regret it."

Boom! The men seemed to try harder. They stepped back, then forward again and swung the heavy steel cylinder. *Boom!* Remi could see the door bump inward without giving way.

Sam reached for a covered switch in the control box and flipped it on. In the monitor, Sam and Remi could see the men on the porch react to a hissing sound. When they looked up, they dropped the battering ram, covered their eyes and faces with their hands, and blindly staggered off the porch.

"What's that?" Remi asked.

"Pepper spray. It's one of the things I added to the security system."

"That kind of paid for itself, didn't it?" she said as she watched men from the woods hurry onto the lawn to pull the injured back to the cover of the pines.

Selma called out, "The phones are dead."

"Use your cell."

"They seem to be jamming 850 megahertz." Selma took another phone out of her desk and they recognized it as one of the ones they'd used in Europe. "Some kind of device. 1900 megahertz too. 2100 and 2500."

"Then send someone you know an e-mail to call the cops for us."

"The Wi-Fi is jammed too. I can't get online. I can't use the phone line because it's dead."

"All right. Of course," Sam said. He manipulated a toggle on his control board to alter the aim of the surveillance cameras. "Wow. We're in trouble," he said. "Look at all the men out there."

"Are Pete and Wendy home?" asked Remi.

"I'll go tell them what's up," said Selma.

Sam said, "Tell them to open the gun safe and bring us—"

"I'll do that," said Remi, already running for the stairs. She took them two and three at a time, but Zoltán seemed to have no trouble staying ahead of her. She reached the second floor and met Pete and Wendy on the way to the third. "Hold it!" she said. "I need you upstairs for a minute."

Pete and Wendy followed Remi upstairs to the fourth floor. There was the big bedroom suite straight ahead from the staircase and to the left were the two big closets. Between the two was a plain panel on the wall that would have escaped notice unless you knew it was there. Remi pushed a spot on it and it opened like a door. Inside was a narrow corridor that held two gun safes and a third safe that looked as though it had come from a small bank. Remi quickly worked the combinations of the gun safes.

Remi said, "Wendy, get five Glock 19 pistols—one for everybody—and two extra magazines each. Then take as much nine-millimeter ammo as you can carry and go to the first floor. You can leave the two for Pete and me."

"What's going on?" asked Wendy.

"Not sure yet. I think it's the people we thought we left in Europe.

Pete, get some long guns and ammo—a couple of short-barreled shotguns and the two semiauto .308s. Lots of ammo."

Pete and Wendy hurried from the fourth floor to the narrow stairway down to the third floor, their arms piled with weapons and boxes of ammunition. Remi closed the two safes without relocking them and then closed the panel that hid them. She went into the bedroom, not looking at Zoltán but feeling him coming in with her. She said, "*Ül*, Zoltán." He sat. She petted his big head. She backed out and closed the door.

She picked up the Glock that Wendy had left her, released the magazine to be sure it was loaded, then put the two spares into the waistband of her shorts and ran down the stairs to the third floor, whirled to go down the next flight to the second floor, and got halfway down when she saw something through a window that made her freeze.

There was a ladder leaning against the side of the house, the end of it just above the top of a second-floor window. A man in a black turtleneck and black jeans scrambled up the ladder in plain sight. He reached the floor, pulled out a hammer, and smashed a large pane of glass, then prepared to step from the ladder onto the empty frame. Remi ran to the nearest window, raised her arms above her head and lifted the long wooden curtain rod off its hooks, dipped it once on each side to let the curtains slide off the ends and ran to the broken window. The man saw her coming and reached for the rifle sling across his chest to bring his automatic weapon to his hand, but Remi was faster. As she ran toward him she aimed her pole out the window into the man's chest. He tried to brush it away, but that caused him to take his hand off the ladder and forget his weapon. Remi pushed him backward off the ladder, then used the pole to push the ladder over after him.

She looked down out the window and saw that a man had run to the aid of the fallen climber and another was picking up the aluminum ladder. When they saw Remi, they fired several shots in her direction. She ran to the opposite side of the second floor, holding on to the curtain rod, and hurried around the stairway.

It was as she had feared. Another man was on a ladder outside the window on that side. He used a tool that looked like a hatchet to break the glass. Remi was already moving, so this time it was easier to catch him before he was ready. She jabbed the long wooden pole through the broken window, still running. But this man still had the hatchet in his hand and he flung it through the window at her. She ducked to the side and it spun past her head and hit something behind her, but she managed to plant the pole in the man's chest and kept running until he went over backward, clinging to his ladder.

Remi saw the control panel for the second floor's systems. She dropped her curtain rod, ran to it, opened the cover, and turned on the switch for the second floor's steel shutters. The lights dimmed, the motor gave a sickly groan, and the shutters came down only about a foot and then stopped.

Downstairs she could hear the booming of the battering ram again. She ran to the head of the stairs and looked down. Sam, Pete, Selma, and Wendy had pushed a lot of heavy furniture against the front door. A pair of desks were on their sides with some steel filing cabinets lying horizontally behind them. The four defenders stood in a twenty-foot circle, watching the door. Pete was on the left, aiming a shotgun, with Wendy on the right pressing the other shotgun to her shoulder, and Selma was at Wendy's shoulder, aiming a pistol with both hands. Sam was in the center with one of Remi's Les Baer Semi-Auto Match rifles. The sturdy steel front door had buckled a little from the constant pounding, and Remi could tell they were almost ready to bend backward enough to let the bolt slip.

As she watched and listened, the battering stopped. Then, from outside, came the sound of a car engine. It grew louder as it came closer, then louder still. It roared for a couple of seconds and then—*Bang!*—the car hit and the front door swung open. The desks and filing cabinets slid inward across the floor as a high-riding pickup, with a crash barrier mounted in front of its grille, appeared in the opening.

Sam had fired a couple of shots as soon as the door had flown open and there were holes on the driver's side of the windshield, but there was no driver. Clearly the pedal had been jammed down with a weight or a stick and the truck aimed at the door.

Men in black clothes appeared a few yards back from the door, hidden by the high bed of the truck, and fired bursts into the house with automatic weapons.

Sam called out, "Get upstairs!"

Pete, Wendy, and Selma, firing at the open doorway, backed their way to the staircase near the center of the house. Sam fired well-placed rounds with the rifle whenever he could see an arm, a leg, or a weapon protrude from behind the pickup. As he did, he backed toward the stairs after the others.

Remi, who had been watching for more ladders, could hardly bear to see Sam down there alone, trying to delay the intruders. She stepped halfway down the stairs and fired rapidly at the opening with her Glock pistol. She was still firing when Sam reached around her waist, picked her up, and forced her up the stairs with him. They climbed the stairs backward, aiming and firing, keeping the intruders outside. Remi ran out of ammunition just as they made it up to the second floor.

As she reached for another magazine, Remi had one last look before Sam and Pete rolled the grand piano down the stairs. It tipped, turned, and then slid with a crash and a disharmonious vibration of hammers against strings, then jammed in the stairwell. But before it stopped, Remi had seen a dozen armed men rushing in past the broken front door. As she reloaded, Sam and Pete ran back to the gym area to get more objects to block the stairs. The first floor was lost.

32

THE SECOND FLOOR

SAM AND PETE PUSHED A HEAVY CROSS-TRAINING MA-
chine, and then a treadmill, into the stairwell. These helped block
the opening so it would be difficult for the intruders to hit anyone
if they fired up the stairs, and the weight alone would probably
keep them from trying to storm the second floor. Remi finished re-
loading and stepped back behind an overturned steel weight table
and watched the stairway for any sign of activity. All at once, from
the floor below, there was a furious rattle of automatic-weapons
fire, none of it directed at the stairwell. "What are they doing?"

"Trying to fire upward at us through the floor," said Sam. "They
won't have much luck because all the floors are reinforced concrete.
Otherwise, we couldn't have a pool up here."

There was an abrupt noise that sounded as though the firing had
grown into a military battle and moved outside. There was a loud,

explosive bang. Pete and Wendy looked out the front windows. "Look!" Wendy shouted.

Outside, in the sky above the ocean, the air turned red, then blue, then white as flarelike pieces floated slowly down until they reached the black water, where they met their own reflections and were extinguished. "Fireworks!"

As they watched, a streak of golden sparks shot upward from a raft tethered to a boat out in the cove. When the projectile reached its apex, it blew up in a starburst, the fiery stars leaving behind burning trails like the drooping branches of a willow tree.

"They're using fireworks to cover the noise!" Selma announced. "Or to explain it. People will think all the shots are part of a celebration."

"Right," said Sam. "A big blowout at the Fargos'."

Another shell was fired into the air and its explosion was green. Another explosion replaced it with bright red, then yellow. Each change was punctuated by an initial bang and then a staccato barrage of pops like the rattle of automatic weapons.

Selma shouted, "The window! No you don't!" There was another man on a ladder at the broken window where Remi had pushed the first man off. Selma held her pistol in both hands and fired four times before she hit him and he fell from the window. Pete picked up the curtain rod Remi had used and pushed the ladder away from the house.

"We've got to get the steel shutters deployed on this floor," said Sam. "Wendy, turn off all the lights. Remi, if you see something down the stairs that looks like part of a human, shoot it. Pete, you watch the windows. If anybody shows up, do what Selma did. Selma, watch my back."

Sam opened a small steel door in the wall by the front windows.

He waited until the lights were off, then engaged the switch. The electric motor groaned, but the shutters descended only another inch or two. Sam took a small hand crank out of the box, knelt to stick it in a socket just above the windowsill, and turned it. The shutter lowered slowly down to the sill. He moved to the next window and knelt again to crank it down. But just as he did, a ladder appeared at the next one.

A man scrambled up the ladder, punched the window in with a hammer, and stuck his arm in holding a Škorpion automatic pistol. Remi shot the arm before he could fire. He dropped the weapon and made his way down a few feet, his arm hanging limp, and Pete pushed the ladder over with the wooden pole.

Sam cranked the shutter down over the window and moved on to the next one. As he cranked, the window next to it burst into a hundred shards as men outside fired at it. Sam shook his head to get rid of the glass in his hair and kept cranking. But after the next window, there was a sudden quiet. He looked up for a second, then ran to the other side of the house and began cranking shutters down.

Aluminum ladders appeared at windows on that side. Two of the climbers got as far as firing weapons into the second floor before Remi or Wendy shot them. Pete pushed the ladders off the house. Sam kept cranking down shutters.

There was a screech of wood against metal, and the piano jammed in the stairwell moved a little. Sam shouted, "Get the refrigerator!"

Pete, Wendy, and Selma ran to the open kitchen and laboriously wheeled the big wide stainless steel refrigerator along the hardwood floor toward the stairs. Sam picked up the .308 rifle he had set down when closing the shutters and ran to the stairs. He stalked around the opening for the well, peeking around the gym equipment for a target, but seeing nobody peeking back. He detected movement at the piano, as though someone were trying to push it. He aimed the rifle at what he guessed was near a leg of the piano and fired through the wood. There was a hush from the stairs so deep that he sensed men must be gathering there. He fired twice more through the piano.

He turned just as another man on a ladder broke a window and stepped toward the windowsill. He shot the man and then saw yet another man on a ladder coming up the opposite side of the house. He shot that man before he could break the window and saw him fall away from the house. He fired twice more through the beautiful mirrorlike finish of the piano into the stairwell.

The others had the refrigerator at the top of the stairs now. He gave them the signal to hold and they moved around behind it and waited. Sam used the time to close more shutters to prevent cross fire from outside. They all heard the sound of the engine of the pickup truck at the front door. Sam sprang to his feet, ran to the edge of the stairwell, and replaced the magazine in his rifle.

The engine outside roared and the piano screeched and then banged down the stairs, dragged by the truck, its strings making an awful noise. It had been holding the gym equipment, which now began to tumble down after it. Sam waved and the others pushed over the big refrigerator. It toppled, crashed, and then slid down and gathered speed like a steel sled. A few men below seemed to get bowled over, but it was hard to see what the damage was.

"Couches," Sam said, and they pushed two big couches into the well together. This blocked the stairs, but a burst of fire came up through them and they had nothing in them that could stop a bullet.

Sam said, "Selma, go up to the third floor and boil water in the kitchen. As much as you can boil, as fast as you can do it. Take a shotgun with you and a pistol, and make sure they're loaded."

"What's that for?" asked Remi.

"We're going to lose this floor too when they clear the stairs. We can make it cost them, but then we have to get upstairs. Those extension ladders won't reach the third floor."

ÉTIENNE LE CLERC, Sergei Poliakoff, and Arpad Bako sat on comfortable chaises on the deck of the yacht *Ibiza* with their feet up and smoking fine Cuban Cohiba cigars. The warm offshore breeze blew the smoke over their shoulders and out to sea.

The second yacht, the *Mazatlan*, was anchored about a thousand yards to their left now because her crew was sending up fireworks from a raft they had spent the afternoon loading.

Through powerful binoculars, Bako watched the distant house above Goldfish Point. "This must be what it was like watching a conqueror like Attila take an ancient city—scaling ladders against defenders with poles, storming the lowest levels of the fortress, and forcing the defenders higher until they surrender and die."

Poliakoff glared at his watch. "Our side had better step up the pace or the distraction of the fireworks will wear thin and someone who lives near them will figure out what's happening."

Le Clerc shrugged. "We cut the power and the telephone in the boxes at the end of the street, and the jammers will keep any sort of phone or Wi-Fi useless for some distance."

Bako said, "There are also men at the intersections to warn our forces if the police come. If necessary, they can close down the roads for a few minutes."

"I just hope Sam Fargo is beginning to feel my hand," said Poliakoff. "What he did to my house in Nizhny Novgorod is exactly what I'm doing to his. And when it's over, if they're not both dead, I'll bring them back with me and make Fargo start where he left off—reclaiming the treasures from the museums and bringing them to me and laying them at my feet to keep his wife alive."

"Don't forget this isn't just you," said Le Clerc. "You're just one of the partners."

"I was going to say that," said Bako. "The treasures were mine to begin with. I just shared them with my partners."

Poliakoff smiled and took a puff on his cigar. "You called me in only after you had failed and been defeated," he said. "I took over when you had done everything you could and lost."

Bako chuckled nervously. "Well, we've all committed ourselves and we'll have them in a few minutes."

There was another volley of shots from the house and then another rocket shot up from the raft in the cove and burst in a ball of blue streaks and gold stars. Each of the little gold stars popped loudly and sent a spray of exploding sparks into the sky above the ocean. Bako said, "Who would believe that the gunshots were not part of the show?"

SAM AND REMI pushed a weight-training machine over into the stairwell as Selma, Wendy, and Pete carefully carried the big pots of boiling water to the railing above.

They waited until the attackers had dragged most of the furniture away and the first men had dashed up the stairs from the first floor to clamber over the weight machine.

Sam made a single downward motion of his arm and Selma, Pete, and Wendy poured the big pots of boiling water down on them. The men shouted, turned and bumped into the men coming up the stairs behind them. The momentum of the others pushed them ahead and some went down on their bellies rather than go under the scorching cascade. As the attackers tussled on the steps, Sam fired his rifle above them, making the retreaters stronger than the chargers. "Go!" he shouted.

Remi, Pete, Selma, and Wendy rushed up the stairs to the third floor. At the top of the stairs, Remi lay on the floor and waited. While Sam backed his way up the stairs, she fired rounds into the second-floor stairwell to make the invaders keep their heads down.

As soon as Sam had cleared the last step up to the third floor, the others pushed over a big wooden sideboard that fell heavily across the stairway like a trap door. They were out of the line of fire for the next few moments, but they could hear the heavy footsteps of the enemy below them rushing up to occupy the second floor.

33

THE THIRD FLOOR

Sam turned to Pete. "We can't keep fighting them on these stairs. We've got to sabotage the one that leads from here to the fourth floor and then make our stand up there. It's held to the steel I beam by bolts—six of them, I think, but you can check. Before you do anything to the stairs, get a climbing rope and tie it to something solid up there and run it down here."

"I understand," Pete said. They were on the third floor where Pete's and Wendy's bedrooms were. He hurried into his room and then the kitchen, collecting tools and equipment, and then climbed the staircase.

Remi walked past Sam and he reached out and held her. "Where's Zoltán?"

"I closed him in our bedroom upstairs. He would have gotten killed down there. He doesn't understand strategic withdrawal. Up there, he thinks he's guarding something important."

"He is," he said. He turned to Selma. "Let's see if the boiling water works again. Get some started in the fourth-floor kitchen."

To Wendy he said, "Wendy, go up and bring more ammunition down. Load all the empty magazines one more time. Load the shotguns too."

Remi was close to Sam's shoulder as they stared hard at the big sideboard covering the stairway, waiting for it to move. "What are they doing?" she whispered.

"We hurt them badly on the last staircase. I think they're tending to the ones who got burned and any who might have been shot. Probably evacuating them."

"What's our strategy now?" she asked.

"We're buying time," he said. "We couldn't call the police or e-mail anyone, but somebody must be figuring out that this isn't just the sound of those fireworks. Probably the ones closest to us don't have phone service either, but farther away they must."

Remi picked up one of the .308 Match rifles and went to the south-side windows. She looked out at the Valencia Hotel backed up to the hillside. She adjusted the mil-dot scope for a thousand yards, adjusted the windage to account for a left-to-right offshore breeze of five miles an hour, unlatched the window, and pushed it open a few inches. She raised the rifle to her shoulder and aimed at the big lighted rectangle of the dining room window of the Valencia. She waited, making sure that there were no people behind it, then squeezed the trigger. *Pow!*

She didn't move, just watched the window through the powerful scope. Two diners who had been hidden by the wall to the left ran across the window toward the doorway. She could see the woman's mouth open in a silent scream. A waiter and a hostess in a cocktail dress appeared, looking up at the broken window with great concern, and retreated out of sight.

"What did you see?" asked Sam.

"The Valencia. I'm pretty sure they're calling the cops about us as fast as they can hit the numbers."

"I should have thought of that."

"We couldn't see the hotels from the windows on the lower floors. The trees were in the way. Now they're not." She picked out a restaurant that was a bit closer but was also brightly lit. After a few seconds, she fired again. "Make that two callers. That makes it more believable."

"Remi," Sam whispered. "I'm hearing movement."

She turned and saw him staring down at the big sideboard over the stairwell with the rifle to his shoulder. She came closer and picked a spot to aim at. "Shouldn't we shoot through it?"

He shook his head. "We're buying time, so any delay helps us. Besides, we don't have enough ammo to shoot people just because they deserve it."

"Just in case we can't buy enough time, I hope I remembered to thank you for rescuing me in Russia."

"You did. Your thank-you was more than adequate."

"And for Zoltán."

"Him too. If anything, you're ahead of me on thanking. Thank you for anything I forgot to thank you for. I've been kind of preoccupied with people trying to kill us."

"Understandable. I just think that Russia thing was really romantic, and if we die tonight, I don't want to have been at all cavalier about it. You should know it was sort of a world-class turn-on."

"If we die, I won't hold it against you. Getting you back was pretty nice too."

"Thanks."

"Of course, I don't plan to die tonight."

"Me neither." She leaned close and kissed him.

Wendy and Selma came down the stairs, carrying loaded magazines for the pistols and the two rifles. "Keep your eyes on the people you *don't* like, you two," said Selma. "And, by the way, everything is loaded, but this is the last of the ammunition."

Pete came down the stairs, holding the railing and walking lightly. "If we do have to retreat to the fourth floor, be careful and hold the rope. It's nearly ready to go. Just one turn per bolt." Wendy handed him a reloaded shotgun and a full magazine for his pistol. "Thanks."

"Use it wisely. This is all there is."

Selma went to the wall of windows on the south side of the house. "Do you hear something?" She listened. "It sounds like cars." She looked out, then quickly pulled her head back. "Oh, no," she said. "They've got those lift things the power company uses."

"What?" said Wendy.

Sam turned to look in Selma's direction. As he did, there was a loud, rapid barrage of fireworks soaring into the sky and exploding into popping starbursts. "Something's coming," he said. "Remember—make your shots count."

The fireworks had certainly been set off to cover this fresh attack. The sideboard began to rise up and Sam fired into the opening the men on the stairs had created by raising it. The sideboard fell back down with a thud.

Two seconds later, Selma fired three pistol shots at something outside the open window.

Wendy and Pete ran toward her just as she ducked to the floor and two windows were blown inward by automatic-weapons fire. Pete crouched behind the stairway and raised the shotgun.

Just outside the window, a shooter was standing in the bucket at the end of the hydraulic arm of a cherry picker. Pete fired, the shooter slumped over and dropped his weapon, and someone below took over the controls of the cherry picker, and lowered it out of sight.

Pete pumped his shotgun and ran to the window. He aimed it downward at the yard and fired, then pumped it again. He jerked back inside and crouched. A burst of automatic fire peppered the ceiling above his head.

Selma was running to the other side of the house. She looked out. "They've got another one!" She and Wendy opened windows along the north side and fired pistols at the man who was in the bucket being raised up to the third-floor window. They couldn't see whether he was hit, but the hydraulic arm lowered rapidly.

At the staircase, the intruders were trying a new tactic. One of them fired a tight burst of bullets through the back of the wooden sideboard to make a splintered hole and then another pushed a Škorpion auto pistol up through the hole and fired wild bursts at floor level, hoping to hit anyone standing near the stairs. Sam was closer to the hand than the pistol, so he hit the hand with the butt of his rifle. The hand quickly withdrew, leaving the Škorpion behind on the sideboard. Another Škorpion appeared a few feet away and Sam kicked the hand that held it hard enough to make the pistol fly across the room. He then stepped away from the sideboard just as a dozen shots punched upward through it.

The third time, Sam and Remi were ready. Three Škorpions appeared at once. Sam and Remi were widely separated, both on their bellies, aiming rifles from behind steel pillars. They each fired at a hand, and then Remi hit the final one.

Sam said to Remi, "Pick up the Škorpions from the floor and go upstairs." He fired a shot at the sideboard, then another at a spot where he suspected men were lurking below.

He turned to look for Selma and Wendy, saw another man rise up to the window on the cherry picker, fired, and saw him collapse into the bucket. "Selma, Wendy!" he called. "Upstairs, one at a time. Remember the steps are loose."

They ran for the stairs, and first Selma, then Wendy, held the climbing rope and climbed to the fourth floor on the rickety steps.

Sam continued putting an occasional shot through the sideboard to keep the men below away from it, and then he heard Pete fire the shotgun again. Sam turned toward him and saw him fire out the window. "Pete!" he called. "Up the steps, and get ready to drop the staircase."

He sensed motion and turned to the stairs from the floor below him. The leading edge of the sideboard popped up and two hands extended from beneath it, holding Škorpions, and began to fire wild bursts onto the third floor.

Sam sprang to his feet, ran and jumped on the sideboard. The sudden impact of his weight brought the heavy piece of furniture down on the two arms and made the hands unable to hold their pistols. Sam used his momentum to make a second jump to the far side of the sideboard, fired three shots into it randomly, scooped up the two automatic pistols by their slings and backed up to the stairs.

He could feel the stairs shaking and wobbling with each footstep and knew the bolts must be working their way out of the nuts that held them to the I beam, but he knew he had to keep firing now and then to hold the attackers off and keep them from charging.

When he reached the top, Remi knelt beside him and fired once, twice, to keep the men below at bay. Sam set his rifle aside on the floor and pulled out his pistol. "Pete!"

Pete, lying flat on the fourth floor, reached down under the narrow staircase with a socket wrench and began to loosen bolts. As each one came loose, he let it fall, then moved to the next one. Sam reached down from the other side and began to unscrew bolts with his hand.

The sideboard below them on the second floor popped upward abruptly and slid aside. Men slipped out from under it and ran to both sides, where they couldn't be seen from above. Just as one of them got his foot on the lowest step to the fourth floor, Pete turned the final bolt and the staircase fell with a horrific crash. The third floor belonged to the enemy.

34

THE FOURTH FLOOR

SAM GRASPED PETE'S ANKLES AND TUGGED HIM BACK from the edge of the opening just as the men below began firing wildly upward through the rectangular hole in the floor that once had held the staircase.

The opening was much narrower than the stairwells on the lower floors because the stairs were narrower up to Sam and Remi's floor. Sam said, "They'll be bringing the aluminum ladders up next. What have we got that will seal that opening?"

Remi said, "How about the safes?"

"Brilliant," said Sam. "Pete? You okay?"

"I'm still alive."

"Then help me with the safes. They're bolted into the wall from the inside. Everybody else, stay back from the opening, but don't take your eyes off it. Fire a shot now and then to remind them we're still here."

Sam went to the wall, pressed the spot to reveal the hidden corridor, stepped in, and opened the safes. He and Pete unbolted the two now-empty gun safes and Sam opened the third one, which held papers. Pete removed the bolts from this last one and then he and Sam pushed all three, one at a time, across the hardwood floor to the edge of the stairwell. As they pushed the last and biggest one, a deep scratch appeared on the floor. Sam said to Remi, "Oops. Sorry."

"It's too late to make *Architectural Digest*, Sam," she said. "The whole place is decorated in vintage Kalashnikov." They pushed the safes over, one by one, across the stairwell. They had sealed the opening completely.

Wendy said, "What do we do now?"

Sam said, "We seem to have just about run out of floors to make them fight for. For the moment, you sit on this safe. They don't have anything with them that can make a dent in it, but the second it moves I want to hear you yell your head off and fire down into any space that appears."

"Okay," she said.

He looked around. "Selma, are you familiar with the way a Czech Škorpion automatic pistol works?"

Selma said, "I did look up the manual online after Remi's problem in Russia."

"Good. We seem to have five of them. Check the magazines and see how much ammunition is left, then consolidate it. We need to have a couple with full magazines. They might buy us some extra time."

"What about the boiling water?"

"Turn down the burners for now so the pots stay hot but the water isn't boiling. We'll get it boiling again if they start moving the safes."

He turned to Pete. "Take my rifle and guard the windows. Those cherry pickers might reach this high."

"Where will you be?"

"Remi and I are going up to the roof. Selma? Are there any matches around?"

"In the kitchen downstairs."

"Great," he said.

Remi said, "I've got some in my backpack." She went to her closet and came out with a small waterproof container of stick matches, two bottles of champagne from the small refrigerator in the closet, and two of her cotton halter tops.

Sam saw her and said, "You figured it out."

"Of course I did. We'll have to pour out the Dom Perignon champagne." She handed him the two bottles.

He went to the sink in his bathroom, popped the two corks, and poured the champagne into the bathroom sink. "I hate to see this go."

"If we make it, there are still five bottles in the refrigerator, and I think three of Cristal."

They went to the back of Sam's walk-in closet. There was a set of flat rungs like the steps of a stepladder running up the back wall and, above them, a round hatch that locked with a lever.

He climbed up, opened the hatch, and looked around on the roof. "All clear."

Remi handed him the matches, the two champagne bottles, and the two cotton tops. He set them on the roof and climbed out after them. He stayed low as he ducked under the awning over the gas generator that had been running since the invaders had cut the outside electric power.

Sam picked up the funnel that he used when filling the generator's gas tank, stuck it in the neck of the first champagne bottle, and used one of the red five-gallon cans he kept there to fill the bottle with gasoline. Then he filled the other.

Remi appeared at his side carrying the second .308 rifle. "Need cover?"

"I might," he said. "Just hold on a minute while I see."

He stuffed a halter top into the neck of the bottle, then tipped the bottle a little so the gasoline soaked it, then repeated the process with the other. He carried one of the bottles to the south side of the house near the front door, glanced over the edge at the scene below, and ducked back where he couldn't be seen. He brought back with him a clear image of what was down there. A man had climbed into the bucket of the cherry picker and he was using the controls to raise himself upward.

Sam struck a match and lit the soaked fabric, leaned over the wall at the edge of the roof, and threw his Molotov cocktail. The flame on the wick elongated and brightened as the bottle fell. It landed on the roof of the truck that supported the cherry picker and broke, splashing a pool of flame on the roof that immediately spread to the sides of the cab and engulfed it.

Sam ran to the opposite side of the roof, stopping to pick up the second bottle on the way. At the other side, he struck a match to light the wick, then threw the bottle at the second truck. This bottle smashed on the truck's hood and the flames rose high. Much of the burning gasoline ran down the sides to engulf the front tires and pool on the ground beneath the engine.

From both sides of the house there were loud bursts from automatic weapons fired at the upper edge of the roof. It was all just noise and wasted ammunition because Sam and Remi were now sitting near the middle of the roof, where they couldn't be hit. After a minute, the firing stopped, replaced by the sound of more fireworks in the cove.

"Is there anything else we can do?" asked Remi.

"Do you know where the gas tank is on one of those trucks?"

"No."

"It's a big cylinder just under the driver's seat."

"You're kidding. That's the dumbest thing I—"

"I didn't design them. If we put a bullet through the gas tank so the gas starts pouring out onto the ground, we might cause them some anxiety at least."

"Starting our house on fire would cause me some anxiety."

"I know," he said. "Just a thought."

She sighed, picked up the rifle, and moved cautiously to the back end of the roof, where the men below would be least likely to anticipate her appearance. She stood, shouldered the rifle, and side-stepped to the edge. As soon as she could see downward she fired and then instantly stepped back out of sight. Within a second or two, there were loud shouts and bursts of gunfire into the sky.

"You must have hit it."

"I should hope so. It's the size of a beer barrel." She walked to the opposite side of the roof, took a stance like the one she had used a moment ago, sidestepped into sight, fired, and sidestepped back. The air filled with more shouts of dismay and random shots.

Then, coming from the opposite side, the evening air seemed to fill with bright gasoline flames as the truck's gas tank emptied into the fire. There was a loud boom as it exploded.

"No!" On the deck of the *Ibiza*, Arpad Bako leapt up from his chair, knocked his drink over, causing the glass to roll toward the scuppers. "No!" he shouted. "What are they doing? What can they be thinking?"

Le Clerc looked at Goldfish Point calmly. "They could be burning the Fargos out. It's crude, but it usually works. I can't quite tell what's burning."

"There could be treasure in that house!" Bako shouted. "Priceless artifacts could be melting into a puddle of gold while we sit here. Ancient jewels the Caesars wore could be destroyed."

Poliakoff sat calmly. "Everything we know says that the treasures are in museums for now. The only way we'll ever get any of it is if we take Remi Fargo back to trade for it. This time, I'll send Fargo a gift-wrapped box with one of her fingers. Sam Fargo made me burn down my own house, did you know that? Once I knew the police and firefighters were on their way, I couldn't let them find a cellar full of smuggled drugs. Two days later my wife drove into the courtyard with my children, saw the pile of wreckage, and told the driver to turn around and head back to Moscow. Just for making me live through that moment, Fargo should be spared no form of pain. I hope they are burning his house down."

Le Clerc smiled slyly. "She's still not talking to you, Sergei? Sleeping alone doesn't agree with you."

"That's none of your business," said Poliakoff. He puffed hard on his cigar, then said, "They're speeding this up. If they don't get the Fargos out of that house soon, we'll have police and firemen rushing there and patrol boats out here."

Bako was at the rail, holding the powerful binoculars on the house. "The flames are coming from the two cherry pickers. The bodies of the trucks are on fire and one of them blew up." As he watched, the second truck's gas tank flared and knocked over the truck, leaving it in flames. The boom of the explosion reached the boat a second later. "Both of them blew up."

Le Clerc said, "You were perceptive, Arpad. It's just like Attila attacking a castle. This time, the defenders set fire to the siege engines."

"It's crazy!" Bako shouted. "What are people like them doing with an arsenal in their house?"

"I suppose if a person finds lots of treasures, other people get jealous and try to kidnap them."

Poliakoff stood too, picked up the radio that sat on the table beside his drink, pressed a button, and said something in Russian over the static.

Bako whirled and reached for the radio. "No!" he shouted. "Don't tell our own men to run away. We're so close! The Fargos and their servants are huddled on the top floor, cowering in fear."

Poliakoff stiff-armed Bako, who stopped and bent over, trying to recover from the hand that had compressed his chest and deprived him of breath. "I'm just checking with my headman to account for all the delay. This should have taken five minutes."

A staticky voice blurted something on the other end. And Poliakoff said in Russian, "Kotzov! What's causing the delay?"

The voice said, "They're on the fourth floor, but it's been a gun battle for every inch. We've got dead men here and quite a few hurt."

"Give me your best advice."

"I'd rather not do that, sir."

"That tells me what I need to know. Collect the dead and wounded. Leave no one behind. We'll take everyone on the boats. Get them to the beach now. We're headed in to anchor."

Poliakoff switched channels. "Stop the fireworks. Cut the raft loose and head for shore. We're picking up our men off the beach with the launches. Leave now."

He shouted up the steps to the man at the helm. "Weigh anchor and head for the beach. We'll be taking all the men with us to Mexico."

"No!" shouted Bako. "Don't do this. Don't be a coward."

Poliakoff turned to face Bako and stood very close to him. His eyes seemed to glint in the flickering light from shore.

Bako looked away, threw his cigar in the water, and sat down on the end of his chair. He held his head in his hands. The anchor chain came up, and they all felt the vibration as the motor yacht's oversize engines moved it forward, slowly at first, and then gaining speed as it headed in toward shore.

THE SILENCE in the house was almost as shocking as the noise had been. Sam and Remi moved to the edge of the roof and looked down at their lawn. Men in black clothes hurried off into the night, carrying casualties on makeshift stretchers consisting of blankets wrapped around the sections of extension ladders or lifting them in over-the-shoulder fireman's carries. The truck that had supported the cherry picker lay on its side, charred and smoking.

"They seem to be leaving," said Remi.

"It looks that way," Sam said. "But we'll see."

She looked at him. "You're so cautious."

He shrugged and put his arm around her. "Perhaps you've heard of a famous siege. When the attackers got really tired of their failure to breach the walls, one really smart one said, 'Why don't we pretend we're going back to our ships? We'll leave a—'"

"Big wooden horse full of soldiers. Are you saying this is the Trojan War? Aren't we taking ourselves a little seriously?"

"I'm just saying I'm not going down there until I can see at least five police cars. Make that twenty."

She looked toward the hotels and the major commercial streets to the south and then pulled his arm to turn him in that direction.

She pointed. There was a long line of police cars streaming up La Jolla Boulevard toward Prospect Street with blue, red, and white lights flashing. In a moment, the distant whoop of the sirens reached the rooftop.

They stepped to the ocean side of the house. Out in the bay, they could see the two motor yachts had come in much closer to the shore. They were holding a position just beyond the outer breaks of surf, launching smaller boats to land on the beach.

From the north, beyond La Jolla Cove, came three police boats, scanning the water with the beams of spotlights and then letting them settle on the two yachts. From the south, the direction of San Diego Harbor, came two Coast Guard vessels, each about a hundred fifty feet long, with crew members scrambling to man the deck guns. The Coast Guard vessels moved into position about six hundred feet offshore and remained there in what amounted to a blockade.

"They're not running," Remi said.

"No," said Sam. "They'd be foolish to try that."

"They could easily outrun the police boats. The Coast Guard too."

"They can't outrun the deck guns."

"So it looks as though we may find out which of our European competitors is a sore loser," said Remi.

"Sore or not, just so long as they're losers," Sam said.

THE TWO COAST GUARD cutters held their places just outside the surf line where the yachts had anchored. Now the yachts' launches were returning against the surf loaded with the men of the assault force who had attacked the Fargos' house. As they returned, the first of the able-bodied men climbed the ladders on the sides of the yachts. Others in the lifeboats had been injured by falls, burns, or gunshots and were in no condition to climb, so some of the yachts' crewmen helped to lift them to the deck. The yachts raised their anchors but kept their bows seaward and held their places by steering into the swells.

The police boats approached on the seaward sides of the yachts, and boarding parties of the San Diego Harbor Police prepared themselves to come aboard.

On the deck of the *Ibiza*, Arpad Bako looked at the police boats, then down at the men struggling to climb aboard the yacht. "Leave the stragglers," he shouted. "There's no time."

Poliakoff turned to Bako. "First you want to stay and then you want to abandon our men? Who's the coward now?"

Bako pulled a pistol from inside his coat and fired.

Poliakoff's face seemed astonished. He looked down at the front of his white shirt, where a red bloodstain was blossoming quickly. His eyes acquired a faraway look, and the next swell arrived to rock the yacht and toppled him onto the deck.

Bako snatched Poliakoff's radio from the deck, pressed the talk button, and shouted, "Take evasive action. Get this boat out to sea now."

"Sir?" said the captain. "Mr. Poliakoff said—"

"Poliakoff's dead. He's been hit. Get going!" As Bako turned, he seemed to notice Étienne Le Clerc again. Le Clerc saw his expression and tried to run for the bridge, but Bako fired three more times, and Le Clerc lay dead. At least there would be no witness.

From the bridge the captain could see that most of the able-bodied men were aboard now, and he knew the others would only be extra trouble. He could also see that if he was going to make a run for it, he'd have to do it before the first police boat brought a boarding party. He shifted to forward and pushed the throttle. The big engines roared into life and the yacht surged forward, leaving a gurgling wash behind it, the twin propellers projecting water into the void behind the stern. As the stern swung about, he heard shouts from men either shaken from the sides of the yacht or chopped by the propellers, but he couldn't help that now. The yacht gained speed, leaving one lifeboat swamped and the other drifting sideways into the surf.

When the *Ibiza* began to move, the captain of the *Mazatlan* saw it and had a small vision of the near future. If the Coast Guard and police had been fooled long enough to let the *Ibiza* pass them to open ocean, they would not ignore the *Mazatlan*. They would have twice the ships and men to devote to preventing the *Mazatlan* and every man aboard from escaping. And then they would blame every crime committed by anyone on the highest-ranking man they had caught, the captain. He shifted his engines into forward gear and hit the throttle. The *Mazatlan* surged forward, just as the *Ibiza* had.

There was a loud amplified voice coming from one of the Coast Guard vessels. He knew it was a warning of the "Stop or we'll shoot" variety and he welcomed it. The more time they wasted shouting into microphones, the less time they'd have for taking action. He pushed the throttle all the way forward, picking up more speed each second. Those Coast Guard cutters probably had a top speed of twenty-five knots. The *Mazatlan* could do sixty. He yelled to his helmsman, "Cut all lights!"

F R O M   T H E   R O O F of the house on Goldfish Point, Sam and Remi watched the yachts, police boats, and Coast Guard vessels. The two yachts sped toward the open sea at incredible speed, roaring out at different angles, one toward the northwest, the other toward the southwest. "They're not taking your advice," said Remi. "They're running."

"Big mistake," said Sam.

The two police boats fired first with small arms set on full auto. Sam and Remi could see the prolonged muzzle flashes, at least four on each boat, peppering the two yachts as they pursued them.

The two Coast Guard cutters remained in position. A trail of reddish sparks soared into the sky from one of them, and it looked as though the fireworks had begun again. There was a flash, but it didn't go away. A military flare hung in the sky, lighting the air above the vessels almost like sunlight.

Sam and Remi watched as the deck guns on the two Coast Guard vessels swung about to aim, then fire. The first two shots took away part of the bow of the *Ibiza*. The third tore into its hull just aft of center and seemed to hit the fuel tank. The deck rose into the air, releasing a fireball that billowed upward and then settled into a large pool of burning gasoline. The gasoline burned brightly, consuming even the parts that had been blown off into the water.

A second later, the bow of the *Mazatlan* dug into the water as the yacht was hit below the bridge. Forward motion stopped, and something big, perhaps one of the engines, tore free and rolled through the yacht, tearing it apart. Then there were five secondary explosions, which left nothing floating on the surface.

"It looks as though they hit the ammo supply," said Remi.

The smaller, nimbler police boats moved in quickly, sweeping the ocean near the surf with spotlights. There was no life near the capsized lifeboats. The Coast Guard vessels sent out launches to the wreckage of the *Mazatlan* and *Ibiza*. Sam and Remi watched them circle the burning spots on the ocean, then crisscross the area, but there were no survivors to pull out of the sea. They had all been shot, blown to pieces, burned, or drowned.

SAM AND REMI CLIMBED down the ladder from the roof into Sam's closet to find Zoltán still standing there, watching to be sure nobody else came up after them. Remi knelt beside the big dog and hugged him. "If it weren't for you, I never would have made it into the house, Zoltán. I'd be heading back to Russia in a barrel. Thank you for being so brave and loyal."

Sam petted Zoltán and whispered in his ear, "*Jo fiu*. Good boy."

They heard the voices of Selma, Pete, and Wendy calling to them. "Sam! Remi! The police! There must be hundreds of them. They're here."

"Oh, darn," said Remi. "We wanted the police to be a surprise."

Sam looked around. "We're going to have to practically rebuild this place from scratch."

"Draw the contractors a picture," said Remi. "Maybe while they're working on it we can give the others a vacation, take Zoltán down to Louisiana with us, and do some more salvage archaeology for Ray. We promised him some help when we left."

"Sure," said Sam. "What could happen to people on an archaeological site?"